*More than just office romances!*

# Not Strictly
# Business!

Three intense and satisfying romances from
three beloved Mills & Boon authors!

# Not Strictly Business!

SUSAN MALLERY

WENDY WARREN

VICTORIA PADE

MILLS & BOON

First published in Great Britain 2011
Harlequin Mills & Boon Limited,
Eton House, 18-24 Paradise Road, Richmond, Surrey TW9 1SR

NOT STRICTLY BUSINESS!
© by Harlequin Enterprises II B.V./S.à.r.l 2011

*Prodigal Son, The Boss and Miss Baxter* and *The Baby Deal* were first
published in Great Britain by Harlequin Mills & Boon Limited in separate,
single volumes.

*Prodigal Son* © Harlequin Books S.A. 2006
*The Boss and Miss Baxter* © Harlequin Books S.A. 2006
*The Baby Deal* © Harlequin Books S.A. 2006

Special thanks and acknowledgement are given to Susan Mallery,
Wendy Warren and Victoria Pade for their contribution to the
FAMILY BUSINESS series.

ISBN: 978 0 263 88338 1

05-0111

Printed and bound in Spain
by Litografia Rosés S.A., Barcelona

# PRODIGAL SON

## BY
## SUSAN MALLERY

**Susan Mallery** is the bestselling and award-winning author of over fifty books.

# *Chapter One*

Samantha Edwards had never minded the interview process, even when she was the one looking for a job. But having seen her prospective boss naked made things just a little tricky.

The good news was Jack Hanson was unlikely to bring up that single night they'd shared. Not only wasn't it relevant to her employment application, it had been nearly ten years ago. She doubted he remembered anything about the event.

Well, not just the one event. Her recollection was completely clear. There had been three "events" that night, each of them more spectacular than the one before.

"Ms. Edwards? Mr. Hanson will see you now."

Samantha looked up at the sixty-something secretary behind the modern metal-and-glass desk in the foyer in front of Jack's office.

"Thank you," Samantha said as she rose and moved toward the closed door.

She paused to tug on her cropped jacket. Her clothing choices had been deliberately conservative—for her, at least. Flowing black slacks, a cream-and-black checked jacket over a cream silk shirt. It killed her to avoid color, but ten years ago Jack Hanson had been the poster boy for straitlaced conservative types. She was willing to guess that hadn't changed.

Except he hadn't been the least bit conservative in bed.

The wayward thought popped into her head just as she pushed open the door to his office. She did her best to ignore it as she drew in a deep breath, reminded herself how much she wanted this job and walked confidently toward the man standing behind his desk.

"Hello, Jack," she said, shaking hands with him. "It's been a long time."

"Samantha. Good to see you."

He studied her with a thoroughness that made her breath catch. How much of his steady perusal was about sizing up the candidate and how much was about their past?

She decided two could play at that game and did a little looking of her own.

He was taller than she'd remembered and he still seemed to exude power and confidence. She wanted to say that was a natural attribute for someone born to money, but she had a feeling Jack would have been a winner regardless of his upbringing. He was simply that kind of man.

Time had been kind, but then time had always preferred men to women, she thought humorously. Jack's face showed character in addition to chiseled features. She wondered if life ever got boring for the physically perfect. While he had to deal with things like broad shoulders and a smile that would have most of the female population lining up to be seduced, she had unruly red hair that defied taming, a stick-straight body, small breasts and a butt that could only be described as bony. Was that fair?

"Please," he said, motioning to one of the chairs. "Have a seat."

"Thanks."

He did the same, claiming his side of the desk. He looked good there—in charge and powerful. But she happened to know he was new to the job.

"I read about your father's death a couple of months ago," she said. "I'm sorry."

"Thanks." He motioned to the office. "That's why I'm working here. The board asked me to step in and take care of the company for a while."

"I'd wondered," she admitted. "Last I'd heard, you were practicing law."

"It would be my preference," he told her.

"But you did so well at business school." She would know—they'd been competing for the top spot, often by working together. He'd been the detail-intensive, organized half and she'd been the creative member of the team.

"Hated every minute of it," he said. "I realized I preferred the law."

Jack thought about the day he'd told his father he wasn't entering the family business. George Hanson hadn't been able to comprehend that his oldest son wasn't interested in learning how to run a multimillion-dollar company. The older man had been disappointed and furious. It had been the only time Jack hadn't done what was expected of him.

Ironically, today he was exactly where his father had wanted him to be.

But not for long, he reminded himself.

"I guess your father's death changed your plans," Samantha said.

He nodded. "I'm on a three-month leave of absence from my law firm. Until then Hanson Media Group gets my full attention."

"Are you sure you want the Donald Trump act to be temporary?"

"I'm not the tycoon type."

She smiled. "I would say you have potential. Word on the street is you're bringing in a lot of new people."

"That's true. My father hated to hand over control of anything. He was still the head of at least three departments. With a company this big, no one has the time or energy to run them and the rest of the business. I'm looking for the best people possible to join the team."

"I'm flattered."

"It's the truth. You're only here because you're good. I need creative types. It's not my strong suit."

She smiled. "A man who can admit his weaknesses. How unusual."

"Samantha, the only reason I passed marketing was because I was on your team. You carried me through the whole class."

"You tutored me through cost accounting. We're even."

She shifted slightly as she spoke, causing her slacks to briefly hug her slender thighs. The other candidates had been highly skilled with incredible résumés, but unlike Samantha, they'd come in dressed in business suits, looking equally comfortable in a board room or law office.

Not Samantha. Despite the conservative colors, she was anything but ordinary. Maybe it was the bright green parrot pin on her lapel or the dangling earrings that hung nearly to her shoulders. Or maybe it was that her long, fiery red hair seemed to have a will and a life of its own.

She was not a conservative businessperson. She was avant-garde and wildly creative. There was an independence about her he admired.

"You left New York," he said. "Why?"

"I wanted to make a change. I'd been working there since graduation."

He studied her as she spoke, looking for nuances. There were plenty, but none of them worried him. Per his research, she was coming off a divorce. Her previous employer had done his best to keep her from leaving.

"You have to know this is a dream job," she said. "You're offering complete creative control of Internet development, with more than a million-dollar budget. How could anyone resist that? It's my idea of heaven."

"Good. It's my idea of hell."

She smiled. Her full mouth curved and he felt himself responding. Subtle tension filled his body.

"You always did hate a blank page," she said, her smile widening to a grin.

"You always did hate rules," he told her.

"Me?" She raised her eyebrows. "You were happy enough to break them when it suited your purpose."

He shrugged. "Whatever it takes to get what I want. What I want now is a great staff and the company running smoothly. Let's get down to specifics."

He passed her information on several current Internet campaigns. After she'd flipped through the material, they discussed possible directions for growth.

Samantha became more animated as the conversation progressed. "Children," she told him. "There's so much we could do for kids. After-school programs on the Web. Not just the usual help with homework, but interactive programs linking kids all over the country."

As she spoke, she leaned toward him, gesturing with

her hands to make her point. "We can also cosponsor events with popular movies or TV shows."

"Cross-advertising," he said.

"Yes. The potential is huge. And that's just younger kids. I have even more ideas for teens."

"They're the ones with the disposable income and the time to spend it," he said. When she raised her eyebrows in surprise, he added, "I've been doing my research."

"Apparently. It's true. With more single-parent families and more families with both parents working, teens are often a real source of information on what items to purchase. They actually influence adults' decisions on everything from breakfast cereal to cars. Plus they're computer savvy, which means they're comfortable downloading information. To them, the Internet is as much a part of their lives as phones were for us."

"So you're interested in the job," he said.

"I distinctly recall the word *heaven* coming up in the conversation. I wasn't kidding. I'd love the chance to grow this part of the company."

Her excitement was tangible energy in the office. He liked that. She'd always thrown herself into whatever it was she was doing and he doubted that had changed.

He'd been surprised to see her name on the short list of candidates, but pleasantly so. He and Samantha had worked well together at grad school. They'd been a good team. Just as important, she was someone he could trust.

"The job is yours, if you want it," he told her. "The formal offer would come from my human-resources person in the morning."

Her green eyes widened. "Seriously?"

"Why are you shocked? You're talented, qualified and someone I'm comfortable working with."

"You make me sound like a rescue dog."

He grinned. "If I could find one that could work a computer…"

She laughed. "Okay, yes. I'm interested. But I have to warn you, I'm very much the creative type. I'll want control of my staff."

"Agreed."

"We're not going to be wearing three-piece suits."

"I don't care if you wear frog costumes, as long as you do the job."

She didn't look convinced. "This isn't like the law, Jack. You can't always find an answer in a book."

"Can I get disapproving and difficult before you give me the lecture?" he asked, mildly amused by her concern. "I get it—creative people are different. Not a problem."

"Okay. Point taken."

She rose. He stood as well. In heels she was only a couple of inches shorter than him. He walked around the table and held out his hand.

"Leave your number with Mrs. Wycliff. You'll be hearing from my HR office first thing in the morning."

She placed her palm against his. As he had when they'd touched a few minutes ago, he felt a slight sizzle, followed by a definite sensation of warmth somewhere south of his belt.

Ten years after the fact and Samantha Edwards still had the ability to drop him to his knees. Sexually speaking. Not that he would act on the information or let her know how she got to him. They were going to work together, nothing more.

He released her hand and walked her to the door. "How soon can you start?" he asked.

"The first part of next week," she said.

"Good. I hold a staff meeting every Tuesday morning. I look forward to seeing you there."

She hesitated before opening the door. "I'm excited about this opportunity, Jack. I want to make a difference."

"I'm sure you will."

She looked into his eyes. "I wasn't sure you'd consider me. Because of our past."

He pretended not to know what she was talking about. He wanted to make her say it. "Why would knowing you in business school make a difference?"

"Not that."

He waited.

Color flared on her cheeks, but she continued to hold his gaze. "Because of what happened that night. When we…" She cleared her throat. "You know. Were intimate."

"Water under the bridge," he said easily, mostly because it was true. He'd never been one to dwell on the past. Not even on a night that had made him believe in miracles. Probably because in the bright light of day, he'd learned that dreams were for fools and miracles didn't really happen.

Promptly at four in the afternoon, Mrs. Wycliff knocked on Jack's office door.

"Come in," he said as he saved the work on his computer, then looked up at his father's former assistant.

"Here are the daily reports," she said, placing several folders on his desk.

"Thank you."

He frowned as he looked at the thick stack that would make up his evening reading. In theory, he knew plenty about running a company. He had the MBA to prove it. But theory and reality often had little in common and this was one of those times. If one of the employees was accused of homicide—that he could handle. Right now, a charge of first-degree murder seemed simple when compared with the day-to-day ups and downs of a publicly traded corporation.

"How is the staff holding up?" he asked the older woman. Although he was confident Mrs. Wycliff hadn't been born into her position, he couldn't remember a time when she hadn't worked for his father.

She clutched the back of the chair and shook her head in refusal when he invited her to take a seat.

"They miss him, of course. Your father was well liked in the company. Of course he would be. He was a good man."

Jack was careful to keep his expression neutral.

George Hanson had been a man of business. He had lived and breathed his company, while his children had grown up on the fringes of his life. That wasn't Jack's definition of *good*.

"Several people have stopped by to tell me how much they miss him," Jack told her. It happened at least once a day and he never knew what to say in return.

She smiled. "We all appreciate you stepping in to run things. Hanson Media Group has been home to a lot of us for a long time. We'd hate to see anything happen to the company."

"Happen?" He'd only been on board a couple of weeks. From what he'd been able to find out, the only problems seemed to be his father's need to micromanage departments. Once Jack got the right people in place, he figured the firm would run smoothly.

Mrs. Wycliff smoothed her already perfect gray hair and absently fingered the bun at the back of her neck. "Your father was very proud of you. Did you know that?"

Jack wasn't fooled by the obvious change in subject, but he figured he would do a little digging on his own before he grilled his assistant for information.

"Thank you for telling me," he said.

She smiled. "He often talked about how well you were doing at your law firm. Of course he'd wanted you to come to work for the family business, but if the law made you happy, he was happy, too."

Jack tried to reconcile that description with the angry conversations he'd frequently shared with his father.

George Hanson had tried everything from bribes to threatening to cut Jack out of the will if he didn't come work for the company.

He'd long suspected his father had shown one side of his personality to the world and kept the other side more private.

"We had a deal," he said. "After law school, I got my MBA. Then I decided which I liked better." He shrugged. "It wasn't much of a choice."

"You followed your heart and your talents," Mrs. Wycliff told him. "That's what your father always said." She smiled. "He brought in champagne the day you made partner."

"Junior partner," Jack corrected absently. Champagne? When he couldn't get hold of his father, he'd left a message with Helen, his stepmother, telling her about the promotion. She'd sent a card and a stylish new briefcase as a gift. Ever polite, Helen had signed both their names, but Jack had known it was all really from her. His father had never bothered to call him back.

"He was a good man," Mrs. Wycliff said. "Whatever happens, you have to remember that."

"That's the second time you've been cryptic," he told her. "Want to tell me why?"

She had dark blue eyes and the kind of bone structure that spoke of great beauty in her youth. If she had been a different kind of woman, he would have suspected something between her and his father. But while George might have been interested, Jack was confident Mrs. Wycliff herself would not have approved.

"I can't," she said, her voice low.

"Can't or won't?"

She clutched the back of the chair more firmly and met his direct gaze. "I don't know anything. If I did, I would tell you. You have my complete loyalty."

"But there's something?"

She hesitated. "A feeling. I'm sorry. I can't be more specific. There's nothing more to say."

He'd known the woman all of two weeks, yet he would have bet she wasn't lying. She didn't know. Or she was a damn fine actress.

Feelings. As a rule, he didn't trust emotion, but gut responses were different. He'd changed his line of questioning during a trial more than once based on a feeling and each time he'd been right.

"If you learn anything," he began.

"I'll tell you. I've been talking to people. Listening." She swallowed. "I lost my husband a few years ago. We never had children and a lot of our friends have retired and moved south. This company is all I have. I'll do anything to protect it."

"Thank you."

She nodded and left.

Mysteries he didn't want or need. As for Mrs. Wycliff, while he appreciated her concern and her willingness to provide him with information, who was to say if they had similar goals? She wanted Hanson Media Group to go on forever, he wanted out. If those two objectives came into conflict, he had a feeling his once-loyal secretary would become a bitter enemy.

* * *

With employment came paperwork, Samantha thought two days later as she sat in an empty office and filled out her formal job application, along with pages for insurance, a security pass, a parking space and emergency contact information.

She worked quickly, still unable to believe she'd landed her dream job with little or no effort on her part. She'd been so excited to get going, she'd come in before her start date to do the paperwork.

"Thank you, Helen," she murmured, knowing her friend had somehow managed to get her name on the short list of candidates. She'd wanted to mention that to Jack during their interview, but on Helen's advice had kept quiet. For reasons that made no sense to Samantha, Jack, along with his siblings, thought Helen was little more than a trophy wife.

Hope I'm around when they all discover that there's a very functioning brain behind those big eyes, Samantha thought.

She signed the application and moved on to the next piece of paper.

"Morning."

She looked up and saw Jack in the doorway to the small office. He looked tall, sexy and just-out-of-the-shower tempting. What was it about a freshly shaved man that got her body to pay attention?

"Hi," she said.

"I heard you were here taking care of details." He

leaned against the door frame. "Thanks for accepting the job."

"I'm the grateful one," she said with a laugh. "I can't wait to get started. But first there's all this to work through." She patted the papers. "I've been promised that if I do everything correctly, I get my own ID badge at the end of the day. And the key to my office."

"I heard that rumor, too. My intrepid assistant informed me we already have a meeting scheduled."

"Monday afternoon," she said. "I'll be working all weekend, bringing myself up to speed. I'll want to discuss parameters with you before I set my team on the task."

"You're not expected to work 24-7," he said.

"I know, but I'm excited and it's not as if I have a lot of things planned. I've just moved to Chicago. I'm still finding my way around."

"All the more reason to get out and explore."

She tilted her head. "Hmm, is my new boss *discouraging* me from working? That's a new one."

"I don't want you to burn out your first week. I need you around longer than that."

She knew they were just joking around, and she enjoyed that she and Jack seemed to have kept some remnant of their friendship intact. But why did she have to be so aware of him?

Even now, with him standing several feet away, she would swear she could hear him breathing. Heat seemed to radiate from his body, in a way designed to make her melt.

It had been like this before, she thought glumly.

Back in grad school, she'd spent two years in a constant state of sexual arousal. She'd needed the friendship more than she'd wanted a lover, so she'd ignored the physical attraction between them. She'd been careful to always seem disinterested.

Until that one night when she'd been unable to stand it a second longer.

"I promise to explore often and well," she said. "But later. Right now I want to get to work."

He held up both hands. "Okay. I give up. Be a slave to your job. I'll stop complaining." He dropped his hands to his sides. "Are you already settled in your new place?"

"I have exactly two suitcases in my hotel room. It didn't take long to settle."

"Aren't you going to get an apartment?"

"Eventually. I'm too busy to look around right now." A partial truth. Apartment hunting would give her too much time to think. She wanted to avoid bursts of introspection whenever possible.

"My building has executive rentals," he said. "They come fully furnished and are rented by the month. That's how I found the place. I took a two-month lease, found I liked the building and bought something larger."

"Sounds interesting," she said cautiously.

He grinned. "Don't worry. It's a huge high-rise. We'd never run into each other."

Did he think she thought that was a problem? Okay, yeah, maybe it was. She had a feeling that running into Jack outside of work could be a complication, if not outright dangerous for her mental health. But hadn't she promised herself to face life head on? Wasn't she done with hiding from the truth?

"I appreciate the information," she said. "Do you have a phone number or person to contact?"

"I have a business card in my office. Let me go get it."

He walked down the hallway. Samantha turned her attention back to the paperwork in front of her, but instead of seeing it, she saw the empty apartment she'd left in New York only three weeks before.

She'd thought she would always live in New York. She'd thought she knew what to expect from her life. Funny how a lifetime of dreams could be packed up into a half-dozen boxes and the man she'd once trusted to love her forever had turned out to be nothing more than a lying thief.

## Chapter Two

"We're working on the, ah, upgrades right now," Arnie said as he shifted in his seat. "The, ah, first set should be, ah, ready by the end of the month."

Jack had to consciously keep himself from squirming in sympathy. In his law practice his clients were usually so distracted by the charges brought against them that they didn't have the energy to be nervous and in court he didn't care if his cross-examination upset a hostile witness.

But Arnie wasn't a client or a hostile witness. He was a techno-geek from the information technology department, or IT, and he was obviously uncomfortable meeting with his new boss.

Jack glanced down at the report in front of him, then

back at Arnie. "Sounds like you're totally on schedule," he said, then smiled at the other man. "Good for you."

Arnie swallowed. "Thanks. We've been trying. Roger, my, ah, boss, sort of said we had to. Oh, but not in a bad way."

"I appreciate your effort," Jack said, wishing Roger, Arnie's boss, had been available for the meeting. Jack couldn't take much more of the poor man's suffering.

"You're going to be working with Samantha Edwards," Jack said. "She started today. She's very creative and energetic. I'm sure you'll be impressed by her ideas."

And her, Jack thought, wondering what Arnie would think of Samantha's tall, slender beauty and infectious smile. Or maybe he didn't have to wonder. Harsh, but true, Arnie looked like the kind of guy who never got the girl. He was pale, with thinning brown hair, light brown eyes and glasses. He wore a plaid short-sleeved shirt and jeans, and his posture yelled, "Please don't hurt me."

Arnie's face contorted as if he were trying to decide if he should smile or not. "I heard there was going to be a lot of Internet expansion. That's good for my department."

"It will be plenty of work," Jack told him.

"We can do it. I'm sure of it."

"I am, too," Jack said. "Once Samantha finalizes her plans, she'll get with you and your guys to work out the details. We may have some capacity issues. I don't know enough about the technicalities to know. I need you to stay on top of that. And help coordinate the launch date. We need to be aggressive, while being realistic."

Arnie nodded vigorously. "Okay. Sure. I can do all that. But, um, you know, George was never interested in the Internet. He always liked the magazine side of the business."

One of the reasons the company was in big trouble, Jack thought. Magazines were expensive propositions when compared with the relatively low cost of maintaining a Web site.

"I see Internet expansion as a quick and cost-effective way to build the business. After the initial start-up costs, we're spending much less." He frowned. Shouldn't an IT guy know this?

"Oh, I agree," Arnie said quickly. "I think it's great. So do most of the guys in my department. But, you know, not everyone will agree."

Jack didn't like the sound of that. "Like who?"

Arnie instantly looked trapped. "Oh, it's—"

"We're a team here," Jack said. "We're only as strong as our weakest member." Hopefully that would be the hokiest thing he had to say this week, he thought grimly. But if it worked…

Arnie squirmed some more, ducked his head, sighed, then said, "Roger, my boss. He's not real big on change."

"Interesting," Jack said, wondering how someone like that rose to the level of running the IT department. Or maybe Jack's father had wanted it that way, considering his disinterest in all things high tech. "I appreciate you telling me that. I won't mention this conversation with Roger. You have my word."

Arnie sighed. "Thanks. I really like my job. I wouldn't want to get, you know, fired." He winced as he spoke, then shook his head. "Your dad was a great man."

"Thank you," Jack said.

"He was patient and kind and really interested in all his employees. We all liked working for him and felt really bad when he died."

Jack nodded. He wasn't sure what to say when people talked about his father this way. They were describing someone he'd never met.

"Knock, knock."

He looked up and saw Samantha walking into his office. She looked from him to Arnie.

"Am I early or late?" she asked with a smile.

"Neither," he said. "Right on time. You're joining our meeting in progress."

Now that she had the job, she'd obviously decided there was no need to dress conservatively anymore—at least her definition of it. Gone were the black slacks and black-and-white jacket. In their place she wore a long skirt in a swirl of reds, greens and purples. A dark green sweater hung loosely past her hips. She had a patterned scarf draped over one shoulder, a half-dozen bracelets on each wrist and earrings that tinkled and swayed as she walked.

"This is Arnie," Jack said, pointing to the man sitting across from him at the conference table. "He's from IT. He'll be working with you on the Internet expansion. You tell him what you want and he'll tell you if it's possible. Arnie, this is Samantha."

The other man rose and wiped his palms on his jeans, then held out his hand. His mouth opened, closed, then opened again.

"Ah, hi," Arnie said, his eyes wide, his cheeks bright with color.

"Good morning." Samantha beamed at him. "So you're going to be my new best friend, right? And you won't ever want to tell me no."

Arnie stammered, then sank back in his seat. Jack did his best not to smile. Samantha had made another conquest.

He wasn't surprised. She walked into a room and men were instantly attracted to her. He was no exception. She was a weakness for which he'd found no antidote. Even now he found himself wanting to pull her close and run his hands through her curly hair. He wanted to stare into her eyes and feel her tremble in his embrace.

Not on this planet, he reminded himself. She hadn't been interested ten years ago and he doubted that had changed.

Okay, she'd been interested *once*. Apparently once was enough where he was concerned. She'd made it more than clear she didn't want a repeat performance.

"Don't let Samantha push you around," he told Arnie. "She has a tendency to do that."

Samantha looked at him and raised her eyebrows. "Me? Are you kidding? I'm the picture of complete cooperation."

"Uh-huh. Right until someone gets in your way. Then you're a steamroller."

Samantha sat next to Arnie and patted his hand. "Ignore him. Jack and I went to grad school together and he seems to remember things very differently. I've never steamrolled anyone." She paused, then smiled. "Well, at least not often. I can get tenacious about what I want, though. And I've read different reports from your department, Arnie. People have been pushing for this expansion for a while."

That surprised Jack. "I hadn't heard that."

Samantha looked at him. "His boss is the reason why. I also read memos from Roger explaining why it was all a bad idea. Apparently he had some backing on that."

She didn't specifically say by who, but Jack could guess. He doubted his father had been a fan of growing technology.

"That was the past," he said. "Let's focus on the future. You two need to get together and talk about specifics."

Samantha jotted down a note on her pad of paper. "I'll e-mail you, Arnie. You can let me know what works for you. I tend to put in long hours. I hope that's okay."

Arnie's pale eyes practically glowed. "It's fine. Sure. I'll be there." He stood and nodded. "Anytime. Just e-mail me."

"Thanks for your help," Jack said.

"Oh, yeah. No problem."

The other man left. Jack waited until the door closed, then turned to Samantha.

"You've made a friend."

"Arnie? He's very sweet, or so I've been told. I think we'll do fine together."

Jack told himself that she would never be interested in the other man and even if she was, it wasn't his business. He didn't care who Samantha wanted in her life as long as she did her job. He very nearly believed himself, too.

"What have you got?" he asked.

"Lots and lots of great ideas," she said with a smile. "I had an extremely productive weekend. I went over the existing Web site. It's pretty basic. There's so much room to improve and that's what I want. I want to start with kids twelve and under as our first target audience and I want to dazzle them."

She set a folder on the conference table and opened it. "We'll deal with the teens later, but first, let's get some buzz going. I want us to be the Web site the kids are dying to go to the second they get home from school. I want to do more than help them with their homework. I want us to be the coolest place on the Web. We can talk about sports and clothes and music. Movies, TV, trends. I was thinking we'd have an 'Ask Annie' kind of column."

He stared at her. "Who's Annie?"

She laughed. "I mean an advice column. Ask the resident expert. Annie, Mark, the name isn't important. But here's the cool part—it will be real-time and inter-active. Like a chat room. I have a lot of ideas for devel-oping all this. But our biggest concern is security. We're going to have to go state-of-the-art so the kids are to-tally safe on the Web site."

"I like it."

"Good."

Her smile widened and he felt it punch him right in the gut. Ever-present need growled to life.

"You don't need to run all this by me," he told her, doing his damnedest to ignore the blood rushing to his groin. "I trust you to run your department."

"I know, but this is big stuff. I'm talking about huge changes."

"That would be the reason I hired you."

She studied him. "You really trust me with all this?"

"Of course."

"Wow. Great. I guess I'll get my team to pull it all together and then we'll have a big presentation."

"I look forward to it." He leaned toward her. "That's how I run things, Samantha," he told her. "Until some-one screws up, he or she has free rein."

"I would have thought you were more the control type."

"Because I wear a suit?"

"Sort of. You're a lawyer. That doesn't help with the image."

"What if I went into environmental law?"

She grinned. "Did you?"

"No. Criminal."

"So it's not just *suits*. It's designer suits."

"Mostly. But even at the law firm, I give my people room to grow and make mistakes. One screwup isn't fatal."

She tucked her hair behind her ear. "That sounds so balanced."

"I like to think of myself that way."

"You were less balanced in grad school. Much more…"

He looked at her. "Stick up the ass?"

Her mouth threatened a smile, but she held it back. "I would never have said that."

"But you were thinking it."

"Maybe a little. You had that study schedule."

"It kept me on track and freed up my weekends. I had plenty of time for fun."

"I remember," she said with a laugh. "Okay, I'll let it go. You weren't that rigid. I think you were just so much more together than any other guy I met. It scared me."

He wondered if that was true. Had he made her uneasy in ways he hadn't understood? Did it even matter now?

"You were the most unstructured successful person I'd met," he said.

"I was kind of crazy back then," she admitted. "I've calmed down some."

"I hope not. I liked you crazy. Remember the time we spent Christmas eve in a stable because you wanted to know what it was like?" he asked.

She laughed. "Yes, and you kept telling me that I needed to pay attention to geography."

"I was right. We were in Pennsylvania in the middle of winter. Not exactly the Middle East."

Despite the cold, they'd had a great time huddled together. He'd wanted her with a desperation that had made him tremble more than the cold. The next morning, he'd driven her to the airport so she could fly home to spend Christmas Day with her mother.

Speaking of which… "How's your mom?" he asked.

Samantha's smile faded. "She passed away about three years ago."

"I'm sorry," he said. "I really liked her."

"Thanks. I miss her. It was hard to lose her. She'd been sick for a while, so it wasn't a big surprise. We were able to say our goodbyes, which made things better." She collected her papers. "Okay, I'm going to let you get back to work. I have to put my presentation together so that you're dazzled, too. You will be, you know."

"I don't doubt it."

He walked her to the door, then returned to his desk. Only a crazy man would continue to want what he couldn't have, he told himself. Which made him certifiable. It was the human condition, he thought.

And now she'd caught Arnie in her web. Jack could almost pity the guy. The difference was Arnie would probably fantasize about happily-ever-after while Jack only wanted Samantha in his bed. He'd learned a long time ago to concentrate on the physical and ignore the emotional. There was no point in engaging his heart—people who claimed to love quickly got over the feeling and then they left.

Samantha hadn't been sure what to expect when she'd signed up for "executive housing," but she was pleasantly surprised by all her condo had to offer. There was a spacious living room with a semi-view, a dining area and plenty of room in the kitchen, especially for someone who made it a point to dirty as few pots as possible.

Her bedroom held a king-size bed, a dresser and an armoire with a television. The closet was huge and she'd already soaked her troubles away in the massive whirlpool tub in her bathroom. There was even a workstation alcove with a desk for her laptop, good lighting and high-speed Internet connection.

The only downside to the space was the fact that it felt…impersonal. The neutral colors were so bland and the furniture so functional. There wasn't anything funky to be found.

Still, the condo worked for now and it was about double the size her New York apartment had been. As she stood in front of the slider leading out to her small balcony and considered take-out options for dinner, she felt a whisper of contentment steal over her.

Coming to Chicago had been a good idea, she thought. She'd needed to leave New York. Despite loving the city, there were too many Vance memories around, and she'd needed to get away from them and him. Here she could start over. Build new memories. There were—

Someone knocked on her door. She crossed the beige carpet and looked through the peephole.

"Jack?" she asked as she pulled open the door.

"I'm presuming," he said, holding up two brown bags. "I come bearing Chinese food. I have wine, too. Sort of a welcome-to-the-building thing. Interested?"

She was delighted, she thought, stepping back and motioning him to enter. Instead, a black-and-white border collie slipped by Jack and stepped into the apartment.

"This is Charlie," Jack said. "Do you like dogs?"

Samantha held out her fingers for Charlie to sniff, then petted him. "I love them." She crouched down in front of Charlie and rubbed his shoulders. "Who's a handsome guy?" she asked, then laughed as he tried to lick her face.

"He likes you," Jack said. "Smart dog."

She laughed. "Okay, now I *really* want to have dinner with you. Come on in."

She led the way to the kitchen where Jack opened the wine and she collected plates for their dinner. As she opened the bags and began pulling out cartons of food, she noticed a bright red plastic bowl and a box with a big *C* on it.

"This is interesting," she said, holding up both.

Jack grinned sheepishly. "They're for Charlie. He loves Chinese, so the place I go mixes up a special rice dish for him. It's beef and chicken, rice, vegetables, light on the salt and spices. He loves it and the vet approves. It's kind of a special treat."

Samantha did her best to reconcile the straitlaced lawyer she knew Jack to be with a guy who would special order food for his dog.

"Now I know who's really in charge," she murmured.

"Yeah," Jack said easily. "He's the boss."

He helped her carry the cartons to the table. Charlie was served, but he waited until they sat down before digging in to his dinner.

Jack held out his glass of wine. "Welcome to the neighborhood. I hope you like it."

"Thank you." They touched glasses, then she took a sip of the red wine. "Very nice. All of this."

"No problem. I thought you might still be feeling out of place."

"Some. I like the apartment, but it's weird because nothing in here is mine. Like these plates." She held up the plain cream plate. "I would never have bought these."

"Too normal?"

"Too boring. Color is our friend."

"Agreed. But you'll get settled, then you can find a place of your own."

"I know. But for now, this is great. They make it very convenient."

Jack passed her the honey-glazed shrimp. "That's why I'm here. Dry cleaning right downstairs. The corner grocery store delivers. The dog walker lives across the street. There are over twenty restaurants in a five-block square around here and a great park close by where Charlie and I hang out on weekends."

She glanced at the dog who had finished his dinner and was now sniffing the floor for rice grains he might have missed. "He's beautiful. But doesn't he need exercise and attention? You're a guy who works long hours."

"He's fine," Jack said. "Is it quiet enough here for you? That's the first thing I noticed when I moved in. How quiet it was. Good construction."

She started to agree, then realized he had not-so-subtly changed the subject. "It's great," she said. "What aren't you telling me?"

He looked at her and raised his eyebrows. "I don't know what you mean."

"About Charlie. You changed the subject."

"From what?"

"How he gets through the day without tearing up your place."

"He keeps busy."

Jack looked uncomfortable. She glanced from him to the dog. "What? He watches soaps and does a crossword puzzle?"

Jack sighed. "He goes to day care, okay? I know, I know. It's silly, but he has a lot of energy and border collies are herding dogs. I didn't want him alone and bored all the time so three days a week he goes to doggy day care. There he plays with the other dogs and herds them around. He comes home so tired that on Tuesdays and Thursdays he pretty much just sleeps. I have a dog walker who comes by twice a day to take him out."

The muscles in his jaw tensed slightly as he spoke.

She could tell he hadn't wanted to share that part of his life with her.

She did her best not to smile or laugh—he would take that wrong—not realizing that women would find a big, tough, successful guy who cared that much about his dog pretty appealing.

"You're a responsible pet owner," she said. "Some people aren't."

He narrowed his gaze, as if waiting for a slam. She smiled innocently, then changed the subject.

After dinner they moved to the living room. Charlie made a bid for the wing chair in the corner. Jack ordered him out of it. The dog gave a sigh of long suffering, then stretched out on the carpet by Samantha.

Jack glanced around at the furniture, then studied the painting over the fireplace. "So not you," he said.

Samantha looked at the subtle blues and greens. "It's very restful."

"You hate it."

"I wouldn't have gone for something so…"

"Normal?" he asked.

She grinned. "Exactly. Too expected. Where's the interesting furniture, the splash of color?"

"I'm sure you'll do that with your next place."

"Absolutely. I miss fringe."

He winced. "I remember you had that horrible shawl over that table in your apartment when we were in grad school. It was the ugliest thing I'd ever seen."

"It was beautiful," she told him. "And it had an amazing color palate."

"It looked like something from a Dali nightmare."

"You have no taste," she said.

"I know when to be afraid."

He smiled as he spoke, making her own mouth curve up in return. It had always been like this, she thought. They rarely agreed and yet they got along just fine. She liked that almost as much as she liked looking at him.

He'd changed out of his workday suit into jeans and a long-sleeved shirt. The denim had seen better days. Dozens of washings had softened and faded the material, molding to his long legs and narrow hips.

A controlled sex appeal, she thought. Reined-in power that always made her wonder what would happen when he lost control. How big would the explosion be? She had an idea from their lone night together. He had claimed her with a need that had left her shaking and desperately wanting more.

Step *away* from the memory, she told herself. Talk about dangerous territory.

"Don't you have some furniture and decorations from your New York apartment?" he asked.

"I have a few things in storage," she said. A very few things. In an ongoing attempt to control her, Vance had fought her over every picture and dish. It had been easier and oddly freeing simply to walk away.

An emotion flickered in his dark eyes. "I know you're coming off of a divorce. How are you holding up?"

The news wasn't a secret, so she wasn't surprised that he knew. "Okay. It was tough at first. I went through the whole 'I've failed' bit, but I've moved on from that. Right now I'm feeling a lot of relief."

"It's a tough time," he said.

She nodded. "I had really planned to stay married to the same man for the rest of my life. I thought I'd picked the perfect guy." She paused. "Not perfect. Perfect for me. But I was wrong."

An understatement, she thought grimly. "We wanted different things in nearly everything. I could have lived with that, but he changed his mind about wanting children." She kept her voice light because if she gave in to her real feelings, the bitterness would well up inside of her. She didn't want to deal with that right now. Talk about a waste of energy.

"I'm sorry," Jack said. "I remember you used to talk about having kids all the time."

"I still plan to have them. I think I have a few good years left."

"More than a few."

She smiled as she spoke. Jack liked the way she curled up on the sofa, yet kept one leg lowered so she could rub Charlie with her bare foot.

She still painted her toenails, he thought, looking at the tiny flowers painted on each big toe. She even had a toe ring on each foot. None of the women he got involved with were the toe-ring type. Of course none of them wore jeans with flowers sewn onto the side seams or sweaters that looked more like a riot of colors than clothing.

"Enough about me," she said. "What have you been up to, romantically?"

"Nothing that interesting," he told her. "No wives, current or ex. I was engaged for a while."

"Oh. It didn't work out?"

"She died."

Samantha's eyes widened. "Jack, I'm sorry."

"Thanks. It was a few years ago, just before Christmas. Shelby's car spun out on an icy bridge and went into the water. She didn't make it."

"How horrible."

Samantha was the sympathetic type. She would want to say the right thing, only to realize there wasn't one. He'd heard all the platitudes possible and none of them had made a damn bit of difference. Not after he'd found Shelby's note. The one she'd written before she'd died.

"Was it very close to the wedding?" she asked.

"Just a little over a week. We were planning to get married New Year's Eve."

She bit her lower lip. "You must hate the holidays now."

"Not as much as I would have thought. I get angry, thinking about what was lost."

Not for him and Shelby—he'd done his best to let that go—but for her family. They were good people and he knew they'd yet to move on.

"Relationships are never easy," she said.

Charlie chose that moment to roll onto his back and offer his stomach for rubbing. Samantha obliged him and he started to groan.

"That dog knows a good thing when he has one," Jack said.

She looked at him and grinned. "Oh, right. Because *you* don't spoil him."

"Me? Never." He sipped on his wine. "Are you overwhelmed by work yet?"

"Almost. Ask me again in two days and I'm sure the answer will be yes. There's so much to do, and that's what makes it all exciting. This is a great opportunity."

He was glad she thought so. He wanted energetic people solving company problems as quickly as possible. "Have you heard about the big advertiser party? It's in a few weeks. It's an annual function and very upscale. Formal attire required."

"Really? You mean I have an excuse to buy a new dress and look fabulous?"

The thought of her in something long and slinky suddenly made him look forward to the party in ways he hadn't before. "It's not just an excuse," he said. "It's an order."

"And you'll be in a tux?"

He grimaced. "Oh, yeah."

"I'm sure you'll look great. All the women will be fawning over you."

"Fawning gets old," he said, doing his best not to read anything into her comment. While he wanted to believe she was flirting, he'd been shot down enough in the past to know that wishful thinking got him exactly nowhere.

"Do you have a lot of it?" she asked, her green eyes sparkling with humor.

"Enough."

"And just how much is that?"

He sensed they were in dangerous territory, but he wasn't sure how to avoid getting in trouble.

"I date," he said cautiously.

"I would guess that you have women lining up to be with you," she said easily. "You're good-looking, successful, well-off and single. That's fairly irresistible."

Except for Samantha, that had always been his take on it, too. So why did he get the feeling that she didn't see the list as a good thing?

"Some women manage to resist," he said. "What about you? Ready to start dating?"

"I don't think so. Not for a while. Divorce has a way of sucking the confidence out of a person. Or at least it did me."

He couldn't believe that. She had always been confident. Smart, funny, gorgeous. "It doesn't show."

She smiled. "Thanks. I'm getting by on sheer determination."

"It's working."

He wanted to tell her she had nothing to worry about—that she was as desirable as ever and he was willing to prove it.

Not a good idea, he reminded himself. So instead of speaking, or acting, he stood. "It's late. Charlie and I need our beauty sleep." He whistled softly. "Come on, boy."

Charlie rose and stretched. He licked Samantha's hand, then joined Jack.

She got up and followed them to the front door.

"Thanks for stopping by. Dinner was great. I appreciated the company, as well." She crouched down and rubbed Charlie's ears. "You're a very handsome boy. We'll have to get together again soon."

Charlie barked his agreement.

Figures, Jack thought with a grin. After all these years, she falls for the dog.

## Chapter Three

Nearly a week later, Jack sat behind what had been his father's desk, cursing his agreement to take over the company, even temporarily. Every day brought a new crisis and, with it, bad news. At this point all he was asking for was twenty-four hours without something major going wrong.

He'd already had to deal with the IT people informing him that their Web pages were nearly at capacity and, to support the Web expansion, they were going to have to negotiate with their server. The previous quarter's report showed magazine subscriptions falling for their three best publications. A train derailment had destroyed nearly a hundred thousand magazines heading to the West Coast markets and he'd just seen the layout for the launch of their new home-decorating magazine and even he could tell it sucked the big one.

There was too much to deal with, he thought. How the hell had his father done all this *and* run several departments?

Jack leaned back in his chair and rubbed his temples. He already had the answer to that one—George Hanson hadn't done it well. Things had slipped and there'd been no time to fix them before the next crisis had appeared. Despite hiring department heads, Jack was still overwhelmed by the sheer volume of work.

As far as he could tell, there was only one way for Hanson Media Group to survive—he had to get more help.

He buzzed for his assistant. When Mrs. Wycliff entered his office, he motioned for her to take a seat.

"I need to get in touch with my brothers," he said. "Do you know where Evan and Andrew are these days?"

If the older woman was surprised that Jack didn't know where to find his brothers himself, she didn't show it.

"I'm sorry, I don't," she said. "Would you like me to try to find them?"

"Please. I suggest you follow the credit-card charges. That's generally the easiest way." Evan favored Europe and Andrew tended to follow the seasons—summering in exclusive beach resorts and wintering in places like Whistler and Gstaad.

Jack knew all the psychobabble about siblings. In

every family each tried to get his parents' attention in a different way. For Jack, it had been about being the best at whatever he did. He'd learned early that he was expected to take over the family business and for a long time he'd worked toward that. But in the end, he'd walked away from Hanson Media Group, just like his brothers.

None of them had made the old man proud.

Did Evan and Andrew ever feel guilty? Jack had tried to make peace with his father more than once, but the old man had never seemed interested. All he'd talked about was how Jack should be at Hanson Media Group instead of practicing law.

Jack regretted losing touch with his brothers a lot more than he regretted disappointing his father.

"I'll get right on that," Mrs. Wycliff told him. "Have you spoken with your uncle?"

"Not about this," Jack told her. "But that's a great idea. Thank you."

She rose. "I'll let you know as soon as I locate them," she said, then left.

Jack buzzed David's office. "Hi. Are you available?"

"Absolutely."

The public relations department was the next floor down, on the main level of Hanson Media Group. Here the bright overhead lights contrasted with the rich blues and purples in the carpet and on the sofas and chairs.

Jack took the stairs and made his way to David's office. His uncle couldn't have been more different from

Jack's father. Where George had lived and breathed business, David always had time for his nephews.

David's secretary waved him in. Jack pushed open the door and walked into David's large office.

The space had been designed to impress and put people at ease. It did both. David walked around his desk and shook hands with Jack, then pulled him close for a quick hug.

"How's it going?" David asked as he led the way to the sofas in the corner. "Still finding things wrong?"

"Every day. I'm hoping for some good news soon. I figure we're all due."

"Toward the end, George wasn't himself," David said. "I think the work became too much for him. I'm guessing. He didn't confide in me."

"Did he confide in anyone?" Jack asked.

"Probably not. You hanging in there?"

"Do I have a choice?"

Jack looked at his uncle. Like all the Hanson men, he was tall, with brown hair. His eyes were lighter and he was nearly twenty years younger than his brother. Maybe that was why David had always been closer to his nephews. Maybe that was why David had been able to be there for them, Jack thought. George had been more like a father than a brother to David.

"You always have a choice," David told him. "You could walk."

"I gave my word to the board. I'm here for three months to clear things up and then I'm gone. I'm trying to get ahold of Evan and Andrew."

David frowned. "Good luck with that."

"Mrs. Wycliff is going to follow the money. That always works." Jack shook his head. "They should be here. We should do this together."

"You've never been close. Why expect it now?"

"Good point." Jack didn't have an answer. "Who am I kidding? If I had the chance to bolt, I'd take it."

"No, you wouldn't," David said. "You could have told the board no and you didn't. You have a strong sense of responsibility."

"Great. Look where it got me—here."

"Is that so bad?"

"It's keeping me from my real job." Jack leaned forward. "Why don't you take over? You know more about Hanson Media Group than any of us. You could run the company."

"Not my thing," David said. "Even if it was, I would respect my brother's wishes. He wanted one of his sons to be in charge."

"We don't know that," Jack said. "And we won't until the will is read." He swore. "What was my father thinking? Why on earth would he want us to wait three months to read the will? It's crazy. Nothing can be settled until then. For all we know, he's giving his majority shares to the cat."

David grinned. "He didn't have a cat."

Someone knocked on the door. "Come in," David called.

His secretary walked in with a tray and set it on the coffee table. "Anything else?"

David smiled at her. "Thanks, Nina. You didn't have to do this."

"No problem. Oh, you had a call from the printers."

David groaned. "I don't want to know, do I?"

"Not really," Nina said cheerfully. "Don't worry. I've already fixed the problem."

With that she left.

Jack reached for one of the cups of coffee. "Tell me Andrew and Evan will at least come back for the reading of the will."

David looked at him. "Are you hoping to cut and run the second their plane touches down?"

"It crossed my mind. I have a law practice to get back to."

"Maybe you'll appreciate your career more if you have to suffer a little here," his uncle told him.

Jack narrowed his gaze. "If you start talking about Zen centering, I'm going to have to punch you."

David laughed. "You know what I mean. You shouldn't take things for granted."

"I don't. I'm not here to learn a life lesson. My father convinced the board that I was the only possible heir and now they're pressuring me to take over. It's all about self-interest. His, theirs, mine. My father didn't give a damn about what I wanted. He's doing his best to control me from the grave."

"George loved you," David said. "In his own way."

"That's like saying the black widow spider doesn't mean it personally when she kills her mate." He took another drink of coffee. "You've always defended him, even as you stepped in to take his place as our father."

David shrugged. "I wanted to help."

"You should have had a family of your own."

"So should you. Speaking of which, I put out a press release about the new people you've hired. One of the names was familiar."

"Samantha was the best person for the job," Jack said, refusing to get defensive.

"I don't doubt that. I'm simply saying it was interesting to see her name again. I remember her from your time in grad school. The one who got away."

"She was never that," Jack told him.

"You talked about her as if she were."

"That was a long time ago. Things are different now."

"Is she married?"

"No."

"Then maybe fate is giving you a second chance."

Jack looked at his uncle. "If you start drinking herbal tea next, we're going to have to have a talk."

David chuckled. "I'm just saying maybe you're getting a second chance."

"I don't believe in them."

David's humor faded and he gave Jack a serious look. "Not every woman is Shelby."

"I know that." He put down his coffee and stood. "Don't worry about me. I'm fine. As for Samantha, she's a co-worker, nothing more."

David grinned. "You're lying. But we'll play your game and pretend you're not."

"Gee, thanks. And if you hear anything on the whereabouts of my brothers, let me know."

"You'll be the first."

"Oh, my," Helen said as she looked around the condo. "It's very…"

"Plain? Beige? Boring?" Samantha asked with a grin.

"I was going to say very 'not you.' But those will work as well." She stepped forward and hugged Samantha again. "I'm so glad you're here."

"Me, too. Getting out of New York was number one on my to-do list. You made that happen."

Helen sank onto the sofa and dismissed Samantha with a flick of her wrist. "Oh, please. I got you an interview. I certainly didn't get you hired. It's not as if Jack would ever think to ask my opinion of anything. You got the job on your own."

Samantha settled next to her friend and touched her arm. "You look tired. How do you feel?"

"Exhausted. Shell-shocked. It's been two months. I guess I should be used to it by now, but I'm not." Tears filled her eyes, but Helen blinked them away. "Damn. I promised myself I was done with crying."

"There's no time limit on grief."

"I know." Helen squeezed her fingers. "You're sweet to worry about me. I'm fine."

"No, you're not."

"Okay. I'm pretending to be fine and that should count for something. Most of the time I do okay. I can now go for an hour or two without falling apart. In the beginning I was only able to survive minutes. So that's an improvement. It's just I miss him so much and I feel so alone."

Samantha didn't know what to say. Helen really *was* alone in all this. She didn't have any family of her own and George's sons hadn't exactly welcomed her with open arms.

"Have you tried talking to Jack?" she asked. "He's not unreasonable."

"I know," Helen said as she dug in her purse. She pulled out a tissue and wiped under her eyes. "He's very polite and concerned, but we're not close. I tried. I tried so hard, but no matter what I did, those boys resisted." She sniffed. "I suppose I shouldn't call them boys. They're all grown men. They were grown when I met them. It's just that's how George thought of them. As his boys."

Samantha angled toward her friend. "I don't get it, either. They should have adored you."

"Oh, I agree. I did everything I could think of. On my good days, I tell myself it wasn't me. George was a wonderful man, but he was never very close with his sons. I don't know why. Whatever problems they had existed long before he met me. Oh, but I loved him so much."

"I know you did."

Helen smiled. "All right. This is stupid. I didn't come here to cry. I want to talk about you. Tell me everything. Are you loving your job?"

Samantha accepted the change in subject. She didn't know how to help her friend, so maybe distracting her would allow her a few minutes away from the pain.

"Every second," she said. "There's so much work, which is great. I like keeping busy. I have so many ideas for the new Web site that I've started keeping a pad of paper and a pen on the nightstand. I wake up two or three times a night with more details or directions or things we could do."

Helen wrinkled her nose. "I can see we're going to have to have the 'balance' conversation in a few weeks."

"Maybe," Samantha said with a laugh. "But for now, I'm really happy. I like the people I work with, I feel I'm contributing. It's great."

"Do you miss Vance?"

Samantha sighed. "No. And I really mean it. I thought I'd hurt more, but I think all the betrayal burned away the love. For the longest time I thought I'd never forgive him. Lately, I've come to see that I don't care enough to worry about forgiveness. He was horrible in so many ways. I have to think about myself and getting better. Not about him."

"Good for you. You've made a fresh start. You can get back on your feet. Look around. Maybe fall in love again."

Samantha held up her fingers in the sign of a cross. "Get back. There will be no talk of love or relationships in the context of my life, thank you very much." She lowered her hands to her lap. "I'm done with men."

"Forever?"

"For a while. I don't need the pain and suffering."

"It's not all like that," Helen said. "Vance wasn't the one for you. You figured that out and moved on. It was the right thing to do. But you don't want to turn your back on love. You don't want to miss the chance to have a great love. I believe there's one great love for everyone."

Samantha nodded. "And George was yours."

"He was everything," Helen said. "I was so lucky to find him. We shared so much. That's what I want to remember forever. How much we shared. How much we mattered to each other. I'll never find that again."

Samantha wondered if that was true. Helen was still a relatively young woman. And a beautiful one. Samantha had a feeling there was at least one other great love in her friend's life. As for herself, she wasn't interested in trying. Not when she'd been burned so badly.

"Speaking of men," Helen said. "What's it like working with Jack?"

"Good. He's very efficient and gives me all the room I need."

Helen raised her eyebrows. "And?"

Samantha shrugged. "And what?"

"Are there sparks? I remember there were sparks when you were in grad school with him. I remember long discussions about whether or not you should risk getting involved with him. I also remember saying you should, but you ignored me."

"He's not my type," she said, sidestepping the sparks question. Mostly because she didn't want to admit they were still there and starting fires every time she and Jack were in the same room.

"Type doesn't always enter into it," Helen said. "Some men simply turn us on."

"If you say so."

Her friend stared at her. "Jack isn't like Vance. He's honest and he's been hurt."

Samantha drew back. She was beginning to think all men were like Vance. "Are you matchmaking? If so, stop right now. It's so not allowed."

"I'm not. I'm making a point. Jack's a great guy."

"For someone else."

"If you say so."

Jack's last meeting finished at four. He returned to his office and found several empty boxes by the wall.

Mrs. Wycliff, efficient as ever, had delivered them while he'd been out. He planned to pack up a lot of his father's things and have them put in storage until his brothers showed up. Then the three of them could sit down with Helen and figure out who wanted what and what to do with anything left over.

He headed for the bookcase first. There were several out-of-date directories and registries. He dropped those into boxes without a second glance, then slowed when he came to the pictures of his father with various clients, city leaders and employees.

"No pictures of family," Jack murmured. No graduation shots, no informal photos taken on vacation or over holidays. Probably because they'd never much traveled as a family and, after his mother's death, holidays had been grim, dutiful affairs at best.

It should have been different, he thought. He knew guys with brothers and they were all tight. Why hadn't he, Evan and Andrew connected? Why weren't they close? They were all dealing with the death of their father. Wouldn't they do it better together?

"Did it matter? I don't even know where they are."

What did that say about the relationship? That he had no idea where to find either of his brothers? Nothing good.

He finished with the bookcase and started on the credenza. He needed room to store reports, quarterly statements and the like. The credenza was perfect. He pulled out old files and glanced through them. Some of them were over a decade old. Was that what had gone wrong with the company? Had his father been unable to stay focused on the present?

Jack had a feeling he would never get those questions answered. He and his father had never been close and any opportunity for that had been lost years ago. What made the situation even worse was Jack could barely feel regret about the circumstances.

He filled more boxes with papers, files and bound reports. When the credenza was empty, he reached for the quarterly reports and started to slide them in place. But the shelf wasn't high enough.

"That doesn't make sense," he said as he looked at the credenza. "They should fit."

He reached inside and poked around, only to realize

the base of the shelf was too thick by a couple of inches. What the hell?

After a little more prodding, he felt a narrow piece of metal, almost like a lever. When he pushed on it, the shelf popped up revealing a long, shallow recessed space and a set of leather books.

Jack's first thought was that his father had kept a diary. He was surprised to find himself anxious to read the older man's thoughts. But when he picked up the first book and flipped through it, there weren't any personal notes. Instead he stared at rows and rows of numbers.

His world was the law and it took him a second to realize he was looking at a detailed income statement. He glanced at the date and felt his stomach clench. This was for the previous year. He'd just spent the better part of the morning looking at the income statement for the past year. He was familiar with those numbers and they weren't anything like these.

Even though he already knew, he still found the first statement and compared it to the one his father had kept hidden. All the entry titles were the same but the amounts were different, and not for the better.

Anger filled him. Anger and a growing sense of betrayal. George Hanson had kept the truth from everyone. Jack didn't know how he'd done it, but the proof was here in the second set of books he'd hidden away.

Not only was the company close to bankruptcy, but his father's concealment had been criminal and premeditated. The company was totally screwed—and so was Jack.

## Chapter Four

Jack carefully went through the books, hoping to find something to show that he'd been wrong—that his father *hadn't* defrauded employees, stockholders and his family. But with every column, every total, the truth became more impossible to avoid.

He stood and crossed to the window where the night sky of Chicago stretched out before him. He could feel the walls closing in and fought against the sense of being trapped. With news like this, the board would pressure him to stay longer. They would insist that a three-month commitment to get things straightened out simply wasn't enough. In their position, he would do the same.

He heard someone knock on his office door, then push it open. He turned toward the sound.

"You're working late," Samantha said as she walked toward him. "I had a feeling you would still be here. You executive types—always going the extra mile. Doesn't being so conscientious get—" She stopped in mid-stride and stared at him. "What's wrong?"

So much for a poker face, he thought grimly. There was no point in keeping the truth from her. He would be calling an emergency board meeting first thing in the morning. Time was critical. The financial information would have to be disclosed, first to the board, and then to the investors and the financial world. His father had insisted on taking the company public, which meant playing by the rules of the SEC.

"I found a second set of books," he said, nodding toward his desk. "My father kept them by hand. I've checked them against the computer financial statements and they don't add up. He was concealing massive expenditures and losses."

Samantha's eyes widened. "Fraud?"

"That's one word for it. I can think of fifty others. We're going to have to do a complete audit and find out the true financial situation. I doubt it's going to be good news. We're talking about a possible SEC investigation, plenty of bad press and downturn in the stock price." He returned his attention to the view. "At least the family owns a majority of the shares. We don't have to worry about a total sell-off. There will be a hit in our price, but it shouldn't be too bad. Not with a new management team in place and complete disclosure."

"I don't know what to say," she admitted.

"You and me, both. Not exactly what you want to hear about your new employer. Ready to cut and run?"

"What? Of course not." She moved next to him. "Are you all right?"

"I'm not happy, if that's what you mean. Just once, I'd like to be surprised by good news."

"Jack, you're talking about your father. That he concealed material financial information. That's a big deal."

"Good thing he's dead, then. Otherwise, he'd be going to jail."

He sounded so calm, Samantha thought. As if all this were happening to someone else. From what she knew, Jack and his father had never been tight, but this had to be hard for him. No one wanted to find out a parent had committed a crime.

"He wasn't a bad man," she said, not knowing if there was any way to make this easier for Jack. "Maybe he just got in over his head."

He looked at her. "You're trying to justify what he did?"

"Of course not. But from everything I've heard, he wasn't evil."

"He doesn't have to be evil to have broken the law. People do it all the time." He shook his head. "I'm almost not surprised. He ran several departments himself. He couldn't give up the control. Maybe this was just another way of holding on tight. The numbers weren't what he wanted them to be, so he modified them. No wonder he wasn't big on change—technology would have made it tough for him to hide the truth."

"But he did," she said.

"In spades. I wonder if David knows about this?"

"Are you going to ask him?"

"I'm going to ask everyone," Jack said. "The only way to ward off a crisis is to have a plan in place to solve the problem and to find anyone who may have helped him."

"You don't think he acted alone?"

"Unlikely. But I know it was his idea."

"You might want to talk to Helen," Samantha said before she could stop herself. "She may know something."

Jack glanced at her. "You think she was involved?"

"What? No! Helen wouldn't do anything like this. But she might be able to tell you if George was acting stressed or if he suddenly seemed to change. She might have some suggestions."

His mouth twisted. "I don't need shopping advice."

Samantha stiffened at the insult to her friend. "Is that what you think of her? That she's a useless bimbo who only cares about clothes and jewelry?"

He shrugged. "I don't really know the woman."

"And why is that? She's been a part of this family for a while now. Why weren't you interested in even trying to get to know her?"

"I'm familiar with the type."

"Helen isn't a type. She's a person and she's not the person you imagine her to be. How interesting. You think your father got himself and the company in this position because he held on too tight to outdated ideas. It seems to me that you're a lot like that, too."

\* \* \*

Samantha took notes as one of her team members wrapped up his presentation. "Great job, Phil," she said. "I really like how you're using colors to coordinate your section. It will make navigating the site really fun."

"Younger kids respond to colors. They're easier for them than instructions," he said with a grin. "I was thinking we could use the same format for the sections for older kids, but with the colors getting darker. Light blue flowing into dark blue into navy. So clicking on anything blue will automatically pop up math-related questions."

"Good idea," she told him, then looked at Arnie. "So, does that make your job harder or easier?"

Arnie rubbed his hand on his khakis. "Once we get it programmed, it's not a problem."

"Good." She found it helpful always to include the IT guys in on the planning stages of any Internet project. Better to get their cooperation and input while the work was still easily modified.

"You could, ah, use drop-down menus, too," Arnie said. "After they click on the color. So it's not just one question. It could be a series. And then based on how they answer, they can go to another place on the site. Like if they get the answer right, they get a mini game. You know, for motivation."

Samantha glanced at her team, who all seemed pleased with the idea.

"Good thinking," she said. "You have a big thumbs-up on that one, Arnie. Thanks."

He shrugged and blushed. His gaze never left her face.

Samantha recognized the signs of a crush and wasn't exactly sure what to do about it. Not only wasn't she looking for love right now, Arnie wasn't her type. He was a nice enough guy, but nothing about him caused her to tingle.

Just then the conference-room door opened and Jack stepped inside. He didn't say anything and quietly took a seat in the back.

Instantly her body went on alert, just in case her brain hadn't noticed his arrival. She hated that even though she was still angry with him, she reacted physically. She found herself wanting to sit up straighter and push out her chest. Of course the complete lack of significant breast-type curves made that gesture futile, but still, the urge to flaunt was there.

Go figure, she thought. Arnie was available and pleasant and smart and probably completely uncomplicated. Nothing about him pushed any of her emotional buttons. Jack might be available and sexy, but he was also her worst-case scenario, man-wise, and totally unreasonable. He made her crazy with his assumptions about Helen.

Which they would deal with another time, she thought as she turned her attention back to the meeting in progress.

"The reward games should be related to the topic," Sandy said. "At least on some level. Like a blaster game based on times tables for the math color or something scientific for the science section."

"The difficulty of the games could increase with each grade level," Phil added.

"We're going to be spending a lot of time on content," Samantha said. "But it will be worth it. We'll need to take these ideas to research and get them going on questions and answers. We can do timed and non-timed quizzes. Maybe coordinate some of the questions with what's being studied in the textbooks. Are they standardized by region? Let's find that out. If we can emphasize what they're already studying, we'll reinforce the teachers' lessons."

"I'm working on the time line," Jeff said. "So a kid can type in a date and find out what's happening all over the world at that time. We're thinking anything date related will reference back to the time line. So if someone is working on a paper on Thomas Jefferson and they go online for information, the Web site will offer a time-line link. That way the student can see not only what was happening in this country, but everywhere. We can also cross-reference, so with the Jefferson paper, they could talk about what was happening in China and how it was the same but different."

"Wish I'd had that when I was in school," Samantha said.

"Me, too," Jeff said. "I would have done better in history."

The meeting continued. Ideas were offered and discussed. They had a limited amount of time to get the Web site up and running, so there would be a final of only the best. Still, she wanted as much to choose from as possible.

As people spoke and offered suggestions, Samantha

was careful not to look at Jack. On the professional side, she knew it was important to put their argument behind them. As someone who cared about her friend, she was still really mad.

"That should take care of it for now," she said. "Good work, people. I'm impressed. We'll meet again on Friday."

Her staff stood and headed for the door. Arnie glanced at Jack, who remained seated at the table. The smaller man hesitated, looked at her, then left. Samantha had no choice but to acknowledge her boss.

"We're getting there," she said as she collected her notes.

"Yes, you are," he told her. "Your team works well together. I like where things are going."

"Good."

"You have an easy working style. You're firmly in charge, but you don't force your will on anyone."

"What's the point of that?" she asked. "I already know what I think. I'm looking for their ideas."

"Not everyone thinks that way."

She didn't know what to say to that.

"You're still mad at me," he said, making it a statement not a question, so she had no reason to deny it.

"I don't understand why you're determined to think the worst of Helen. From what I can tell, you barely know the woman. If you'd spent time with her and she'd been horrible, I would understand your less-than-flattering opinion. But you're basing it all on a few casual meetings and the mythology that stepmothers are inherently evil."

One corner of his mouth twitched. "It's not about her being my stepmother."

"Then what is it?"

He hesitated. "She's much younger than my father," he began. "My father was not a kind man."

Samantha stood. "Oh, I see. You're saying she married him for his money? Is that it?" Anger filled her. "I've known Helen for years. In fact, she used to be my babysitter. We've stayed close. She's like family to me. She loved your father. Maybe you and he didn't get along so you're having trouble with that concept, but it's true. She considers him the love of her life. I can't help defending her. It's like you're attacking my sister."

Jack rose. "You seem very sincere."

"I am."

They stared at each other. His dark gaze never wavered. At last he shrugged. "Then you must be right."

She nearly collapsed back in her chair. "What?"

"You've never lied to me, Samantha. I knew you pretty well back in grad school. You were never dishonest and you weren't stupid about people. So I'll respect your opinion on Helen."

Okay, she heard the words, but they didn't make sense to her. "What does that mean, exactly?"

"That you believe she's a good person. You're right, I haven't spent much time with her. I don't know the woman at all. Maybe she's nothing I've imagined."

Just like that? She studied him, looking for some hint that he was toying with her, but she couldn't find it. And to use his own words, she'd known *him* pretty well back in grad school and he hadn't been a liar, either. A little rigid maybe, but that was hardly a crime. Not that he'd done anything to admit *he* might be wrong in this case.

"Okay, then," she said. "That's good."

"So we're not fighting anymore?" he asked.

"I guess not."

"You sound disappointed."

"I have a lot of energy floating around inside of me," she admitted. "I'm not sure how to burn it off."

The second she said the words, his body stiffened. Tension filled the room and it had nothing to do with them not getting along. Every inch of her became aware of every inch of him and some of those inches were especially appealing.

Her mind screamed for her to run as far and as fast as she could. Her body begged her to stay and take advantage of the situation.

He broke the spell by glancing at his watch. "I have to prepare for the board meeting tomorrow."

"Is everyone flying in for it?" she asked.

"Most. A couple will tap in by phone. It's not going to be pretty."

She couldn't begin to imagine how that conversation would go. "I checked the papers this morning. There wasn't a leak."

He shrugged. "I didn't expect there to be. As of eight last night, only you and I knew."

"Oh." She'd assumed there were more people in the loop. "I didn't say anything to anyone."

"I knew you wouldn't."

With that, he excused himself and left. Samantha sank back in her chair and waited for the ache inside to fade.

What was it about Jack that got to her? He was everything she didn't like in a man—well-off, controlling, powerful. And yet he'd just said he was wrong about Helen. In all the years they'd been married, Vance had never once made a mistake—at least in his mind. Certainly not one he would admit to. So in that respect the two men were different.

But it wasn't enough, she thought. And she couldn't take a chance on making another mistake like the last one. If she did, the next one could kill her.

Three of the board members lived in the Chicago area. Two flew in and two would be on speakerphone. Mrs. Wycliff arranged for coffee and sandwiches, but Jack doubted anyone would be in the mood to eat. Not when the news was this bad.

He waited until exactly eleven-thirty, then walked into the boardroom. The five people standing there turned to look at him.

He knew a couple by sight, having met them at various functions. The other three introduced themselves, then introduced the two who hadn't been able to make the meeting. The chairman, a craggy man in his late sixties named Baynes, motioned for everyone to take a seat. Jack found himself sitting at one end of the long conference table, while Baynes took the other. Jack had filled each of them in by phone so now they could get right to it.

"Sorry business," the older man said. "How did it happen?"

Everyone looked at Jack. "I have no idea," he said. "Until you asked me to step in for my late father, I'd been busy with my law practice."

"He never talked about the business with you? Never mentioned how things were going?"

"No." Jack didn't see any point in explaining he and his father had never spoken much at all, about the company or anything. He set the second set of books on the conference table. "I found these when I was cleaning out his credenza. There was a false bottom on one of the shelves. He didn't want anyone to find them."

He pushed the books to the center of the table. No one seemed to want to be the first to touch them. Finally Baynes motioned for them and the lone woman on the board pushed them in his general direction.

"The chief financial officer has made copies of everything," Jack said. "She's already running the numbers to find out where we really are. We should have some accurate information by the end of the week."

"The auditors are going to have hell to pay," Baynes said absently.

Jack nodded. Every publicly traded company was required by law to be audited by an independent accounting firm. Somehow George's double books had gotten past them.

But their problems were the least of Jack's concerns.

"I've prepared a statement," he said. "We'll issue it after the board meeting."

Several of the board members looked at each other, but no one suggested not going public. Just as well, Jack thought. He didn't want to have to remind them of their legal or fiduciary responsibilities.

"You asked me if I knew about this," he said. "What about all of you?"

Baynes looked at him. "What are you suggesting?"

"That you were his board. Many of you had known my father for years. He would have talked to you."

Baynes shook his head. "George didn't confide in anyone. This was his company. He made that clear before he went public. Things would be done his way."

"So you just let him run the company into the ground?"

The woman, Mrs. Keen, leaned forward. "George presented us with financial reports. We had no reason to doubt their validity or his. Your father wasn't a bad man, Jack, but clearly he was in over his head."

That seemed to be the consensus, he thought. "Shouldn't you, as his board, have noticed that? Shouldn't you have made sure the man running Hanson Media Group knew what he was doing?"

"Attacking us isn't going to solve the problem," Baynes said firmly.

Right. Because they were all more concerned about covering their collective asses, Jack thought grimly.

"We need to present a united front," Mrs. Keen said. "Perhaps the board should issue a statement as well."

"Do what you'd like," Jack told her.

"Things would go better if we could announce that you would be taking on your father's job permanently," Baynes said.

Jack narrowed his gaze. "I agreed to three months and that's all. I'm not changing my mind."

"Be reasonable," the older man said. "This is a crisis. The company is in real danger. We have employees, stockholders. We have a responsibility to them."

"No, *you* have one."

"You're George Hanson's oldest son," Mrs. Keen said. "People will look to you for leadership."

"I'm not his only son," he pointed out. "I have two brothers."

Baynes dismissed them with a wave of his hand. "Who are where? They don't have the experience, the education or the temperament for this kind of work."

Jack did his best not to lash out at them. Losing his temper would accomplish nothing. "Three months," he said. "That's all. In the meantime, I suggest you start looking for an interim president. Hire someone who knows what he or she is doing."

"But—"

Jack stood. "There's no point in having a conversation about me staying or going. I'm not changing my mind. Besides, we don't even know who owns the majority of the company. My father's shares are in limbo until the reading of the will. Who knows—maybe he'll want them sold on the open market."

The board members paled at the thought. While they

were still taking that in, he made his escape. As he walked down the hall, he loosened his tie. But that wasn't enough to wipe away the sense of being trapped.

"Come on, come on," Samantha called as she stared at the basket and willed the ball to slide cleanly through the hoop. There was a moment of silence, followed by a *swish* of net.

"Woo hoo." She held up her hand to Patti, one of her directors. "Two more for our team. We're up by six."

Patti gave her a high five, then went back into position. Perhaps playing basketball in the corridor right outside her office wasn't standard corporate procedure, but Samantha found it really helped her people clear their heads after a long day of brainstorming.

"Lucky shot," Phil said as he dribbled the ball. He jogged in to take his shot. Samantha moved in front of him. When he stretched up to shoot, she batted the ball away and it bounced off the wall before rolling down the hall.

The game went quiet as Jack rounded the corner and picked up the ball. Samantha could feel her staff looking at her. She knew Jack had endured the meeting from hell with the board and braced herself for him to take that out on her.

He raised his eyebrows. "Who's winning?"

"My team," she said quickly. "We've been brainstorming all day and we're—"

"No need to explain," he said, then bounced the ball. "Got room for one more?"

She glanced at Phil, who shrugged. "Sure," she said.

Jack tossed the ball back, then took off his jacket. After pulling off his tie, he went to work on rolling up his sleeves.

"Who's on the other team?" he asked.

"I am," Phil said, then he quickly introduced everyone else. "Any good at this?"

Jack grinned. "Just get me the ball."

Ten minutes later, Samantha knew they'd been had. Jack wasn't just good—he was terrific. He could shoot from any angle and he rarely missed. His team pulled ahead and then beat hers by six points.

"You're a ringer," she said, trying to catch her breath.

"I've had some practice."

"Where'd you play?" Phil asked, after slapping him on the back.

"Law school. We all did, to unwind. Grad school, too, but not so much."

Samantha remembered that Jack had attended law school before going to Wharton. She also vaguely recalled him hanging out with friends on the basketball courts, but she'd never paid much attention.

Now she knew she'd made the right decision. Being close to Jack while he ran, dodged, threw and scored bordered on dangerous. She liked the way his body moved and the energy he put in the game. She liked how he worked with his team and how, when his shirt came unbuttoned, she got a glimpse of some very impressive abs.

Bad idea, she reminded herself. Lusting after the boss could only lead to trouble. Okay, so she wasn't ready for a real relationship—maybe it was time to find rebound guy.

"Thanks for letting me play," Jack told Phil.

"Any time."

"There's that pub on the corner," Jack continued. "Why don't I buy you all drinks." He glanced at his watch. "Say half an hour?"

"Great." Phil grinned. "Thanks."

"No problem."

Samantha waited until everyone else had disappeared into their respective offices. "You didn't have to do that."

"Buy them drinks?" He shrugged. "I wanted to. They let me play. I needed the break."

"The board meeting?"

"Yeah." He shrugged into his jacket. "You're coming, aren't you?"

She shouldn't. It wasn't smart. It wasn't a lot of things. "Sure. I'll be there."

"Good."

He smiled and her toes curled. She walked into her office. Rebound guy—absolutely. She would have to get right on that.

Jack didn't just order drinks, he ordered platters of appetizers, then proceeded to talk to each member of her team individually. Samantha watched him work the crowd and did her best not to react when he smiled at one of her female staffers.

Finally he settled in the stool next to hers. "You've

done well," he said in a low voice. "You have good people working for you."

"Thanks."

Despite the easy conversation around them, she was aware of being watched. Some of her team were mildly interested while a few—the single women—were trying to figure out the score.

"How did it go?" she asked.

"About as expected. They're more interested in protecting themselves than what really happened. We're making an announcement first thing in the morning. I have two phone calls scheduled with investors. The first is to tell them what happened, the second will come later when I announce our specific plan to rectify the situation."

"Do you have a plan?"

He sipped his drink. "Not yet, but I'm hopeful." He glanced around. "They're all working their butts off. I want to make sure it's not for nothing."

"It won't be. There will be some bad press, but we'll get through it."

"Until the next crisis."

"The company is in transition," she said. "There are always adjustments."

"I know. What I don't understand is why my father never had a successor picked out. He had to know he wasn't going to live forever."

"Maybe he was waiting for one of his sons to get interested in the company."

Jack took another drink. "Probably. I don't see Evan

and Andrew making a beeline to Chicago and, honestly, I can't see either of them being willing to take things over."

She touched his arm. "You don't have to do this if you don't want to."

"I'm aware I can walk away at any point."

But he wouldn't. Jack had a sense of responsibility. She respected that about him.

Once again her body reminded her that he was nothing like Vance, but her head wasn't so sure. On the surface her ex had been a great guy, too. Successful, a caring father. He'd said and done all the right things—right up until the wedding. Then overnight he'd changed.

Her father had done the same thing. In a matter of weeks, he'd gone from a loving, supportive man to someone who'd walked out and had done his best not to have to support his only child.

Powerful men often hid dark, guilty secrets. As much as she was attracted to Jack, she was determined to keep their relationship strictly professional. She couldn't afford to take another emotional hit right now.

"I should go," she said, collecting her purse.

"I'm heading out, too," he told her. "Want a ride home?"

Ah, the close confines of a car. So tempting and so dangerous.

"No, thanks. I have a few errands to run on my way home. I'll walk."

"Are you sure? I don't mind."

She smiled. "I appreciate the offer, but I'll be fine on my own."

She'd learned it was the only safe way to be.

## Chapter Five

Roger Arnet was a tall, thin blond man in his mid-fifties. He shook Jack's hand, then sat in the visitor's chair on the other side of the desk.

"How are you settling in?" Roger asked pleasantly. "Your father was a great man. A great man. You won't find filling his shoes easy."

Jack didn't know how to answer the question. News of the second set of books had been released to the public. The response in the press had been relatively mild since Hanson Media Group wasn't a major player in the city, but there had been plenty of uproar in the office. He wondered if Roger had any way of reconciling his insistence that George had been a great man with the reality of a company president who lied to his entire staff.

"I'm finding my way," he said, going for a neutral response.

"Good. Good." Roger smiled. "I understand you're a lawyer."

"Yes. I attended law school, then went on to business school. It was my deal with my father. I would study both and then pick."

"You chose the law. George was very disappointed."

Had his father spoken about him with everyone in the firm? "I'm here now," Jack said. "Which is why I wanted to talk with you. We're making some changes."

"I heard about them," Roger said. "I've been on vacation and when I got back, everyone was buzzing. The Internet, eh? Are you sure about that?"

"Very sure."

Roger took off his glasses and pulled out a handkerchief. "Arnie's been filling me in on your plans. Very ambitious. Very ambitious. A bit too much, if you ask me."

Jack leaned back in his chair. "Are you saying we're not capable of expanding our Web sites?"

"Expansion is one thing, but what you're proposing is something else. But then it's not you, is it? It's that new girl. Samantha something."

"Edwards. And she has my full support."

"Of course. She's very energetic, but in my experience, it's better if we take things slowly. Sort of feel our way. Technology is all fine and good, but this company was founded on print media."

"Magazines are expensive and change slowly," Jack

said. "We don't have any publication that has circulation over a million. We're barely breaking even on thirty percent of our magazines and we're losing money on the rest. The Internet is a significant part of our culture. It's not going away. Changes can be made there relatively inexpensively."

Roger nodded. Jack felt as if he'd just stepped into an alternative universe. If Roger was the head of IT in the company, shouldn't he be pushing for *more* technology, not less?

"Arnie mentioned all of this to me," Roger admitted. "But he's young and he tends to get ahead of himself. I hope he wasn't filling your head with a lot of nonsense."

Jack was willing to respect those older than him and he was certainly willing to listen to qualified opinions; however, he wasn't willing to be treated like an idiot.

He straightened and stared directly at Roger. "Let me be as clear as possible," he said. "This company is on the brink of financial ruin. I'm sure you've read about our recent problems. The announcement that my father kept a second set of books wasn't happy news. Doing business the old way isn't going to keep this company going. We need change and we need it quickly. I believe that technology is our best solution. Now you can get onboard with that program or you can find another company that is more to your liking."

Roger blinked. "That's very blunt."

"Yes, it is. I've heard good things about you and I hope you'll decide to stay, but if you do, be aware that we have a new direction and I expect everyone to be excited about it."

"All right. I'll consider what you said. As far as the Internet expansion, I'm concerned about the safeguards. Your target market is children and there are many predators out there."

Jack wasn't sure how to read him. Still, the truth would come out quickly enough. Either Roger was with him or Roger was gone.

"Protecting the children using our site is our first priority," Jack told the other man. "Samantha's first presentation was on Internet safeguards. She and Arnie are working very closely on that project. I appreciate your concern as well and I would ask you to oversee their work. Feel free to report back to me on any weak areas."

Roger seemed surprised. "Why should you trust me?"

"I believe you're genuinely concerned about the children," Jack said. "You're also slightly mistrustful of the changes. That will make you a good custodian of the security programs. You won't let anyone cut corners."

"Thank you for that. Let me think about all that you've said and get back to you."

"Of course. Thanks for coming in."

Roger shook hands with him, then walked to the door. Once there, he turned back. "I wish you could have seen your father at work here, Jack. He was brilliant. Simply brilliant."

"So I've heard."

\* \* \*

Restless after his meeting with Roger, Jack headed to Samantha's office.

"Got a minute?" he asked as she hung up the phone.

"Sure. Have a seat."

He glanced at the light wood furniture, the bright prints on the walls and the purple sofa by the corner. In a matter of a week or two, Samantha had taken the space and made it her own.

"Interesting decorating," he said as he settled in a chair.

She grinned. "You hate it."

"Hate is strong."

"There's a lot of really cool stuff in the company storage facility."

"Some of it dating back to the sixties," Jack murmured.

"You're right. I didn't want to get too wild, but I like having color to inspire me."

Which, apparently, applied to her clothes, he thought as he took in the orange-and-gold tunic top she'd pulled on over black slacks. Her hair was loose, in a riot of red curls that tangled in her beaded dream weaver earrings.

By contrast, his suit that day was gray, his shirt white and his tie a traditional burgundy. They couldn't be more different. Which is what had always made their relationship interesting, he reminded himself.

"What's up?" she asked.

"Have you met Roger Arnet?"

She wrinkled her nose. "Arnie's boss, right? I shook hands with him in passing, but we haven't spoken."

"Be prepared. He's not one to move with the times. He's opposed to the Internet expansion on many levels. He thinks the plans are too ambitious."

"Great. Just what I need. The person in charge of a critical department for me not getting onboard."

"I know he's going to be a problem. I told him he could get with the program or get out."

Her eyes widened. "That's not subtle."

"It's my style. I think he's a little more willing to compromise now. He does have one legitimate concern and that's to keep the site secure. Children are vulnerable."

"I agree and I've been working with the IT guys on different ideas for that. We're going cutting edge. No stalkers allowed."

"Roger felt very passionately about it, as well. You might want to put him on the team."

Samantha recoiled physically. "Do I have to?"

She sounded more like a twelve-year-old than a responsible adult.

"No, you don't," he said, holding in a smile. "It's your show. You can do what you like. I'm simply pointing out that sometimes it's better to find a way to work with those who don't agree with us. If you make Roger feel important and really use him on the project, you're more likely to win him over. I'll fire him if I have to, but I would prefer not to. He knows the company and he knows his job. All my reports about him are excellent."

"Good point," she murmured. "I'll do the mature thing and work with him. But I won't like it."

"No one is asking you to."

"Good to know."

She stood up and walked to a coffeepot on a low table by the window. When she held it out to him, he nodded. She poured two cups.

He took the one she offered and watched her walk back to her seat. He liked the way she moved and the way her clothes swayed with each step. When she sat back down, she sniffed her coffee before sipping, as if making sure no one had accidentally changed her drink for something else.

She'd been doing that for as long as he could remember. He used to tease her about it, which always sparked a furious argument during which she denied the action. Then he would hand her coffee and she would sniff and they would both laugh.

But this time he didn't say anything. A couple of nights ago, at the pub, she'd shut him down good. She'd been doing it in various ways ever since they'd first met. At some point he was going to have to accept the truth. Samantha simply didn't want him.

In his world, chemistry usually went both ways, but she was the exception to the rule. No matter how powerful the need inside of him, she didn't feel it. It was time to accept that and move on.

"Nothing about this job is boring," she said. "You have to admit that."

"Right now I'd be happy with a few days of boring. That would mean no new crisis."

She sighed. "You've been going from one to the other. That can't be easy."

He shrugged. "It is what it is. I'll deal with it. Are you still enjoying your condo?"

"Very much. You were right—the location is fabulous. Have you had pizza from that place across the street?"

"I'm a regular."

She sipped her coffee, then sighed. "I ordered it the other night. It's amazing. It was so good, I actually had some for breakfast. I've never done that in my life—not even in college. Until I tasted their pizza, I never really understood the whole deep-dish thing. But now I get it. Heaven. Pure heaven."

"Wait until you order their pasta."

"Really? I might do that tonight. I'm hoping to get out this weekend and explore a little more of the neighborhood. So far all I've seen is work and my building."

He consciously had to keep from offering to be her guide. He generally spent Saturday mornings with Charlie in the park, but a walking tour would give his dog plenty of exercise. They could—

No, he told himself. Samantha had made her position incredibly clear. He wasn't going to push anymore.

"You can go online," he said. "There's lots of information about the city there. Points of interest, planned walks, that sort of thing."

"Thanks," she said, sounding a little puzzled. "I'll do that. But if you're not busy we could—"

Mrs. Wycliff knocked on the open door. "Mr. Hanson, you have a call from Mr. Baynes."

He rose. "I need to take that," he told her, aware

she'd been about to suggest something for the weekend. While he wanted to accept and spend more time with her, he knew it would be a mistake. He'd spent too much time wanting what he couldn't have where Samantha was concerned. He needed to move on.

Saturday, Samantha dressed for the cool, clear weather, then collected what she would need for a morning spent exploring. As she stepped out of her condo, she thought about going up to Jack's place and asking him to join her. Except she had a feeling he would say no.

Not that she could blame him. She'd been so careful to shut him down time and time again, shouldn't she be happy that he finally got the message? It was better for both of them if they were simply work colleagues.

She walked to the elevator and hit the down button. It was better, she told herself. Sure Jack was a great guy, but he was also the type of man to push all of her buttons and not in a good way. As much as she liked him, she was also wary of him. He was too much like her father and Vance. Too much in charge. She'd been fooled already—she wasn't willing to go there again.

Not that she was even looking for a serious relationship, she reminded herself. The best thing would be to find rebound guy and make that work. If only Jack weren't so sexy and smart and fun to be with.

She stepped out into the crisp morning and drew in a deep breath. Enough, she thought. For the rest of the day, she refused to think about Jack. She would simply enjoy herself and—

Something bumped into the back of her legs. She turned and saw Charlie. The border collie gave her a doggy grin, then barked. Jack smiled.

"Morning," he said, looking delicious in worn jeans and a sweatshirt.

"Hi."

"Out to see the sights?"

She tugged on the strap of her purse/backpack. "I have everything I need right here. Maps, water, money for a cab in case I get lost."

"You picked a good day. It won't get too hot."

Was it just her, or had things taken a turn for the awkward? "So you and Charlie are headed for the park?"

He nodded. "Every Saturday, regardless of the weather."

She rubbed the dog's ears. The smart choice was simply to walk away. But she was lonely, she liked Jack and she wanted them to be friends.

"Can a non-dog owner come along?" she asked.

He hesitated, but before she could retract the question, he smiled. "Sure. When I get tired of throwing Charlie the Frisbee, you can take over."

"I'd like that." She fell into step beside him. "So how did you get Charlie? Did you grow up with dogs in the house?"

"No. I wasn't actually looking for a pet. Then a buddy from my law firm invited me over for dinner. I learned later it was with an ulterior motive. His dog had six-week-old puppies he was looking to sell to unsuspecting friends. Charlie and I bonded over a game of tag."

She laughed. "I wouldn't have thought a hotshot-attorney type could be influenced so easily."

"Don't tell anyone. He moved in a couple of weeks later and I quickly found out that puppies are a ton of work. For a year he chewed everything he could get his teeth on. Then I took him to obedience training and now we understand each other better."

They stopped at the red light on the corner. Charlie waited patiently until the light changed, then led them along the crosswalk.

"Have you been reading the papers?" Jack asked.

She had a feeling he didn't mean the fashion reports. "I've noticed there was some local coverage on Hanson Media Group, but I could only find a couple of articles in the national papers. You're right—there wasn't all that much press."

"Sometimes it's good to be small, relatively speaking. Now if we were one of the networks, it would be a different story."

"I'm surprised no one ever made any offer to buy the company out," she said. "So much of entertainment is now controlled by conglomerates."

"For all I know my father's been fighting off offers for years. He wouldn't sell and risk losing his name on the letterhead."

He sounded bitter as he spoke. "You don't agree?" she asked.

"It's not my thing. I don't need to be the center of the universe, at least as my father defined it."

They'd reached the park.

"The dog zone is on the other side," he said. "Hope you don't mind the hike."

"Exercise is my friend," she said with a grin. "At least that's what I tell myself."

"There's a gym in the building."

"They showed it to me on my tour. Very impressive." There had been several treadmills and ellipticals, along with weight machines and three sets of free weights.

"I work out every morning," Jack said. "It's pretty quiet at five."

"In the morning?" She shuddered. "That's because more normal people are sleeping. I can't believe you get up that early."

"I'm lucky. I don't need a lot of sleep."

"Apparently not. Most of the year, it's dark at that time."

"They have lights in the gym."

They'd need more than that to get her there. Coffee, for starters. And bagels.

"I'm not really into the whole sweat thing," Samantha told him. "I've been lucky. I don't seem to gain weight."

It sort of went with what was kindly referred to as a boyish figure. She decided it was a trade-off. Sure she didn't have anything to fill out her bras and padding was required to hint at anything resembling cleavage, but she'd never counted calories or given up carbs. She could eat what she wanted and still have the world's boniest butt.

"Exercise isn't just about weight loss. It keeps you healthy."

"So does getting enough sleep. Besides, I'm a big walker. I can go for miles." As long as there was plenty of food along the way. One of the things she missed about New York. All the street vendors and little delis where a pretzel or ice-cream craving could be instantly satisfied.

They walked through a grove of trees and came out in a huge open area. There were already a half-dozen dog owners and their pets running around. Jack found a spot in the sun and set down his backpack.

"Equipment," she said. "So what exactly is involved in your Saturday-morning ritual?"

He pulled out a blanket. "For me," he said. Then a ball. "For Charlie. We start with this and work up to the Frisbee."

He unclipped Charlie from the leash, then threw the red rubber ball what seemed like at least a quarter mile.

Charlie took off after it, grabbed it and raced toward him.

"Impressive," she said. "The dogs don't get crabby with each other?"

"Not usually. Most people know if their dogs are social or not. There have been the occasional fights, but it's rare."

Charlie bounded toward them and dropped the ball at her feet. She winced.

"I throw like a girl," she told the dog. "You won't be impressed."

Jack laughed. "Come on. He's not going to be critical."

"Uh-huh. You say that now, but neither of you has seen me throw."

She picked up the slightly slobbery ball, braced herself and threw as hard as she could. It made it, oh, maybe a third of the way it had before. Charlie shot her a look that clearly asked if that was the best she could do before running after the ball. This time when he returned, he dropped it at Jack's feet.

"So much for not being critical," she said.

Jack laughed and tossed the ball again.

They settled on the blanket. The sun felt good in the cool morning. She could hear laughter and dogs barking. Families with children in strollers walked on the paved path that went around the dog park. There was the occasional canine tussle, but as Jack had said, no real trouble.

After about fifteen minutes of catch, Charlie came back and flopped down next to them.

"He's just resting," Jack told her. "Soon he'll be ready for the Frisbee. Then watch out. He can catch just about anything."

She rubbed the dog's belly. "I can't wait to see him in action."

"He'll show off for you."

"I hope so."

Charlie licked her arm, then closed his eyes and wiggled in the sun.

"What a life," she said. "I used to see dogs in New York all the time. I wondered what it was like for them to be in a city, but Charlie is hardly suffering."

Jack narrowed his gaze. "Is that a crack about the doggy day care?"

"No. Of course not. Why would I say anything about that?" She was careful not to smile as she spoke.

"Somehow I don't believe you, so I'm going to change the subject. Do you miss New York?"

She crossed her legs and shrugged out of her jacket. "Sure. It's a great city. But I can already see the potential here. The feeling is different, but in a good way. In New York I always felt I had to be going or doing or I'd miss something. I don't feel so frantic here."

"I like it. And the people. Are you missing your ex?"

A subtle way to ask about her divorce, she thought. It was a fair question. "No. The marriage was over long before I left. Unfortunately, I didn't notice."

"Did he agree with that?"

"No. Vance wasn't happy about me leaving." She ignored the memories of fights and screaming. "I just couldn't trust him anymore and once trust is destroyed, it's over."

"He cheated?"

The question surprised her until she realized it was a logical assumption, based on what she'd said. "Nothing that simple. I met Vance through my work—a fundraiser I worked on. He's a cardiologist. He has an excellent reputation and everyone who knew us both thought we'd make a great couple. So did I. He was divorced, but was still really close with his kids. I thought that meant something."

Jack frowned. "You wanted kids."

"I'm surprised you remembered."

"You used to talk about it."

She laughed. "Right. You thought two was plenty. I wanted four. You were uncomfortable with three because an odd number would make travel difficult. Ever practical."

"It's true. Try finding a hotel room that sleeps five."

"Okay. Good point. Anyway Vance knew I wanted children. We discussed it at length." That's what got her, she thought. That he'd agreed. "We even discussed names."

"He changed his mind?"

"More than that. He lied." She shook her head. "I was such a fool. We decided to wait a little, get settled in our marriage. Then, when I was ready to start trying, he kept putting it off. I never suspected anything. Finally I pressured him into agreeing it was time."

She paused as she mentally edited her past. There were so many other reasons she'd left Vance, but this was the easiest to explain.

"Nothing happened," she said. "Months went by. Finally, I spoke to my doctor, who agreed to do some tests. It made sense for me to go in first. After all, Vance had already fathered children. I came through fine and then it was time for Vance to make an appointment. Only he wouldn't. He finally came clean. He'd had a vasectomy after his youngest was born. He'd been lying the whole time."

Jack hadn't known where the story was going, but he sure as hell hadn't guessed the ending. "Samantha, I'm sorry."

"Me, too." She ducked her head and rubbed Charlie's chest. "I was so angry, but more than that, I was hurt. I couldn't understand why he hadn't told me the truth when we'd first started dating. It would have been so easy. He lied. Worse than that, he let me believe there was something wrong with me. He even hinted at it by telling me his first wife hadn't had any trouble getting pregnant."

He heard the betrayal in her voice and didn't know what to say. The man's actions made no sense. Why lie about something that was going to come out eventually? Why marry Samantha knowing she wanted kids and he didn't?

"What did he say?" he asked.

"Not much. That's what got me. He never took responsibility for his actions. He never thought he was wrong." She pulled her knees to her chest and wrapped her arms around her legs. "I can't tell you how much it hurt to find out the truth. It was as if I'd never known him. I thought he was different. I thought he was special, but I was wrong."

There was still pain in her eyes. Jack didn't know how long it would take to get over something like that. He knew a little of her past—that her father had walked out with no warning and had abandoned her and her mother. No wonder she was wary around men.

"Okay, this is boring," she said, a smile trembling on her lips. "Let's talk about something a little more perky. Like you. A lawyer, huh? Who would have thought."

"That's me—a man interested in the law."

"Really? But it's so stodgy."

He grinned. "Not to me."

"I don't know. All those thick books you have to read. Case law. So not my thing."

"Not to mention the clothes."

"Yeah. The dark suits would really depress me. So what's the game plan? You work your way up to senior partner, then torture new associates for sport?"

"That's one possibility."

"And the other?"

He didn't usually talk about his future plans with many people. Not that he didn't trust Samantha. "I want to be a judge."

She stretched her legs out in front of her. "Wow— that's pretty cool." She tilted her head and studied him. "I think you'd be good at it. You're very calm and you reason things through. If only the robe weren't black."

He chuckled. "Every career has drawbacks."

"True, and that's not a big one. Judge Hanson. I like it. All the more reason to get back to your law firm."

"Exactly."

"Which means every disaster is something you can almost take personally," she murmured. "That's got to be hard on you."

He wasn't surprised that she understood. He and Samantha had never had a communication problem. Their friendship had been based on long nights spent talking, arguing and seeking common ground.

"I've agreed to stay for three months," he said. "When that time is up, I'm going back to my real job."

"The company won't be the same without you," she told him. "But I understand why you want to leave."

Charlie stretched, then stood and looked meaningfully at the backpack. Jack pulled out the Frisbee and threw it. Charlie raced after it and caught it in midair. Samantha scrambled to her feet.

"Did you see that? He's incredible. Does he always catch it?"

"Most of the time. Border collies are athletic dogs."

"I guess."

Charlie trotted the Frisbee back and put it at Jack's feet. Jack threw it farther this time.

"Amazing," Samantha said. "What a fun way to spend your Saturday morning. Do you always come to this park?"

"Mostly. There are a few other dog parks around the city. Sometimes we jog along the lake. You'll have fun exploring."

"I know," she said absently, watching his dog. "Although my travels will be limited by my lack of driving."

"What? You don't drive?"

She crossed her arms over her chest. "No, I don't. I never learned before I went to college and once there, I didn't have the opportunity. Since then I've been living in Manhattan. I did fine with public transportation or walking."

"You don't drive?" He couldn't imagine it. How could someone not know how to drive?

"No matter how many times you repeat the question, the answer's going to stay the same," she said. "It's not that big a deal."

"It's a little scary," he said. "Want me to teach you?"

The invitation came out before he could stop it. Instantly he braced himself for her standard refusal. What was wrong with him? Why couldn't he accept the fact that Samantha just wasn't into him that way?

"I've seen your fancy car," she said. "Too much pressure."

Was that a yes? Did he want it to be? Wasn't he done trying to make points with her?

"I can get my hands on an old clunker."

"Really? I'm tempted. I've always felt, I don't know, weird about the whole driving thing." She studied him. "You wouldn't yell, would you?"

"Not my style."

Charlie barked, urging the Frisbee game to continue. Jack ignored him.

"Then thank you for asking," she said. "I'd be delighted to take you up on your offer. But if you change your mind, you have to tell me. I don't want you doing something you don't want to do."

"Again, not my style."

She laughed. "Jack, you're currently doing a job you hate because it's the right thing to do."

He chuckled, realizing she had a point. "Not counting that."

Charlie barked again. Then he picked up the Frisbee he'd dropped and brought it to them. Jack reached for it, as did Samantha. Their arms bumped, their shoulders crashed and the two of them tumbled onto the blanket.

Jack twisted and put out his hands to pull her against him, so he could take the weight of the fall. They landed with a thud that pushed out most of his air.

Her hands were on the blanket, her body pressed intimately against his. His legs had fallen apart and she lay nestled between his thighs. He could feel her breasts pressing against his chest.

Their eyes locked. Something darkened hers and all he could think about was kissing her.

There were a lot of reasons not to and only one reason he should.

Because he wanted to.

*Chapter Six*

Samantha felt the light brush of his mouth on hers. She knew she could easily stop him by saying something or simply rolling off him. It was the sensible thing to do. And yet she found herself not wanting to move. Her recollection of her previous kisses with Jack, from that one extraordinary night they'd shared, were still vivid in her mind. She was confident that she'd inflated their impressiveness over time. A kiss now would allow for comparison.

When she didn't move, he cupped her face with his hands and angled his head. Then he kissed her again, this time moving his lips back and forth. She felt heat and soft pressure. Blood surged in her body, making her want to squirm closer. She was already right on top of him, their bodies touching in so many interesting places, but suddenly that wasn't enough. She needed more.

He moved his hands, easing them past her ears so he could bury his fingers in her hair. Then he parted his mouth and bit down on her bottom lip.

The unexpected assault made her breath catch. He took advantage of her parted lips and slipped his tongue inside.

It was like drowning in warm, liquid desire. Wanting crashed over her, filling every cell until it was all she could think of. His fingers still tangled in her hair, which made her impatient. She wanted him touching her…everywhere.

Even as he circled her tongue with his, teasing, tasting, arousing, her body melted. She felt herself softening, yielding, kissing him back with a desperation that made her the aggressor.

She took control of the kiss, following him back into his mouth, claiming him with quick thrusts of her tongue. At last he moved his hands to her back where he stroked the length of her spine. Her hips arched in an involuntary invitation, which brought her stomach in contact with something hard, thick and very masculine.

Memories crashed in on her. She remembered how he'd touched her and tasted her everywhere. She recalled the sight of him naked, of how many times he'd claimed her. She'd been sore for nearly two days, but the soreness had only reminded her of the incredible pleasure they'd shared and had made her want to do it again. But she'd resisted—because of who he was and what he could do to her heart.

She hated the logic filling her brain, the voice that asked what was different now. She wasn't interested in danger or reality or anything but the way their bodies fit together. If she—

But an insistent barking distracted her and at last she lifted her head only to find Charlie's nose inches from her face.

Below her, Jack groaned. "I'm going to have to have a talk with that dog."

She became aware of their intimate position and the very public location. Without saying anything, she slid off him, then scrambled to her feet.

"We're in the park," she said more to herself than him. "In public."

Jack rose more slowly. He reached down for the Frisbee and tossed it, all without looking away from her.

"I doubt anyone noticed," he told her.

"Still." She pressed her hands to her heated face. Talk about acting out of character. She had always been a strictly-in-bed, lights-off kind of date. The only exception to that rule…was standing right next to her.

Of course. She was fine as long as she resisted Jack's particular brand of temptation, but if she gave in, even for a second, she completely lost her head.

"I, ah…" She glanced around, then returned her attention to him. "I'm, um, going to let you get back to your morning."

His dark eyes glowed with passion. "You don't have to."

"It's for the best."

His mouth straightened. "Let me guess. This was a mistake."

His tone of resignation caught her more than his words. He expected her to pull back because that's what she always did. There were several good reasons, but he didn't know them. If she had her way, he never would.

"Thanks for everything," she said, trying to smile. "I'll see you Monday."

She hesitated, then walked away when he didn't speak. A slight feeling of hurt surprised her. What did she expect? That he would come after her? Not likely after all the times she'd turned him down.

Jack watched her go. Once again Samantha was the queen of mixed signals. She had been from the beginning. Is that what made him want her? He never knew where he stood?

"Not exactly the basis of a great relationship," he murmured, throwing the Frisbee again.

The good news was Samantha wanted him sexually. The truth had been there in her response. For some reason, she couldn't handle the idea of it, but at least she didn't find him repulsive.

Was it him in particular or would she have run from anyone?

But she still liked to run and a guy with a brain in his head would let her go. Funny how he'd always been smart, everywhere in his life but with her. What was it about her that made him want to keep trying? It wasn't that he thought that they were soul mates. He didn't believe in that sort of thing and he sure as hell wasn't interested in a serious relationship. What was the point?

He was in it for the sex. Not a one-night stand. That wasn't fun anymore. He liked to take a lover for a few months, make sure they were both completely satisfied, then move on when one or both of them got restless.

Somehow he doubted Samantha would be up for anything like that.

Which left him where? Wanting a woman who didn't want him? There was a way to start the weekend. Okay, he was back to his original plan—forgetting about her as anything other than an employee.

Easier said than done, he thought as he remembered the feel of her body on his. But not impossible.

Jack reached for his coffee and cursed whoever had invented speakerphones and teleconferences. Spending an hour explaining to stock analysts and trade journalists how he had found a second set of books was not his idea of a good time.

"You're sure the investigation into how this happened has already begun?" a disembodied voice asked.

"Of course. It started less than twelve hours after I found the books. It would have started sooner, but I couldn't get an independent accounting team in here until morning."

"You're not using your regular accountants, are you?"

"No. No one who has ever been associated with

Hanson Media Group is involved. As soon as we have a preliminary report, I'll make it public. Until then, I don't have any answers."

"Do you think more people were involved than your father?"

Jack hesitated. "I don't have any specifics on that, but my personal opinion in that my father acted alone."

"Has his death been investigated? Are the company's troubles the reason he died?"

The not-so-subtle implication that George Hanson had killed himself infuriated Jack. He spoke through gritted teeth. "My father died of natural causes. There was an autopsy. He didn't kill himself." And he would sue any bastard who reported otherwise, Jack thought. He might not have been close to the old man, but he wouldn't let any member of his family be dragged through the press that way.

"Is the company going to make it?" someone asked.

Jack stared at the phone. In truth, he didn't have a clue. He continued to ride the bad-news train, with a new crisis every day. From where he sat, he couldn't imagine how this could be pulled off. In his opinion, it would take a miracle or a buyout for Hanson Media Group to survive, but he wasn't about to tell them that.

"We're going to come through this just fine," he said, wondering if saying it would make it reality.

Samantha had spent much of the weekend giving herself a stern talking-to. Being afraid was one thing, but acting like an idiot was another. She had to pick a side—any side. Either she was interested in Jack romantically or she wasn't.

She hated the mixed messages she sent every time they hung out together. She didn't like that she had become that sort of woman. In truth, she found him sexy and funny and smart and pretty much everything any reasonable single female would want in a man. But he was also rich, powerful, determined and used to getting his way, which terrified her.

There were actually two different problems. First, that however much she told herself she *wasn't* interested, that she only wanted a platonic relationship with him, her body had other plans. No matter how much her head held back, the rest of her was eager to plunge in the deep end and just go for it. The attraction was powerful and ten years after she'd first felt it, it didn't seem to be going away.

The second problem was also a head-body issue. However much her head could intellectualize that Jack was nothing like Vance or her father, her heart didn't believe. So she got close, he made a move, she reacted, then the fear kicked in and she bolted. It was a horrible pattern and short of never seeing him again in any capacity, she didn't know how to break it.

Whoever said acknowledging the problem was half the battle had obviously never lived in the real world. Understanding what was wrong didn't seem to move her any closer to solving it.

But solution or not, she owed Jack an apology and she was going to deliver it right now. Or in the next few minutes, she thought as she paced in front of his office. Mrs. Wycliff glanced at her curiously, but didn't say anything. Finally Samantha gathered her courage and walked purposefully toward the door. She knocked once and entered, careful to close the door behind herself. She didn't need any witnesses for her potential humiliation.

"Hi, Jack," she began, before starting her prepared speech. "I wanted to stop by and—"

She came to a stop in the center of the room and stared at him.

He sat at the conference table, the speakerphone in front of him, notes spread out. He looked as if he'd received horrible news.

She hurried to the table. "What happened? Are you all right?"

He shrugged. "I'm fine. I had the phone call with several investors and some people from the street. It didn't go well."

Of course. The problems with Hanson Media Group. As if he weren't dealing with enough from that, she was torturing him on weekends. How spiffy.

"I'm sorry," she said, sinking into the chair across from his. "I'm guessing they had a lot of questions."

"Oh, yeah. Plenty of suggestions, too. None of them especially helpful. But this is why they pay me the big bucks, right? So I can take the heat."

Maybe. But Jack wasn't interested in the money or the job. "Talk about a nightmare," she murmured.

"One I can't wake up from. But that's not why you stopped by. What's up?"

"I wanted to tell you I'm sorry about what happened on—"

"Stop," he said. "No apologizes required."

"But I want to explain. It's not what you think."

He raised his eyebrows.

She sighed. "Okay. Maybe it is what you think. I'm having some trouble making up my mind about what I want. I'm working on that. The thing is, I don't want you to think it's about you. It's not. It's about me, and well, who you are. Which isn't the same as it being about you."

He smiled. "None of that made sense, but it's okay. Let's just forget it and move on. You didn't like what happened and I'm okay with that."

She started to tell him that she *had* liked him kissing her, but stopped herself. That wasn't the point…at least she didn't think it was.

"You push my buttons," she admitted instead. "You have some qualities in common with my ex-husband."

Jack winced. "Not the good ones, right?"

"Sorry, no."

"Just my luck." He glanced out the window at the view of the city. Rain darkened the horizon and made the lights sparkle. "Life would be a lot less complicated without relationships."

"Not possible. Then we'd be nothing but robots."

"Or just very sensible people. Like Vulcans."

She smiled. "I'm not sure we should aspire to pointed ears."

"But their philosophy—no emotion. I understand the appeal."

"Too much pressure?" she asked, already knowing the answer.

"Too much everything. I remember when I was a lot younger. My brothers and I really got along. My father was busy with work, so there was just us and whatever nanny worked for him that month."

"I'm guessing the three of you were a handful."

He grinned. "Full of energy and imagination. It was an interesting combination. What I can't figure out is when we stopped being a family. That's David's big complaint and he's right. We don't pull together. I want to blame my father, but that only works so long. The three of us are grown-ups. We need a new excuse."

"Or maybe a way to change things. Would you like to be close to your brothers now?"

He nodded slowly. "Maybe together we could figure out how to fix this mess. But I can't get Evan and Andrew to return my calls. When it's time to read the will, I'll have to drag them back here. It's crazy."

"But they will come back," she said. "You could talk to them."

"I don't know what to say anymore. How sad is that?"

She had to agree it was pretty awful. If she had a brother or sister, she wouldn't ever want to lose touch.

"Maybe if you talk to Helen," she said without thinking. "She might have some ideas."

Jack looked at her. "No, thanks."

Samantha felt herself bristle. "What is it with you?" she asked. "Why won't you even give the woman a chance? Name me one thing she's done that you don't approve of. Give me one example of where she screwed up big time."

"I don't have any specific events," he said.

"Then what's the problem? You said you trusted my opinion of her and were going to stop assuming the worst." He made her crazy. Jack could be so reasonable about other things, but when it came to Helen, he refused to be the least bit logical.

"I don't think the worst," he said.

"You certainly don't think anything nice. She's pretty smart. Why don't you talk to her about the business?"

"My father wouldn't have told her anything."

"How do you know?"

"He didn't talk to anyone about the company."

"To the best of your knowledge. Did it ever occur to you that he might have married her *because* she's smart and capable? That maybe when things went bad, he talked to her." She held up both hands. "I'm not saying I know anything. But neither do you. You treat Helen like she's a twenty-one-year-old bimbo your father married because she had big breasts. It's crazy. You have an asset there you're not using."

He looked at her. "You're a very loyal friend."

"Helen makes it easy to be. Will you at least think about what I've said?"

He nodded. "Promise."

She was fairly sure she believed him. Jack had never lied to her. But why was this an issue in the first place? Why didn't he already know his stepmother's good points? Every family had secrets, but this one seemed to have more than most.

"It was just my mom and me," she said. "I can't relate to problems inherent in a large family."

"Want to trade?" he asked, then grimaced. "I'm sorry. I know you and your mom were close. You must still miss her."

She nodded, thinking she'd missed her most during the last few months of her marriage. When she'd wondered if Vance was really what she'd thought or if she'd been overreacting.

"We'd always had a special relationship," she said, "but we got even closer after my dad left. There was something about worrying about our next meal that put things in perspective."

"The man was a first-class bastard," Jack told her. "You haven't talked to him since?"

"He never wanted to talk to me. When I got older, I tried a few times, but eventually I gave up. He just wasn't interested. I heard he passed away a couple of years after my mom."

"I won't say I'm sorry. Not about him."

"I always think that things could have been different. I wasn't interested in him for what I could get. I just wanted a relationship with my father. But he never understood that. Why do relationships have to be so complicated?"

"Not a clue."

She stood. "Okay, I've taken up enough of your time. I just wanted to tell you that I'm sorry."

"Don't be."

"Thanks, Jack."

She left, not sure if she'd made things better or worse between them. She had a feeling that the only way to really solve the problem was to make a decision one way or the other and stick to it. If she was going to keep things business only, then she should not go to his office to chat. If she was interested in something else, then she should do that.

Complications, she thought. Questions and no answers. At least her life was never boring.

Jack returned from his working lunch meeting with the vice president of finance to find his stepmother waiting for him in his office.

Helen smiled when she saw him. "I was in the neighborhood," she said.

Under normal circumstances, he would have been polite and done his best to get her gone as quickly as possible. Since his last conversation with Samantha, he was curious to find out what Helen wanted.

He motioned to the leather sofa in the corner. Helen crossed the room and took a seat. He followed and settled in a club chair, then tried to figure out what was different about her today.

She was still pretty, blond and only a few years older than him. Not exactly a bimbo, as Samantha had pointed out, but still very much a trophy wife.

While she wasn't dressed in widow's black—did anyone still do that today?—she'd replaced her normally bright clothes with a navy tailored pantsuit. She'd pulled her hair back and, except for simple earrings and her wedding band, she seemed to have abandoned the heavy jewelry she usually favored.

"How are you doing?" he asked. "Is everything all right at the house?"

She frowned slightly. "I don't understand."

"You're alone in the house. I know it's large and I wondered if you were coping all right."

Eyebrows rose slowly. "You can't possibly be concerned about me."

He shrugged. "I'm asking."

"Hmm. All right. I'm doing fine. Yes, the house is big and empty, but your father worked long hours, so I'm used to being there alone."

Jack shifted in his seat and wished he'd never started the damn conversation in the first place. But he was already into it. "Are you, ah, sleeping?"

She sighed. "Not really. I still expect George to walk in and apologize for working late again. But he doesn't." She smiled. "Enough of my concerns. They're not why I stopped by. I wanted to check on you. It's been a difficult couple of weeks."

"You've been reading the paper."

"Several. There wasn't a lot of mention in the national press, which is something, but we're getting plenty of local coverage. I feel just horrible, Jack. I wish I could make this all better."

So did he. "Did you know about the second set of books?"

He watched her as she spoke to see if she got uncomfortable, but her cool gaze never flickered.

"I didn't. George didn't talk about the business very much with me. I wanted him to. I was interested. But he just wasn't one to do that. I do know that for the last year or so before he died that he was under a lot of stress. I had an idea there were problems with the company, but I had no idea they were this bad."

He wanted to believe her. Right now he had enough bad news without thinking there was someone making trouble from the inside. Not that Helen worked for the company, but until the will was read, she controlled his father's stock. Speaking of which…

"Do you know what's in his will?" he asked bluntly.

"No. He never discussed that with me, either."

"So what did you talk about?"

"Everyday things." She crossed her legs. "Jack, I'm not the enemy here. I always thought things would be better if you, your father and your brothers could reconcile."

"How magnanimous of you."

She drew in a breath. "So you still don't like me."

"I don't know you. Why is that?"

"I don't know," she said, surprising him. "I wanted to get to know you and Evan and Andrew. I invited you all over several times. You were the only one to come."

Jack remembered the lone uncomfortable dinner he'd attended. His father had spent the entire time telling him that his decision to go into the law instead of joining Hanson Media Group was foolish at best. That no good would come of it. Jack recalled walking out sometime between the salad and main course.

"He wasn't an easy man," he said.

"I know, but for what it's worth, I don't think he meant to be so difficult. He tended to see things one way."

"His."

"He wanted you to be happy."

Jack grimaced. "He wanted me to run his company, regardless of what I wanted."

"Here you are," she said softly.

"Lucky me."

"I wish things were different," she said. "I wish he weren't dead. Not just for me, but for you. I wish you didn't have to do this."

"There isn't anyone else," he reminded her. "I'm stuck."

"You're the best choice. I'm sorry this is taking you away from what you love but the company is important, too. We all have to make sacrifices."

"Not from where I'm sitting. So far it's a sacrifice committee of one. I wish I knew what was in the will. Maybe he left everything to you and I can screw up enough that you'll fire me."

She shook her head. "Don't hold your breath on that one. George was always interested in surprising people. I doubt he wrote a boring will."

He believed that. "If he left the company to me, I'm selling."

She stiffened. "Just like that? Your father gave his life to this company."

"I know that better than anyone, except maybe you."

"I loved him, which means I can forgive his flaws."

The implication being Jack should do the same.

He wanted to ask her how that was possible. How could she give her heart to a man who made sure she always came in second. But he didn't. There wasn't any point. People who were supposed to love you left, one way or the other. Some disappeared into work or circumstances. Some walked away and some died. But at the end of the day, everyone was alone. He'd learned that a long time ago and he didn't plan to forget it.

## Chapter Seven

Samantha was reasonably confident that driving lessons were a bad idea all around. For one thing, Jack should be really mad at her. For another, the situation had the potential to turn into a disaster.

"Second thoughts?" he asked from the passenger seat of the old import parked in an empty parking lot.

"Oh, I'm way past them. I'm on to deep regret and remorse."

"You'll be fine," he said. "It's easy. Think of all the crazy people you know who can drive."

"Telling me I'm likely to encounter the insane isn't a way to make me feel better," she told him. "Really. Let's talk about all the safe drivers instead."

"There are a lot of them. You'll be one of them. All you have to do is relax."

Oh, sure. Because that was going to happen. She peered out the windshield and was dismayed to note there wasn't a single cloud in the sky. Not even a hint of rain or bad weather or impending anything that would give her a good excuse to call off the session.

"You don't have to do this," she said. "I could hire someone."

"I don't mind. It will be fun."

Maybe for him. She curled her fingers around the steering wheel and sighed. "I don't think I'm up to it."

"Of course you are. You're afraid, which makes sense, but once you let go of the fear, you'll be fine. Think of the end goal. You'll be driving. You can go anywhere you want. You won't be dependent on bus schedules or trains. You're free. Close your eyes."

She looked at him. "I may not know much about driving but even I know that's a bad way to start."

He laughed. "You'll open them before we go anywhere. Close your eyes."

She did as he asked.

"Now imagine yourself driving on a big highway. The lanes are wide and it's divided so you don't have to worry about oncoming traffic. There are only a few cars and none of them are near you. It's a pretty day. You're going north, to Wisconsin. Can you imagine it?"

She did her best to see the road and not the flashing telephone poles or trees beckoning her to crash into them. She imagined herself driving easily, changing lanes, even passing someone.

"Now see yourself getting off the highway. At the top of the exit, you stop, then turn into a diner. You're completely comfortable. You're driving and it's easy."

She drew in a deep breath, then opened her eyes. "Okay. I'm ready."

"Good. We've been over the basics. Tell me what you remember."

She talked her way through starting the car, putting it in gear and checking her mirrors. Long before she wanted him to, he told her it was time to replace visualization with actual doing.

She started the engine. Of course it sprang to life. She carefully shifted into D and then checked her mirrors. They were blissfully alone in the parking lot.

"Here I go," she murmured as she took her foot off the brake and lightly pressed on the gas.

The car moved forward. It wasn't so bad. She'd had a couple of driving lessons back in college and she'd enjoyed those. These weren't all that different.

"Signal and turn right," Jack said.

Signal? She flipped on the indicator then turned. Unfortunately, she pulled the wheel too far and they went in a circle. Instantly she slammed on the brakes.

"Sorry."

"It's fine," he told her. "Don't worry about it. We're here to practice. If you could get it right the first time, why would you need to practice?"

He was being so logical and nice, she thought. Vance would have been screaming at her the whole time.

"Let's try that turn again," Jack said.

"Okay." She drove straight, put on her signal, then eased the car into a turn. It did as she asked.

"Wow. That was pretty easy."

"Told you," he said with a smile. "We'll make a couple more laps of the parking lot, then go onto the street."

"The street?" she asked, her voice a screech. From the back seat Charlie raised his head as if asking what was wrong.

"You can't stay in this parking lot forever," Jack said.

"Of course I can. It's a great parking lot. I like it. I could live here."

"You'll be fine. Come on. More driving. That way."

He pointed in front of them. She drove for another five minutes, making turns and coming to a stop when he told her. Despite her protests, he managed to convince her to head out onto the actual street.

"This is an industrial park," he said. "It's Saturday. There aren't going to be a lot of cars. Deep breaths."

She held in a small scream then took the plunge. Or, in this case, the driveway onto the street. Up ahead was an on-ramp to the highway and all the open road she could want. Like a cat let out of a carrier, she traded freedom for safety and took a side street. The highway would still be there tomorrow.

"And?" he asked as they cruised the produce section of the local market.

"You were great," she said. "Just terrific. Patient, calm and happy to explain everything fifty times."

He shook his head. "While I appreciate the compliments, they weren't the point. Admit it. The driving wasn't so bad."

It hadn't been. After nearly an hour in the industrial park, she'd actually driven back into the city. There had been a single harrowing experience at an intersection when some jerk had jumped the light and nearly hit her, but aside from that it had been…easy.

"You're a good teacher," she said.

"You're a good driver."

She sighed. "I am, aren't I? Soon I'll be really good. Then I'll have my license."

"Then you can buy a car."

"Oh. Wow." She'd never thought in actual terms of getting a car. "I like it. There are so many kinds. I could get a little convertible."

"Not a great choice in winter."

"Hmm. You're right. But maybe something sporty. Or an SUV. Then I could haul stuff on weekends."

"Do you have anything to haul?"

"I don't think so. Is it required?"

"The dealer isn't going to ask."

"Okay. Or maybe I could get a hybrid. That's more environmentally friendly and I always recycle."

He looked at her as if she'd suddenly grown horns.

"What?" she asked.

"Nothing. You about ready?"

She eyed the strawberries, then nodded. "I'm always tempted by out-of-season fruit. It's a thing with me."

He pointed to her overflowing basket. "You know, this store delivers."

"I heard, but I like to buy my own groceries. Check stuff out. What if I change my mind about what I want for dinner?"

"What? You don't carefully plan a menu for the entire week and then stick with it?" he asked.

She felt her eyes widen a split second before she realized he was teasing her. "No, I don't. But you rigid types plan everything."

"I've had a few surprises lately."

She was sure he was talking about the company, but she suddenly wished he were talking about the kiss they'd shared. That had been...nice.

She'd enjoyed knowing that her nerve endings hadn't died in the divorce and that, yes, eventually she would want to be with another man. Although she had a feeling that her powerful sexual reaction had specifically been about Jack, there was still hope for her future. Eventually she would find someone else to be interested in.

They went through the checkout, then Jack helped her load her bags of groceries into the trunk.

"Let's go," he said, opening the passenger door.

She stood on the sidewalk. "Wait. I can't drive back to our building."

"Why not? It's just around the corner."

"Yes, but once there, I'd have to park. I might even have to back up." She wasn't ready for backing up. Not on her first day.

"You can do it," he said and closed the door.

She glared at him for a full minute, but he didn't budge. That forced her to get behind the wheel and consider her options.

"I could just walk home," she said.

"What about your groceries?"

"You could carry some."

"But I won't."

He might not have screamed during their lessons, but he was very stubborn.

"Fine. I'll drive back, but if anything bad happens, you have to take over. And I'm seriously reconsidering the dinner I promised as a thank you."

"You don't have to do that. I was happy to help."

She looked at him. His eyes were dark and she couldn't tell what he was thinking. Maybe he didn't want to have dinner with her. After the way she'd over-reacted to his kiss, who could blame him.

"I'd like to cook you dinner," she said. "But I'll understand if you don't want to come over."

"We're friends, right?"

She nodded.

"Then sure. I'll be there."

Friends. The way he said the word made her wonder if the statement had been to help him remember their relationship, or if it had been about telling her. Maybe he was making it clear that where she was concerned, he'd made his last move.

Jack arrived at Samantha's apartment exactly at seven. He'd brought Charlie, even though the dog was tired from his day and would only sleep. Still, if conversation got slow, they could always talk about the dog.

Pathetic, he told himself. He was completely pathetic. Yeah, he wanted to do the right thing where Samantha was concerned. Be a friend, a boss and let the rest of it go. But no matter what he told himself or how many times she rejected him, he couldn't seem to stop wanting her. Even now, standing outside of her door, he felt his body tighten in anticipation.

He knocked and promised himself that when he got home, he was going to figure out a way to get over her for good. But until then, a man could dream.

"You're here," she said as she opened the door and smiled at him.

"Was there any doubt?" he asked.

"I hoped there wasn't. Come on in."

He let Charlie lead the way, using the microsecond before he entered to brace himself to withstand the assault of color, gauzy fabric and perfume.

She'd changed out of her jeans and sweatshirt—both covered in sewn-on flowers—and into a loose top and flowing skirt that nearly touched the top of her bare feet. She was a kaleidoscope of color, causing him not to know where to look first.

There was her hair, long and flowing and curly, but pinned up on one side. Her blouse that fell off one shoulder, exposing pale, creamy skin. Her feet with painted toes and at least two toe rings. Her arms, bare except for jingling bracelets.

"So you're back," he said.

She closed the door behind him. "What do you mean?"

"You've been a little conservative since you moved here. Oh sure, you've been playing basketball in the halls and wearing bright colors, but not in the way I remember. This is the first time you're exactly like you were."

She smiled. "That's about the nicest thing you've ever said to me. Thank you."

"You're welcome."

"Come on," she said, grabbing him by the arm and tugging him toward the kitchen. "I have wine and I'm going to let you be all macho and open it."

"It's what I live for."

They settled in the dining room with a bottle of wine and some appetizers. Charlie retreated to an ottoman where he curled up on the cushy surface and quickly went to sleep.

"I can get him down if you want," Jack said, jerking his head toward the dog. "He's great, but he sheds."

"No problem. A few dog hairs will make the condo seem more lived in. Right now it's still too perfect."

"And we wouldn't want that."

She dipped a chicken wing into spicy sauce. "Life's beauty is found in the irregular and unexpected. Ever see a perfect waterfall? A symmetrical sunset?"

"Technically the sun goes down in the same way every—" He broke off and grinned when she swatted him with the back of her hand.

"You know what I mean," she said. "I'm talking about the clouds, the colors and you know it."

"Maybe."

"My point is, dog hair is fine."

"Great. Maybe you'd like to take over grooming him, too."

"I wouldn't mind it. He's a great dog."

"I agree."

She sipped her wine. "I've noticed a bit more positive press in the past couple of days," she said. "There were at least two mentions of the upcoming advertisers' party. How Hanson Media Group is getting some things right."

"I saw them, too. David is doing a hell of a job trying to counteract the negative stories."

"You really like him."

"In some ways he's more like my father than George ever was. Or maybe a big brother. He's not that much older than me. He was always there, making time in ways my father wouldn't. Even though he traveled a lot, he kept in touch. He took the time. Sometimes that's all that's required."

"I know." She grabbed for a piece of celery. "After my father walked out, I missed him terribly. Sure there was the whole trauma of going from the rich princess to the kid in castoffs, but it was more than that. Given the choice between getting the money back and getting my father back, I would have gladly picked him. But either he didn't get that or he didn't care."

"I know he walked out on your mom, but didn't he see you at all?"

She shook her head. "One day he was just gone. That played with my head. How was I supposed to believe my father had ever loved me when he walked away and never looked back?"

She sipped her wine. "Mom was great. She really fought him. Some of it was about the child support. It's crazy that a guy that wealthy paid almost nothing. But he could afford excellent lawyers and they knew all the tricks. As for seeing me, he would make promises and then not show up. There was always a good reason. Eventually my mom stopped pushing. She saw that it was hurting me more to hope."

Jack couldn't imagine what kind of man simply walked away from a child. His own father—no poster child for perfect parenting—had at least gone through the motions. He'd shown up to graduations and big events.

"It was his loss," he said.

"Thanks. I used to tell myself that, too. Most of the time I even believed it. I grew up determined not to repeat my mother's mistakes. I didn't care if the guy had money, as long as I was important to him and we wanted the same things."

Her words hit him hard. Ten years ago, he'd been that guy, but she hadn't been willing to see that, or maybe she'd just never thought of him as more than a friend.

"Vance?" he asked.

"I thought so. He'd been married before, so he was cautious. I liked that wariness. It made sense to me. I could tell he liked me a lot, but he wanted to take things slowly and I respected that, too. In hindsight, I was an idiot."

"In hindsight, we all are."

"Maybe. But I was a bigger idiot. He talked about how his first wife had been obsessed with how much money he made. She wanted the best, the biggest, the newest. I decided not to be like her, so I didn't ask for anything. It took me a while to figure out that had been his plan all along."

Jack didn't like the sound of that. "He set you up?"

"I think so." She sighed. "Yes, he did. It's hard for me to say that because it makes my choice even more crazy. He's a cardiologist in a big, successful practice. When we talked about getting married, he was concerned about losing that. I wanted to reassure him."

Jack grimaced. "Prenuptial?"

"Oh, yeah. I was sensible. I read the whole thing. But I didn't bother to get a lawyer. Why spend the money? Later, I realized he'd played me. He'd made a joke that his first wife was so stupid that she wouldn't have been able to get past the first page. But that I was really smart and would understand it all."

She shook her head. "I don't know if it was ego or my need to prove I wasn't her. Either way, I did read it, but I didn't get a lawyer to and I missed all the subtleties."

Jack practiced criminal law, but he'd heard enough horror stories from co-workers practicing family law that he could guess the outcome.

"It wasn't what you thought."

"Not even close. Not only couldn't I touch his practice or any income from it, but everything of mine was community property. I got nothing of his and he got half of mine. The only bright spot is I didn't have a whole lot to take half of."

He reached across the table and covered her hand with his. "I'm sorry."

"Don't be. I learned an important lesson. My mother used to tell me the trick was to marry a rich man and keep him. I think the real trick is to not need a man at all."

"Speaking on behalf of my gender, we're not all jerks."

"I know." She squeezed his fingers. "I blame myself as much as Vance. There were warning signs. I didn't pay much attention to them."

While he knew intellectually that she was right— that she did have to take some responsibility—his gut reaction was to hunt down Vance and beat the crap out of him. Talk about a low-life bastard.

"Want me to have someone look over the settlement and see if anything was missed?" he asked, suspecting she wouldn't appreciate the offer of physical violence.

"Thanks, but I'm okay. I'm doing my best to put my past behind me. It's been hard. Not because I'm so crazy about Vance, but because I tried to be so careful and he made a fool out of me in so many ways."

"Which makes you naturally wary," he said.

"Oh, yeah. Between him and my father, I'm now

convinced any man I meet is out to screw me, and not in a sexual way." She grabbed another chicken wing.

"Ah, isn't this where you say present company excluded?" he asked.

She looked at him. "I want to. You're a great guy, Jack. I know that."

"But?"

"You're still a rich, powerful man. I'm having a little trouble letting go of that fact."

"I see your point. Here we sit, you thinking if you trust a guy he'll take off and dump on you in the process. I'm convinced anyone I care about will leave. We're not exactly a normal couple."

She grinned. "I like to think there is no normal."

"Do you believe that?"

"Sometimes. I know that I can't be afraid forever. I'm trying to get myself back." She tugged on the front of her blouse. "Dressing like this, for example. Vance hated my bohemian ways. He kept telling me I had to grow up."

Jack frowned. "Your free spirit is one of your best qualities. I'm sorry he didn't see that."

"Me, too. But there it is. He liked me to dress a certain way, that sort of thing."

"Controlling?"

She shrugged. "He was a cardiologist. He had an image."

"I know lawyers like that. It gets bad for their wives after they make partner. Suddenly what was great before isn't good enough anymore. I don't get it."

"That's because you're reasonable. Not everyone is." She released his hand and leaned back in her chair. "Now that you know the basic story of my pathetic divorce, I hope you'll understand why I'm becoming the queen of mixed messages where you're concerned. I know my past doesn't excuse my actions. I don't expect it to. I just hope you'll understand and accept my apology."

He stared at her. Until that second he'd never considered there was a reason for her behavior that had nothing to do with him.

"What?" she asked. "You have the strangest look on your face."

He shook his head. "I was just thinking that you being cautious around me was about you, not me. On the heels of that I realized I can't separate myself from who I am. I come from a wealthy family, I have a challenging, professional career. I am, on the surface, a walking, breathing manifestation of everything you're not looking for."

"Exactly."

At least she was being honest, he thought grimly. "A lot for us to overcome," he said, going for a light tone of voice. "I guess I should stop trying so hard."

She winced. "I feel really horrible. You've been nothing but nice to me. And before, in grad school, I loved us being close. You were terrific. I know in my head that you'd never hurt me."

"It's the rest of you that can't be convinced," he said.

"Yeah. But I've also decided it would be a good thing for me to face my fears."

While he liked the sound of that, he wasn't sure why she should bother. "You don't have to."

"It's the mature thing to do and I like to think of myself as mature. I want us to be friends."

Great. So much for making progress. "We *are* friends."

"I'm glad. I really love my job and I don't want to blow this opportunity."

"You won't," he told her.

"I hope not. It's just that…" She pressed her lips together and looked at him.

In any other woman, he would swear he was being given an invitation. But with Samantha? He wasn't sure. Better to stay on the safe side of the road.

"Remember that time we were studying in the park and that woman's dog got away from her?" he asked. "She was running around calling for him and you said we had to help."

She grinned. "Yes. And you told me that a dog would never come to strangers so I said we had to tempt it with food. So we went to that butcher and bought bones."

He'd felt like an idiot, he thought, but he'd been with Samantha so he hadn't cared.

"There we were, running around, calling for a dog and throwing bones around. Every stray in a three-mile radius started following us."

"It was sad," she said. "I felt so badly for those dogs."

"You felt badly? You're the one who insisted we find a rescue place for them. Then it was my car we crammed them into. Of course you hadn't realized that dogs like to mark what they think of as new territory."

She winced. "I felt really horrible about the smell, but the dogs got adopted. So that's something."

"Unfortunately none of the new owners was willing to buy my smelly car."

He'd been forced to get rid of it for practically nothing. Still, it had been worth it, he thought, remembering how happy she'd been about the dogs.

She leaned close. "Doesn't taking the moral high ground ease some of the financial sting?"

"Not as much as you'd think," he said, finding his gaze riveted on her mouth.

Dumb idea, he told himself. On a scale of one to ten, ten being somewhere between stupid and idiotic, this was a twelve.

But there was something about the way she smiled and the light in her eyes. Something that spoke of promise and desire.

Hadn't he always been an idiot where she was concerned?

He shifted toward her and lightly touched her cheek with his fingers. He thought that if he gave her plenty of warning, she would have time to bolt before he kissed her.

But she didn't. Instead she parted her lips slightly and drew in a quick breath.

He took that as a yes and kissed her.

He moved slowly, only touching her mouth with the lightest of brushes. He kept his hands to himself, or at least didn't do more than rest one on her shoulder and the other on her arm. He waited for her to kiss back.

And waited. One heartbeat. Two. Then slowly, almost tentatively, her lips moved on his. She pressed a little harder, then touched his bottom lip with the very tip of her tongue.

It was as if she'd just taken a blowtorch to his bloodstream. Heat and need exploded and he was instantly hard. He'd heard that it took longer for a man to get aroused as he got older. Apparently he hadn't crossed that threshold yet.

But as much as he wanted to pull her close, to rub his hands all over her until she was wet and weak and begging him to take her, as much as he wanted to take off her clothes and run his tongue over every inch of her, he did nothing. He sat there letting her take control of their kiss. Let her set the pace.

When she touched the tip of her tongue to his lip again, he tilted his head and parted for her. She slipped into his mouth and traced the inside of his lower lip.

Everything got hotter, harder and more intense. The need to take control, to claim her, threatened to overwhelm him, but he was determined not to screw up again. She'd made it clear that he pushed all her buttons, so it made sense to go slowly.

But when she circled his tongue with hers and sighed, it took every bit of self-control he had not to reach for her. Instead he mentally ground his teeth in frustration. He kissed her back, but slowly, without letting her know how deep the passion flowed. And when she withdrew slightly, he straightened, as if he were un-affected by what they'd just done.

She ducked her head and smiled. "That was nice."

"Yes, it was."

She glanced at him from under her lashes. "I'm a complete adult and I accept responsibility for what just happened."

Was that her way of saying she wasn't going to back off and run this time?

"And?" he asked, knowing there had to be a punch line.

"No *and*. Just that. And me saying thanks for being patient."

"My pleasure." Although pleasure didn't exactly de-scribe his painful state of arousal. He reached for an-other chicken wing and bit into it. In time, the need would fade to a manageable level. His erection would cease to throb with each beat of his heart and the tem-perature in his body would slowly cool. But until then, life was hell.

"You're going to have to go to a few Cubs games when the season starts," he said.

She laughed. "You're deliberately changing the subject."

"You noticed."

She smiled. "This is in an effort to erase the tension here and keep me from feeling awkward."

"Something like that." Some of his motivation was selfish. Thinking about baseball was a time-honored way to keep from thinking about sex.

Her smiled widened. "Okay. Then tell me everything you know about the Cubs."

"At least the news isn't getting worse," David said.

"Not exactly the sign of forward progress I would like," Jack said. "But it beats the hell out of our string of bad news. You've been working hard to get us favorable play in the press."

"It's my job."

Jack leaned back on the sofa in his uncle's office. "Helen came to see me last week. She wanted to talk about how I was doing. It was almost as if…"

David raised his eyebrows but didn't speak.

Jack shook his head. "It was almost as if she was worried about me."

"Is that impossible to believe?"

"Yes. Why would she care?"

"Why wouldn't she? You don't know anything about Helen."

"Do you?"

"Not really. George and I haven't been exactly tight these past few years. But I've spoken with her, spent a few dinners with her. She seems reasonable and intelligent. You might want to take the time to get to know her."

"That's what Samantha says. She's a serious advocate."

David smiled.

Jack narrowed his gaze. "What?"

His uncle's smile turned into a grin. "There's something about the way you say her name. So things are progressing."

"No and no. We're getting along. She works for me. That's it."

"Like I believe that."

"It's true. She is just getting over a divorce. I'm not interested in getting involved in that process."

"Have you considered the fact that you already are?"

Was he? Jack thought about the weekend, when he and Samantha had spent so much time together. Hearing about her past and her marriage made a lot of things more clear to him. But that didn't mean he was interested in her. Not in any way but sexually.

"I'm not involved," he told David.

His uncle nodded. "Keep telling yourself that. Eventually it will be true."

## Chapter Eight

The company had gone all out for the advertisers' party. As this was the first one Samantha had attended, she didn't know if the stunning decorations, incredible view and fabulous food were normal or if this party was a little bit extra-special in an effort to soothe their accounts.

Either way, she was excited to be there and felt just like Cinderella at the ball. For once, she'd left her loose and comfy clothes behind and had instead worn a form-fitting strapless gown in dark apple-green.

The shimmering fabric very nearly matched the color of her eyes. She'd gone simple in the jewelry department, wearing vintage paste earrings that looked like amazing diamonds. The antique settings made them look like the genuine article. Last, she'd spent nearly two hours on her hair, curling it on big rollers and then drying it. But the effort had been worth it. Her normally tight, natural curls were now loose and sexy. She'd pinned up the sides and left the back to cascade over her shoulder blades.

She felt good and knew she looked her best. The question was had she done enough to dazzle Jack?

"Not that I care," she murmured as she made her way to the bar for the glass of white wine she would hold on to for most of the evening. She refused to define herself by a man.

Not that she was. Wanting to knock Jack's socks off had nothing to do with definition and everything to do with the fire she'd seen in his eyes last weekend when they'd kissed.

She saw David and moved toward him. It was early and most of the guests hadn't arrived.

"You look beautiful," he said with a smile.

"Thank you. Great place. I love the view."

From one set of floor-to-ceiling windows was the lake and from the other were the lights of the city.

"We have a lot on the line," David told her. "Are you rethinking your decision to take this job? This isn't Hanson Media Group's most shining moment."

"Jack asked me that as well. I meant what I said then. I'm excited about the opportunity to create something wonderful."

"I've seen the preliminary designs on the Web site. They're great. And I've been over the security you want to put in place. It could be called obsessive."

She laughed. "I'm sure I'll hear worse before the launch. The point is to make this a safe destination for children. I'm willing to do everything possible to make that happen. Even if it means driving the IT guys a little crazy."

David grinned. "Good for you. Next week let's set up a meeting to talk about publicity for the launch. I've already reserved some space in a couple of kid magazines and there will be a few Saturday morning cartoon spots."

Samantha stared at him. "Television advertising?" She knew how much it cost.

"Jack said you were going to be the one to save the company. So he told me to think big."

She doubted Jack had ever said she would save the company but she knew the Web site could go a long way to boosting the bottom line. Still, she was surprised and pleased to find out how much he was supporting her.

"I'll call you," she said. "I have a lot of ideas for the advertising."

"Why am I not surprised?"

She laughed. "I have ideas for pretty much everything."

"That's what Jack said."

There was something in David's voice that made her wonder what else Jack had been saying about her. Not that she would ask.

Several clients walked into the ballroom. David excused himself and went over to greet them. Samantha followed more slowly, wanting to give him a moment to talk before she moved close and introduced herself.

She'd done plenty of industry parties. They had a simple formula for success. She had to make sure she spoke with everyone, was charming and friendly and remembered their names. Then, during the second half of the evening, she needed to circulate, chatting about anything and finding subtle ways to talk up the company. She'd also learned to pay attention to anyone who seemed to be on his or her own. Being lonely at a party was never a good idea. Taking a little time to be a friend and then introduce the shy person to others went a long way to making the evening a success.

David spoke with the group of eight men and women. She waited for a lull in the conversation then moved in closer.

David smiled at her. "This is Samantha Edwards, one of our newest and brightest additions to Hanson Media Group. Samantha is working on an incredible expansion of our Internet site for kids."

One of the women raised her eyebrows. "Do I want my children spending more time on the computer?"

Samantha smiled. "Probably not. Aren't they on there so much now?"

The woman nodded.

"It's a real problem," Samantha told her. "One I've been working on. My goal isn't to trap them inside for more hours, but to make their computer time more efficient, fun and safe, all the while making sure their homework gets done and their parents are happy."

"That's a big order," one of the men said. "Can you do it?"

She nodded. "Absolutely. Let me tell you how in two minutes or less."

She launched into the pitch she'd spent the last week perfecting, then stayed long enough to answer a few questions. When the group had moved away to sample the buffet, David took her by the elbow.

"Well done," he said.

"I believe in being prepared."

"Good. Let's go over here. I have some more people I want you to meet."

About an hour later, Samantha felt a distinct tingling on the back of her neck. Careful to continue to pay attention to the conversation, she casually looked around to find the source of her hyperawareness.

It didn't take her long to locate Jack standing by the window with two older men.

At the sight of him, she felt her blood surge a little faster. Her skin seemed to heat as her toes curled.

He looked pretty amazing in his tailored tux, but then he had the James Bond sort of good looks that were made for formal wear. The stark white of his shirt contrasted with his black tie.

Yummy, she thought, instantly recalling the kiss they'd shared and how her body had reacted to his nearness. Despite the fears left over from her previous marriage and her general wariness of men like Jack, she found herself wanting a repeat of their make-out session along with the time and privacy to take things further.

She forced her attention back on the conversation and away from Jack. After a few minutes, the tingle increased, then she felt a warm hand on the small of her back.

"Having a good time?" he asked everyone, even as he continued to touch her.

"Great party," Melinda Myers, the president of the largest string of car dealerships in the Midwest said. "Your father would be very proud, Jack."

Samantha guessed she was the only one who felt him stiffen slightly.

"Thank you," he said graciously. "Despite everything that has happened recently, I wanted to keep the family tradition going. Your business has been very important to us."

Melinda smiled. "Hanson Media Group has been a good partner for me. I don't want that to change."

"Nor do I," he told her.

Melinda nodded at Samantha. "I've been hearing great things about the new Internet site. Impressive. Samantha was just telling me about her plans and some innovative ways for my company to be a part of it."

"I hope you take her up on her offer," Jack said.

Melinda smiled coyly. "Of course I will. I know a good deal when I hear one. That's how I got to where I am now."

Samantha did her best to pay attention to the banter but it was difficult with Jack's fingers pressing against her skin. Heat radiated out from him, feeling hot enough to burn.

Warmth spread out in all directions, making her breasts swell and her thighs melt. She wanted to blame her reaction on the liquor, but she'd yet to take more than a sip of her wine. Her next best excuse was that she hadn't had much to eat that day.

A tall older man approached and asked Melinda to dance. Several other people excused themselves, leaving Samantha and Jack standing together beside the dance floor.

"So what do you think?" he asked, his dark eyes locking with hers.

She assumed he meant about the party and not her awareness of him. "The night is a hit," she said. "I had wondered how our advertisers would react to all the recent bad news, but they're taking it in stride. A lot of that is you." She grimaced. "I'm sorry. I know you don't want to hear that, but it's true. They see you as a capable replacement for your father."

"Nice to know they think I can do as well as a man who defrauded investors."

She touched his arm. "They don't mean it that way."

"I know." He set down his glass on a nearby tray. "Want to dance?"

She would never have thought he was the type to be comfortable on the dance floor and, to be honest, the thought of being that close to him was two parts thrilling and one part pure torture. Still, she'd never been able to resist things that were bad for her.

She set down her wine. "Absolutely."

He took her hand and led her to the edge of the parquet dance floor, then drew her into his arms. She went easily, finding the sense of being against him and swaying to music almost familiar. Had they done this before? In grad school? She didn't remember a specific time when they'd—

"You're frowning," he said. "I'll admit my moves are pretty basic, but I didn't think they were frown-inducing."

"What? Oh. Sorry. I was trying to remember if we'd ever danced together before."

"We haven't."

"You sound so sure of yourself."

"I am. I would have remembered."

Which meant what? But rather than pursue the question, she drew in a deep breath and consciously relaxed into the rhythm of the music.

The slow song allowed them to sway together, touching from shoulder to thigh. He clasped one of her hands while her other rested on his shoulder.

"Did I mention you look stunning?" he asked, his voice a low murmur in her ear.

"No, and because of that, I think you should have to say it at least twice."

"You look stunning. The dress is nearly as beautiful as the woman wearing it."

Ooh, talk about smooth. He certainly was a man who knew his way around a compliment. "I don't get much chance to dress up these days. It's fun for a change."

"And worth the wait."

The song ended, leaving her feeling as if she wanted more. A lot more. But this was a work-related party and she still had rounds to make, as did Jack.

"I'm off to dazzle," she said. "Thanks for the dance."

"You're welcome."

He held her gaze a second longer than necessary, and in that heartbeat of time, she felt her body flush with need. All the tingles and whispers and little touches combined into an unexpected wave of sexual desire.

Then Jack turned and disappeared into the crowd.

She stared after him, trying to remember the last time she'd felt safe enough to want a man. She'd spent the last two years of her marriage simply going through the motions of intimacy because it had been expected, but she hadn't enjoyed herself. She'd been too hurt and broken to let herself feel anything.

Had time begun to heal her wounds or was her reaction specifically about Jack? She knew what it was like to make love with him. The memory of their single night together had been burned into her brain. She remembered everything from the way he'd kissed her to the feel of him inside of her. He'd coaxed more orgasms from her that night than she'd had in the previous year.

Funny how a month ago she would have sworn she would never be interested in getting physical with a guy again in her life. But suddenly there were possibilities. Maybe not with anyone else, but certainly with Jack.

\* \* \*

Jack didn't bother counting the number of times he was compared with his father and told he was nearly as great as the old man had been. He couldn't believe so many people could know about his father's mismanaging of the company and still call him a good man.

By eleven, he was tired and ready to be done with the party. But there were more advertisers to schmooze and more hands to shake. It came with the job.

Helen walked over and offered him a glass of scotch. "How are you holding up?" she asked.

She looked beautiful in a fitted gown that showed off perfect curves. Her blond hair had been piled on her head, giving her a regal air. He didn't doubt there were plenty of men willing to take her home for the night, or as long as they could get.

Had she done that? She was substantially younger than his father. Had she taken lovers to keep herself satisfied?

Then he pushed the thought away. Why was he once again assuming the worst about her? He'd lived in the city and traveled in similar social circles as his father and Helen. There'd never been a whisper of gossip about either of them.

"Not my idea of a good time," he said. "What about you?"

She glanced around the crowd and shrugged. "Last year I came with George. I can't stop thinking about that and I keep expecting to turn around and see him. It's difficult."

She took a sip of her drink. As she shifted and the

light spilled across her face, he could've sworn he saw tears in her eyes.

He did swear, silently, calling himself several choice names for his earlier thoughts. "You really loved him."

"Stop sounding so surprised when you say that," she told him. "Of course I loved him. I'm very intelligent and very capable. I didn't need to marry someone to get what I wanted from life. I could have done that on my own."

He wanted to ask why his father. What qualities had the old man shown her that he'd managed to keep from his sons?

"They're saying good things about you," she said. "They're happy you're in charge."

"So that sharp clanging sound I hear is the door closing on my freedom?"

"I don't know," she told him. "No one wants you to keep a job you hate."

"Except the board of directors."

"It's not their job to be compassionate. I suspect, over time, they would come to see that an unhappy president wouldn't be best for Hanson Media Group."

"I don't think I have that much time."

"You could be right." She took another sip from her drink. "I saw you dancing with Samantha. You make a very attractive couple."

"She's a beautiful woman."

"And a friend. You're a great guy, Jack, but I know how you are. Serial monogamy is great in theory, but sometimes someone gets hurt."

She wasn't being subtle. "You don't want that person to be Samantha."

"She's just been through a difficult time."

"I know about her divorce."

Helen smiled. "I wonder if you really do."

"What do you mean?"

"Be kind to my friend."

"I'll do my best." He shook his head. "You put her name on the short list. I'd wondered how it got there."

"I knew she would do a good job and I thought she was someone you could trust."

There was something in her voice that implied she knew more than she was saying. How much had Samantha told her about their previous relationship?

"Good call on your part," he said.

"Thanks. I have my moments." She looked around at the large gathering. "Ready to plunge back into the hordes?"

"No, but there's not much choice."

She glanced back at him. "I know you don't care or even want to hear this, but your father would have been very proud of you."

He didn't say anything because he was starting to like and respect Helen, but as she walked away he acknowledged she was right. He didn't care about what his father thought.

Samantha knew she was babbling. It was late, she was tired and hungry and she couldn't seem to stop talking.

"I think the party had a real positive impact on our relationships with our advertisers," she said as Jack stopped at a light. "There was so much good feedback and I have some great ideas to bring to the next creative meeting for the Web site."

He drove through the quiet, empty streets, nodding every now and then. She knew neither of them was really interested in business and that he already knew everything she was saying.

"The band was good, too," she added with a bright smile. "A lot of people were dancing. That doesn't usually happen at parties like this. But everyone seemed really relaxed. Didn't you think so? Weren't you relaxed?"

He stopped for another light and turned to glance at her. "You don't have to entertain me on the drive home," he said. "It's okay if we don't talk."

Great. So she'd bored him.

She firmly pressed her lips together and vowed not to say another word between here and the parking garage at their building. From there it was a short elevator ride to her condo.

Silence, she told herself. She could do silence.

"I like your car," she said before she could stop herself. "Is it new?"

"About two years old. Why are you so nervous?"

"Me? I'm not. I'm fine. I had a good time tonight."

"You sure didn't drink. As far as I could tell you didn't eat. So what's going on?"

"Nothing. I'm fine. Perfectly. See? This is me being fine."

He pulled into the parking garage and drove to his space. When he turned off the engine, he shifted so that he faced her.

"Are you worried I'm going to make a pass at you?" he asked.

The blunt question shocked her into silence. If she looked at things from the right perspective, life sure had a sense of humor. For the past few weeks she'd been hoping Jack wouldn't notice her as anything but a co-worker. Now she wanted him to see her as a desirable woman and he was worried she thought he was going to come on to her. Which meant he wasn't.

She'd spent the entire evening in shoes that made her feet hurt for nothing.

"Why would I worry about that?" she asked, not able to meet his gaze.

"Because of what happened the last time we were alone together."

Ah, yes. That magical kiss. "It was nice," she whispered.

"I thought so, too. Still do." He leaned across her and opened her door. "Come on. I'll walk you home."

He came around and helped her out of the car, then took her hand as they walked to the elevator. Seconds later the doors opened and they stepped inside.

She wanted to say something. Maybe invite him inside or at least come off as cool and sophisticated. But she couldn't think of anything good and she didn't know how to tell him she wasn't exactly ready for the evening to be over. Maybe in her next life she would understand men and deal with them better. In this one, she was batting a big, fat zero.

The elevator stopped on her floor. She turned to say good-night, only he was stepping off the elevator and leading her to her door.

She dug for her key in her tiny evening bag and clutched it in her hand.

Her place was at the end of the hall. Jack took the key from her, opened the door then cupped her face and smiled at her.

"You've told me no plenty of times," he said quietly. "Tonight your eyes are saying something different. Which should I believe? Your words or your eyes?"

Her stomach flipped over, her throat went dry and it was all she could do to keep hanging on to her purse.

It all came down to this. What did she want from Jack?

"Talk has always been overrated," she whispered.

"I agree," he said as he eased her into the condo and closed the door behind them.

She heard the lock turn just before he bent down and kissed her.

She instinctively leaned into him, wanting to feel his mouth on hers. When his lips brushed against her mouth, she wrapped her arms around his neck to hold him in place.

They surged together, need growing until her mind overflowed with images of them together, naked, craving. Even as she tilted her head and parted her lips, she dropped her purse on the floor and stepped out of her shoes.

He took advantage of her invitation with a quickness that heated her blood. He nipped at her lower lip, then swept his tongue into her mouth where he claimed her with an eagerness that made her thighs tremble.

His hands were everywhere. Her shoulders, her bare arms, her back. She touched him, as well, stroking the breadth of his shoulders, before starting to tug on his jacket.

He quickly shrugged out of it, letting it fall, then he pulled off his tie. He broke the kiss, then turned her so her back was to him.

"Cuffs," he murmured as he pushed her hair over her right shoulder, then held out his hands in front of her.

But removing the gold-and-diamond cuff links was more difficult than it should have been. Even as she reached for the fastening, he nibbled on her bare shoulder, then licked the same spot.

Goose bumps erupted on her arms. Her nipples got hard and she felt the first telltale wetness on her panties.

At last she managed to free the cuff links. She started to turn, but he stayed behind her, put his hands on her hips and drew her back against him.

He was already hard. She felt the thickness of his need as he rubbed back and forth. Wanting filled her, turning her body liquid. He moved his hands up her body until he cupped her breasts.

Her curves were modest at best, but exquisitely sensitive. Even through the fabric, she felt his thumbs brush over her nipples in a way designed to make her his slave.

"I've wanted to do this all evening," he breathed before biting down on her earlobe. "That damn dress. You were driving me crazy. I couldn't decide which would be more erotic—coming up behind you and touching you like this or just saying, 'The hell with it,' and shoving my hand down the front of your dress."

Either would have taken her breath away.

"I want you naked," he murmured as he kissed her neck. "I want to touch you all over until we're both exhausted and then I want to do it all again."

He'd talked to her before, she remembered, her brain turning mushy from too many hormones and too little sex. She hadn't been with a lot of men, but except for Jack, they'd all been silent.

She loved his words. They not only turned her on, but they left no doubt that she did the same to him.

She turned in his arms and pressed her mouth to his. He kissed her with an intensity that shook her to the core. When she felt his fingers on her zipper, she trembled in anticipation of being naked with him.

Her dress fell in a whisper of silk. Underneath she wore tiny panties and nothing else. He continued to kiss her even as he brought his hands around to cup her breasts.

While she'd always wanted to be voluptuous, she had a theory that her small breasts had the same number of nerve endings as big ones, so hers were more sensitive. Apparently Jack remembered, because he touched her gently as he stroked her hot skin.

Fiery sensation shot through her, making it hard to

keep breathing. Every part of her being focused on his touch as he moved closer and closer to her nipples. At last he touched them, first with just his fingertips. He lightly rubbed the very tips before squeezing them oh so gently.

She gasped with pleasure. He groaned, then broke the kiss and pushed her back. Seconds later three books, her mail and a plastic container of fake flowers crashed to the floor. Before she could figure out what he was doing, he lifted her onto the top of the wood console in her foyer, bent his head and sucked on one of her nipples.

Suddenly the mess didn't matter at all. She closed her eyes and arched her chest toward him. Her fingers tangled in his hair.

"More," she breathed as he circled her tight, quivery flesh. "Don't stop."

He didn't. He sucked and licked and circled and then moved to her other breast. He replaced tongue with fingers, arousing her with everything he did.

He put one of his hands on her thigh and moved it steadily toward her center. She parted her legs, then cursed the panties still in place as he rubbed her through the silk.

"Off," she begged, shifting on the console. "I need them off."

He grabbed them and pulled them down. When she was fully naked, he reached for her and slid his fingers into her swollen, waiting heat.

Heaven, she thought, barely able to breathe. Heaven

and then some. He explored her, quickly finding her favorite spot, then teasing it. He shifted so that his thumb rubbed there and his first two fingers could slip inside of her.

Passion grew as her body tensed. She clung to him, barely able to absorb all the sensations. It was too fast, too soon. And yet…

"Jack," she breathed as she felt herself spinning higher and higher.

His only response was to suck harder on her breasts. The combination of pleasures was too much, she thought as she felt the first shuddering release of her climax. It overtook her body, leaving her unable to do anything but hold on for the ride.

She felt herself tighten around his fingers. He moved in and out, imitating the act of love. Toward the end, he raised his head and kissed her on the mouth. She kissed him back, then sighed as her contractions slowed.

She opened her eyes and smiled at him. "Wow," she breathed, both pleased and a little embarrassed at the speed of her response.

He grinned and then picked her up in his arms. She shrieked and wrapped her arms around his neck.

"What are you doing?" she asked.

"Taking a naked woman to bed. What does it look like?"

"A plan I can get into," she said, then lightly bit his earlobe. "Once we're there, you can get into me."

"I will," he promised. "In a second."

"What do you… Oh!"

He dropped her onto the bed, then quickly stripped out of his clothes. She gave herself over to the show, remembering how good he'd looked before.

Time had been kind. He still had a hard, sculpted body and his arousal was very impressive. She reached for him as he joined her on the bed, but he shook his head.

"Protection?" he asked.

She pointed at the nightstand and held back the need to explain that they were, in fact, very new. She'd bought them the day after he'd kissed her. More than a little wishful thinking on her part.

He pulled out the box of condoms and removed one. But instead of putting it on, he slipped between her legs and knelt over her.

"I want you," he said.

She saw the desire in his eyes and felt her body quicken with an answering need.

"Me, too. Despite my recent thrill ride."

"Good."

He bent down and kissed her belly. As he moved south, she knew what he was going to do. Politeness dictated that she at least offer him his own release before taking another of her own, but as she tried to speak, she remembered what it had been like that one night they'd spent together. How he'd kissed her so intimately, with an understanding of her body that had taken her to paradise so quickly.

"Just for a couple of minutes," she told him as he pressed his mouth against her. "Three at most."

He chuckled. She felt the movement and the puff of warm air. Then his tongue swept against her with the exact amount of pressure. He circled her most sensitive spot once, twice, before brushing it with the flat part of his tongue.

She was lost. Rude or not, she couldn't stand the thought of stopping him. Not when he made her feel so good. She pulled her knees up and spread her legs apart, then she dug her heels into the bed.

He moved faster, pressing a tiny bit harder. It was the most intimate act she knew and she'd trusted no one but him to do this to her. She might have trusted Vance, but he'd claimed it was disgusting, although he'd been plenty willing for her to do it to him.

Without warning, her body shuddered into orgasm. She lost control in a way she never had before. He kissed and licked and moved his fingers back and forth as she screamed her release into the night.

She lost track of time and reality. There was only the waves and waves of pleasure filling her. At last her body slowed. She felt him pull back. She reached toward him, not wanting to lose the connection, but then he was there, between her legs, pushing, filling her.

She opened her eyes as he slowly thrust himself inside of her. He was much bigger than his fingers and she felt herself stretching. The delicious pressure made her shudder again and again. She came with each thrust, milking him.

He braced himself on the bed and made love to her. Their eyes locked and she watched him get closer and closer. She wrapped her legs around his hips, holding him inside, feeling him climax and contracting around him as he did.

## Chapter Nine

Jack opened the drapes and returned to the bed to watch the growing light creep across the room. He gently shifted the lock of hair curling across Samantha's cheek so that he could see the pale skin and the curve of her mouth.

She was beautiful, which wasn't news, but still struck him this morning. She lay across rumpled sheets, with the blanket tangled in her legs. Her bare arm stretched toward him and he could see her naked right breast.

Just looking at the tight nipple sent blood surging to his groin. He wanted her again, but after last night, he didn't think he should indulge himself. Three times was impressive, four was greedy. Besides, he didn't want to make her sore.

He touched her curls again, rubbing his fingers against the soft texture of her hair. He didn't even have to close his eyes to remember what it had been like the second time, when she'd straddled him, claiming him, moving faster and faster as her body gave itself over to pleasure.

He'd watched her as she'd arched her back, her breasts thrusting toward him, her hair spilling down, swaying with each thrust of her hips.

They were good together, at least in bed. But would she see that? Or would she revert to type—second-guessing what had happened and telling them both that this was all a mistake?

She stirred slightly, then rolled onto her back and opened her eyes. The sheet pooled around her waist, leaving her breasts bare and even after she'd seen him, she didn't try to cover herself.

"Good morning," she whispered. "Did you sleep?"

He nodded.

Her mouth curved into a smile. "You're looking so serious. What's wrong?"

"I'm fine."

She rolled toward him and touched his bare chest. "Then what?" she asked, her smile fading. "Are you sorry about last night?"

"That's your line."

"Oh."

He saw the hurt flash in her eyes and groaned. "Samantha, no. I didn't mean it like that."

She sat up and pulled the sheet so she was covered

to her shoulders. Her messy hair tumbled across her bare shoulders and her mouth twisted.

"You did mean it like that and you have every right to expect me to bolt," she said firmly. "Based on how I've been acting, what else could you think? I'm sorry I was a total change-o girl."

He stared at her. "A what?"

"You know what I mean. I've been the queen of sending mixed messages. I hated that I was doing it and I didn't know how to stop. I've since given myself a stern talking to. I'm working on being in the moment and letting the future take care of itself. You've been nothing but terrific since I moved to Chicago. You're a great guy and I have no regrets about last night." She shook her head. "I take that back. I have one regret. That it took me so long to get you into bed."

He'd braced himself to hear a lot of things, but that wasn't one of them. "You're not sorry."

"Nope. Are you?"

He grinned. "Are you kidding? Last night was incredible."

"I do have a special talent," she said modestly, then smiled. "Okay, what happens now? What are your usual rules of play."

"You assume I have rules."

"All guys do. Tell me what they are and I'll tell you if I agree."

Dangerous territory, he thought. Although maybe not. Samantha was coming off a rough divorce. He doubted she was looking for anything serious any more than he was.

"Serial monogamy," he said. "We stay together as long as it's good. No forever, no hurt feelings when it's over."

She batted her eyes. "So you'd be, like, my boy-friend."

He chuckled. "If that's what you want to call it."

"Would we get matching tattoos?"

"Never."

"Would we make love?"

"Almost constantly."

She flopped back on the bed. "What makes you think I want you?"

"Last night you were screaming."

Her cheeks darkened with color. "I don't remember that."

"Trust me. You screamed."

Her humor faded. "You've been really patient with me, Jack. I've been so scared about messing up and being taken. I thought it was best to just avoid any kind of relationship. But that's no way to live. Complicating the situation was my reaction to you."

He took her hand in his and rubbed her fingers with his thumb. "What reaction?"

"You know, mine."

"You have to be a little more specific."

She sighed. "Look at the situation logically. If I didn't want to get involved, why didn't I just stay away from you? Why did I keep coming back for more?" She shrugged. "You've always been something of a temptation."

He liked the sound of that. "Since when?"

"Since before. When we were in grad school."

What? "You blew me off. You said it was a mistake."

"I was scared."

"Not of me. What did I ever do wrong?"

"Nothing. That's my point. My fears were about me. But even they weren't enough to keep me away. I was so torn. You were a lot like my father in that whole rich, powerful way and I didn't know how to handle it."

Which meant he was also like her ex-husband. How did he convince her that he wasn't the enemy? That he wasn't interested in hurting her?

"I never forgot that night we shared," she said, not quite meeting his gaze. "After a while I convinced myself that I'd made it better than it was in my mind. That no one was that good. After last night, I know I was wrong."

He wanted to tell her that their incredible time in bed together had a whole lot more to do with chemistry than with him, but it was kind of nice having her think he was special.

"At least half of last night was about you," he said. "You're very responsive."

"Not all the time. Pretty much only here. So is this okay? Is this what you want?"

He nodded. "I'll be your boyfriend."

She laughed. "That sounds nice. I could use a little normal in my life right now."

"Normal?" He moved in close and pressed his lips against her ear. "Not normal. I have some very kinky fantasies in mind."

"Really? Like what?"

Samantha finished her speech to nods and smiles. She collected her materials and returned to her seat at the side of the room.

This had been her first ever presentation to a board of directors and it had been pretty high up on the nightmare scale.

"Sort of like facing down seven stern principals in school?" David asked in a low voice.

"Worse," she whispered. "Do they all have to look so disapproving?"

"It comes with being on the board. They're supposed to take things very seriously."

"Obviously. I'm just glad I wasn't trying to do stand-up."

She reached for her cup of coffee and swallowed the tepid liquid. When this was all over, she owed Jack a big apology. He'd insisted everyone practice their presentations several times before the board meeting. They had all endured long evenings, perfecting their pitches.

At the time, she'd thought his anal obsession was foolish. Wouldn't spontaneity be more interesting? But having just endured the stern expressions and pointed questions, she realized the importance of being prepared.

"I'm up next," David said as he was called.

Samantha leaned back in her chair and did her best to relax. She'd heard all the talks so many times, she knew what to expect and could tune out the words. So she found herself with a little time on her hands.

She used it to good advantage, turning her head so she caught sight of Jack sitting at the end of the long conference table.

He looked good—all buttoned up and formal in his black suit. If she didn't know him, he could have seriously intimidated her. But she did know him—every inch of him. And there were some mighty fine inches.

She watched the way he listened intently—as if he hadn't heard every sentence at least a dozen times—and took notes.

He was a great guy, she thought happily. Smart, caring, funny. The man owned a dog. How was she supposed to resist that? If she hadn't known about—

Samantha stiffened in her seat as a single thought flashed through her brain, on and off, over and over again. She wasn't able to think about anything else, and as she considered the truth of the statement, she wondered what on earth she was supposed to do about it.

Jack wasn't just some guy she'd hooked up with. He wasn't just an old friend or a new boss or a terrific lover. He was all that and much more.

He was the one who got away.

The board meeting was endless and three kinds of torture, Jack thought when the presentations finally finished. The board excused everyone but Helen and him.

He thanked his team as they left and braced himself for the inevitable confrontation. He'd put it off as long as he could, but there was no going back now.

Baynes, the chairman, waited until the door closed before looking at Jack. "You've pulled the team together. I'm impressed."

Jack nodded, but didn't speak.

"Obviously our goal is to keep Hanson Media Group alive. Between the bad stories in the press and troubles internally, that's a challenge. You're well on your way here. The new programs are very exciting. But we need to do more. We need to provide stability over the long haul."

Several of the board members nodded in agreement. Helen shook her head.

"We don't have to do anything right now," she said. "I know where you're going and it's too soon. If we simply announce Jack as the new president, it will be seen as a knee-jerk reaction. Let's think this through."

Samantha might sing her friend's praises, but obviously Helen, like the board, was ready to sell him out if that's what was best for Hanson Media Group.

"Helen, it's necessary. Do you want to see George's legacy bankrupt, or worse, lost in some mega-conglomerate takeover?" Baynes shrugged. "I don't. The only way to keep Hanson Media Group going is to announce a permanent president. Jack, I know you're anxious to get back to your law practice, but we all have to make sacrifices. It's time for you to make one. I'm asking you to accept the job."

Jack looked at the older man. "What sacrifices are being made aside from mine?" he asked calmly.

"You know what I mean," Baynes told him.

"Actually, I don't. I'm not interested in running Hanson Media Group any longer than the three months I've already agreed to."

Several of the board members started speaking at once.

"This is a family company. Always has been. You owe it to your father."

Not an argument designed to get his vote, Jack thought grimly.

"Think of the stockholders. What about them?"

"You're the best man for the job. The only man."

Baynes quieted them. "Jack, your family owns the largest percentage of stock, but we still have an obligation to the financial community."

"I find it hard to believe you can't come up with a single qualified person to take over this company," Jack said. "Have you even been looking?"

"You're the one we want."

"Has it occurred to any of you that forcing Jack to stay when he doesn't want to is incredibly foolish?" Helen asked. "Someone unhappy in the position isn't to anyone's advantage. Now if he wanted to be here…"

"I don't," Jack said flatly.

Baynes narrowed his gaze. "I would think you, Helen, of all people would want a family member in charge of the company."

She leaned forward. "I agree that Jack is very qualified and I trust him implicitly. But I see no advantage in guilting him into staying on. It's a short-term solution and I don't want that. We're doing fine for the moment. Let's not make a change before we have to. Leave Jack alone to do his job. In the meantime, we can be looking for a suitable replacement. If there isn't one, then Jack gets my vote."

"I don't like it," Baynes said.

"Just so we're all clear," Helen continued, "until George's will is read, I control his voting stock, which means I get the final say." She looked at Jack. "I still believe you owe your father but I'm reluctant to put his legacy in the hands of someone who doesn't respect his vision."

Not respecting his father's vision was the least of it, Jack thought. But before he could protest, Baynes cut in.

"What do you know about the will?" he asked Helen.

"Nothing," she said. "I'll find out when everyone else does. That's not my point. We have time to think this through and make the right decision for Hanson Media Group. As long as the company is moving in the right direction, then I say let it be."

Samantha paced the length of Jack's office, then turned around and walked back the other way. He'd already been in with the board for nearly twenty minutes. What on earth did they have to talk about for that long?

Finally he walked in. She hurried over to him.

"All you all right? Did they pressure you to stay?" she asked.

He pulled her close and kissed her forehead. "You're worried about me."

"Well, duh. What did you think? Now tell me everything. You didn't accept the job permanently, did you?"

"What makes you think they asked?"

"It's just a matter of time until they start pressuring you. You're doing a great job. Why wouldn't they want to keep you?"

He led her over to the sofa, then pulled her down next to him. "You're right. That's what they wanted. Helen held them off, saying they should make sure they had the right candidate. While I'm not interested in staying, at least she bought me some time." He took her hand. "She's not on my side in this. She cares about the company."

She leaned back into the leather sofa and sighed. "You don't know that."

"Actually, I do. I respect her position. If I were her, I'd do the same thing."

"But you're not her. You still want to leave."

"I *will* leave."

She looked at him. "Were they all upset?"

"They weren't happy but until the will is read, Helen controls the majority of the stock. That puts her in power." He pulled her close. "Don't kid yourself, though. If she decides she needs me to stay, she'll be the first one holding out the employment contract."

"I don't want to argue about Helen," she told him.

"Me, either." He stood and crossed to a glass cabinet by the window. After opening one of the doors, he held up an empty glass. "Want a drink?"

"No, thanks."

He poured one for himself and took a sip. "I don't know where everything went wrong with my dad and his sons."

"You probably never will. Sometimes families have trouble connecting."

"If Mom hadn't died…" He shrugged and took another sip.

She stood. There was something different about Jack. He was hurting and that pain made him vulnerable. She'd never seen him as anything but strong and powerful, so this side of him surprised her.

She crossed to him and put her arms around him. "You did the best you could."

"Maybe. Can we change the subject?"

"Sure." She gazed up into his eyes. "You were right about making us practice. It made a big difference."

He smiled and put down his drink. "I'm right about a lot of things."

"Yes, you are."

He put his arms around her and drew closer. "I was right about you and the job."

She laughed. "So we're going to make a list of all your perfections?"

"I have the time."

She glanced at the closed door. "Or we could do something else."

He raised his eyebrows. "Ms. Edwards, it's the middle of a workday."

"Yes, it is."

"Are you making advances at me?"

"Actually, I was just sort of noticing how very big your desk is. I like a big desk."

## Chapter Ten

"You've sent them e-mails?" Jack asked, frustrated because he already knew the answer to the question.

"Repeatedly," Mrs. Wycliff said. "I also sent letters using overnight delivery. I know the letters were received—Evan and Andrew had to sign for them."

His brothers were ignoring his attempts to get in touch with them. He suspected they were following the financial news and knew about the trouble with the company. He had a feeling neither of them would resurface until things were better or it was time for the reading of the will—whichever came first.

Someone knocked on his open door. He glanced up and saw David standing in the doorway.

Jack excused his assistant and waved in his uncle.

"Did you hear?" he asked.

"Most of it," David said. "Evan and Andrew are still refusing to get in touch with you?"

Jack nodded. "I don't suppose either of them has contacted you and asked you not to say anything about it."

"Sorry, no."

"We haven't spoken in years," Jack said. "How the hell did that happen? When did this family get so screwed up?"

"Your mother's death didn't help."

"I was just thinking that a few days ago. If she'd been alive, so much would have been different, but with her gone it was easy to go our separate ways."

"George didn't help," David admitted. "He was more interested in the business than in his family."

Jack nodded slowly. "I remember when I was young, people would tell me I was just like him. That always scared me. I knew I loved my father, but I wasn't sure I liked him. I wanted more than that from my kids."

"You don't have any kids," his uncle reminded him.

"I noticed that, too. After Shelby…" He shook his head. No reason to go there. "I think one of the reasons may be it's the only way to make sure I don't repeat his mistakes."

"Kind of like cutting off your arm to make sure you don't get a hangnail."

"You're saying I'm taking things to the extreme."

David shrugged. "You know what your father did that you didn't like. So don't do that."

Sounded simple enough. "When I was a kid, I didn't know what I was doing that made people think I was like him, so I didn't know how to stop doing it."

"You're not a kid anymore."

"None of us are," Jack said. "I haven't talked to Evan and Andrew in years and ever since I've been working at this damn company, I miss them. Oh, sure, I want them home to do what they need to be doing. I want them to help out. But I also want to talk to them. Hang out. Like we used to. We were a family once."

"Maybe it's time to make that happen again," David said. "Maybe it's time to start pulling together instead of pulling apart."

"I'm willing. What I don't know is how to do it. I can't even get my brothers to return my e-mails. I'm ready to resort to threats."

"Might not be a bad idea. Get them back for any reason, even if it's just to protect their personal interest."

"I agree," Jack said, "but I don't like it. They're my brothers. I shouldn't have to use threats to get them to communicate with me. There has to be another way."

"I'm out of ideas," David told him.

Jack was, too, but he knew someone who might not be.

"How do I get my brothers back?" Jack asked.

Helen raised her eyebrows. "Why do you think I would know the answer to that?"

"Because I've finally figured out you know us a whole lot better than we know you. I need them here and I'll do anything to get them in Chicago."

"Even ask for my help." She smiled. "Evil step-mothers are often invisible. It can come in handy."

"I never thought you were evil."

"I know. You simply didn't think of me at all. I wasn't trying to be your mother. I just wanted to be a friend."

"I couldn't think of you as anything but my father's wife."

"His *second* wife," she said. "We all know what that means."

Had she wanted more? Had she wanted it all?

She didn't have children, he thought. And at her age, she was unlikely to have any. Had his father been the reason there weren't any little Helens running around? Maybe George would have had better luck with a sec-ond family.

She held up both her hands. "Okay, this conversation is getting out of hand. Since your dad died, I've been liv-ing on the emotional edge and if we continue like this any longer, I'm going to find myself sobbing uncontrol-lably. I think we'd both find that uncomfortable. So let's talk about your brothers. Who do you want to start with?"

"I'll let you pick."

She considered for a moment. "Andrew will come home for money. You're going to have to be blunt. Ei-ther he shows up or you cut him off. Cruel but effective. You might want to start by cutting off one of his credit cards so he gets the message."

"Done," Jack said. "And Evan?"

Helen sighed. "He'll come home for the reading of the will. He always wanted to be close to George and he'll be looking for closure."

"Then if Dad left him anything, it would prove Evan mattered to him?"

"Something like that."

"I hope he's not disappointed," Jack muttered.

"Me, too."

"I know you loved the old man, but he wasn't exactly father of the year."

Helen nodded slowly. "He tried, in his own flawed way. He loved you all."

"He loved the business more."

"No. He loved it differently. It was safe to let everyone know how he felt about the business. It never went away and did something he didn't approve of."

"Like his sons," Jack said.

"Some parents have trouble understanding that when a child makes a decision that the parent doesn't approve of, it's not personal. Children are their own people—they have to make their own lives."

"My father wanted me to live his life."

She smiled. "He couldn't understand that what you chose to do for your career had nothing to do with him. He's the one who gave you choices, and then he was angry with what you picked."

"So was I," Jack admitted. "It was as if he'd changed the rules partway through the game."

"He had, but he still loved you."

Jack studied the woman who had married his father.

She looked different since the funeral. She'd become elegant in her sorrow.

He could see why his father had been drawn to her. The combination of brains and beauty.

"You were good to him," he said.

She smiled. "You don't actually know that."

"Yes, I do. It's there in the way you talk about him. You were more than he deserved. He got lucky when he picked you."

"Maybe I was the lucky one."

She was consistent. He would give her that.

He narrowed his gaze. "You're good at this, at listening and offering just the right amount of advice and encouragement. You should have had children of your own."

Helen stiffened slightly, which answered the question he hadn't asked.

"I, ah—"

"It was him, wasn't it? He said he didn't want to start another family."

She sighed. "It seemed like the right decision at the time."

"And now?" he asked.

"There's no going back."

He had the feeling that she hadn't asked for much in her marriage, but his father had refused her the one thing she'd really wanted.

"He was a selfish bastard."

"Don't say that. I made my choices and I loved your father. Knowing what I know now, I wouldn't change anything. He was a great man." She held up her hand.

"You don't have to agree with me on that, but I know it to be true. I loved him. I will never love that way again."

There was a certainty and a power in the way she spoke. For the first time in his life, he envied his father. Not because he had any romantic feelings for Helen, but because the old man had been loved completely. Helen saw his faults and accepted them. She believed he was the great love of her life.

At one time Jack had wanted that for himself. He'd believed he'd found it with Shelby, but he'd been wrong.

"Back up," Jack said.

Samantha held in a low moan. "See, I was thinking I could go through life in Drive rather than Reverse. Sort of like letting go of the past. Don't you think that's important? To always move forward? It's a Zen thing. Or if not Zen, then something else Zen-like." She smiled brightly.

Jack looked at her. "We're talking about driving, not your life, and one isn't a metaphor for the other. You're going to have to learn to back up the car at some point, so why not now?"

She'd been afraid he was going to get all logical on her. "The Zen thing didn't move you even a little?"

"No."

"But you have to admit it was clever."

"Very clever. Now back into the parking space."

Had he always been this imperious? she thought as she carefully checked the empty parking lot.

There weren't any other cars to be seen, just ominous white lines marking parking spaces. Very small parking spaces.

"Go slowly," Jack told her. "Think about where you want the car to go, not where it is. Check for anything in the way, then back up slowly."

She wasn't sure when this had become the advanced class, but she was determined not to balk, despite nearly blinding fear.

She drew in a deep breath and looked at where she wanted the car to go. There was a tree there, spindly and gray. She briefly imagined the car's rear bumper only a foot or so from the tree, then she put the car in reverse and slowly began to back up.

"Keep your eyes on where you want to be, not where you are," he said.

"Hey, don't try to out-Zen the Zen master," she muttered, still watching the tree. She got closer and closer, then put on the brake and slipped the car into Park.

Jack grinned. "Pretty good," he said and opened his car door. "Check it out."

She jumped out and ran to the front of the car. "It's perfect," she yelled, ignoring the slight angle of her car. "Perfect. I'm in between the lines and in the middle of the space." She tilted her head. "Almost."

Jack walked over and studied the car. She bit her lower lip. Not that she cared what he thought, except she did.

He put an arm around her. "Great job. Let's do it again."

Later that evening, Samantha showed up at his condo with salad fixings and two large slices of chocolate-chip cheesecake. As she shifted the bakery bag to her other hand so she could ring the bell, she realized she'd never been to his place before. All their rendezvous had taken place at her apartment.

"Why is that?" she asked as he opened the front door and waved her in.

"Why is what?"

She waited for his kiss before asking, "Why haven't I been here before? Are you keeping secrets?"

"Have a look around and see for yourself," he said as he took her packages from her. "I'll open the wine."

An invitation to snoop. How often did that happen? But before she could take him up on it, Charlie came racing toward her.

She dropped down and hugged him. "How's my handsome guy?" she asked as she rubbed his ears. "Did you have fun this morning at the park?"

Charlie yipped his response, then led her into the condo.

The foyer opened onto a large living room with a to-die-for view of the lake and shoreline. To the left was a U-shaped kitchen with a high granite bar and three stools. Beyond that was a dining alcove that also looked out on the water.

"This place must be terrific during thunderstorms," she said.

"It is. Most weather looks pretty good if you're up high enough."

She took the glass of wine he offered and sipped. The color palette was typical guy—cream walls, beige furniture, black accent tables and cabinets for way too many electronics. Except for the fact that everything was new and expensive, the room reminded her a lot of what he'd had in grad school.

"Despite your fear of it," she said with a grin, "color doesn't kill. Imagine what this place would be with a red accent pillow or a bowl of green apples."

"Imagine."

Even his artwork was subdued—the two seascapes were muted and dark. There was an impressive abstract in the dining room that was mostly reds and oranges.

"This looks out of place," she said. "I'm guessing you didn't buy it."

He stared at the painting for a long time. Samantha got a twisted feeling in her stomach. There were memories in that painting. Good or bad? she wondered, knowing there was danger in both.

"Helen gave me that when I made partner," he said quietly. "It was her way of reaching out to me. I should have seen that before, but I didn't."

Samantha studied the painting again and felt the relief sift through her. "Helen always had great taste."

He waved toward the entrance to the hallway. "Have at it."

"If you insist."

The first door on the right opened to a small powder room with a pedestal sink. Next was a home office with a television on the wall and more law books than she'd ever seen in her life. There was also a very large and squishy-looking bed for Charlie. She found a linen closet—mostly empty and painfully neat, and, last but not least, the master bedroom.

Once again beige ruled the day. A beige-and-cream bedspread covered the dark wood sleigh bed. There weren't any throw pillows, nothing decorating the nightstands. Just lamps, a clock and a TV remote.

An armoire stood opposite the bed. She would bet money that inside there was a television, because God forbid he should miss a single play of whatever sports game he was watching. More massive windows offered an incredible view, while the master bath had a steam shower and a tub big enough for two.

Gorgeous, she thought, but impersonal. There weren't any family pictures, no little items picked up on travels, no magazines lying around. No memories.

"What do you think?" he asked as he walked into the room and leaned against the door frame.

"Beautiful, but a little too beige for my taste."

"Sorry. I tried to get out and buy a throw for the bed, but time got away from me."

She laughed. "Do you even know what a throw is?"

"Sure. It's something that you, ah, throw."

"What does it look like?"

"It's brown."

She grinned. "You're hopeless."

"You should even be impressed that I could use *throw* in a sentence."

"I am."

He walked toward her and took her hand. "Come

on," he said. "I'll build us a fire. We'll get wild back here later."

"I like that idea."

She curled up on the sofa while he put in kindling, then actual wood logs. Minutes later, when the fire had taken hold, he joined her on the sofa.

"Comfy?" he asked.

She nodded as she angled toward him. Then, thinking about the lack of personal touches, said, "You know all about my past, but you never talk about your own."

Nothing about his expression changed, still she sensed him pulling back a little.

"Too sensitive a topic?" she asked.

"Not for me. What do you want to know?"

"What you've been doing for the past ten years," she said, speaking honestly. "Romantically, I mean. I know all about your checkered career path."

"Checkered? I was a lawyer."

She smiled. "Exactly. Environmental law I could have understood."

"Because you have an inherent love of tree huggers."

"Absolutely. But criminal law. That's a little scary."

"Everyone deserves the chance to be defended."

She sipped her wine. "I don't actually agree with that. Some people don't deserve anything but punishment."

"How can you know they're not innocent?"

He was being logical, one of his more annoying features. "Sometimes you just know." She sighed. "Okay, perhaps it's best I'm not in charge of our criminal justice system. Which is why you'll be a much better judge than me. But this isn't what I wanted to talk about."

"You want to know about my love life."

"Pretty much."

He shrugged. "Shelby's the most significant relationship and you know about her."

That she'd died. "That must have been so horrible."

"It wasn't fun. After her, I didn't date for a long time."

"Because you were still in love with her?"

His mouth straightened, which didn't tell her all that much about what he was thinking. She tried to read the emotions in his eyes, but they flashed by too quickly.

"I'm not sure it was love as much as I didn't want to answer questions. I never knew when to tell someone I was dating that my fiancée had been killed shortly before the wedding. Too soon and it looked like I was fishing for sympathy. Too late and I was accused of keeping secrets. It was easier not to get involved at all."

Which all sounded reasonable, she thought, but she didn't buy into it. He didn't date because it was too hard to explain his past? Maybe for someone else, but not Jack. He was used to thinking on his feet. As for making a convincing argument, it was what he did for a living.

"So you avoided relationships?" she asked.

"Serious ones. I've fallen into a pattern of serial monogamy and it's working for me."

"Don't you get lonely and want more?" She held up

her free hand. "I'm asking intellectually. I'm not fishing."

"You mean love and happily-ever-after." He shook his head. "I'm not a big believer in that. Are you?"

"I shouldn't be," she said slowly. "What with my divorce and all. But I know love exists. I loved Vance, at least at first. Helen loved George."

"Maybe it's something women are good at," Jack said.

"Meaning men aren't? There's an abdication of responsibility."

"I don't know a whole lot of guys who are in happy relationships. Did my father really love Helen? I hope so, for her sake. But from what I saw about the old man, it seems unlikely. My brothers have sure stayed away from anything serious. Even David, who is the most normal, centered guy I know, has managed to avoid marriage."

"Are you saying it's a bad deal for men?"

"No. I'm not advocating that guys need to screw around. I don't know how anyone gives with his or her whole heart. How do you take that step of faith? In my world, people you love leave."

"Including Shelby?"

"Especially Shelby."

But his fiancée had died, Samantha thought. Was it fair to blame her for something that wasn't her fault?

"Is that why there aren't any pictures of her around?" she asked. "Because you're angry with her?"

"I stopped being angry a long time ago. It's not about anger. It's about letting go."

She took another sip of her wine and sighed. "It's funny—I'm fighting you on your theory about giving it all and truly falling in love when I know Vance didn't love me. Not the way I loved him. I don't know what he felt. If you were to ask him, he would swear he loved me. He would talk about all the ways he proved it. But that wasn't love."

"What was it?"

She didn't mean to say anything. The word just sort of slipped out. "Control."

Jack raised his eyebrows, but didn't speak. She found herself filling the silence.

"He wasn't like that before we got married. At least not so much. He might make a suggestion about something I was wearing, or what I planned to cook for dinner. I thought he was interested. I thought it was a good thing."

"It wasn't?"

"No. He began to monitor my life. How much time I spent at work, how long it took me to get home. He wouldn't let me wear certain things. He said they were too sexy. He accused me of being interested in a couple of guys at work, which was crazy. I wasn't interested in anyone. Then he started telling me it didn't matter because no one…"

She swallowed. Okay, how had she gotten into *this* conversation. Big mistake.

"Because no one what?" Jack asked.

She stared at her lap. "Because no one else would want me. He said I was lucky he wanted me."

"He abused you." Jack's words were flat.

She looked at him. "He didn't hit me." She made a harsh sound that was supposed to be close to a laugh. "Isn't that horrible? I told myself that for more than two years. He wasn't hitting me so it couldn't be abuse. He was just tired, or I'd made him angry. But he would scream at me and make me feel useless and small. I told myself I was letting it happen, because no one can make you feel anything if you don't let them, right? So there was something wrong with me. But I didn't know how to fix it and Vance was always there, in my face, speaking my worst fears."

She felt the tension in Jack and didn't want to know what he was thinking. Just talking about her past made her feel small and ashamed.

"I was a fool," she said quietly. "I equated attention with love. Vance was attentive. Too attentive. He separated me from my friends, my mom, he didn't like me spending long hours at work. I saw what I had become and I hated it. But I didn't know how to make it better."

"You left," he said.

She nodded. "I can't even tell you what happened. One day I came home and he was complaining about my clothes and my body and telling me I was stupid and I just snapped. I threw a vase at him. It hit him in the chest, then dropped to the floor. He screamed louder, saying I was in trouble now. It was like he was my father and I was his child. I suddenly realized I didn't have to be there. So I left."

Jack didn't say anything, but she could hear him thinking.

"You're judging me," she said, feeling defensive and vulnerable.

"No. You got out. That takes courage."

All the right words, but why was he staring at her as if she were a bug? "But?" she asked.

"I'm surprised it happened at all. You're strong and powerful. I wouldn't have thought a guy like that could mess with you."

"You're saying I should have seen it coming."

"No. Why would you? You trusted this guy. Any signs would have been…"

"Signs?"

He shifted uncomfortably. "No one changes overnight."

"I see. So you think I missed big clues. That I'm as much to blame?"

"No. Not to blame. If you'd never been in the situation before, you couldn't have known. You got out. You fought."

She stood. She hated this. Hated what had happened, hated telling him. She felt exposed and flawed. Unworthy.

"We can't all make perfect decisions," she said, trying not to get angry, knowing her temper was a defense mechanism. "I screwed up with Vance. While it was happening, I kept wondering what I'd done wrong. Was I listening to my mother? Subconsciously trying to keep a rich powerful guy around so I would be safe?

Only I wasn't safe. And if I knew that, why was leaving so hard? That's what I hate. How hard it was to go. How long it took me. I'm sure this is all too confusing for you. Your world is simply black and white. You don't get involved. You don't risk anything. That does make things simpler, doesn't it?"

"Samantha." He stood and moved toward her.

She flinched, then put her wine on the coffee table. "This wasn't a good idea. I need to go."

"Wait. We should talk."

Suddenly, she couldn't. The past was there, pressing down on her. He was wrong—Vance *had* changed so completely. There had been no warning. Vance had been so much like Jack.

She hurried out of the condo and ran for the elevator. Jack followed. The doors opened and she slipped inside.

"Samantha, wait."

But she didn't and when she got back to her apartment, he didn't bother to come after her.

# *Chapter Eleven*

Jack had no idea what had gone wrong with Samantha. He mentally went over their conversation several times and still wasn't sure where they'd derailed. What had he said to upset her? Did she think he wasn't impressed she'd gotten away? A lot of women didn't. There were several cases in his law office, abusive husbands who had murdered their wives. Those women hadn't been able to get away, but Samantha had.

He clicked on another computer file, hoping work would distract him. Unfortunately, it didn't. He kept seeing the hurt in Samantha's eyes, the pain as she ran from him, as if he were just like Vance.

Vance. Is that where he'd gone wrong, saying that there had to be signs? He believed that was true. Maybe

Samantha hadn't seen them, but he, Jack, was willing to bet that there had been clues.

Not that he would say that to Samantha now. He doubted she wanted to speak with him about anything personal. He hadn't heard from her in a couple of days and he sure as hell didn't know how to open the lines of communication.

Under normal circumstances, he would simply accept that the relationship had unworkable flaws and move on. He'd told himself to do that just this morning. The only problem was he didn't want to move on. He wanted to know that Samantha was okay. He wanted to explain that he'd never meant to hurt her, and then he wanted to find a way to make it all right between them.

Yeah, right—because he had so much success in his personal relationships. Based on his track record, Samantha should stay as far away from him as possible.

He glanced at his watch and groaned. The last full staff meeting before the Web site launch was due to start in ten minutes. So he was going to have his desired chance to speak with Samantha. Unfortunately, it would be in front of her entire team and the IT guys.

He collected his notes and walked to the main conference room. Samantha and her people were already there, setting up for their PowerPoint presentation. Jack nodded and took a seat at the conference table, doing his best not to notice how feminine and sexy she looked in her loose, flowing blouse and long skirt.

"Morning," Samantha said, her smile bright, but still not reaching her eyes. "We're on schedule with every-

thing. If you'll just give us a minute to get a few last minute glitches out of the flowcharts, we'll be good to go."

"Take your time," Jack told her.

Arnie burst into the room and hurried to her side.
After an intense, whispered conversation, Arnie handed
over a memory stick, then grinned and took the seat
next to Jack's.

"Hey," the younger man said. "Pretty exciting stuff,
huh? We've been working day and night to get the Web
site ready to launch. Some of the interactive links are
going to blow everyone away."

"That's what we're looking for," Jack said as Roger
walked into the room.

Arnie's boss sat across from Jack.

"Morning," Jack said.

Roger nodded, not looking happy. "This has all been
rushed through," Roger said. "I hope we can meet the
deadline."

Jack looked at Arnie, who shifted uncomfortably in
his seat. "We'll get there, boss. You'll see."

Jack knew that the Web site wasn't Roger's idea of
a good time. What he didn't understand was how someone could get to be the head of the IT department and
not be interested in innovation.

Samantha stepped in front of the conference table.
"All right, we're ready. Welcome to the new and improved Hanson Media Group interactive Web site for
children. Today I'm going to give you a detailed look
at the Web site—what's available, what's new, what we
can expect to launch over the next six months. If you'll

please direct your attention to the large screen on the wall, I'll begin."

Over the next ninety minutes, she outlined the Web site. Jack took a few notes, but mostly he divided his attention between the screen and Samantha.

She spoke with the confidence of someone who knew her material and believed in what she was doing. She fielded questions and offered opinions. When the discussion got too technical, she handed control over to Arnie, who explained things to the point where Jack was lost in a sea of computer terms.

When they'd finished, Samantha invited them all to the launch party Wednesday afternoon, when the site went live.

Everyone rose. Jack lingered until he and Samantha were the last two in the room.

"Good job," he said. "Arnie's worked out well for you."

She nodded. "He's been great. He's not only good at the technical stuff, but he understands the creative process. He's a big fan of yours and your dad's. He talks about George all the time. How George was really there for him."

"Good to know," Jack said. "Think he would be interested in running the department?"

She frowned. "Why do you want my opinion?"

"You've worked with him. You know how he thinks, what he's like. Could he do the job?"

"I think so. You're going to fire Roger?"

Jack sighed. "I don't know. I'm going to talk to him about his attitude. If he can't get onboard with what we're doing, then yes. It's never my first choice, but sometimes it has to be done. Given that, I would prefer to promote from within."

"Arnie's really popular with the IT team. That can be both good and bad. He might not enjoy the transition from one of the guys to being in charge."

"Once I decide what I'm doing with Roger, I'll talk with Arnie," Jack said. "I appreciate your candor."

She smiled. "No problem. As you know, I have opinions on nearly everything. Anything else you want to know about?"

What went wrong between the two of them, he thought, but before he could ask, she collected her files and computer.

"Never mind," she said quickly. "I have another meeting."

And then she was gone.

She'd always done that, he reminded himself. Disappeared when the going got tough. Ten years ago, when he'd pushed for more, she'd resisted and then she'd retreated. She proved his point about people leaving.

So he should just forget about her. It was the intelligent thing to do. And he would. Just as soon as he figured out how to get her out of his head…and his heart.

"So what exactly is the problem?" Helen asked.

Samantha writhed on the cream-colored sofa and covered her face with her hands. "Nothing."

"Of course I believe you, what with how calmly you're acting."

"It's crazy. It's dumb."

Her friend curled up in the club chair opposite and tucked her feet under herself. "You screwed up."

Samantha looked at her. "Do you have to be so blunt?"

"It seems called for. What's the problem? Did you blow it with Jack? I know it's not work related. I've only been hearing good things about you in that respect."

"Really? What kind of things?"

"They would not be the point of this conversation. What happened?"

Samantha flopped down on the sofa and groaned. "I blew it. Seriously. I'm going to be a cautionary tale."

Helen waited expectantly but didn't speak.

Samantha groaned. "Fine, I'll tell you, but it's not pretty."

She detailed the conversation she'd had with Jack at his place a few days ago.

"I freaked," she admitted after she'd shared the specifics. "He didn't really say anything that bad, it was all me. I felt guilty and embarrassed and stupid. As if I'd disappointed him somehow. As if it were my fault. I didn't like feeling that way. I didn't know how to deal with it so I overreacted. Worse, I blamed him."

"Actually, I think the worse part is that you walked out without explaining."

Samantha raised her head and glared at her friend. "You're not being helpful."

"Of course I am. I'm telling you the truth. The problem isn't that Jack couldn't handle the past, it's that you still can't. You don't want to believe you were that stupid." Helen smiled. "I'm saying this with love. You know that, right?"

"Yes. I feel the love. Sort of. It's me. It's all me. I'm ashamed and I feel like an idiot. I'm strong and tough, just like Jack said. How did I let some guy abuse me? How did I let him cut me off from my support system? Why couldn't I see the signs?"

"Because you weren't looking for them. You took Vance at his word. That's not exactly a crime."

"Maybe not, but it turned out to be poor judgment on my part. I feel horrible."

"I'm not the one you should be sharing your feelings with."

Samantha rolled onto her side. "You're saying I need to go talk to Jack."

"I can't think of another way to fix the situation."

"But what if he hates me?"

"Gee, what if you stopped being so dramatic?"

Samantha grinned. "Okay. Hate is strong. What if…" She sat up. "What if he doesn't respect me anymore?"

"What if he does? There's only one way to find out what he's thinking and that's to ask him."

Samantha knew her friend was telling the truth. "So when do I get to be the mature one in the relationship?"

"Next time."

"Ha. Like I believe that. You're so good at this. I guess it's because you had a great marriage. I want that. I want someone to love me and care about me, all the while seeing me as an equal."

"If you really want it, it will happen."

"Sort of like if you build it, they will come?"

"Yes, but this time in a romantic sense. If you know what you want, it's within your grasp."

Meaning Jack. Did she want him? Them? "We're doing the serial monogamy thing," she said. "Nothing long term."

"Okay, then after Jack."

After. Right. Because what were the odds of finding someone better than him? Someone more honest and funny and charming and better in bed?

"He doesn't want more," Samantha said. "He told me so."

"Do you know why?"

"Sort of. He doesn't believe people stay."

"A lot of people have left him, including you."

"I don't want to think about that."

"Maybe it's time you should," Helen said. "Why did you go?"

"Because I thought he'd hurt me. I thought he was too much like my father. But he's not. Although Vance was. This is confusing."

"What do you know for sure?"

"That I have to tell Jack I'm sorry."

Helen smiled. "Want me to show you out?"

Jack was home and he answered the door right away. Samantha had been hoping for a bit more time to figure out what she was going to say to him.

"Hi," he said and stepped back. "Want to come in?"

Just like that. No recriminations, no questions as to whether or not she was going to bite off his head.

"Thanks. Is this a good time?" she asked as she moved into the foyer and looked around for Charlie. Dogs were always a good distraction.

"Sure. What did you have in mind?"

He looked so good that she wanted to skip the conversation and suggest they move into the bedroom. He'd pulled on a sweater over worn jeans and pushed up the sleeves. He wore socks, but no shoes and had that weary end-of-the-day stubble that made her want to rub her hands against his jaw.

"I have a couple of things I'd like to say," she told him instead, not because it was the mature thing, and therefore the most Helen-like, but because she had a bad feeling he wouldn't be interested in sleeping with her right now.

Charlie came strolling down the hall, his yawn betraying his most recent activity.

"Did you just get up?" she asked the dog as she bent over and rubbed his ears.

"He had a tough day at doggy day care," Jack told her. "Apparently he played until he dropped from exhaustion."

That's right. Big tough ol' Jack took his dog to day care. How was she supposed to resist that?

"Come on," he said, leading the way into the living room. "Have a seat."

"Okay." She followed him, then perched on the edge

of the seat cushion. "I just wanted to apologize for what happened the last time I was here. I kind of lost it."

He sat at the other end of the sofa and faced her. "You seemed upset."

"I was. And hurt and embarrassed. I sort of took all that out on you." Wait. There was no *sort of.* "I *did* take that out on you. I thought you were judging me."

"Samantha, I wasn't," he told her. "Never that."

"I figured that part out later. By then I was home and giving myself a stern talking-to. The thing is, I'm not proud of what happened with Vance. I still don't know how I let him take control of me, of the situation. I've tried to learn from what happened. The control thing started so small. With little tiny suggestions. They grew and before I knew it…"

She shrugged. "My point is, it was my problem. Your comment about seeing clues was valid."

"Maybe, but it was poorly timed," he admitted. "It's a guy thing—wanting to fix. I know better."

"You didn't do anything wrong. I just hated believing you think badly of me."

"Not that." He moved close and took her hands in his. "Never that. I admire what you did. You found yourself in a hellish situation and you got out. You fought. Shelby didn't."

What? "What does your late fiancée have to do with my poor judgment with men?"

He released her hands and stood. "I told you Shelby died shortly before our wedding, but there's more to it than that. She'd been depressed for a while. Looking back, I suspect she'd been depressed all her life. We met during one of the times when she was feeling good. It didn't last." He walked to the window and stared out at the city.

"I didn't understand what was happening," he admitted. "She would get so sad and withdrawn. It was almost as if she disappeared from life. I thought it was me. I thought I was doing something wrong. But then the depression would ease and we'd be fine. She started seeing a therapist and she put her on medication. It helped. For a while. That's when I proposed. I figured this was just a manageable disease, like diabetes. I was wrong."

Samantha didn't know what to think. Jack was so vibrant and full of life. She couldn't imagine him with someone who was too depressed to deal with the world.

"Planning the wedding was too much," he said, his back to her. "I figured that out too late to do anything. Her mother tried to help. Helen offered, but I wasn't willing to deal with her. We had a bad storm and Shelby went driving in it. She lost control. At least that's what the police said. It was an accident."

Samantha couldn't breathe. Her heart ached for him. "It wasn't, was it?" she asked with a gasp.

He shook his head. "She left me a note. I burned it as soon as I read it. I knew the truth would only hurt her parents. They thought she was doing better, that she was finally happy. They actually thanked me for that at the funeral."

He turned to look at her. "I knew it was better to let

them think what they wanted. Why hurt them after she was gone? Why tell them she would rather be dead than married to me?"

Samantha sprang to her feet and hurried to him. "Is that what you think? It's not true, Jack. Don't you see? She was sick. You were right to call what she had a disease. Blaming yourself for her depression is as crazy as blaming me for Vance's abuse. You were there for her. You tried to help. In the end, she couldn't handle life and that has nothing to do with you."

She touched his arms, his back, trying to make him see. "You have to believe me," she whispered.

"I want to. You don't know how much. It's been a long time and I've let it go. But every now and then I wonder what I could have done differently. How I could have saved her."

"You can't save someone who won't save herself."

He turned then, and looked at her. "You saved yourself. That's what I was thinking the other night. You saved yourself."

They stared at each other. All their polite pretenses and shields were down. There was only the moment and the raw pain swirling around them, taking them to a level of emotional intimacy that was so real, so deep, it hurt.

Her first instinct was to run. If she stayed, if she let him in and they dealt with this together, there might not be an escape. She might start to care too much. She might get lost inside of him.

But there was no denying the truth. That they'd each

shared their most intimate secret. They knew the worst about each other. So where did they go from here?

He must have read the question in her eyes, because he answered it by grabbing her, pulling her in close and kissing her. She responded by surging toward him, silently begging for more.

He wrapped his arms around her as if he would never let her go. She welcomed the heat and power of his embrace. He was not a tentative lover—he claimed with a forceful need that took her breath away. Right now she had to know he wanted her, she had to know this mattered, and he told her over and over again as his mouth claimed hers in a kiss that touched her soul.

Wanting grew as she tasted him and felt her body sigh and swell and dampen. She ran her hands up and down his back, then across his broad shoulders. His strength excited her. She loved the feel of his muscles bunching and releasing. When he dropped his hands to her hips and urged her closer, she arched toward him and felt the satisfying hardness of his desire.

"More," she breathed.

He took her at her word and raised his hands to her breasts. He cupped her slight curves, teasing the sensitive skin before lightly brushing her hard nipples. Pleasure shot through her. She gasped, then let her head drop back as she lost herself in the tingling, burning, arousing sensation of his gentle touch.

Over and over he teased her, rubbing her breasts, stroking her. Even through the layers of her blouse and her bra, the feelings were exquisite. He leaned in and kissed the side of her neck, then gently bit down on her bare skin.

She shuddered in anticipation of them making love. Her brain filled with images of them naked, reaching, surging, claiming. Suddenly she needed him naked and inside of her. She stepped back and reached for his clothes.

"Now," she commanded.

Either he wanted the same thing, or he understood exactly what she needed. He reached for her blouse as she reached for his sweater. Their arms bumped and it probably would have made more sense for them to each undress themselves, but she didn't want that. She wanted to be the one to reveal his warm, naked flesh. She wanted to undo his belt, push down his jeans and briefs and reach for him, even as he jerked her skirt and panties to her ankles.

She stepped out of both, along with her clogs. Then they were naked and reaching and they were touching everywhere. Even as he kissed her deeply, thrusting his tongue into her mouth, he reached for her bare breasts. She ran her hands down his back, pausing when she reached his butt. Once there, she caressed the high, tight curve, then squeezed.

His arousal flexed against her stomach. So hard, she thought, loving how much he wanted her. She was already wet—she ached with readiness.

Once again, he seemed to read her mind. He pushed her back until she felt the sofa behind her. They dropped onto the cool, soft surface, a tangle of arms and legs and need. He shifted her until she sprawled across the cushions, her legs parted, her body exposed. He slid onto the floor, then bent forward, bringing his mouth into contact with her most intimate spot.

Samantha surrendered to the magic of his tongue and lips as he explored every sensitive inch of her. He licked her thoroughly before focusing his attention on that single spot of pleasure. Even as she felt herself both melting and tensing as she strained toward her completion, he slipped a finger inside of her.

The combination was too much for her to stand. Her breath quickened as her muscles clenched. Her climax became a certainty so all she had to do was simply brace herself for the explosion.

When it crashed into her, she gasped her pleasure. Her body contracted and stiffened, only to become boneless. Still he moved in and out, while kissing and licking and circling. As long as he touched her, she came—again and again. The orgasm stretched out until every cell in her body sighed in delight.

At last he slowed and her contractions eased. When he raised his head and looked at her, she found herself feeling more exposed than she ever had. Raw emotion made her uncomfortable. But she was trapped and naked and there was no escape.

Then Jack smiled. "You're so incredible," he murmured. "So beautiful. I could do that for hours."

With a few simple words, he made her feel special and at ease. She opened her arms and welcomed him. He moved close, shifting so that he could slide his arousal into her waiting warmth. Her body tensed slightly and he groaned.

He put his hands on her hips and drew her closer, then he shifted one hand so he could touch her breast. She wrapped her legs around his hips, urging him deeper and deeper, wanting to get lost in him, as he was lost in her.

She felt him harden, stiffen, then still. His release claimed him. She kept her eyes open and watched his face tighten. At the last possible moment, he opened his eyes as well and they stared at each other.

It was a perfect moment of connection, she thought in wonder. She was truly one with this man. And in love with him.

The revelation stunned her but, once admitted, the truth wouldn't go away.

She loved Jack.

She didn't know if the feeling was new or if it had been in hiding for the past ten years, but she loved him and she didn't have a clue as to what she was going to do about it.

## *Chapter Twelve*

"We have plans, Jack," Harold Morrison said as he handed a glass of scotch to Jack's boss.

Jack held his drink until everyone was served, then waited for the toast.

"To men who have the potential to go places," Morrison said.

Everyone glanced at Jack. He nodded, rather than smiled. "I appreciate the support and encouragement," he said before taking a drink.

"We think you can make it all the way," Morrison told him. "We've been talking about you."

Jack glanced around at the ten other people in the room. There were the four senior partners from his law firm, two congressmen, the junior senator and three of-

ficials from the state party office. Six men and four
women, all of whom had the power to influence his future.

Morrison patted Jack on the back. "You need to get
things squared away at Hanson Media Group. You're
doing a good job. We're getting excellent reports. Sure,
you're not practicing law, but you're being a leader,
making decisions. That bodes well. Just don't screw up
there."

Everyone laughed but Jack.

"You'll be back at the law firm in another couple of
months," Morrison continued. "Once that happens,
you'll be put on the short list for an appointment to the
circuit court as an associate judge. The law firms like
to send good people into the judicial system. It makes
us look good."

More laughter.

"I'll do my best," Jack said, knowing there was little he could do to move the process along. The launch
of the Web site was only days away. Once that was up
and running and adding to the cash flow, he could focus
his attention on the many other problems. Two months,
Morrison had said. Was it enough time?

Jack knew that legally he could walk away any time
he wanted. Without signing a permanent contract with
the board, they couldn't stop him from leaving. But
legal obligations were different than moral ones. Hanson Media Group was the family company. Could he
turn his back on it and let it fail so he'd be free to pursue his own dreams?

It was a question he had yet to answer.

Sarah Johnson, one of the firm's senior partners, leaned her hip on the conference-room table. "After working as an appointed judge, you'll run as an elected one. We'll have an organization in place to help with that. We've seen how you think and we like what we see. You're fair without being sentimental and you consider all your options. That's good for everyone. If you do as well as we expect, it won't be long until you're appointed to the federal bench." She raised her glass. "I like the sound of that."

"Agreed," Jack said, then took a sip of his drink. Big plans. Why did it have to come down to a choice between doing what he wanted and doing what was right for a family business he didn't care about?

"Was it wonderful?" Samantha asked as she walked into Jack's office for their quick lunch together.

"It's the first time I've had liquor before noon." He frowned as he thought about college. "At least in a lot of years."

"Oooh, you were drinking. That's good, right?"

"I'm not sure the drinking mattered, but there was a spirit of celebration."

She moved toward him and smiled. "I like the sound of that," she said as she raised herself on tiptoes and lightly brushed his mouth with hers. "They're impressed with you—just like me."

As always, her closeness made him aware of his ever-present need for her. It didn't seem to matter how many times they made love, the wanting wouldn't go away.

She set a tote bag on the coffee table and sank onto the sofa. After pulling out two wrapped sandwiches, she held one in each hand.

"Turkey or ham?" she asked.

"Either."

She passed him the ham, then dug around for take-out cartons of salad, two bags of chips and napkins. He took two sodas out of the small refrigerator in the corner and settled next to her on the sofa.

"There's a plan in place," he said as he unwrapped his sandwich. "I have the support of the senior partners, along with a couple of guys from congress and our junior senator."

"That's great," she said. "Did you get to meet them?"

He nodded. "They said they like the way I think. Plus having a former member of a law firm moving up the judicial food chain is always good for getting clients."

She frowned. "Because they think they'll get a break in cases?"

He smiled for the first time that morning. "No. Because it means they can pick and groom talent. Any sign that I was favoring one side over another in a case would mean getting thrown off the bench. I haven't busted my butt to get this far only to screw up over something that stupid."

"Okay. That makes sense. So if you look good, they look good."

"Yeah. There's only one thing standing in the way of all that."

She tilted her head. "I don't even have to guess. What are you going to do?"

"I haven't decided. Part of me wants to call a board meeting and resign. What do I care about this company?"

She touched his hand. "Except you do care. You don't want all the employees to be out of a job and there's a tiny part of you that can't face losing the company your father loved so much."

He stiffened. "I don't give a damn about my father." Why would he?

But instead of backing off, Samantha stayed exactly where she was and took a bite of her sandwich. The silence lengthened. Finally he exhaled sharply.

"Fine. I might not care about the old man, but you're right. I can't let this all be destroyed. It would be wrong."

She swallowed, then smiled. "Why was I afraid of you back in grad school? I kept seeing you as exactly like my father, but you couldn't be more different."

"Why were you afraid of me?"

"Because I thought you'd hurt me, then leave me."

Instead she'd been the one to walk out, he thought. "I'm not like him or Vance," he said.

"I know that now."

Better late than never, or was it? In the ten years they'd been apart, they'd both learned lessons. Unfortunately, his had been to be wary of trusting anyone to stay.

"I want to talk to Helen," she said. "About getting you back to your law firm. She can take on the board, she's good at that kind of stuff. There has to be someone else who can run things around here."

He leaned close and lightly touched her face. "Not your concern."

"I want you to have your heart's desire. Why wouldn't I?"

Very few people bothered to look out for him these days, he thought. David had when he'd been younger. Now Samantha was stepping into his life and doing her best to make his dreams come true.

"Why does it matter?" he asked, when what he really meant was "Why do *I* matter?"

She smiled. "It just does." She pushed his sandwich toward him. "You'd better eat. Mrs. Wycliff said you had a full afternoon."

He unwrapped the paper and took a bite, but his mind was busy elsewhere. Her words, her actions, all spoke of caring about him. He'd wanted that for a long, long time. Was it finally happening? Could he trust her not to bolt? And if she was willing to stick around this time, was he willing to open himself up or had he been burned one too many times?

"I'm going to throw up," Samantha muttered, doing her best to stay calm and keep breathing.

Arnie hovered at her side. "You'll be fine. We're all fine."

She laughed. "You look like you're going to pass out.

That's hardly fine." Her humor faded. "Jeez, I hate this. Why can't it be tomorrow? Why can't the launch be behind us?"

"Because it's now."

And it was. She stood in the corner of an after-school center in the middle of the city. The large computer lab was filled with excited kids, members of the media and most of her team and the IT staff.

Dozens of conversations competed with laughter and loud music. There were bright balloons, plush toys licensed from animation on the Web site and a cake big enough to feed a hometown Bears crowd.

They had been live for all of eighteen minutes and she was still scared to go see how it was going.

"It's my job," she muttered to herself and took a step toward the computers.

"What do you think?" she asked the boy sitting closest to her.

He was maybe eleven, with bright red hair and freckles. "It's fun. I can do my math homework and get help when I need it. Plus, there's this game."

He clicked on several icons faster than she could follow and ended up in a math-based jungle where three different paths offered three different games.

Samantha made a few notes and then moved on to another child. About a half hour later, David Hanson strolled up and said, "You can't hide from the media forever," he said. "They have questions."

"I'm nervous," she admitted.

"It doesn't show. Come on. It won't be so bad."

Samantha followed him to the row of reporters and newspeople. David introduced her.

"We'll start with general questions," he said, "then we can schedule individual interviews and tape segments for the local news."

A pretty woman in a tailored navy suit jacket grinned. "I'm actually the network feed. This is going national."

"That's great," Samantha said, knowing it was amazing publicity and ignoring the sudden aerial formation of butterflies in her stomach. "Ask away."

She fielded several questions about how the new Web site worked.

"What about security?" one of the reporters asked. "How are you protecting our children?"

"In every way possible," Samantha told her. "We have all the usual safeguards in place, along with specific security triggers to flag potential stalkers. There's a special section for parents on the Web site. They can set up parameters, determining how much access each child in the family has. Older kids can do more, younger kids less. We're interested in feedback on the issue as well." She smiled. "I have the time logs in my office. On this project, we've spent as many hours on security as we have on content and we're very proud of that."

The next few questions were for the director of the after-school program. Samantha took the time away from the spotlight to look around and enjoy the success. She'd had the idea of making this a reality and now it was.

"We also owe a specific debt of gratitude to Hanson Media Group," the director was saying. "Not just for the wonderful Web site, but also for the new computers and high-speed Internet access they've donated to our center."

Samantha joined in the applause, but she didn't know what the woman was talking about. As soon as the media interviews were over, she found David.

"The company donated computers to the center?" she asked.

David nodded. "It was Jack's idea. He didn't think it was right to use them to get publicity without giving something back. Their computers were pretty old."

She glanced at the man in question and saw him sitting in front of a monitor with a little girl on his lap. Two more girls leaned against him, all raptly intent on the screen.

"The donation isn't mentioned in the PR material," she said. "I reviewed it last night."

David shrugged. "Jack didn't want to exploit the moment. I told him he was crazy, but he didn't listen. He's stubborn that way."

She knew he hadn't done it for her. In fact, she was confident she'd never crossed his mind. He'd quietly given thousands of dollars worth of computers because it was the right thing to do. That was simply the kind of man he was.

She'd let him walk out of her life once because she'd been afraid....

But not of him, she suddenly realized. Her fears had

never been about him. They'd been about herself. About how she would react. About how her world would change. She'd been afraid of depending on someone who would let her down and that she wouldn't be able to handle it.

Ten years ago she'd let Jack go, not because of who he was, but because of who *she* was.

She walked toward him and as she got closer, her chest tightened. There he sat with those girls, typing in what they told him to, patiently exploring the site with them. One of the girls pointed at a colorful animated parrot and laughed. Jack smiled at the child and nodded.

Samantha got it then—she saw it all. The acceptance, the caring, the goodness of the man inside.

She'd always wanted children. She'd put her dreams on hold because of her marriage to Vance. She'd lost so much time, but she'd been given a second chance. Was she going to blow it again? Or was she going to reach for the happiness waiting there, well within her grasp?

Friday night the Web site flashed with bright colors. The man at the keyboard typed furiously. This was wrong. All wrong. George wouldn't have wanted this. George would have wanted things to stay the same. He never approved of all this new technology.

It was the wrong direction for the company. How many times had George said Hanson Media Group was about magazines? Not this. Never this.

It was all going so well, too. Jack would get the credit. Jack who had never cared about his father. Jack who had broken his father's heart by refusing to go into the family business. The board and everyone else would say Jack was the hero.

He typed more quickly, working links into the software programming, putting them in places no one would think to look. Because they *would* look. The IT people always wanted to fix the problem themselves.

What they would forget was that he was better than all of them. The more they dug, the farther away they would get from the actual problem.

He tested the links, then smiled. All done. Now all he had to do was crash the system. The techs on duty would work frantically to get it up and running again. When they did, they would see everything working fine. What they wouldn't see was that the Web site automatically linked to a porn site. They wouldn't know there was even another problem to deal with until it was too late.

That should punish Jack. That should punish all of them.

A fire crackled behind the grate. Jack felt the warmth on his legs, but only barely. He was far more interested in getting Samantha's bra off. But she wasn't cooperating.

"I want you naked," he murmured against her mouth.

She laughed and kissed him. "Do you see me protesting?"

"You're trying to get my shirt off. Bra first, shirt second."

"But I want to see you," she said. "You look good naked."

"See later. I want to touch now."

She smiled. "Touching is good. I would support touching."

He stared into her eyes and found himself wanting to get lost there. This is how it was supposed to be, he thought. This is what mattered. Being with someone he cared about. Someone he could trust.

A voice in his head warned him that Samantha had run before and she would probably run again, but he didn't want to listen. He didn't want to think about her leaving. Not now.

But what to say to convince her to stay? After all, he wasn't one who truly believed in relationships working out. They certainly never had for him. Was this time different?

Maybe the difference was this time he wanted it to, he thought as he bent down and kissed her.

She parted for him and he stroked her tongue with his. He tilted his head so he could deepen the kiss, then claimed her with a passion that seared him to his soul.

"Samantha," he breathed as he rolled onto his back and pulled her with him.

She draped across his chest, her body warm and yielding. Her hands were everywhere, touching, pulling at clothes, teasing and exciting. She shifted so she could rub herself against his arousal.

The sharp sound of the phone cut through the night.

He swore and considered not answering it. It was

after eleven on Saturday night—what could be that important? Only an emergency, he thought grimly as Samantha sat up and handed him the phone.

"Hello?"

"Jack? Is that you? Are you watching the news?"

"What? Who is this?" Then he recognized the frantic voice. "Mrs. Wycliff?"

"Turn on the news. Any channel. It's on all of them. Oh, Jack, it's horrible. This is the end. I don't see how the company can survive now."

He grabbed the remote and turned on the television. The local late-night news anchor appeared and behind her was a screen showing a raunchy porn site. Certain body parts were blacked out, but it was easy to see what the people on the screen were doing.

Jack swore and increased the volume.

"No one from Hanson Media Group was immediately available for comment," the news anchor said. "From our best guess, the new Web site for children has been linking to this porn site for the better part of the afternoon. Parents across the country are furious and no one knows exactly how many children were exposed to this sort of smut."

## Chapter Thirteen

"It's been twelve hours," Jack said, more than ready to yell at the people assembled in his office.

Most of Samantha's team was in place, as were the IT guys, along with David and Mrs. Wycliff. Although he hadn't told his secretary to come in, she'd been waiting when he'd arrived.

"Twelve goddamn hours since the site crashed and no one—*no one*—thought to call me?"

His words echoed in the large room, followed by an uncomfortable silence. Right now he didn't care about anyone being uncomfortable. He wanted answers.

"Everyone has my home number," he continued. "I've told you all to get in touch if there's a problem and the only reason I know now is because Mrs. Wycliff watched the late news. How long would this have gone on otherwise? When exactly did you plan on letting me know?"

He directed the last question at the IT staff. Roger stepped forward.

"The site crashed yesterday morning. We're not sure why. I have a team investigating. They had the site up and running in about two hours."

"At a porn site?" Jack asked sarcastically. "Wouldn't it have been better to wait until our content was available?"

Roger swallowed. "Our content is available. But when our Web address is typed in, users were redirected to the porn site you heard about. Our Web site is fine."

Jack narrowed his gaze. "I don't think I'd use that word to describe things right now." He turned to Arnie. "Did you pull the plug?"

The smaller man nodded quickly. "Yes. As soon as I heard, I came right in. When you type in the Web address, the user gets an error message."

That was something, Jack thought grimly. At least no more children would be sent to view raunchy sex.

"Do we know what happened?" Jack asked in a quiet voice. "Do we know what went wrong?"

No one answered.

He leaned against the edge of his desk. "How bad?" he asked David.

"It's too soon to tell. We have to figure out how many hits we had this afternoon. With the publicity blitz all week, we were expecting a couple million."

Jack swore. A couple million? Was that possible? Was this company really responsible for exposing two million children to that kind of horror?

"We were supposed to be helping them," he said. "We were supposed to be providing a safe environment for children. A place where they could learn and have fun, away from everything bad. Instead we sent them right into the heart of the worst of it."

"Our stock might take a hit, but it will recover," someone said.

Jack stared at the man, not sure what department he belonged in and knowing it would be unreasonable to fire him for expressing an opinion.

"You think I care about the stock price?" he asked. "Do you think it matters to me if this company goes out of business tomorrow? We have done the one thing we vowed we would never do—we have hurt our kids. Nothing makes that right. And there's nothing we can do to make it right."

But people would try. He looked at David again. "Has the legal team been notified? Come Monday morning, people are going to be lining up at courts across the country."

"I have calls in."

"Good. I'm guessing most of the board members have heard, but in case some of them are out of town, I'll call them in the morning." He glanced at his watch. "Later this morning."

Arnie stepped forward. "Jack, I know it's not worth much, but I don't think it was us. Oh, sure, the site crashed, but when we got it back up, it was working fine. The, ah, techs monitoring the site never saw the porn site because it wasn't there. I think there was an override in our server."

Jack stared at him. "You're saying the redirect was external to our system?"

Arnie shrugged. "It's a place to start looking."

The meeting broke up an hour later. After telling everyone to be in by six on Monday morning, Jack sent them home. Samantha stayed on the sofa, not only because she'd come with Jack but because she felt too sick to move.

He collapsed in a club chair and rubbed his temples. "This is completely and totally screwed."

"I feel so horrible," she whispered. "I can't believe this happened. We checked so many times. The security was all there. That's what gets me. The site wasn't compromised. It was the server."

"Regardless of the technicalities, Hanson Media Group is still responsible," he said.

"I know. No one is going to care how it happened, only that it did." She crossed her arms in front of her midsection. "All those children. Who would have done it and why?"

"Not a clue," he admitted. "But I'm going to find out and then that person is going to be prosecuted if I have to do it myself."

Her eyes burned, but she blinked the tears away. Crying wouldn't help anyone. Still, it was hard not to give in to the pain. So many people had worked so hard, only to have everything ruined by someone bent on destroying the company.

"This is revenge," she said. "Or an act of rage. It feels personal."

"To me, too. So who hates me that much and why?"

"Does it have to be someone hating you?" she asked. "Can it be someone who hates the company? A recently fired employee? Someone with a personal grudge against George, or one of your brothers. Who has enemies?"

"Who doesn't?" he asked.

She stared at him. "I'm so sorry, Jack. I thought the new Web site was the answer to all the company's problems. Now I find I've just made things worse."

"You filled all the holes you saw."

"And missed a really big one."

She'd also gotten in the way of his future, she thought as her stomach clenched tighter. Jack wanted to do his job and get back to his dreams. What were the odds of that happening now? The board was going to be furious and they would blame Jack.

So not fair, she thought frantically. But how could she keep it from happening?

"Jack, I—"

A knock on the door cut her off.

"Come in," he called.

Mrs. Wycliff stepped inside. "The police are here."

Samantha's breath caught. "The police?"

Jack shrugged. "What did you expect?"

Not that. Some of her shock must have shown on her face. He stood and walked toward her.

"It's all right," he said gently. "David is waiting in his office. He'll take you home."

"I don't want you to have to deal with the police by yourself."

He touched her cheek. "Don't worry. You'll get your chance to answer their questions later today or Monday. Try to get some sleep."

Before she could try to convince him to let her stay, Mrs. Wycliff had ushered her out of the office and into the hallway. There she saw several police officers. They nodded politely.

She walked past them toward David's office. A part of her couldn't believe this was really happening. It was all wrong and there didn't seem to be anything she could do to stop it.

Jack grabbed a couple of hours of sleep Sunday night and was at the office before five on Monday morning. He had multiple crises to deal with.

While it all hit the fan over the Web site disaster, there was still a company to be run. The emergency board meeting started at nine, followed by an afternoon with in-house legal counsel. At last count, there were over a hundred lawsuits ready to be filed as soon as the courts opened. If this didn't kill the company, it would be sheer luck. Best case scenario, Hanson Media Group survived as a smaller, less proud organization which meant cutbacks and massive layoffs.

He was surprised to find Roger waiting outside his office when he arrived.

"Here to confess?" he said, then regretted the words as soon as they were out.

Roger looked at him. "I didn't do it. I'll take a lie detector test if that will help."

Jack looked at the lines of exhaustion on the other man's face, then waved him into the office. "Sorry. I shouldn't have said that. I have no reason to suspect you."

"No more than anyone else with the technical expertise," Roger said bluntly, then handed over a tall cup of Starbucks.

Jack was as startled by the coffee as by Roger's statement. "I was under the impression that you were more a manager than a techie."

Roger sipped his own coffee, then shrugged. "I'll admit that my first experience with a computer was with punching cards, but I've worked in the business all my life. I might be older and not as fast, but I can code with the best of my team."

News to Jack, as he tried to remember where he'd gotten the idea that Roger didn't know what he was doing on the technical front.

"We've continued to investigate over the weekend," Roger said. "As I suspected from the first, it's not our Web site. The content there never changed and the address wasn't hijacked. Instead, someone got inside the server and messed with it. When the server started to route the user to our site, it made a quick left turn to porn central."

Jack didn't know if the information made a difference or not. "Who did it?"

"I'm still working on that. My guess is someone from this end rather than the server, but the police will be investigating them. I'm in touch with the detective in charge of the case."

"Why do you think it's someone from this company?" Jack asked.

"The attack feels personal. That's just my opinion."

"I appreciate hearing it," Jack told him. "Anything else?"

Roger nodded. "The detective thinks there's a good chance the feds will get involved."

More trouble, Jack thought. No one wanted that. "It's all out of our control," he said. "What are you doing this morning?"

"Continuing the investigation."

"Stay available. I have an emergency board meeting. They may want to ask you more questions."

Roger nodded, then left. Jack stared after him. He'd never liked the man, but suddenly Roger was stepping up to take charge during a crisis. Did he need something like this to show his true nature, or was he the guilty party looking to be close to the action?

Several hours later Jack sat with the board and wished to hell he'd never left his law practice. They were angry and out for blood and right now they didn't particularly care whose.

Baynes, the chairman, led the discussion.

"This has to be fixed, Jack, and the sooner the better."

Jack sat forward and braced his forearms on the table. "I agree, and I'm working on the problem. The in-house IT people are doing what they can to find out who's responsible. I've also hired an outside team to work backwards from the server problem."

"Hired guns?" Baynes asked.

"Independent agents. They don't evaluate what they find, they simply report it. Someone told me this morning that the Web site crash feels personal and I agree with him on that. Someone somewhere wants Hanson Media Group to crash and burn. I want to find out who and I want to know why."

Baynes looked surprised by the information. "A personal attack? Against the company?"

"Until I know who did it, I can't answer that," Jack told him.

"You're working with the police?"

"Yes."

Baynes looked at the papers in front of him. "Samantha Edwards was in charge of the new Web site."

"That's correct. She handled content while coordinating with the IT team on technical aspects."

"According to previous reports, she came up with the whole idea."

Jack saw where they were going and didn't like it. "She had nothing to do with the crash and subsequent rerouting."

"You don't know that for sure," Baynes said.

"Actually, I do. Samantha simply isn't that kind of

person and even if she were, she doesn't have the technical expertise."

"She could be working with someone."

"She's not. I know Samantha personally and I'm telling you she's not the one. You're wasting your time with her. She is as devastated as anyone by what happened."

Baynes didn't look convinced, but he changed the subject.

The board broke at noon. Jack barely had an hour until he met with the company's legal counsel. As he hurried into his office, he yelled for Mrs. Wycliff to get Samantha in to see him right away.

He didn't have time for any of this, he thought as he poured coffee and ignored the sandwich his secretary had thoughtfully left on his desk.

Samantha arrived less than five minutes later.

"What's up?" she asked as she walked toward him. "Is it awful? They all have to be furious, but they have to know none of this is your fault."

"They don't know what to think," he told her. "Right now they're looking for information. They want to talk to everyone involved in the project, including you."

She nodded. "Especially me. I was in charge and it was my idea. I thought this would happen. When do they want to see me?"

"After lunch."

"Okay. No problem. I'll clear my calendar."

She looked tired, but then they all did. It had been a long couple of days. Perhaps anticipating her presence before the board, she'd dressed conservatively—at least for her. A simple blouse over a long, dark skirt. Her hair had been tamed by a clip at the base of her neck.

He led her to the sofa and urged her to sit. He settled next to her.

"They're going to ask a lot of questions," he said. "You don't have very long to prepare. Stay calm and answer as best you can. It would help if you had information to back up your plans."

She frowned. "What kind of information?"

"Your notes. How you came up with the idea of the Web site, the various forms it took. Logs of meetings with your team and the IT people. Transcriptions of discussions."

Samantha stared at him. "You have to be kidding," she said, knowing there was no need to panic, but wanting to all the same. "I don't keep records like that. I barely record the dates and times of our meetings in my date book. Jack, this was a very creative process. We would brainstorm together for a few hours, then go off to work individually. When we got back together, we compared what we had. No one took notes. Sometimes we worked over a game of basketball. You know that."

He nodded. "You'll need to go through the process as logically as you can. Our board members wouldn't be described as creative, so they're not going to understand what you're talking about. They'll want to see your e-mail assigning a task to someone."

"It doesn't exist."

He touched her hand. "It's okay. This is just a conversation. They're going to push you, but that doesn't mean you have to let them. Stand your ground."

She appreciated the advice, but wished she didn't need it. "Are you going to be at the meeting?" she asked.

"I wish I were, but I have to be with legal."

Which made sense, but didn't make her happy. Somehow all this would be easier with Jack in the room.

"I'll be fine," she told him, as much to convince herself. "I have nothing to hide, so what's the worst that can happen? They'll get crabby and I'll endure it. In the meantime I'll go through my notes and see if I can figure out a time line for putting the Web site together. I wonder if Arnie has any information."

"Don't check with him. It will look too much like collusion."

Until that moment, Samantha had only been nervous. Suddenly she was scared. "Jack, do they think it's me?"

"They think it's everyone. The only thing singling you out is that you were in charge. So you've come to their notice. That's all." He squeezed her fingers. "I mean that. I trust you completely."

She saw the sureness in his gaze and allowed herself to draw comfort from it. "You know I would never—"

He cut her off with a quick kiss. "Don't say it. You don't have to. I would suspect myself before you. This isn't about that. It's about an angry board looking for answers. Nothing more."

"Okay." She stood. "I'd better go get ready."

He rose and smiled. "Before you go…"

"What?"

He pulled her close and kissed her. Even as his mouth brushed against hers, his arms came around her. She leaned against him, savoring the heat and strength of his body.

This was where she belonged, she thought. This was home.

He licked her lower lip and when she parted for him, he slipped his tongue inside. They kissed deeply for a few minutes before they both drew back.

"That could get out of hand in a hot minute," he teased.

"You're right and neither of us have time."

He kissed her lightly. "Rain check."

"We don't even have to wait for bad weather."

"Good to know." He walked her to the door and opened it. "If it gets rough, if they start to get out of hand, excuse yourself and come get me. I mean it, Samantha. Don't let them get to you. They're just regular people."

"Crabby regular people," she told him.

"You'll do fine."

"I'll do my best."

"Ms. Edwards, what made you come up with the Web site expansion in the first place?"

The woman questioning Samantha was elegant, well-dressed and obviously furious.

"When I heard about the job at Hanson Media Group, I spent several days researching their positioning in the market. I knew cash flow was a problem and that while they needed to grow, another magazine wasn't the answer. The Web site offered a way to expand quickly, and with relatively little start-up capital."

"You've done this sort of thing before? Launched a Web site?" a man asked.

Samantha wished they would all wear name tags, because except for Mr. Baynes, the chairman of the board, she had no clue who anyone was.

"I've been part of a launch," she said. "I've never been completely in charge."

The board members sat on one side of a long table, while she sat on the other. There was a vast expanse of space on either side of her, giving her the sensation of being very, very alone. She knew she could call Jack and he would come defend her, but she wasn't going to take him up on his offer. She would get through this on her own.

"How exactly did you come to work for Hanson Media Group?" Mr. Baynes asked. "You've been hired fairly recently."

"I heard about the job and applied."

"Heard about it how?"

"Helen Hanson told me. We're friends." Samantha clenched her teeth. Should she have admitted to the relationship? She didn't want Helen dragged into this.

"You've known Helen a long time?"

"Over twenty years."

The board members looked at each other.

"Were you jealous of Helen?" the woman asked. "Did you resent her successful marriage, her personal wealth?"

"What?" Samantha couldn't believe it. "Of course not. What does my relationship with Helen have to do with the Web site?"

"We're looking for a motive, Ms. Edwards."

"I didn't do it," Samantha told them firmly. "I love my job and I'm very supportive of what the company is doing. I would never endanger any child. The team and I worked very hard to make sure we had state-of-the-art security in place. While I do accept responsibility for this happening on my project, I would like to point out that the site itself wasn't compromised. It couldn't have been. Someone got into the server. As that is an outside company and beyond our scope of control, I don't see how we could have prevented that."

"Perhaps if you'd considered the threat," Mr. Baynes said sharply. "Perhaps if you'd looked past your quest for glory."

"My *what?*"

"You were very careful to take the spotlight in all the media interviews, weren't you?"

"No. This is crazy. I was in charge of the project, so it made sense for me to represent the company."

"Something that is normally David Hanson's job," Baynes continued.

Samantha shook her head. "David was with me. We coordinated our activities."

"So you say."

She got it then. She wasn't sure why it had taken so long for her to see the truth. Jack had been wrong—this wasn't an angry board. This was a board looking for a scapegoat. For reasons she couldn't understand, they'd decided that scapegoat was her.

She stood. "However much you search, you are not going to find a motive for me to have sabotaged Hanson Media Group. I wasn't involved in what happened in any way. I don't have a grudge against the company or anyone working for it. I was hired to do a job and I did it to the best of my abilities."

"Hardly a statement to reassure us," the woman said with a sniff.

Samantha ignored her. "I would never endanger any child. That was my mission from the first. To provide them with a safe environment to learn. Every memo, every e-mail, ever letter I've written on the subject supports that."

Baynes narrowed his gaze. "We've spoken with your ex-husband, Ms. Edwards. He describes you as a very emotionally unstable person. After walking out on him for no good reason, you filed for divorce only to change your mind. You begged him to take you back. You threatened his children."

Samantha felt as if she'd been shot. There was a sharp pain in her chest and she couldn't seem to catch her breath. Damn Vance. He'd vowed he would get back at her for leaving him. He'd hated giving up control. By calling Vance, Baynes had handed him a perfect way to get revenge.

"My ex-husband is lying," she said, trying to stay calm. "However, it's very clear to me that you're not going to believe anything I say. What do you want from me?"

"Your resignation," Baynes said.

Right. Then they could issue a press statement and say the person responsible had been punished. The board didn't care about finding the person who had actually done this. They simply wanted to make the news cycle with good news. Something they could toss out in an attempt to salvage the company and the stock price.

"You want me to resign because you don't have any reason to fire me," she said.

"We'll get it soon enough," Baynes told her. "If you go quietly, we won't give the information from your husband to the press."

Talk about a low blow and a threat.

Indecision filled her. Her instinct was to stay and fight, but to what end? Wouldn't her leaving make things easier for Jack? With the board off her back, he could focus on getting the company back on its feet.

She could deal with lies and innuendo, but she didn't want to hurt Jack.

"I'll resign," she said.

## *Chapter Fourteen*

Jack and the legal team took a break close to three. They had already developed a strategy of crisis control and cleanup. Jack did his best to remember his position as president of the company. He knew he was responsible for making sure Hanson Media Group survived. But every time he thought about what had happened, he wanted to throw a chair through the floor-to-ceiling windows.

He left the conference room and headed for his office to pick up his messages. David fell into step beside him.

"The board is still meeting," his uncle said. "But they've already found one victim."

"That's fast work." He hadn't expected them to act for several weeks. Investigations took time.

"It's Samantha."

Jack didn't break stride. He simply changed directions and headed for the stairs that would take him to the floor where the board met. David stayed with him.

"I know what you're thinking," the older man said.

"I doubt that." Worried, furious, frustrated didn't even come close. Dammit, he'd sent Samantha in there by herself. She'd had to face a firing squad alone and he hadn't been there to protect her.

"Jack, I know you care about her, but think before you act."

"Why? They didn't. How long did they question her? Fifteen minutes? We all know that Samantha isn't guilty of anything. She had great plans for the company. Someone deliberately screwed with that and I'm not going to let him, her or them get away with it."

"What are you going to do?" David asked as they climbed up to the next floor.

"Take control."

He walked into the conference room without knocking. The board was in the middle of questioning several of the IT guys. Jack jerked his head toward the now-open door and the three of them scuttled out.

Jack crossed to the long table, pushed the now-empty chairs aside and leaned toward the seven people who wanted to control his destiny.

"I understand you've had an admission of guilt," he said. "Why didn't you tell me someone had confessed?"

Baynes glared at him. "You're out of line, Jack."

"Not even a little. Come on, Baynes, how are you

going to threaten me? Do you want to say you're going to fire me? That would only make my day. So how did you get the confession?"

"Ms. Edwards didn't confess. But as she was ultimately responsible for the program we all thought it was best if she—"

Jack slapped his hands on the table. "*I'm* ultimately responsible. While I'm in charge, then this is my company. You do not have the right to go behind my back and fire my employees for no reason."

"They had a reason," David said, his voice cold. "Tell him, Baynes."

The chairman of the board looked uncomfortable but didn't speak.

"They want to make the news," David said. "They want everyone to think they're making progress so the stock price doesn't tank."

"We care about this company," Baynes said. "Which is more than I can say about either of you."

Jack swore. "I've given everything I had to keep Hanson Media Group from going down. You were all happy about our new program."

"Until there were problems," Baynes said. "Obviously you have incompetent people running things around here. Ms. Edwards has a history of problems and I'm sure they—"

Jack leaned forward and glared at Baynes. "What the hell are you talking about? What problems?"

"We spoke with her ex-husband. He was very forthcoming."

"I'll bet he was."

Jack straightened and took a step back. If he didn't get out of here, he was going to beat the crap out of Baynes and anyone else who stuck around. Samantha must hate him right about now. To think the board had pried into her personal life. He had to find her. He had to know she was all right.

"You want someone to blame," he said. "Blame me. I quit."

Baynes stood. "You can't. We don't accept your resignation. We have a contract, Jack. You violate that and we'll haul you into court. We'll win, too. Then what will happen to your law career?"

Jack started for the old man. David grabbed his arm and pulled him out into the hallway.

"Think," his uncle told him. "Don't make things worse than they are. They're not going to let you go."

"You're right." Jack started for the elevators. "Where's Samantha? Has anyone seen her?"

"Here I am again," Samantha said as she reached for another tissue. "Curled up on your sofa and crying. Isn't this getting boring?"

"Not yet," Helen said with surprising cheer. "You always come for a new and exciting reason. That keeps it interesting."

"Thanks." Samantha knew her friend was trying to keep her from falling too far into the despair pit by using humor but it wasn't exactly working. "I never want to go through anything like that again."

"I don't blame you," Helen said. "I swear, if George leaves the majority shares to me, I'm going to consider firing the board."

Samantha wanted to take that as personal support, but she knew her friend well enough to know that Helen was making a business decision.

"I don't know what to do," she admitted. "I really wanted to stand up to the board, but I don't want to make things worse for Jack. I hate that this is happening to him. Taking over the business was his way of doing the right thing. I know he and his dad weren't close, but when it was important, Jack gave up the job he loved to help out. Now he's getting hit with this. I just wanted to make it better."

"Have you talked to him?" Helen asked.

"No. I sort of lost it and came right here. I guess I should put a call in to him."

Helen smiled. "I have a feeling he'll be looking for you."

"Why?"

"Gee, I don't know. The woman he's been involved with just got bullied by a board of directors he's already annoyed with. Don't you think that will make him react? I won't be surprised to hear he punched out Baynes."

Samantha sat up. "He wouldn't do that."

"Wouldn't he?"

She thought about all the ways Jack had been there for her. How he'd been patient and supportive and more than a little understanding.

"Oh, no," she breathed. "You're right. He's going to be furious." She felt her mouth drop open. "He really cares about me."

Helen rolled her eyes. "You think?"

Samantha grinned. "I care about him, too. I have since we first met."

"That would be the time when you were too scared to hang on to the fabulous guy who was crazy about you?"

"Pretty much." She stood. "What if he thinks this is me running again? What if he doesn't know I'm doing this to help him?"

Helen shrugged. "Have I mentioned how communicating would be a good thing?"

Samantha bent down and kissed her friend's cheek. "You're the best. You know that, right?"

"I've been told before."

Samantha laughed, then grabbed her purse. "I have to go find Jack. If he calls here, would you tell him I'm looking for him?"

Helen reached for the phone. "Just go back to the office. I'll call Mrs. Wycliff so she can let him know you're on your way."

Jack paced in his office, not willing to believe the message until Samantha actually walked in.

"I wasn't leaving," she said as she rushed up to him. "Well, okay, I was leaving the company, but not you. I thought it would make it easier for you."

"Letting the board pin all this on you?" he asked

gruffly, as he pulled her close and stared into her eyes. "Why would having you gone help?"

She smiled. "I had a momentary loss of brain function. It won't happen again."

"Good."

She felt right in his arms. Warm and soft and feminine. Also stubborn, difficult and outrageous and he didn't want her to change a thing.

"Oh, Jack," she said quietly. "This is a really big mess."

"Yeah, but we're going to fix it. For one thing, I've refused to accept your resignation, so don't think you can get out of working here."

"I don't want to try, but I did think of something that may be significant. While I was in the cab from Helen's I wrote out a time line." She pulled a small piece of paper from her purse. "There's something we've all overlooked. The Web site crashed."

He stared at her. "What?"

"Remember? The site went down. The tech guys got it up and running. From this end, the site was fine. But when the site came back online, something happened in the server, switching everyone who logged on to the porn site. I think the two incidents are related. I think the whole thing was rigged to be triggered by the rebooting of the Web site. Which means it could still be an inside job."

He grabbed her shoulders and swore. "It has to be. That's the only thing that makes sense. We've been talking about how this all feels personal. You haven't been around long enough for anyone to hate you—"

"Neither have you," she reminded him.

"I've been around my whole life. Even if I wasn't here, people knew who I was. They knew I wasn't involved. Then my father dies and I come in and take over."

"Or maybe someone was angry at your father and wanted to get back at him through the company."

A real possibility, he thought. He released her and lightly kissed her. "You're pretty smart."

She smiled. "One of my many good qualities. So we have this great theory. Now what?"

"We call in a friend." He walked to the phone and dialed a number. "Roger? It's Jack. Samantha and I have come up with a possible scenario. If I tell you what it is, can you tell me who is capable of doing it?"

He listened carefully, then thanked the man and hung up.

"Well?" Samantha asked. "Are there any names?"

"Two, and one of them is Arnie."

The two men arrived at Jack's office less than ten minutes later. Samantha took one look at them and knew Arnie was the culprit. The truth was there in the way he wouldn't meet her eyes.

Jack invited the two men to sit in the chairs by his desk, but before he could start questioning, she walked up to Arnie.

"Why?" she asked softly. "I thought we were friends. We put in all those late nights together. You had great ideas and I listened. I trusted you. I don't know why you wanted to punish the company and I'll accept that you probably had a good reason, but you hurt children. Innocent children. What about them?"

Arnie stared at her and slowly blinked. "I have no idea what you're talking about."

The man with him, Matt, shifted in his seat. "Me, either. I didn't do it, if that's what you want to find out. The site went down and I worked on that, but I never touched the server." He swallowed. "I have kids of my own. Two. I wouldn't do this."

Samantha never took her gaze off Arnie. "But you would. I thought we were friends."

Jack moved up behind her and put his hand on her arm. "It's not about you, Samantha. It's about me. Am I right, Arnie? It's about me and my father and the company. Because I have it all now. The old man is gone and I have everything."

Arnie sprang to his feet. "You don't deserve it," he yelled. "You don't. You never cared about the business. You never respected your father. Did you think I didn't hear what you said about him? He was a great man. You'll never be like him. Never."

Samantha nearly forgot to breathe. "But you were so supportive of the Web site."

"He was playing you," Jack said tonelessly. "He played us all."

Arnie's lip curled. "You made it so easy. Both of you. I knew your father. We were friends. He liked me. Did you know he talked about you all the time? He missed you and wanted you in his life and you couldn't be bothered. George Hanson was a great man and now he's gone and you don't deserve to run his business. You don't deserve to even sweep the floors."

"So you wanted to take me down," Jack said. "You knew there was a good chance that I would be ruined by the scandal."

Arnie shrugged. "I had high hopes."

Samantha couldn't believe it. "This was your plan from the beginning?"

"Sure thing, babe. Did you really think you were all that?" His expression turned contemptuous. "I had you all fooled. I don't care about what happens to me because the company is ruined. You'll never recover from this. Face it, Jack. You're screwed. You'll stay on to save the sinking ship, but it can't be saved. I made sure of that. The lawsuits will bankrupt you and even before that, no one will ever want to do business with your company again. You're in charge of a worthless empire. And you have me to thank for it."

The door opened and Mrs. Wycliff led in the detective and several uniformed officers. They read Arnie his rights and took him away.

Matt excused himself, as did Mrs. Wycliff, leaving Samantha and Jack alone.

He led her over to the sofa and pulled her down next to him.

"I want to say that was easy," he told her, "but it's just beginning. Knowing Arnie did it and why doesn't clean up the mess any faster."

She snuggled up against him. "At least it gives us a place to start."

He kissed the top of her head. "Maybe I should just give the board what they want. It's going to take years to get the company back on its feet."

She shifted so she could look at him. "Don't you dare. I mean it, Jack. Your dreams are too important to give up. You have a commitment here, so stay for now. But only on your terms. Don't walk away from everything you've ever wanted just because of this."

"What if what I want is you?" he asked.

Her heart flopped over in her chest. She felt the movement, along with a rush of gladness. Her mouth curved in a smile.

"I would say that's a good thing because I want you, too."

He stared into her eyes. "Seriously?"

"Yes. I've spent so much of my life running from the things that frightened me, but I never once stopped to think about what I might be missing out."

He took her hands in his. "Me, too," he murmured. "I haven't wanted to believe love lasts. For me, it didn't. Now I'm wondering if the reason I couldn't give my heart to someone else is because I'd already given it to you. I love you, Samantha."

Her breath caught. "I love you, too. I think I have from the first moment we met."

"So we wasted ten years?"

"No. We became the people we needed to be to find each other now."

"I like the sound of that."

He pulled her close. She went willingly into his arms. They kissed, their lips clinging.

"We can do this," she told him. "We'll fix Hanson Media Group, then we'll get you back to your law firm. You need to become a judge. You'll look good in black."

He laughed. "Hell of a reason."

She grinned. "Okay. You'll be great at it, too. How's that?"

"I like how you think." He kissed her again. "In fact, I like everything about you."

"I feel the same way about you."

"Want to get married?"

"Yes."

"Just like that? You don't have any questions."

She stared into his eyes. "I love you, Jack. I trust you and I want to spend my life with you. What questions could I have?"

"I'll do everything I can to make you happy," he told her. "I'll be there for you."

She knew he would. He always had been.

He put his arm around her. "I've been thinking about my brothers. I want to get them to come home. Not just because of the company but because we need to be a family again. You think I could get them back here for a wedding?"

She leaned against him and sighed. "Absolutely. And if they don't agree, we'll hunt them down and drag them back. That could be fun."

He chuckled. "This is why I love you. You always have a plan."

"It's one of my best features."
"And the others?"
"How much I love you."
"Right back at you, Samantha. For always."

\* \* \* \* \*

# THE BOSS AND
# MISS BAXTER

BY
WENDY WARREN

**Wendy Warren** lives with her husband, Tim, a dog, a cat and their recent—and most exciting!—addition, baby daughter Elisabeth, near the Pacific Northwest's beautiful Willamette River. Their house was previously owned by a woman named Cinderella, who bequeathed them a gardenful of flowers they try desperately (and occasionally successfully) not to kill, and a pink General Electric oven, circa 1958, that makes the kitchen look like an *I Love Lucy* rerun.

A two-time recipient of the Romance Writers of America's RITA® Award for Best Traditional Romance, Wendy loves to read and write the kind of books that remind her of the old movies she grew up watching with her mom—stories about decent people looking for the love that can make an ordinary life heroic. Wendy was an *Affaire de Coeur* finalist for Best Up and Coming Romance Author of 1997. When not writing, she likes to take long walks with her dog, settle in for cosy chats with good friends and sneak tofu into her husband's dinner. She always enjoys hearing from readers, and may be reached at PO Box 1208, Ashland, OR 97520, USA.

For Patricia Giacolini, as beautiful a friend as she is a poet. With all my heart, thank you for being Libbi's auntie and playmate so I could finish this book! And thank you for gifting your friends with the grace and wisdom of your elegant words.

## Chapter One

"Tell *no one* that I did this."

"It's between us. I swear." Nina Baxter smiled at her friend and former co-worker. The smile felt forced and phony, but at least the words were sincere.

Burying her bunched fists more deeply into the pockets of her jacket, Nina stood by as Carolyn Ahearn fitted her master key into a polished brass doorknob and unlocked the heavy oak doors protecting Hanson Media from the rest of the world.

Nina felt her stomach clench as the door eased open. She'd crossed this threshold countless times over the past thirteen years—five days a week, Monday through Friday—but couldn't remember ever being here on a Sunday.

Nor could she recall ever being this nauseous when she'd come to work, and that included the months she'd slogged through morning sickness.

"I'm going to make a run to Noah's for a bagel and latte," Carolyn said, pocketing the key. "It'll probably take twenty minutes. Is that enough time?"

Nina nodded. "I'll meet you back here." She reached out to take her friend's hand. "I can't thank you enough, Carolyn. I'm sorry you had to interrupt your weekend for me. I just couldn't face—"

"I know." Giving Nina's cold fingers a reassuring squeeze, Carolyn shrugged. "It could have been you opening the door for me, kiddo. It was just the luck of the draw. Layoffs bite."

Nina's laugh sounded watery. "Big-time." She'd been *laid off* on Friday, told she could come back to collect her things on Monday if she needed to, but she wanted to wave goodbye with a modicum of grace—not stumble to the elevators with her arms full of items from her desk, and her eyes bloodshot and teary.

Even now, as tears gathered at the back of her throat, she clung to her stiff upper lip like a drowning man to a life preserver. "Go eat a bagel," she told Carolyn. "Extra cream cheese."

"Oh, sure," Carolyn mumbled as she turned back toward the elevators that had carried them to the offices of Hanson Media Group. "Easy for you to say. You can't eat when you're stressed. I devour my weight in carbs." She walked down the lushly carpeted hallway without looking back, and Nina quietly shut the door, listening for the click that locked her in.

With what she hoped was poetic dignity, she made her way past the imposing reception desk against the wall that sported a huge gold *H* in a circle, and continued round to the circular bank of desks where the secretaries worked.

Hanson Media Group had been her home away from home since she'd first walked through the doors at nineteen—newly married, delighted to start her first "real" job and pregnant with her first child. The clerical position she'd applied for had required office skills she hadn't possessed at the time and formal business attire she hadn't owned. She should have been daunted by the opulent surroundings and by co-workers who had made her look like a junior high intern. But Nina had needed the job too much to let a little intimidation thwart her. And she had been naive then. Wonderfully, happily naive.

Arriving at the desk that had become hers the day she'd been promoted to secretary, Nina trailed her fingers mournfully over the nubby back of her ergonomically correct chair. Monday through Friday, no matter what insanity had pervaded her personal life, she'd had this chair to sit down on, this desk to work at. She'd had self-respect—a single mom making a living and securing the future for herself and her kids.

All gone. All the security, everything she'd worked for—gone in one lightning-swift chop of the corporate guillotine.

A rush of anxiety made Nina feel as if she were about to internally combust. Her nausea intensified. Trying to cool off, she discarded her coat, pulled a knitted purple hat off her head and got down to business.

Opening the large shoulder bag she'd brought with her, she began to stuff personal items inside. Two pictures of her kids…her favorite pens…the lavender notepad in the shape of a hippo… She moved rapidly, packing her purse at random until she came to the plastic gold trophy cup her daughter had given her last year after the annual Take Your Daughter to Work Day. World's Best Secretary.

Perusing the packed in-box and watching her mother's fingers fly across the computer keyboard, Isabella had looked at Nina with such respect that Nina had thought she could have been standing atop an Olympic podium—she'd felt that triumphant, that proud.

Suddenly her hands began to shake. She pushed the trophy into the depths of her bag and kept packing, but she couldn't stop shaking. Nor could she halt the anger that sparked like flash fire in her belly.

It wasn't *her* fault that Hanson Media was in trouble. It wasn't the fault of anyone who'd been laid off. The trouble had started at the top, but did the big dogs care about that? No. Even when they dug their own holes, it was the little guy who wound up with a mouthful of dirt.

And what had Nina done on Friday after being let go? She'd hugged her supervisor. That's right. She'd felt sorry for her obviously stressed supervisor, told her not to worry then brought her two aspirins and a glass of water.

Such a faithful employee; such a thoughtful person.

"Such a *doormat!*" Nina growled, feeling a surge of power that came from resentment, pure and simple. Who at Hanson would bring her an aspirin when she got a headache from searching the classifieds? Who would care whether she got a job before she had to move her kids' bedroom to the back seat of their Toyota?

"No one!" Nina answered her own question. And even though it was not nice, even though it was downright *wrong,* she picked up the first thing she spied—a plastic container filled with multicolored paper clips—and threw it as hard as she could against the solid oak door of David Hanson's office.

He was a big dog—emphasis on *dog*. He was a Hanson. Would he skip even one steak while his laid-off employees stocked up on Cup-a-Soup?

The paper-clip container made a satisfying *ping* against the door, but it wasn't nearly satisfying enough. So Nina picked up her Strunk and White's *The Elements of Style* and threw that against the door as well. Then she reached for her *Pocket Roget's The-saurus*.

With each article she grabbed—and hurled—she said a naughty, naughty word she'd never used before.

And began to feel a little bit better.

"What the—"

David Hanson looked up from the paperwork covering his desk and stared at his closed office door. At first he'd thought someone was knocking—strange enough on a Sunday—but when he heard thwack after thwack against the solid wood, he realized he'd heard not a *knock* but a *smack*.

There was someone in the outer office, and that someone was throwing things at his door.

David didn't take long to think, and he didn't pause to consider calling reinforcements, like someone from building security. He rose, strode to the door and stood by, waiting for a lull in the assault. When it came, he jerked open the door....

And was almost decapitated by a stainless-steel travel mug.

"Holy—!" A timely duck saved him. Straightening, he locked eyes with a wild-haired blonde whose pitching arm was poised again. "Whoa!" David ordered, raising a hand to halt the action. When she froze, he turned his open hand into a warning index finger. "Excuse me. What the hell is going on out here?"

The blonde seemed incapable of speech. Or of

moving at all now that she'd been caught in the act of vandalizing his office.

David took a quick glance around. She was definitely alone, which he supposed was a good thing: one of her, one of him. Next, he noted that she had a strong arm (stood a good thirty feet from his door and still managed impressive velocity). And finally, he saw that she needed a tissue.

Tears filled the woman's eyes and streaked her face; her nose was red, and her cheeks were rapidly turning the same fiery shade. She looked so miserable, in fact, that he began to feel sorry for her until he reminded himself she was a vandal. He really ought to let security handle this. With all the other trouble he had right now, he didn't need a nutcase on his hands. He stepped one foot back toward his office. But then…

David leaned forward. And squinted. "Miss Baxter?"

With her arm still poised, the blonde blinked several times rapidly to clear her eyes. She attempted a smile that wobbled treacherously around the edges. "Yes?"

*Jeez, it was her.* He'd been thrown off by the exploding-firecracker effect of kinky blond curls and clothing that was more suited to a swap meet than the office. The Miss Baxter he was used to seeing during the week wore suits or skirts and blouses, like the other secretaries, and she wore her hair…well, hell, he couldn't really recall…in a bun?

David frowned. "What are you doing?" He was going to add *here,* but *what are you doing* seemed more apropos under the circumstances.

To her credit, she was obviously determined to make the best of the situation and shrugged with what appeared to be a miniature potted plant in her still-raised hand. "Cleaning."

He looked at the floor outside his door. A small paper-clip explosion had occurred; plus, there were two books and a silver mug lying on the carpet. "Cleaning?"

"My…desk…off. Sir."

After three of the most difficult and unpredictable months in his career, David should have been used to expecting the unexpected. But Nina Baxter had him knocked for a loop. Had there always been a psych case lurking behind the face of the mild-mannered secretary?

And then David realized…

*Aw, hell.*

Nina Baxter was one of the casualties of his late brother's screwups.

David squeezed the bridge of his nose as the headache he'd been battling for days took a sudden turn for the worse. Obviously he was not going to escape the mess his life had turned into. Not even on a Sunday.

While David Hanson hid behind his hand, Nina thought of the job reference she'd been counting on and figured she ought to start rehearsing, "Would you like fries with that?" as soon as possible.

Good God in heaven, what had she been thinking? Lowering her hand, she stared at the potted cactus her grandmother had given her. She was not a violent person. And yet she'd been about to smash the bit of flora into David Hanson's unsuspecting head. What if she'd already thrown the plant by the time he'd opened his door? The tiny needles could have lodged anywhere.

"I could have killed you!" The words burst out of her.

Obviously self-control was not her forte this morning. David Hanson's expression had already changed from anger to frowning distrust.

*Note to self: Forget leaving Hanson Media Group with grace and dignity.* She wasn't even going to look *sane*.

And if Mr. Hanson discovered how she'd gotten into the office, poor Carolyn might wind up in the unemployment line right behind her.

"I'm so terribly sorry," she said, rushing toward the scattered paper clips and other office weaponry. The closer she got to David Hanson, the more the sound of the ocean filled her ears. She had never felt comfortable in his presence, not in over a dozen years of working around him. In fact, she often avoided him when she could. He was so formal, always polite and correct and distant.

And tall. He was a good ten inches taller than her five foot three, and she had this thing about tall men. Fear of height.

"I'll clean up this mess and—" Realizing she still had the cactus in her hand, Nina looked for someplace to set it.

Surprising her, David reached for the pot. When their fingers brushed, she jumped at the contact and let go. He caught the plant in a deft save and stared down at her.

"Miss Baxter, may I suggest you sit down." He pointed to one of the desks several feet away from him. "Over there."

Yep, he thought she was crazy.

"I'm not usually like this," she said in her own defense. "Really. I'm usually calm. It's just that today I…" She searched for the correct word, for some way to explain her change from composed and trustworthy to certifiably wacko. "I'm very…"

Nina's mind scanned the options…*tired…worried…nervous?*

All accurate, but when her exhausted brain landed on exactly the right adjective, she knew it because her chest nearly burst with the effort to contain her grief, and her stomach pitched. Perhaps she shouldn't have said anything else at that point, but her body seemed to bring the words up of its own volition.

"It's just that I'm very…*UNEMPLOYED!*"

The tears she'd thus far managed to keep at bay

began spouting like geysers. Through them she spied David reaching out a hand. She pulled back before he could touch her.

Diving to the floor, she gathered the scattered paper clips, every last one, and the books and the mug. David watched her silently. The paper-clip container had obviously broken, and she wasn't sure where the pieces were, so she held out her fist.

"These…paper clips," she said, trying not to do that humiliating hiccup-sob thing, "are…not… mine."

When he made no move to take the clips, she pressed them into the soil around the cactus. Then she indicated the books. "These…*hic*…are mine."

David raised a brow. "Okay."

Nina turned and marched back to her desk. Grabbing the few remaining personal items, she stowed them in her bag, zipped it shut and snatched her coat and hat. She heard David call out, "Miss Baxter," but knew she had to get out before she broke down completely or Carolyn returned or both, so she picked up her pace and scurried to the outer doors—which was when she remembered that she was locked in and that Carolyn had the key.

It seemed like a good time to consider which window she could hurl herself from, but then David reached in front of her, slipped his own key into the lock and said, "Should I ask how you got in?"

Wordlessly she shook her head.

"Miss Baxter, I—"

Nina didn't wait. Ignoring the elevators, she hit the stairs running, fleeing like Cinderella from the ball.

For thirteen years, despite numerous challenges, she had maintained a spotless employment record and earned the respect of her co-workers. On Friday the clock had struck midnight. Now, two days later, she knew the party was over for good.

When Nina opened the door to her own apartment, the first thing she noticed was the aroma of chicken soup and something baking.

After telling Carolyn that she'd "run into" David Hanson, but that he didn't know who had let her into the office, she had walked around downtown Chicago for half an hour then bought a Sunday paper, a package of Rolaids and caught the El home. Before her stop, she'd wiped her eyes, blown her nose and applied a little lipstick to offset her red cheeks and bloodshot eyes. She hadn't eaten anything all day, and she still didn't want to, but she was determined to put up a good front for her family.

"I'm home!" she called into the quiet apartment.

As if her announcement had released a herd of gazelle, Nina's two children ran into the living room from opposite ends of the apartment. As always, they managed to sound as if, between them, they had ten pairs of feet rather than two.

Isabella arrived first, wrapping her arms around

her mother's waist and craning her head to look up. "I helped Bubby make matzo balls and *mandel-brodt!*" The exuberant ten-year-old's dark blue eyes sparkled with pride. "And guess what? Bubby says these matzo balls are lighter than air 'cause I have just the right touch!"

Nina smoothed a hand over Isabella's brown hair, gloriously wavy, but not frizzy like her own. "I can't wait to taste these matzo balls," she told her daughter. "Did you save me any?"

"We haven't eaten lunch yet." Isabella stepped back, making room for her brother, Isaac—Zach for short—to greet his mother. "I'm going to help Bubby some more." She loped back to the kitchen, preteen awkwardness and grace rolled into one lean body.

Nina looked at her son. At twelve years of age, Zach was old enough to contain his enthusiasm over seeing his mother a mere two hours after he'd last seen her. He stood back a bit, more interested in the *Chicago Sun-Times* than in Nina's return.

"Hi, Mom. Can I have the sports section?"

"Sure, honey." Stepping forward to run a hand over his short-cropped curls—because she wasn't too old to exhibit enthusiasm over seeing her son—Nina asked, "How were you today, Zachie? Any problems?"

Increasingly impatient of late when asked about his health, Zach ducked away from his mother's touch. "I'm *fine*." He reached for the paper. "I want the movie section, too. Okay?"

"Just save me—" *The classifieds,* Nina almost said, but caught herself in the nick of time. She had not yet told her family about the layoffs. She would love not to tell them anything at all until she had a new job lined up.

Even at twelve, Zachary worried too much. Nina figured that came with the territory of being the man of the house before you'd shaved your first whisker. But when he worried, his asthma kicked in…and then *she* worried.

"Save the rest of the paper for me," Nina told her son, refraining from asking if he'd had to use his inhaler today.

"Okay. When's lunch?"

"I think it may be ready, so stick around."

Zach took his paper to the couch and sat down to read, neatly separating sections and placing them aside until he came to the sports. He was so much like her, Nina mused—calm, methodical….Abruptly she amended her thought. No, he was the way she'd been *before* she'd gone secretary on her boss.

Deciding to leave the classifieds until she had some private time, she deposited her heavy bag by the door and halfheartedly followed the aromas to the kitchen.

Under her great grandmother's watchful eye, Isabella dusted a pan of *mandelbrodt* with cinnamon sugar.

"Now that smells wonderful." Nina reached over her daughter's shoulder to sample one of the long cookies.

Bubby's gnarled hand, made quick from years of baking and hand slapping, shot out to admonish her granddaughter. "Not so fast. You'll have soup first."

Nina exchanged smiles with her daughter. "Well, when you put it that way. Anything I can do?"

"Go sit," her grandmother directed, and gratefully Nina retreated to a small 1950s-style Formica-topped table that nestled near the window of their third-floor apartment. Feeling immeasurably tired, she watched her daughter and grandmother and thanked God for Bubby, five foot nothing, but with strength that couldn't be measured in inches and a love for family that made her seem mountainously large.

Bubby didn't live with them—she liked to keep her own apartment—but she babysat anytime Nina needed her, and she was a steady, loving influence in her great grandchildren's lives, as she'd always been in Nina's.

"Izzy dolly." Bubby put a hand on Isabella's shoulder. "This is a special lunch you made. Go change into something nice, very nice, so we can dine like civilized people."

The opportunity to wear one of her fancy dresses sent Isabella running happily to her room.

Bubby poured two mugs of coffee from the electric pot on the counter and stacked a plate with the warm *mandelbrodt*. Dressed cozily in dark blue polyester stretch pants and a matching blue sweatshirt that read If You Don't Like It, I Didn't Cook It, she ambled to the table with the skill of a career waitress. Nina knew better than to offend Bubby by offering to help.

"Huh, so I do get cookies before soup?" she asked, then looked down at her own clothing. Faded jeans and a beige cable-knit sweater with floppy sleeves were more suited to moving day than to the "civilized" family lunch Bubby requested. "Don't you want me to change my clothes, too?" Nina eyed the steaming mugs of caffeine and hoped the answer was no.

"Stay put," Bubby directed, setting everything down, then lowering herself to a chair with an exaggerated groan. "The weather in Chicago is not good for my bones. I should move to Orlando. Me and Mickey Mouse."

Nina had heard the I'm-moving-to-Florida threat too often to take it seriously. "The Wilkens Senior Center would be lost without your *rugelach*," she said, and Bubby nodded.

"True."

Deciding the cinnamon sugar would settle her stomach, Nina sampled one of the *mandelbrodt*. "Mmmm."

"What's wrong?"

Dunking the bitten tip of her cookie into the coffee, Nina cocked her head at her grandmother. "Nothing. It's delicious."

Impatiently, Bubby slapped a hand at the air. "Not the cookie." She leaned forward, sharp blue eyes narrowing. "You got something to tell me?"

So much for hoping the cinnamon would settle her stomach. Nina took her time pulling a napkin from the Lucite holder on the table and set her cookie neatly on top of the white square. "Well…offhand, I can't think of—"

"Ellie Berkowitz gets the Sunday paper. She likes the coupons. Today she read the business section. I don't know why." Bubby shrugged. "Maybe she wants to sleep with Morty Rosenfeld. He's a retired CEO, and she was always a floozy." Bubby took a sip of steaming coffee then waved a hand. "But that's not the point."

She leaned farther over the table, her aging bosom resting on the Formica. "The point is Ellie called here this morning, because she knew I'd be here, and she asks me, 'Rayzel, why didn't you tell me there were more layoffs at Hanson?'" Bubby jerked back as if struck. "Layoffs at Hanson! Who knew? Not me." She placed crooked fingers over her chest. "But they couldn't affect my Nina, or she would have told me. Besides, I said to Ellie, Nina is at the office right now to drop off some work she did over the weekend."

Nina frowned morosely at her coffee, her mind hopping from one barely plausible excuse to another. She needn't have bothered.

"Of course," Bubby continued, "I said all this before I knew that Ellie Berkowitz's niece, Carla, got a job at a new coffee store downtown—Some Like It Hot. Good for her."

"What does this have to—"

"I'm getting there. I'm old. Be a little patient, maybe." Bubby licked her dry lips. She looked her granddaughter in the eye. "Carla's son Anthony goes to school with Isaac—another thing I didn't know, and Carla called Ellie, because she recognized you walking down the street this morning. It looked like you were crying, she said. She was concerned. Some Like It Hot is right near your office." Bubby sat back in her chair, hands resting atop the table. "Carla read the paper, too."

Plowing fingers into her thick curls, Nina wagged her head then looked toward the kitchen door to make sure neither of her children was on the way in.

"I didn't want to worry you or the kids," she said softly. "I thought if I had a few job prospects when I told you, you wouldn't worry so much."

She must have sounded as miserable as she felt because Bubby turned immediately comforting. "Me worry? Who's worried?" She reached across the table to clutch Nina's hand. They sat in silence for several moments.

"I'm sorry you had to hear the news from Ellie Berkowitz," Nina murmured.

"Ah, she's such an old gossip." Leaning back in her chair, she looked around the kitchen. "How much did you say your rent was going up?"

Nina winced at the mere mention of the notice she'd received two weeks before. The older building they were in had been sold. The new owners planned to remodel the exterior and make other upgrades. The rent was going to jump a hundred dollars a month, effective on the first of the month—ten days away.

"It's the timing of this that stinks," Nina said, propping her head in her hand. "I had a little savings, but then Izzy needed a Girl Scout uniform and Isaac's music teacher said he needed a better violin to practice on."

Since the kids had been in kindergarten, Nina had been squirreling away just enough money each paycheck to buy a savings bond here, a savings bond there, always in their names and hers. She'd sworn to herself, though, that she would never dip into their savings for the household needs.

"I have some money," Bubby began, but Nina squeezed her hand to halt the offer.

"You're not touching your Social Security. You'll need it for your own rainy day. No," she said when Bubby opened her mouth to protest. "We're going to be okay. I have an excellent employment history, and I'm a hard worker. And I haven't looked in the Sunday paper yet. I bet just the right job is going to be in there." She smiled then raised her thumb to her lips and nibbled unconsciously on the cuticle.

"I thought David Hanson was such a nice man," Bubby said sadly, wagging her salt-and-pepper head. "He gave Isabella that cute bear."

"That was ten years ago." Nina pushed back her chair and leaned her head against the windowpane.

The day she'd had Izzy by C-section had also been the day she'd received her final divorce papers by mail. Nothing, not even flowers, had come from her ex, but a giant stuffed teddy bear had arrived from Hanson Media. When Nina had called to say thank-you, the temporary receptionist had told her that David Hanson himself had gone out on his lunch hour and brought the bear back with him. He'd been off on one of his many trips to the Far East when Nina returned to work, so she'd left a thank you note, which he'd never acknowledged. That had been the end of that, but he'd won a fan in Bubby for life.

"You'd think he could have found you another job in the office," Bubby insisted. "Maybe if he knew the situation—"

"I've already seen David Hanson," Nina said to squelch any thought that she might go see him again. "He knows how I feel." A careful understatement.

Bubby rose to stir her soup. "I suppose you never know about people," she said sadly. "And he even attends the Special Olympics every year."

"Yeah. Well." Nina wasn't entirely sure what that had to do with the layoffs, but she chose not to pursue it.

As she watched Bubby taste the soup and add a pinch of pepper, Nina tapped her unpolished fingernails on the Formica, knowing she was too antsy to sit still for lunch. Regardless of what she'd said about her ability to get a new job, she knew the market was tight and that even a few-week lapse of employment could be devastating given her rent increase. Worse, she would now have to pay for her family's health insurance out of her own pocket.

"Lunch is ready. I'll call the children." Bubby wiped her hands on her flowered apron.

Nina jumped from the chair. "I'll be right back."

"Where are you going?"

"To talk to Mr. Goldman."

Bubby scowled. "What for? He likes my chicken soup all of a sudden?"

Arthur Goldman was the manager of Nina's apartment building, and Bubby had never thought much of the man. He didn't keep the hallway clean enough in her opinion, and he smoked clove cigarettes in a nonsmoking building.

"I don't want him to come to lunch," Bubby said.

"I'm not asking him to come to lunch." Nina fished a rubber band out of the "everything" drawer and scraped her hair into a ponytail. "I'm going to explain my situation and ask him to talk to the new owners on our behalf or to give me their number. Then I'm going to remind him that we are stellar tenants, that stellar tenants are not easy to come by, and that I have never once complained about the stench his clove cigarettes leave in the hallway."

"You'd be better off talking to David Hanson. I bet

he sweeps his hallway!" Bubby called as Nina headed toward the door.

"I bet he hires someone to sweep his hallway," Nina tossed over her shoulder without breaking stride. "I doubt David Hanson would know which end of a broom to put on the floor, and I am absolutely certain he has better things to do than to concern himself with my problems. Or the problems of any of his *ex*-employees."

Entering the living room with Bubby at her heels, Nina assured herself that her son was still deeply engrossed in the sports section. She reached for the doorknob. "I'm going to buy myself a little leeway, and then I am going to blow the Hanson dust off my shoes and not look back." She paused briefly to meet Bubby's doubtful gaze. Despite her grandmother's brave claim, Nina could see worry fading the aging blue eyes.

She took her grandmother by the shoulders. "I've got you and the kids," she said quietly. "And you've got me. I refuse to worry. I've got smarts and I've got chutzpah."

Feeling stronger almost instantly with a simple change in attitude, she admonished herself for allowing someone—anyone—else's actions to frighten her. Hadn't she learned better over the years?

Standing as tall as her five-foot-three frame allowed, she opened the door and stepped into the hall. "I don't need anyone to rescue me," she reassured

Bubby, summoning her first genuine smile in the past three days, "least of all a corporate suit who, despite having laid off half his employees, will not miss a single meal at his favorite five-star feedlot, I am sure. Know what I mean?"

"I think I get the picture."

Nina jumped, literally jumped in the air, as she whirled around.

David Hanson stood in the hallway of her modest apartment building. Dressed in the designer clothes he wore, apparently, even on weekends, he frowned at the purple hat and scarf in his hands.

"You left these on your desk, Miss Baxter." He raised unreadable brown eyes. "As the day is chilly, and I'm about to be responsible for turning off your heat, I thought you might need them."

## *Chapter Two*

While her family entertained David Hanson in their living room, Nina stood in her bathroom and wondered how long it would take for anyone to discover she'd climbed out the window.

Immediately upon seeing David in the hallway, Bubby had pulled him into the apartment, sat him on the couch next to Zach and shooed Nina toward the bedrooms.

"Go! See what's taking Izzy so long," her grandmother had said in an overly hearty voice and with an overly cheerful smile. *Put on some lipstick,* Bubby had mouthed to Nina as she'd shoved her down the hallway.

Turning to gaze into the mirror, Nina shook her head at her sad reflection. She'd been grateful for any excuse to escape David's serious, censorious gaze, but lipstick, she feared, would not cure what ailed her.

Leaning toward the glass her children routinely splattered with toothpaste, she shook her head. Could she have been any more of a doofus today?

Probably not, because according to her calculations, she had just run out of feet to put in her mouth.

Morose but dutiful, she plucked a lipstick from the basket of makeup she kept on the sink. She uncapped the tube and raised it to her lips, then halted. She wore no other makeup. Scooped into a ponytail, her curly hair looked like a profusion of yellow ribbons exploding behind her head. No wonder David Hanson hadn't immediately recognized her in the office.

For work she always, but always, tamed her flyaway kinks into a twist or bun or French braid. And she'd always dressed conservatively, in suits and blouses. Neat. Respectful. Appropriate.

Recapping the lipstick, she dropped it into the basket. Why bother? No matter what Bubby thought, an attractive appearance was not going to help her get her job back. And Shell-Pink Long-Lasting Lipwear would not erase David Hanson's memory of how she had behaved today.

All she could do now was go to the living room, thank Mr. Hanson for very kindly returning her hat and scarf, and bid the man a permanent if not overly fond farewell.

Snapping off the light, she headed down the hall. Before she reached the living room, she heard Bubby say, "Not too many *mandelbrodt* now, David. You'll spoil your appetite."

*Oh, dear Lord, no.* Bubby couldn't have…she wouldn't have…. Nina practically sprinted the remaining steps to where her children and grandmother were entertaining a bemused David Hanson. He held a coffee mug in one hand, a cookie in the other. Busy chewing, he looked up as she skidded to a stop.

"David is having lunch with us," Bubby announced.

"No!" Nina blurted. She glanced frankly at David. "I appreciate your bringing my things. I do." Offering what she hoped was an ironic and understanding smile, she said, "You don't have to have lunch with us."

It took David a moment to swallow his cookie. Another moment to respond, "But I'm hungry."

He looked dead serious.

"Can I show David my room?" Zach turned toward his mother. "He likes chemistry sets."

"And I want to show him Jo-Jo," Izzy said, referring to her giant bear. Dressed in her fanciest pink dress, Izzy sat close to David on the couch. "Bubby said he gave me Jo-Jo when I was born."

"He" looked at Nina with an expression she could not read. Four sets of eyes were trained on her, each anticipating her response. She couldn't believe David

Hanson wanted to eat chicken soup with a laid-off employee, her obviously besotted grandmother and her hungry-for-any-male-attention children.

Seated rather stiffly between Izzy and Zach, holding his cookie and drink at right angles to his body, he resembled a big, gangly new kid in school—willing to be included, but not quite certain what to do with the people around him.

What was he up to? Nina felt like she was slogging her way through some weird dream, the kind where you tried to speak, but no sound emerged.

*"Kinderle,"* Bubby said, motioning for Isabella and Zach to come to her. "Help me set the table. We'll call Mr. Hanson and your mother when we're ready."

She ushered the children into the kitchen, turning back to Nina and gesturing madly for her to take her ponytail down. David, fortunately, was still looking at Nina and missed the fervent signal.

When her children and Bubby were safely in the kitchen, Nina looked at her ex-boss and shook her head ineloquently. "I have no idea what to say." Spreading her hands, she shrugged. "You have seen me at my absolute worst today. I'm very embarrassed." A wry laugh warbled from her chest. "Humiliated, really. I can't imagine that you honestly want to have lunch with us. I realize you're trying to be polite…which is more than I can say for myself today…but it's not—"

David stood. "I'm not polite." He set his mug on the coffee table and held up the biscotti-shaped *mandelbrodt*. "I like this. Your grandmother is a good baker. You have a nice family."

The best Nina could offer was a bemused frown. "Okay."

"And I am hungry." Without the slightest change in his sober expression, he added, "I missed lunch. My favorite five-star feedlot is closed Sundays."

Nina felt her face flush, a lovely complement, she was sure, to her firecracker hair.

"You fired me," she said, unwilling to remain on the defensive. That had to be a good excuse for feeling testy.

David's chest rose and fell on a long breath. "There were layoffs," he corrected. "You got caught in them and for that I am sorry. The board hired an external accountant to thoroughly examine Hanson's finances, and it was determined quickly that the company cannot support a full staff at present and survive."

David felt some of the tension leave his body. There. He had said exactly what he had come to say. When he'd recognized Nina in the office and realized she was one of the layoffs, he'd felt a stab of highly unprofessional guilt. In truth, he felt guilty for every one of the layoffs. Hell, lately he'd been feeling guilty simply for bearing his last name.

As CEO of Hanson Media, his brother, George, had made mistakes that caused suffering throughout the company and cost Hanson its reputation. David had been working daily—and often nightly—to repair the damage. He'd been in Tokyo recently, solidifying relationships with Hanson's existing Asian partners.

He'd arrived home last night and was still exhausted and jet-lagged today. He'd missed the board meeting at which the layoffs had been finalized. He hadn't had time yet to scan the list of dismissed employees. Or perhaps he'd been avoiding that task.

In any case, David was glad he was here, explaining the situation more clearly to Nina Baxter, helping her to understand.

"Layoffs aren't personal," he said in a tone he hoped was reassuring, soothing. He wanted to smooth the frown from her face. "I realize it's difficult not to feel rejected—"

"Rejected?" she interrupted, her big blue eyes blinking several times, rapidly. She shook her head like a swimmer clearing water from her ears. "You think I feel 'rejected'? Mr. Hanson, I'm not upset because you didn't ask me to the prom. I'm the head of a one-income household." She tapped her chest. "Me. All alone. I couldn't care less about getting my feelings hurt. I am worried about my children's ability to grow to the age of thirteen on a steady diet of boiled potatoes and boxed macaroni with fluorescent cheese."

On a roll, she barely inhaled before continuing. "I

know the company is in trouble, but I didn't cause that trouble. Janet Daitch from sales has been with Hanson for eight years. She's a grandmother. She was hoping this would be her last job. She didn't cause any of the problems, either. And Joe from the mailroom?" She raised a hand in a gesture that said *ditto.* "Maybe the board of directors should call another meeting to determine how *they* could help ease some of the burden. Maybe the executives should, too. Last week I was told to make reservations at Season's Restaurant for an *informal* dinner meeting."

She didn't have to say any more. Season's was one of the most expensive restaurants in the city.

David felt the tension seep—no, flood—back into his shoulders, neck and head. He was going to be an old man before his time, thanks to his careless brother and the burdens George had bequeathed to the family.

"I can't mandate the location of business meetings," David said carefully, taking one last shot at conciliation. "But I'll mention your point at the next board meeting. And I will see to it that the severance packages are dispersed promptly."

"What severance packages?" Nina Baxter looked blatantly disgusted with him. "Janet Daitch got two extra-strength Excedrin from the head of HR when he broke the bad news, but from what I've heard, that's the most anyone was offered." Folding her arms, she stared at him in challenge. "We stood by your company, Mr. Hanson, when you were in trouble. We believed in you. Well, now we're in trouble. And no matter how you put it or how reasonable the layoffs were, it still…sucks."

An alien sense of failure stabbed David's gut. He was head of public relations; he ought to be able to fix this.

"Lunch is ready!" Her grandmother's voice carried from the kitchen. A moment later the woman he'd met only as "Bubby" poked her head around the corner. "Come, children. It's only soup and a few latkes I pulled from Nina's freezer, but the latkes are to die for. Such a cook, this granddaughter of mine. Come. Eat while it's hot."

David glanced at Nina. She wanted him to leave. Nothing could have been plainer. The situation was awkward and unsatisfying for them both. He had only words with which to appease her, and she didn't need words.

Regretfully, David geared himself up to disappoint a good-hearted seventy-year-old woman. "It's been a pleasure meeting you…" he began. With that brief opening, he saw Nina's shoulders drop in relief. She knew he was about to beg off and didn't bother to mask her pleasure.

Returning his attention to her grandmother, he continued. "And I'm looking forward to trying your soup, Bubby." Closing the distance between him and Nina, he held out an arm. "Shall we?"

Nina's brows hitched almost comically then swooped into a scowl. Pretending not to notice, David smiled.

Bubby clucked her approval from the kitchen. The approval, however, quickly turned to exasperation when Nina failed to move. "Nina dolly, a man holds out his arm, he's not asking if you want to hang your hat. So, come on, already."

She turned and disappeared into the kitchen, leaving Nina to stare warily at her former employer. "I haven't told my children yet that I was fired—"

"Laid off."

She snapped her fingers. "Yes, laid off. And I will explain that difference to them. Right after I sell their computer for lunch money. Now, as I was saying, I haven't told them I was fired. I will do that in my own way and in my own time. Please do not blow it for me. My children tend to worry. If Isaac has to use his inhaler today because you slip up, Mr. Hanson, I will escort you out of my home even if you have one of Bubby's matzo balls hanging halfway out of your mouth."

David grinned. "Miss Baxter, your way with words is exceeded only by your hospitality." He raised his arm a bit higher. Nina ignored the offer, but walked by his side toward the kitchen. "What's wrong with Isaac?" he asked.

"Nothing's wrong with him. He has asthma."

"Serious?"

"Asthma is never a joke." She'd already lowered her voice, but now she dropped it to a near whisper. "He doesn't like us to discuss it. Please don't mention that, either."

He frowned but said nothing else. As they were about to step into the kitchen, he took her hand despite her protest and tucked it into his arm. "Your grandmother will like this," he said, holding her firmly when she tried to pull back. "And I like making elderly people happy. My karma needs a good deed today, so humor me."

Nina endured lunch. That was really the most she could say for her lack of contribution to an otherwise lighthearted meal.

Her children kept David entertained with accounts of their experiences in music and dance classes and the field trips they'd taken during the current school year. At first, David responded to her children's breathless chattering as if he were viewing a foreign species. Then he began to relax…and smile. He laughed outright at Zach's impression of his teacher's dismay when a papier-mâché volcano prematurely exploded during a school science fair, and he told Isabella that he thought she must be a very good dancer because he could see that she looked like Julie Kent. When Isabella asked who Julia Kent was, David told her that Ms. Kent was the greatest ballerina dancing today and asked if Izzy had ever attended a professional ballet.

Nina wanted to ask if he knew what tickets to the ballet cost these days, but she bit her tongue and just listened. He was good with the kids—easily admitted what he didn't know (had not a clue about Maroon 5 or Captain Underpants)—and didn't talk down to them. But his very presence at her table underscored the chasm between his world and hers. He'd never had matzo balls before, he ate his latkes with a knife and fork, and he chewed *and swallowed* before speaking. Dining mostly with children for the past twelve years, Nina had forgotten that was an option.

After lunch, Zach and Izzy dragged David to see their room. Nina immersed herself immediately in cleaning up.

"I like him," Bubby said without preamble as she joined Nina at the sink, picking up a towel to dry the dishes Nina washed.

Hoping to avoid conversation about David at least until she could gather her thoughts, Nina urged, "Bubby, have a cup of tea and relax in the living room. You did the cooking." She reached for the towel, but her grandmother whipped it away.

"I relax better in the kitchen." Wiping off a soup bowl, Bubby eyed Nina shrewdly. "You don't want me to talk about him, but why not? He didn't want to fire anybody. I can tell."

"You can?" She felt her lips curl into an unflattering twist. "How's that?"

"He looked at your plate when you weren't watching. It bothered him you didn't eat."

Nina released a hoot of laughter. "That's how you know he didn't want to lay off half his staff? Because he was eyeing my matzo balls? Maybe he just wanted more food. The Hansons love acquisitions."

"I don't know what's this 'acquisitions,' but I know what's guilt, and that man feels terrible."

"I don't think so."

"Ah, maybe you're right." The gray head wagged sadly. "Maybe he doesn't care. But then why does he come here? Why does he have lunch with an old woman and two children and his secretary?"

"I was never 'his' secretary," Nina corrected. "Except for a very brief time when his AA was out of the office and I filled in. Really, I've never had that much to do with him other than working in his department."

Bubby raised sparse but eloquent brows. "So? Even more strange that he should care enough to come talk to you."

"All right, he feels guilty. Big whoop. A flash of guilt does not make him Nelson Mandela. David Hanson is part of the problem, he is not the solution, so don't romanticize him. He didn't ride here on a white horse to save the day." Scrubbing the pan Bubby had used to reheat the latkes, Nina muttered, "More likely he double-parked his Porsche."

"Actually I drive a reconditioned Mustang that

belonged to one of my uncles. It was a college-grad-uation present. I still love it."

The latke pan clattered into the sink as Nina whirled. David filled the kitchen entrance. "How much did you hear this time?" she demanded.

"Not much." When she scowled doubtfully, he raised his right hand. "Honest, Your Honor."

His eyes glinted with deprecating humor, but Nina got the point: She was judging him, had been judg-ing him all day. And that was strange for her, really, because she'd always liked the Hansons. She'd never before begrudged them their wealth. Or felt sorry for herself. She shook her head.

"Oy." Bubby bent side to side from the waist. "My aching back. Standing on hard linoleum is not so good for me anymore."

Nina reached for her arm. "Here, come sit at the table."

"No." Bubby edged away. "You know me. I can't relax in a kitchen." Heading for the living room, she handed David her dish towel. "Here. You dry. You don't mind? I'll sit on the sofa and put my feet up. And watch a little TV. I'll turn the sound up. I don't hear a thing when the sound is up."

David smiled as he watched her go, then, dish towel at the ready, he approached the sink and Nina.

She shook her head. "You do not have to—"

David's placed two fingers on Nina's lips. "Why bother?"

His smile was ironic, his brown eyes warm as they watched her. She'd never thought of David Hanson as warm before.

Immobilized by the unfamiliar and unexpected contact, Nina couldn't recall ever seeing him touch anyone at the office, not even at the company parties. His late brother, George, had been the back slapper, the inveterate shoulder patter. David was the head of public relations, but he was no schmoozer.

Slowly he lowered his fingers. "Hand me a plate, Miss Baxter. We'll get this show on the road."

Nina did as he asked. It was easier than arguing, and perhaps that was his intention, too: Get the job done and go. She handed him a bread dish, a soup bowl, a water glass.

And discovered that he didn't know squat about doing dishes.

He took too much care, polishing them as if he were waxing an automobile. She had to slow down the rinsing considerably. No one at the office could speak knowledgeably about his personal life, so all she knew came from the bits her grandmother had read in the Lifestyle pages. He was single, dated socialites, lived downtown. And obviously had a housekeeper.

"You don't do this much, do you?" For the first time since he'd arrived, she felt a bubble of humor. "That's not a judgment," she hastened to add when he glanced up and frowned. "I'm just asking, because you're very…diligent."

David arched a brow. "Dead giveaway?"

Nina nodded. "Pretty much. You can't be overly concerned about water spots when you don't have a dishwasher and you serve three meals a day. You'd never get out of the kitchen."

He looked ruefully at the plate he'd been polishing then at bowls and glasses waiting to be dried and the pot that hadn't even been washed. "You're going to do this again tonight?"

"Gotta clean 'em if you want to eat off 'em."

"And on workdays?"

"Well, then it's two meals a day." She almost restated that in the past tense, but decided to give him a break. "Do you eat any meals at home?"

Reaching for a new plate, he slid her a look. "A few. Not many. Is that a strike?"

"A strike? Against you? No." She shrugged. "I mean, it's not my business, anyway." After a moment, she grew wistful. "Although truthfully, I suppose that if anything, I envy you. I'd love to eat out more. Just put in our orders and send the plates back when we're done."

He accepted another bowl from her. "And where would you eat, Miss Baxter? If you could eat out every night?"

She smiled. "Good question. When we do go out, I usually choose a place I know the kids will like, so that means burritos for Isabella and burgers for Zach. But even that's a treat if I don't have to cook."

David was quiet after that, so they washed and dried—more quickly—in companionable silence. Nina insisted on putting everything away on her own, so when the last cup was clean, David folded his towel and hung it neatly over the sink. It was almost two o'clock.

"I'd better get back to the office," he said, his gaze on her but his mind someplace else. She could see the moody thoughtfulness that had crept in on him. He seemed distant and distracted: the remote Mr. Hanson she was used to seeing at the office.

"Do you usually work on Sundays?" she asked.

"No, not usually." His lips curved briefly. "Not *often*. But Hanson isn't experiencing 'usual' circumstances." He focused on her more closely. "You know that when my brother died, he left the business with unusual debts. And you were present for the Internet screwup last month."

Nina nodded. The Hanson Media Group Web site had been hijacked, and for twenty-four hours every visitor who had attempted to log on to Hanson's new interactive Web zine for kids had been mistakenly directed to a porn site. "My son was one of the visitors to the site that day."

David's brows shot up. "Zach?" He pressed a hand to his eyes and swore beneath his breath. "I didn't know that. I'm sorry."

It was one of the most sincere and regret-filled apologies Nina had ever heard. Hanson Media's reputation had been hit hard by the mix-up, and Nina knew that as head of public relations for the company, David must have been dancing as fast as he could to repair the damage. At the office, however, the stress rarely showed. Now, looking at the lines around David's tight mouth, she actually felt concerned by the stress she saw him carrying.

"Zach wasn't overly damaged by the experience," she said, injecting a note of wry humor into her voice. "In fact I'd say it was a rite of passage. And it forced that conversation I'd been meaning to have about hormones and teenage boys."

Lowering his hand, he looked at her gratefully. "You ought to be a spin doctor. I'm sorry you had to have that worry with your son."

His brown eyes grew more troubled. "A week ago we received notice that one of the major charities to which we contribute has 'grave concerns' about accepting our most recent donation. We believe that if they publicly sever ties, the damage to our reputation could be irreparable. It takes time to rebuild public trust, and time isn't something we have. We're walking a financial tightrope." His expression asked her to appreciate the import of what he was telling her. "None of the other…released employees has been given this information."

Because, Nina realized, if the information was leaked before David had the chance to ease the charity's concerns, the public damage would be a done deal. Not a bad way to wreak revenge on the company that had "released" you.

"I appreciate your telling me," she said. "It won't go any further."

He nodded. "It's time for me to go, I think. Thank you for sharing your family with me. I like them."

*Aw, crud.* Nina had been hoping to hang on to her resentment at least a little while longer, but he was making it darn hard. With the death of his brother, David had become the senior Hanson, the head of a Chicago dynasty. He was forty-four, well traveled, sophisticated. But his somber sincerity—and the humility with which he'd uttered the last sentence—made him seem more endearingly awkward than suave.

"Well, I think it's safe to say they like you, too."

They stood uncomfortably a moment, aware that neither of them had mentioned liking the other. David broke the lingering silence. "Goodbye, Nina."

His farewell held the ring of finality. Which was appropriate, Nina thought, absolutely appropriate. The truth was they didn't have a reason to see each other again and were unlikely to meet by chance—unless he had a sudden urge to watch a middle-school talent show or she was invited to the Oak Park Country Club.

"Goodbye, Mr. Hanson. Best of luck."

She thought he winced slightly, but recovered before saying, "You, too."

He headed for the kitchen's arched entrance then

stopped and turned. "By the way, where were you headed when I showed up at your door?"

Nina had to concentrate for a moment. "Oh! I was going to see the building manager. Our rent is going up next month, and I wanted to…"

Her voice trailed away when David's brow furrowed. Lord, she did not want to sound any more desperate than she had already today. In over a decade of fending mostly for herself, she'd learned to present a confident front. And she finally believed Bubby was right: David Hanson was a man plagued by his responsibilities. His conscience didn't need the weight of her burdens as well.

Backpedaling, she assured him, "The rent increase is no big deal. That was only my *excuse* to go see him, because…" She had no idea what she was going to say, hesitated and watched David's frown drop lower. "Because…" *Dang it!* Lying was not her forte. "I…have…a crush…on him. The building manager." She laughed. "Go figure."

She ushered David out of the kitchen and toward the front door.

"Bubby! Kids! Come say goodbye to Mr. Hanson!" she called, glad for the first time today that her family doted on him. In a matter of seconds, they claimed David's attention. The general consensus was that they didn't want him to leave, but after a few fawning moments, they allowed him to open the door and wedge out.

Saying her final goodbye before her children yanked off his arm in an attempt to pull him back into the apartment, Nina closed the door and sagged against it. *Thank heavens that was over.*

"Can we come to your office to see David? He's nice!" Izzy jumped up and down.

"I want to invite David to my violin recital." Zach was more calm than his sister, but equally enthusiastic.

"So what's this about the building manager?" Bubby stood with her arms crossed, her countenance unsmiling.

Nina remained where she was, back to the door, one hand on the knob. *There were days,* she thought, *that should have ended at dawn.*

She looked at her son. "Where's the paper?"

## *Chapter Three*

David's jaw remained clenched as he descended the stairs leading to the foyer of Nina's apartment building. He'd spent an interesting afternoon. *Why* he had chosen to have lunch with Nina's family despite his hostess's obvious reluctance remained a mystery to him.

Or maybe it wasn't so mysterious.

She intrigued him. Nina Baxter had turned out to be a fascinating blend of hyper-responsible and Kewpie-doll charming, even when she was trying to insult him behind his back. David felt guilty about her job loss and concerned for her and her family's future. When he returned to the office, he intended to review the employee records and to attempt to work out some sort of severance package. He'd been in Asia during the last board meeting; call him a fool, but he'd had no idea that severance packages had been disregarded.

Nina Baxter, with her shock of blond curls, her emotion-filled blue eyes and her outspoken voice of the people, had wreaked havoc on his peace of mind. And that last comment, about the building manager…

"Has nothing to do with the layoffs and is none of your damned business," David muttered as he stepped off the last stair.

He had made it a policy never to nurture an attraction toward anyone with whom he had a work relationship.

Or toward anyone who had children.

Or who looked like the type to carve Halloween pumpkins and invite him to meet her family over the holidays.

If he'd ever gone on one of those bachelor TV shows he'd have failed miserably. He was a dyed-in-the-wool realist, actually got heartburn when he heard people say they'd fallen in love at first sight.

David enjoyed physical attraction, he enjoyed women, but those feelings were transitory. They could be managed. If a couple decided to marry, they should do so, he believed, only because they both supported the institution of marriage and believed it would enhance their lives. Not because of transient feelings, either physical or emotional.

Wishing he'd brought his coat from the office, rather than opting for only his sport jacket, David prepared to face the punishing Chicago wind, which had kicked in considerably since he'd left work. He'd come here on the train and planned to return the same way. He'd work a couple more hours then head home to get ready for a charity function that he hoped would help Hanson Media Group's reputation. The company had to show that it was still functional, still able to give.

Though not, apparently, to its own employees.

Chewing on that thought, David missed the other person in the lobby until he heard a phlegmy cough.

"Blowing like a sonovabitch."

A stout man, almost bald save for a rim of artificially dark hair that circled three-quarters of his head like a laurel wreath, stood at the glass-walled entrance and pointed with a cigarette held between his thumb and index finger.

"I beg your pardon?" David asked.

"The wind," the other man clarified. "Bastard's getting worse, not better. I gotta replace a window screen in 102. Gonna freeze my keister off." He dragged on the cigarette and shook his head. "I shoulda moved to Philly when I had the chance."

David focused on the man's comment about the window. "You're a handyman?"

"Yeah. Handyman, collection agent, and the building shrink, too. Apartment managers—we're like barbers. Everyone wants to tell you their troubles."

"You're the manager of this building?"

"Yeah."

"Is there a second manager?"

Instantly the man's unibrow swooped. "Why? You got a complaint?"

"Not at all." David looked at the man upon whom Nina supposedly had a crush and decided that no, he had no complaints at all. "Actually, the building is very well-kept," he commented. "I was wondering how one manager alone could be responsible." Perhaps he'd spent too many years in public relations, but the fib flowed smoothly. And had the desired effect.

The round, stubbled face bobbed in satisfaction. Nina Baxter's apartment manager stabbed a thick thumb at his chest. "I'm responsible, all right. Only me. When I'm on the job, one super's all you need."

Puffed with pride, the burly man pointed his cigarette in David's direction. "You looking for a place to hang your hat?"

David began to reply in the negative then thought better of it. Nina Baxter had lied about having a crush on her super. He didn't know her well, but he knew that. Now the question was, why had she done it?

"I may be interested," he said. "What can you tell me about the apartments? Start with price."

* * *

On Monday morning, Nina sat on the floor in her living room, Sunday classifieds spread out over her coffee table, a red felt-tip marker in hand and the cordless phone lying by her side with only a small charge left to give it life.

She knew just how the depleted phone felt.

Stretching backward over the couch, she heard something in her body pop, but was too tired to pinpoint exactly what or where. It was 11:00 a.m.; she'd been sitting here circling help-wanted ads and making phone calls since she'd dropped the kids off at school. A mug of bitterly strong coffee sat on the table, too, because she'd only had two hours of sleep…*maybe* two hours…the night before. Isaac had been up twice needing to use his inhaler.

Watching her son struggle to find a useful breath had always terrified her beyond anything else she could imagine. Last night was the worst. Without a job, without the knowledge that she could take care of her family, Isaac's fight for air on Sunday scared her more than ever before. She'd wanted to rush him to the emergency room immediately, before knowing whether the inhaler would help. She'd wanted to phone the paramedics and to ask one of the EMTs to hold her hand.

In the end, she'd kept her cool—outwardly at least. After a decade of parenting alone, she had come to believe that was sometimes enough. She'd dealt with Isaac the way his doctors had instructed, the way she had too many times before, and she'd held him in the aftermath, the two of them quietly reassuring each other that everything was okay and then reassuring Izzy, who had woken up at the height of it all.

Because her children had school the next today, Nina had lured them back to sleep with the promise of chocolate-chip waffles in the morning. She'd stayed awake, though, listening for the sound of Isaac's breathing, and creeping to their door several times in the dark early morning, not falling asleep until exhaustion overcame maternal fear...which happened as it usually did, about five minutes before her alarm went off in the morning.

Now, as she struggled to stay awake despite the infusion of caffeine, she wondered why she didn't just get back into bed till the kids came home. Scouring the want ads wasn't getting her anywhere. Most of the office positions available were part time; the full-time jobs with benefits often required experience in fields that were unfamiliar to her. With multitudes of applicants for the better positions, employers could afford to be choosy.

She felt defeated, and it wasn't even mid-day.

And then the phone rang.

"I have a proposition for you."

He did not have to add "Miss Baxter" for Nina to identify the voice. Measured, cultured, as rich as

brandy, David Hanson's voice sent a shiver of feminine response down Nina's back and put a buzz of
foreboding in her belly.

"What kind of proposition?"

"Are you busy?" he asked.

"Now?"

David paused, and Nina pictured him checking his
watch. "In thirty minutes. I'll have an hour free then.
I can come to you, or we can meet somewhere. Have
you had lunch?"

"It's only eleven." She hadn't yet managed breakfast. There was a cold chocolate-chip waffle with
her name on it in the kitchen.

"Hmm. How about if we meet at twelve then? I
can work that out. If I head to your neck of the
woods, can you direct us to a good lunch place?"

"I haven't said I'm going to meet you," Nina replied
baldly, then almost added *sir*. She'd never been anything but unfailingly polite to her bosses. Reminding
herself that the events of the weekend had changed the
status quo, she said, "Why do you want to see me?"

There was a brief pause. "Have you found a new
job yet?"

"No. But I just sat down to look at the paper," she
lied.

"Maybe you could look at it after lunch…that is,
if you don't like what I have to say. You may not need
to look at the classifieds at all, Miss Baxter." She
heard the sound of papers being shuffled…then a

muffled voice…and his response as he held the phone away from himself. "I've got to go. Pick a lunch spot near your apartment."

He waited for her response, and Nina hesitated only briefly. "I'll meet you near your office. In front of Some Like It Hot." Give Mrs. Berkowitz's niece Carla a thrill.

David rang off without further ado, obviously needing to get back to business. Nina looked at her phone, pressed End and remained where she was a considerable time, staring at nothing. Her mind hopped along several scenarios, all of which featured her being rehired at Hanson Media. She was sure that was why David had called and why he wanted to meet, and she began to feel immense relief, along with a healthy measure of vindication.

David Hanson, business mogul, must have been moved by something she had said yesterday when she had been too distraught to be tactical. Perhaps he planned to rehire a number of the other laid-off staffers as well. The thought was invigorating.

Abandoning the newspaper and the red marker, Nina sprang from the floor with more energy than she'd had in three days. She had an hour to shower, dress and get downtown. Like on any other workday.

Even with the short notice, Nina was in front of Some Like It Hot with several minutes to spare. David was waiting for her.

"Miss Baxter," he nodded politely in greeting. "Thank you for meeting me."

As always, the combination of his suave good looks and his almost nerdy formality bemused her.

"Are you hungry yet?" he asked.

With the chocolate chip waffle growing stale on her kitchen counter, Nina was aware of a growl deep in her belly. She had a strong aversion, however, to spending the money in her wallet on lunch at an overpriced Hanson-style restaurant. The mother in her would rather bring home a treat for her kids. Also the worrywart in her said, *He hasn't given you your job back yet. Celebrate after you're sitting behind your desk.*

Staring at the lapel of David's elegant gray suit, she said, "Something light, maybe. A sandwich?" She hitched a thumb over her shoulder. "There's a deli down the block…."

"Roseman's? I love that place." He put a hand beneath her elbow. "Let's go."

Surprised that David knew about, much less loved, the no-frills deli that had never even bothered to cover their subfloor, she fell into step beside him. They walked the block to the restaurant without small talk, which Nina thought was rather nice and rather awkward at the same time.

At a few minutes before noon, the deli was crowded, but mostly with the take-out crowd. Nina's eyes darted in several directions as she realized they could easily bump into someone from the office—someone whose brows were sure to rise when they saw David with a recently laid-off female employee, someone with whom he'd never had much personal contact in the office.

David, however, seemed unconcerned by the possibility, or perhaps he hadn't considered it, which seemed odd for a man who ran a public-relations department. Nina would have thought that appearances would be uppermost in his mind, but he smiled as the hostess greeted them, put a hand on the small of Nina's back and didn't demur when the young woman led them to a table in the center of the room.

When the hostess left, he picked up his menu and scanned it as if there were nothing more pressing in this moment than deciding between the "mile-high" turkey and the pastrami on rye.

"What do you like when you come here?" he asked.

Nina leaned toward him. "I like the table near the kitchen."

David looked up, quizzical. "Really?" He glanced over. "Seems cramped." Sending her a dazzling smile that made her forget for a moment why they were there, he shrugged. "It's empty. We'd better grab it now."

She put a hand on his arm as he started to rise. "My point is we could run into someone from the office. What will people think if they see us here, knowing I was laid off, and then I show up at my desk again?" She still didn't know *for sure* that he was planning to rehire anybody else. "It could look—"

The arrival of the waitress, who clearly wanted to get their orders in before the lunch rush began in earnest, temporarily halted their conversation, but Nina was glad she'd addressed the concern out loud.

David chose the mile-high turkey sandwich with a side of potato pancakes. "I'm addicted since yesterday," he admitted, and Nina put in her considerably smaller order: a dinner salad with a scoop of tuna. David frowned at her choice. "She'll take an order of pancakes, too."

Taken aback, Nina shook her head at him. "No, I won't." Turning, she shook her head at the waitress. "No, I won't."

David frowned. "Hmm." He glanced again at the menu. "One of the dough things then, with the potatoes inside. What are those called? Knishes?" He smiled at the young woman whose pencil was poised above her check pad. "We'll have a potato *nish,* too," he ordered, mispronouncing the word.

"It's *k-nish,*" Nina corrected, smiling when he pursed his lips and frowned at the menu. He wore the same expression Zach did when studying for a spelling test.

*Vulnerable,* she thought, surprised the word popped into her mind, but the truth was that the dignified, distant David Hanson she knew from work seemed almost endearingly vulnerable when he was up-close and personal. Then again, maybe she only thought that because she'd insulted him so much.

She handed her plastic menu to the waitress. "Kibosh on the knish."

Flipping easily from eraser to pencil tip, the waitress adjusted the check and beat a hasty retreat.

David took a sip of water. "Not a potato eater, not hungry or you prefer to order for yourself?"

"The latter."

He nodded, set his water glass back on the table. "I'll make a mental note."

There was no further talk of changing tables, and they settled into the utilitarian wooden chairs.

David rested one wrist on the table. "Now where were we? Oh, yes. You were worried about running into someone from the office." He shook his head. "That's not an issue, I'm afraid. Hanson Media isn't going to be able to re-staff for some time."

Nina was so attached to the notion that he was rehiring her and so hopeful that he would rehire at least a few of her co-workers that she didn't immediately grasp what he was telling her. "Hanson isn't rehiring any *other* people, you mean?"

David pursed his lips. His dark eyes grew concerned. "Hanson isn't rehiring at all." He rubbed his temple. "I should have explained the situation better when we were on the phone."

Nina's heart sank. She was not returning to her favorite desk and her ergonomically correct chair? "Then why am I here?" she asked. *Spending eight dollars for iceberg lettuce and a can of tuna when my family is about to lose the roof over their heads?* She looked around for the waitress, so she could cancel her order. Or change it to hot tea and two aspirin.

"You're here, Miss Baxter, because although our current circumstances do preclude rehiring at the office, I find that those same circumstances require me to do a great deal of work from my home. I can't ask my secretary to take on the extra load. So I would benefit from a personal assistant who would work out of my house." He steadily held her gaze. "Are you interested?"

"You want me to be your in-home personal secretary?"

"There wouldn't be a great deal of computer work, other than keeping track of schedules and budgets involving work-related expenditures. I'll handle my personal accounts. Your job description would include coordinating the details of business parties and attending the functions as well, or at least some of them. I'd also ask you to run errands and coordinate the household staff—things I would not ask you to take on if we were in the office."

He let her absorb that info while he studied a bowl of pickle slices. "Do you think these are sweet and dill or all dill?"

"All dill."

"Hmm." He started to dig in then lifted the bowl to her even though it had been sitting on the table between them since they sat down. "Would you like one?"

Mechanically she took a pickle slice, but while he bit into his, she merely stared at hers.

"Is this a pity thing?" she asked. "Or a guilt thing?" She held up a hand before he could answer. "Never mind. I'm not sure I want to know."

She didn't want a reason to turn him down before he told her all the details. A job was a job, after all, and she was desperate. The longer she waited in the hope of finding something she really liked, the harder it would be ever to recoup her losses. As long as he wasn't asking her to do anything illegal or morally unsound, did it matter whether she worked in a home office or a high-rise building?

"You're wondering if I really need an assistant," David remarked, wiping his hands on a napkin. "Miss Baxter, I am by no means broke, but given Hanson Media's current state, neither can I afford to throw money away. I need a personal assistant and you need a job. You have a good work record, I like you—when you're not insulting me or throwing desert flora around my office—and I like your family. That seems a good start to our association. Assuming, of course, your feelings toward me have…gentled somewhat since yesterday? I don't want to be brained by a cactus when I least expect it."

He made the comment with a remarkably straight

face. And certainly, in light of yesterday, the comment was reasonable enough. Nina felt a blush infuse her cheeks, nonetheless. Something about David's formality actually made his question regarding her feelings seem more intimate.

"You know, when you talk like that you sound like Rex Harrison." Nina's hands flew to cover her mouth. She was never rude. Ordinarily, she never even came close to risking rudeness. "I'm sorry! I shouldn't have said that. I just meant…" She shook her head, not sure, really, what she meant.

David's brow puckered. "Hmm. I always liked Rex Harrison. If you hadn't apologized, I'd have thought you were complimenting me."

"No." Her eyes widened in dismay. "Oh! I mean—"

"Never mind. I'm not sure my ego can weather the explanation." He paused while the waitress set salad and sandwich in front of them.

"I'll be back with the latkes," she said and zoomed off. David looked at Nina for clarification. "Latkes. These are the potato pancakes, right?"

"Yes." Nina looked at her lunch, but felt too guilty to think it looked appetizing.

"Ah." He removed the top slice of bread from his sandwich and reached for the mustard. "Did you grow up on this type of food, Miss Baxter?" His tone indicated that he was prepared to forgive her faux pas.

"Yes. And on Rex Harrison films," she said. "I always liked him very much, just for the record."

He smiled, not broadly, but with irony. "But you thought he was stiff? Formal?"

"No. Not exactly." He didn't believe her at this point, of course, so she admitted, "I thought he was…remote. You know, kind of set apart from other people." David's pensive expression made him look vulnerable again, so she added hastily, "But in a good way!"

David winced. "Uh-oh. You've gone from insulting me to placating me. The situation must be worse than I realized." Replacing the bread he'd spread with mustard, he picked up half his sandwich. "Tell me, does this…remoteness…impact my effectiveness at the office?"

"No! Not at all." She was glad she could be honest about that. "Probably the opposite. You seem so completely professional. No one even talks about your love life anymore." As soon as she heard the words, Nina closed her eyes and lowered her head. "Maybe we should just shoot me now." She looked at him earnestly. "You may not believe me, but this is the least tactful I've been in my life. I'm usually too polite. My ex-husband called me Miss Manners."

"Not a compliment, I take it?"

"Not hardly."

Before David took a bite of his sandwich, he asked, "How long were you with your ex-husband?"

"We met when I was seventeen." She picked up her fork and began dissecting the scoop of tuna. "By nineteen I was pregnant with Isaac and by twenty-two I was having Izzy…alone."

"I remember."

Nina felt David's eyes on her as she toyed with her salad. "You do?"

He waited until she looked at him again. "I remember seeing you run out of Edward Karlson's retirement party when the garlic chicken was served. And I remember stepping off the elevator one day and watching you beeline toward the bathroom with your hand over your mouth."

"Oh, charming."

"You appeared to be pretty far along in your pregnancy by then. When I asked my secretary what was wrong, she said you were one of the unlucky women who had morning sickness for all nine months."

"True." The mere memory made Nina's tuna salad seem menacing, like a live shark. She looked ruefully at David. "It was miserable. Whatever I ate seemed to hit my stomach and bounce."

He winced. "And yet you were pregnant twice."

"Unintentionally the first time. But absolutely worth it."

"My secretary also said your marriage was failing. I checked the employee records. You didn't miss a day of work."

"You checked?"

David adjusted the knot of his tie. "Strictly business, Miss Baxter. You looked young enough to leave work and head straight for cheerleader practice. I wondered how you would handle two children, work and single parenthood. And then I realized you wore a sense of responsibility like some women wear expensive perfume—it followed you everywhere. I was impressed."

Dumbfounded, Nina fiddled with the paper napkin on her lap. "I'm not sure what to say. Is that why you sent the bear for Izzy? And the check?" Along with the gift of the bear, there had been a check for one hundred dollars. Perhaps naively, Nina had assumed that all pregnant employees received a cash gift. "Was that from the office…or from you?"

David began eating. After he swallowed the first bite of his sandwich, he said, "Does your ex-husband help with the kids? Time-wise? Financially?"

Nina decided that she knew enough about David Hanson now to know that if he chose not to respond to her question then the answer was yes. She was too discomfited by the discovery to push the topic. Keeping her eyes on her plate, she wondered why he'd taken special interest in her situation. Pity? Self-esteem had been hard to come by for a young woman whose husband had walked out. To know people had pitied her would have been too much to bear.

Though David had evaded her question, he was awaiting an answer to his. Nina toyed with her salad while she considered whether she wanted to talk about her ex and decided, *What the heck?*

"We never see him. The kids don't remember him. Parenthood didn't agree with Peter, and I didn't want to fight him for money." She shook her head. "In the end I suppose I thought it would be easier on the kids and me if he was out of our lives entirely. He didn't want to be a father or husband."

A muscle tightened in David's jaw. He stared at his plate, but his thoughts were clearly on something other than food.

Nina wondered if to his ears she sounded like a man-hater. That was far from the truth, but David Hanson had never married or had kids...that is, she didn't *think* he'd ever had kids. He kept his private life so private—who knew? Perhaps he could relate to the type of man her ex had turned out to be.

On that happy thought, Nina plunged her fork into her salad and chewed lettuce until David pinned her with his pensive gaze.

"In light of what you've shared with me, Miss Baxter, it seems like a good time to discuss the second half of my proposition."

## Chapter Four

Friday afternoon had always been busy at Hanson Media Group. The end-of-the-week push, the force of George Hanson's larger-than-life personality and the sheer number of employees had often generated a sense of chaos.

Standing inside the door to his private office, David surveyed today's scene and thought his brother would rise from the grave if he could feel the tense and exhausted energy of the decimated Hanson staff. People did not bustle; they trudged through the tasks at hand, tasks that had multiplied since the last round of layoffs. It appeared to David that his employees felt overburdened and defeated before they even arrived at work.

They needed a pep talk; the kind George, who could have talked a snail into speeding, would have been able to give them.

The kind of pep talk David did not have inside him right now.

George had been twenty years David's senior, born when their parents were young, had the time and, presumably, the interest in a child—three conditions not present in David's youth. George had fit into the family better than David ever had. Like their father, he had been bigger than life and, as an adult, fascinated by money—making it, keeping it, flaunting it.

Even family dinners had revolved around business discussions, with George and George Sr. animatedly debating whether to merge or acquire. David recalled one evening in particular, when he was six or seven. He'd watched a superior episode of *Johnny Quest* on TV that day and believed that finally he had something worthwhile to share. His father had responded to his overeager, babbling recount by telling his mother they needed to fire the nanny; clearly she allowed him to watch inferior programming.

George hadn't said anything, just sipped his wine and grinned at his brother. From that time on, David had learned to please by being seen and not heard. At age ten he'd taken to wearing ties to school and listening intently at dinner so he could ask pertinent questions, whether the topic interested him or not.

David had not enjoyed hearing Nina's estimation of him yesterday, but she hadn't been off the mark. He'd been a stuffy, formal kid; it stood to reason he'd become a stuffy, formal man.

Lunch with Miss Baxter had happened four days ago; he'd been replaying it in his mind ever since. And accomplishing crap, because he couldn't get her...or the feeling of being with her...out of his mind.

Forcing himself away from the door, he headed down the hallway to his nephew Jack's office. Jack had temporarily taken George's place as CEO after his father's death. Perhaps he could rev up a skeleton staff that had stopped trusting the upper brass and had stopped thinking of Hanson as their company, too.

*I know how they feel,* David thought, scanning the empty desks as he passed down the hall. There were days—and today was one of them—when he thought he might be happier if he simply got out of the business and attempted something new.

He tried not to grit his teeth in an obvious way as he nodded to the employees who bothered to look up. He'd been dissatisfied for a long time; being with Nina Baxter highlighted his restlessness.

He'd had no word from her since their lunch. And that, he'd decided, was a direct result of the second half of his proposition.

When he reached Jack's door, he turned to Mrs. Wycliff, his nephew's secretary, who'd been with the company almost as long as David had himself. "Is he in?"

"He just buzzed me and asked that I hold all calls.
I'll tell him you're here."

Before her fingers touched the phone, Jack's door
jerked open. Barreling through, Jack, who was not
normally a barreler, almost slammed into his uncle.
"I'm on my way to see you." He blinked as if he were
a bit disoriented by a circumstance he hadn't arranged.

"Here I am," David said helpfully.

Jack headed back into his office, then turned and
told the woman whose hair had been gray as long as
David could remember, "Hold all my calls."

"I got that part," David heard her murmur as he
followed his nephew into the spacious corner office.

Jack hadn't changed the furnishings since his father had occupied this office, though his fiancée, Samantha, had clearly influenced the decor. Where a
Waterford crystal bowl used to sit, there was now a
large African basket filled with fresh fruit, and vibrant Mayan weavings had replaced the black-and-
white Hirschfeld portrait George had commissioned
of himself.

David saw the details in a way he hadn't before.
The change in decor was more than superficial; it reflected the profound influence Samantha had on
Jack's very personality. Of all George's children, his
eldest son had been the least like his father. A conservative person at heart, Jack tended to keep the
tones of his life low and mellow…at least he had before Samantha had upped the tempo.

"What kind of tie is that?" David peered at his nephew's neck.

"It's from Guatemala. It's woven." Jack patted the tie protectively, as if afraid his uncle might have something negative to say.

David shrugged. He wasn't going to slight his nephew's fashion statement. The material changes Samantha's presence had effected were nothing compared to the influence she had on Jack's personality. In fact, the recently relaxed and buoyant Jack hadn't looked this tense in awhile.

"What were you on your way to talk to me about?" David saw clearly that his nephew's thoughts were now on the woman who had undoubtedly purchased the tie, and he rather reluctantly brought Jack back to the business at hand. "You look like you need a long vacation. What tragedy has befallen Hanson Media today?"

David spoke tongue in cheek, but his concern spiked when the question etched deep furrows on his nephew's otherwise smooth face.

Jack remembered the letter in his hand and passed it toward his uncle. "Read this."

It took David mere seconds to realize that Hanson had, indeed, suffered another blow. He swore.

"I used that word in front of you when I was ten," Jack said, "and you threatened to wash my mouth out with the garden hose."

"I'm a lot older than you were." *And a lot more*

*tired.* David wanted to crumple the letter, toss it in the wastebasket, not give a damn. He was so freaking fed up with the chain reaction of problems his brother's deceit had left behind.

"Has anyone contacted Angel's Harbor yet?"

Jack shook his head. "I just got the letter."

Angel's Harbor was a group home for kids who had to be removed from their birth families, but for whom there was no foster care. Instead of further stressing an already overburdened foster-care system, Angel's Harbor was a not-for-profit alternative that sought to provide a safe and loving environment for kids in crisis. It was a great project, and Hanson Media was proudly one of the Harbor's biggest supporters. A large and celebrity-studded fund-raiser was coming up to generate the funds for a second Angel's Harbor in Illinois. Hanson Media was going to host the affair.

Or rather, had planned to host the affair. According to the legally worded letter in David's hand, Hanson's involvement through the years, "while greatly appreciated" was no longer "advisable." Apparently rumors of bankruptcy, layoffs and the recent problem of misrouting young Web visitors to a porn site made Hanson Media an undesirable name to have on one's sponsor list.

"This will be all over the media in twenty-four hours." David rubbed his eyes, but it would take more than a brief massage to stay the headache he felt building.

"What can we do?" Jack had never wanted to be the CEO of Hanson, but apparently he'd inherited enough of his father's competitive streak not to let the company die under his leadership.

"We try to make this better, and if we can't, we go shopping for another high-profile charity." Jack winced. "That sounds worse than it is," David assured. "Hanson has never supported an organization we didn't believe in. We're going to have to do some serious media schmoozing. You up for it?"

"Whatever it takes. Samantha will be onboard, too."

David nodded. He folded the letter, knowing he needed to get back to his office and start making phone calls. He felt overwhelmingly weary, though, a far cry from his usual response to business challenges.

Wandering to the wall of windows in Jack's office, he gazed at downtown Chicago. "Nice view," he murmured to Jack, then without any segue at all, asked, "How are things between you and Samantha?"

Turning to watch his nephew's reaction, David found himself fascinated by the transformation of Jack's features. Apparently the mere thought of the woman he loved was enough to wipe the concern from Jack's face. David didn't even need to hear the response, which was a simple "Great."

The sweeping restlessness that had plagued David lately hit again full force. Immediately he thought of Nina Baxter and her family, and of the feeling he'd had in their home…or, rather, he thought of the feeling in their home. The life, the exuberance, the familiarity among them.

He knew why he'd pushed so hard for Nina and her children to move in with him: He was like a leech, trying to feed off their happiness.

He had a disconnected family, and though he'd been physically intimate with women, he didn't feel that close to anyone.

"Do you want to come to dinner tonight?" Jack asked, clearly entertaining the idea on the spur of the moment. "Samantha's trying her hand at lasagna."

"Is she a good cook?"

"No. This recipe feeds ten. She's afraid she might ruin it if she cuts it down, so there'll be plenty."

David tried to remember the last time he'd had a non-business dinner with one of his nephews. Clinton had been in office.

Being an uncle to George's three boys had never come naturally. It might have gone better if the position had come with a job description. Or if David had figured out first what it meant to be a brother. As it was, despite being only nine years older than Jack, the oldest of his nephews, he'd always felt a bit awkward. A little too…formal.

*Thank you, Nina,* he thought wryly, *for giving voice to my conscience.*

He would definitely have dinner with Jack and Samantha. But not tonight. Tonight he would be awful company, and Jack didn't need an uncle who was moody and distracted. This time, he wanted to get the uncle business right.

"I think I'll let you do the first lasagna taste test," he said. "I'll take a rain check, though. Soon."

"All right. Deal." Jack gestured to the letter in David's hand. "Anything I can do to follow up on that?"

"I'll take care of it for now, but when the serious schmoozing starts, I'll let you know."

Jack nodded, but he was staring at the phone and fiddling with some wooden beads in a bowl on his desk, his mind obviously elsewhere.

"The reading of my father's will is coming up."

*My father's,* David thought, not *Dad's.* Jack's worried frown elicited a similar expression from his uncle. *If I had kids, I'd want them to call me Dad, even after I'm gone. And I wouldn't want them to look tense or nervous when they spoke about me.*

"What's on your mind, Jack?"

Exhaling forcefully, Jack said, "Evan and Andrew." He picked up a handful of the wooden beads then chucked them angrily back into the bowl. "My brothers haven't responded to Father's lawyer or to me. They were too busy to take an interest in the business. Now they're too 'busy' to be bothered with the will." Jack muttered an expletive.

Concern for his eldest nephew sparked David's irritation at Evan and Andrew. The younger Hanson brothers seemed to be MIA from the time they were old enough to say, "See you later." If they harbored resentment toward George, who had been a better boss than a father, that was one thing. But they were allowing Jack to shoulder the entire family burden, to upset his own life path in order to save a business that would ultimately benefit them, too. That was a circumstance David found intolerable.

Perhaps it was time to exercise an older relative's authority. Assuming this older relative had any.

"Have Mrs. Wycliff give me their contact information," he said to Jack, his tone sharp enough to indicate that he would not take no as an answer when he summoned his nephews home. "They'll be present for the reading of the will."

Jack nodded, obviously relieved to share one more burden he'd taken on after his father's sudden passing. "You don't mind dealing with this and the check?" He indicated the temporarily forgotten letter in David's hand.

"I don't mind," David assured. He felt fatigued by the problems his family continued to have, yet he realized that helping Jack made him feel more like an uncle, especially when he saw his nephew's shoulders relax. "You should take the rest of the day off," he said, surprising Jack and himself, too. "Help your fiancée make lasagna."

Jack's lips betrayed vestiges of the love-sodden smile he acquired now whenever Samantha was mentioned.

Exiting the office, David tried to focus on business

and not on his rapidly plunging mood. Ordinarily the letter he held would burn itself into his hand and his brain; his mind would wrap around that challenge and little else.

He told his secretary to hold all calls as he entered his office, but when he picked up his phone, it was not the charity's number he dialed.

Nina sat curled on one end of her couch, a magazine borrowed from the library in her lap. The article she'd been reading—"Six Home Businesses that Made a Million"—had turned out to be of little use. Unless she intended to conduct corporate headhunts out of her kitchen or mass-produce DVDs about achieving multiple orgasms, it was back to the drawing board job-wise. She glanced again at the article about multiple orgasms. Definitely not her area of expertise.

Closing the magazine self-consciously, she looked at her kids, who were home this Friday for a school in-service day. They sat in the living room with her, finishing their homework so they'd have the weekend free. Izzy used the family computer to write a book report and Zach was immersed in math. They each had a mug of hot apple cider and a toasted bagel sandwich next to them. As usual, Zach had eaten only the filling of his sandwich. It was a cozy scene. Nina sighed. She was such a good mother.

Except that she wasn't sure where they'd all be living next month and still hadn't mentioned her job loss to her children. She supposed she was still holding out hope for this Sunday's classifieds.

"Mom, how do you spell *porcupine?*" Izzy asked without looking up.

Zach jumped to the answer first. "P-o-r-c-u-p-i-n-e. Porcupine."

"Thanks, *Mom.*"

Nina smiled, but weakly. Her children liked to study, God bless them. They deserved to go to college. They deserved music lessons and dance lessons and a class trip to New York to see *The Lion King* onstage.

After her own parents had died and she'd moved in with Bubby, there had been little money for extras. To save Bubby from worrying about her, Nina had pretended not to want to go on "juvenile" school trips or to continue her "boring" violin lessons. She had watched her friends continue to be kids while she had grown up overnight. She didn't want her own children to face such concerns.

But how could she afford the extras when she was worried about keeping a roof over their heads?

Was it horrible of her not to leap at the opportunity David Hanson offered?

"Zach, do you want any more of that bagel?" she asked. In the past few days she'd gone from a nervous inability to eat to a nervous desire to eat everything in sight.

"Nope," her son answered.

"Toss it here." Part of her was so attracted to the idea of living in someone else's home with someone else's too-high rent and someone else's leaky faucets. She liked the idea of not worrying about the details for a while.

But she liked the idea of general peace of mind better, and she would not gain serenity by becoming dependent on the *idea* of David Hanson. And that's what would happen.

Because she'd been fantasizing about him all week already.

Burrowing more snugly into the corner of the couch, as if she thought she could hide there, she bit down hard on the chewy bagel. David Hanson was sophisticated, awkward, social, reserved, formal, funny—a study in contradictions. He was also solicitous, yet when he'd dropped the bomb about her moving into his apartment, he'd seemed forceful and protective.

And she'd liked that.

Shifting again and shoving the magazine with its money-making "multiples" idea between the sofa cushions, she thanked her lucky stars that Bubby was in a keno tournament at the senior center this week. Had she been able to hover over her granddaughter, the astute septuagenarian would have picked up immediately on Nina's restlessness and ambivalence.

David had stated that Nina's living situation was a

concern because he needed her on call in the evenings to oversee business parties, and he knew she would be more comfortable if her children were close by. Also, he didn't want her to be distracted by housing issues, which would certainly come up again. Even if she hadn't been laid off, she'd have struggled with the rent increase, and she couldn't imagine finding lower rent in a decent neighbourhood.

Nina didn't know if David was a control freak or boss of the year. She didn't know whether to accept his offer and deal with the disturbing thoughts she'd been having about him or to reject the job outright and put the Hansons—David especially—out of her mind. Socially, he was way out of her league. Romantically, they weren't even on the same planet. She'd married at eighteen. He was still single at forty-four.

*Why* was he still single at forty-four? Nina frowned, working her jaws around another big bite of the bagel. Was it a chronic condition? Lord knew he hadn't suffered for a lack of exquisite female companionship over the years. He'd been photographed with some of the loveliest women in Chicago.

*Photographed with them. But never married.* Nina couldn't recall even a rumor about an engagement. Did David Hanson date for publicity? Could he be—

Nina looked at her children, making sure they were focused on their work, as if they'd be able to read her thoughts if they looked at her.

Gorgeous, formal, a little awkward, never married…

What if David Hanson was gay and trying to hide it?

She began to chew the bagel with nervous intensity. The more she thought about it, the more it made a kind of sense. Hanson Media garnered much of its financial support from family-slanted groups. The kind that typically frowned on alternative lifestyles. And certainly, after the problems with his brother and the Internet gaffe, now would not be the time to come out of the closet.

If David Hanson turned out to be gay, Nina wouldn't have to brood a bit about her silly attraction. Or that odd feeling of wanting to be taken care of. All that would be a moot point.

In that case, she could kind of, almost, sort of see herself accepting the job offer.

"I'll get it!" Izzy jumped up.

"Get what?" Nina said around a cheekful of bagel before she realized the phone was ringing.

Call it a sixth sense, which she'd never really possessed, but somehow she knew who was on the phone before her daughter returned, holding out the receiver.

"He asked to speak with 'Miss Baxter,'" Izzy said in a stage whisper that left much to be desired, and grinning girlishly as if this were hysterically funny.

Nina didn't bother to ask *who?* "Well, I'm not

married anymore," she reminded her daughter as she unfurled from the sofa and stood on cramped legs. Shooing her nosy child back to the computer, she stumbled to the kitchen before her knees had warmed up and held the receiver to her ear. "Hello."

"What should I call you?"

David's voice was smooth and rich, as always. And, as always, she detected a little frown in his tone.

"Miss Baxter is fine," she said. She kept her married name because it belonged to her children, too, but asking people to call her Ms. was too much trouble. Most people called her "Mrs."; she didn't bother to correct them. "Or you can call me 'Nina,'" she added. "Your brother always called us by our first names."

"Yes." Nina heard him sigh as if the mention of his brother were a heavy weight. "He should have run the PR department."

"You seem to do all right."

"Apparently not," David countered. "I can't even get prospective employees to phone me."

She winced. "Guilty. Sorry. I've been…" she hesitated.

"Busy?" he supplied. "Searching the classifieds? Ambivalent?"

Tucking the phone between her shoulder and cheek, Nina smiled reluctantly as she opened the refrigerator and poked at a defrosting chicken. "All of the above," she admitted.

"Hmm. And did you find anything in the classi-fieds?"

*Why lie?* "No. Not yet."

"And you are still searching, because…?"

Leaving the poor chicken alone, she shut the re-frigerator and walked to the window to put a little more distance between her and the living room. Qui-etly she said into the phone, "Because having an of-fice job and my own apartment would be less complicated than working and living in someone else's home."

"Not if you can't find a job or an apartment to suit your situation," he said with a characteristic business-man's confidence. "My offer is actually less chal-lenging than trying to find and maintain housing given Chicago rents and the fact that you need at least a two-bedroom place. And very few office jobs will allow the adequate time and flexibility to parent your children without significant child care. I'm sure you've already come to that conclusion, which must be why you haven't phoned to categorically reject my offer."

"Well, now that we've worked that out," Nina mumbled, gazing out the window at the old neigh-borhood in which they lived.

He was correct about thing: She and her children were going to have to move. She couldn't come up with the rent the new owners of the building had re-quested. She'd already asked for a break on the basis of being a good tenant of long-standing. It was a long shot, but she'd had to try. Unfortunately she'd received only a swift and politely worded response thanking her for her loyalty to the apartment complex and rejecting her request.

"I have more questions," she told David. "About the job. And the living situation."

"Name the time and place," he said, understanding before she said a word that she didn't want to discuss this over the phone.

"Your schedule is fuller than mine. At the moment."

"Tonight. Seven o'clock."

The one night she had restrictions. "It's Shabbat—the Jewish Sabbath," she said. "The kids and I are serving shabbos dinner at my grandmother's senior center. The other servers are down with the flu, so I can't cancel."

The pause on the other end of the phone was brief. "Need an extra pair of hands?"

The pause on Nina's end of the line was quite a bit longer. "You?"

"I'm free tonight." He sounded offhand, as if he volunteered to serve challah and Manischewitz wine to seniors whenever he had an open Friday. "Just give me a street address and a time."

"I don't think that will be the best place—"

"Serving usually requires some cleaning. That ought to give us a few minutes." She heard him shuffle papers. "I've got to go. Give me an address and a time, and I'll meet you there. You can ask your questions or watch me wash dishes while you come up with an alternative meeting."

"Wouldn't it be easier to just—"

"Address and time, Miss Baxter. I'm on the clock."

She came up with the requested information, and they hung up.

Nina gazed out the window and amended her opinion of David Hanson. He might be concerned and genuine, but he was also wily and persistent and surprisingly skilled at getting his way.

Once more, she wanted to kick herself in the tush for being charmed by his tactics.

She shook her head and tried to ignore the desire to race to her closet and try on clothes. She wasn't sure what else she was going to discover about David tonight or how it would affect her decision to take the job. But suddenly, that was not her greatest worry. She was far more concerned with all the things she was discovering about herself when David was around.

## Chapter Five

Fifteen minutes into Shabbat, Nina decided David had to be gay, after all. No straight man she'd ever met was as willing to have his cheeks pinched by senior citizens as he was.

Bubby was overjoyed to see her "Davy." She introduced him to her friends as "My Nina's David. You know, used to be her boss. He likes to come visit."

*Likes to come visit* may have been an overstatement; they'd only seen him twice outside of work in thirteen years, but the comment had the desired effect on Bubby's friends. For years, the denizens of the Wilkens Senior Center had read about the Hansons, Chicago's upper crust. Bubby had made sure of that. She'd brought in every newspaper clipping that had anything to do with the Hansons since Nina had started working for the company in 1993. Now her women friends were meeting a Hanson in person, and they were positively giddy. Only bringing in Oprah would have been a better show-and-tell.

One of Bubby's octogenarian gal pals tried to coax David into sitting down to dinner, but he declined, reminding her that he was there to serve, not to be served. In all these years, it was the first time Nina had seen him turn on the charm, and she realized he had an abundance of it.

When the last bite of kugel was eaten and the plates cleared, Nina told her children to head to the multipurpose room to join the services.

"We're supposed to help the whole night," Izzy protested, though Isaac, who loved Friday services, was already halfway out the kitchen door.

"Mr. Hanson is here to help me," Nina said. "And I don't want you to miss Rabbi Jackie. She's a Renewal rabbi visiting from California. I'd like you to hear a woman rabbi."

Izzy, who had learned from her mother and grandmother that women had not even been allowed to hold the Torah when Bubby was a girl, appeared unconvinced.

"And, I understand she raises quarter horses," Nina added. "I'm sure she'll talk to you about that after the services."

*Bingo.*

Izzy raced her brother to the multipurpose room, leaving Nina alone with David in the kitchen.

Nina stood at the sink, which was filled with dirty dishes, and watched David sample a chocolate-chip *rugelach* from the dessert tray they would bring out later.

"What are you doing?" she asked him.

He looked up from the cookie and smiled. "Sorry. I couldn't help myself." Popping the rest of the cookie into his mouth, he spoke around it. "Let's get to work."

He appeared so boyish, so ingenuous, Nina had a crazy impulse to hug him as he approached the sink and stopped in front of her. He was still wearing his dress shirt from work, but the sleeves were rolled up and his tie was loosened. So formal. She shook her head.

"That's not what I mean. I mean, what are you doing *here?* Why were you cutting kugel for two dozen octogenarians when I know you could have found twenty free minutes to meet with me?"

"What's *koo-gul?*"

"The noodle casserole."

"The one that smelled like cinnamon?"

"Yes."

"I wanted to try that." He glanced around.

"It's all gone. Don't change the subject." Grabbing a dish towel, she flicked him on the middle with it. But privately she added *cute* to the list of descriptive adjectives she was compiling about him. "You aren't here for the food," she insisted. "What's the deal? Is Hanson targeting seniors as a hot market? Are you building a Web zine for the over-eighty crowd?"

Golden-brown eyebrows lowered over almost similarly golden-brown eyes. David's lower lip jutted beyond its mate. The expression made Nina instantly sorry she had teased him, and she told him she was kidding. "I just can't figure out why you wanted to meet here, that's all."

"I suppose I thought you'd be more relaxed on familiar turf," he admitted. "More yourself. I want you to work for me, Nina. I didn't want to sit across a table from you while you come up with a hundred sound reasons to turn me down."

"You think there are a hundred sound reasons for me to turn you down?"

"I think there are a few," he said honestly, looking her straight in the eye. "But I think there are more reasons to say yes, and they're just as sound."

The hair he usually wore brushed straight back had gotten mussed during his runs from kitchen to table. A gold-tinged lock fell over his forehead. Nina put both hands behind her back and clutched the towel, resisting the urge to reach up and push his hair off his brow if only to see how he would respond.

"Why do you want to hire me? It's certainly more complicated than hiring someone who has no dependents. Not to mention secure housing."

David nodded slowly. For well over an hour now, he'd been with Nina, working under her direction, putting food on plates held out to him by quivering veined hands and watching her fill needs both practical and emotional. Nina's warmth and genuine interest in others spread over the people in her immediate vicinity like the perfect blanket on a chilly night. Watching her, feeling her beside him, he became more and more convinced that his *life* was a chilly night.

He began to wonder if he was heading toward a midlife crisis, dissatisfied suddenly with a path that had suited him well until now.

"I like your dependents," he said carefully, keeping his voice light and casual. He didn't want to scare her away. He didn't want to scare himself. He didn't know what he wanted from her, really. It seemed pathetic to believe that he wanted to borrow her life for a while, to experience family by sharing the one she had created with such obvious care. David feared that might be the truth, however, as his own parents' agenda had not included making their youngest child feel warm and fuzzy.

He looked at the lovely blonde who was watching him closely with a wariness and suspicion he probably merited. She'd dressed nicely but conservatively in a pale blue sweater and long wool skirt. Her hair was pulled back in a thick bun, but she hadn't completely tamed the curls. He liked that.

"Nina," he said, the first time tonight that he'd used her given name. Up to now he'd stuck with *Miss Baxter,* which had made the old women smile. "You have the qualities I want in a personal assistant." He decided to keep his reply and his thoughts on the business plane. "I can enumerate your assets if you like. You're efficient, a fast thinker, easy to get along with—" Her brows shot up, and David smiled. "I like people who tell me the truth. You're also warm and gracious, which will be critical at the business functions I'll expect you to supervise and attend. And, you're available. That's not good for you, but it does work out for me. I don't have time to interview people."

"Your secretary could—"

"She has more than enough to do right now."

"I have children. Have you ever lived with two pre-teenage children?"

He rested his palm on the sink, leaning into it. "No. I don't have kids of my own. I'm not planning to have kids of my own. But yours are already housebroken, and they seem docile enough."

He enjoyed the rich, free sound of her laughter. "Housebroken and docile, huh? You sure you don't want to hire someone with, say, a Boston terrier?" She shook her head. "You cannot count on my kids to be quiet."

"Silence is overrated."

"They're messy. I don't want to worry that we're

ruining a Persian rug every time Isaac brings mud in. And Izzy likes to tap dance on hard surfaces."

"I have wall-to-wall carpeting."

Nina began to chew her lip—unconsciously, he thought. "I need the job," she murmured, and though he heard the reluctance in her inflection, the hope that grew in his chest felt surprisingly good.

Angling toward the sink, she turned on the faucets to fill the basin.

David picked up a sponge. "I'll wash this time. You dry."

She eyed him doubtfully, but didn't demur. Instead, she pulled two aprons out of a drawer, insisted he don one and rolled up her sleeves to swish bubbles into the soapy water.

"Have at it, mister."

As they began to clean the dinner mess, the sound of voices raised in song drifted in from the multipurpose room. The melody was moving and joyful, but the Hebrew words were unfamiliar to David. He was about to ask what they meant when he heard Nina begin to sing softly under her breath.

Silently he handed her the wet plates he had scrubbed and stole glances at her profile. Somehow, from her lips the foreign words acquired meaning for him. He could tell that the song was filled with anticipation, that it was about waiting and hoping for something.

Nina Baxter, he decided, was beautiful. With curly

blond hair, baby-doll blue eyes and a figure like Betty Boop's, she could easily be termed *cute* or *adorable;* but that would discount the depth of her attractiveness. She was a woman, certainly not the girl who'd first come to work over a decade ago.

As she sang, her soft features seemed to mature before his eyes. The song held meaning for her. He had no intention of interrupting and was content to work and listen to her sing, but she stopped abruptly to ask, "Have you ever wanted children?"

Caught off guard, he didn't temper his response. "No."

She looked mildly surprised, but not disappointed. "That's it, huh? Just 'no'? Have you ever thought about it? Or is it something you've actively avoided?"

The pan David was scrubbing slipped from his fingers and clattered into the sink. Frowning, he fished it out, made sure no harm was done and wondered just how complete his answer ought to be. There were lines of decorum, he'd always felt, that shouldn't be crossed. Somehow, though, with Nina he wasn't at all certain the usual rules applied. "All right, I'm going to be blunt here. My answer involves you."

This time, Nina's head reared back with considerable surprise. David kept working, but angled his attention toward Nina. "I remember when you were pregnant for the second time and not throwing up in a business meeting seemed like a Herculean effort for you. Then I found out you were single and had to make a living on your own…." He narrowed his eyes in an expression both wry and a bit sheepish. "I went out," he admitted, "and bought a very large box of condoms."

Nina stopped drying a water glass. She blinked at him. "That was *really* honest."

"You asked."

"So what was the deal, exactly? You didn't trust the woman to use birth control? You didn't trust yourself to stick around if you did make a baby?"

He scowled and spontaneously flicked sudsy water at her nose, not something he recalled ever doing to a woman—or an employee—before. "No. Jeez, no. I trusted myself to act with integrity." He shook his head, working harder to scrape some kind of casserole out of a pan. "I didn't trust myself to act with joy—that was the problem. I thought a child—and a woman—deserved both."

After a pause, Nina responded softly, "You're right. On both counts." She kept her eyes on the glass she was still drying…well beyond the point of dryness…then looked up at him. "Hey, so you're not—"

She cut herself off.

"What?" David gazed at her. Her expression was five parts surprise, five parts mortification. "Don't stop now. We're building trust here. I'm not…?"

"Not…going…to get the stuff off the pan that

way. Use the scrubber." She nodded to a nylon ball on the sink.

He cocked a brow at her, tossed the sponge aside and picked up the scrubber. "I'm not what, Nina? Come on, cough it up. You were about to insult me again. It's all over your face."

Nina considered a fervent denial, but fervently *lying* on the Sabbath would be bad karma. Also, David didn't seem particularly disturbed by the prospect of her insulting him again.

"It's not an insult this time. Really," she said, setting aside the glass she'd wiped to a squeaky-clean shine and turning her focus on a dinner plate. "I'd just wondered—just briefly, I mean I didn't dwell on it— whether you hadn't married because you might be…" She lowered her head, not at all sure she should say it. "…ay."

"What?" He leaned toward her. "I didn't catch the last word."

She mumbled it a second time.

"I can't understand you. I might be what?" He shook his head. "Gray?"

"No! Gay," she said loudly and clearly. "I thought maybe you were gay."

He looked utterly shocked. Speechless, in fact.

"It's a reasonable assumption," she defended.

"Really?"

She stood her ground and looked up at him. *Now* he seemed a little peeved.

Nina sighed and set the plate on top of some others. "You see? This is why a boss and a secretary should not even contemplate living together. We're going to cross all kinds of unspoken boundaries."

"No, I think this one *is* spoken."

"Well, I didn't mean anything negative."

"That settles it, you're moving in. My reputation is at stake."

"If you and I move in together—with my children—*your* reputation is the last thing we're going to worry about," she contradicted, the topic of his sexuality losing ground to the issue of her children's well-being. "I will insist that we make it very clear to everybody that there is nothing romantic or sexual going on. I won't even consider moving in unless we're agreed on that."

"Agreed that there *is* nothing romantic or sexual going on or agreed that we *tell* people there is nothing romantic or sexual going on?"

She folded her arms.

"All right. I will take swift and decisive action to correct any mistaken impressions. Including my own. Kidding," David said when she opened her mouth to retort. "Meet me at my place, Sunday. I'll show you around, you can ask invasive questions and make your decision."

Temporarily nonplussed, Nina stared.

"This is the easy part, Miss Baxter. Just say yes to Sunday. We'll take it from there."

\* \* \*

Two days later, on a Sunday afternoon, David stood in the steamy bathroom of his downtown condo and slapped cologne on his freshly shaved face and neck.

Nina was due to arrive to inspect his place at 4:00 p.m. And he was preparing for their meeting as if he were about to embark on the hottest date of his life.

Setting the cologne on the granite counter, he abandoned his preparations and headed for the kitchen. This wasn't a date, but he did want her to say, "Yes." Yes, she would work for him; yes, she and her kids would move in. His reasons, he had decided while he'd run on the treadmill this morning and again as he'd pushed through several sets of flies, were sound. She'd be a great personal assistant, and if she worked for him he could stop feeling guilty that she'd been fired. He was thinking clearly.

When the doorbell rang, he was downing a glass of orange juice and blaming it for the sudden burn in his stomach.

His heart began to pound uncomfortably as he walked to the door. *Damned acidic fruit juices.*

Nina stood in the large light-filled hall of his twenty-third-floor condo and met his gaze with what he was coming to view as her characteristic this-will-never-ever-work expression.

Standing so close he could smell her shampoo, she said, "This will never ever work," before she bothered with "Hello."

David smiled, a deep smile that started low and rose until it parted his lips in a full-fledged grin. The sight of her relaxed him.

"Bummer, Miss Baxter." He put a hand beneath her elbow. "Come in."

Nina tugged on the lapel of her long coat. It was lightweight for spring, a powder-blue color that looked great with her eyes. "All right," she agreed. "But only because I've never seen an apartment like this before, and I'm curious. *Not* because I'm still considering moving in, because now that I've seen this building—" She silenced abruptly as they entered the living room. "You said you had carpeting."

David looked at the room, genuinely bemused. "Ahh, yes, I do."

"It's white," Nina said in a tone that sounded faintly accusing. All David could think about was taking her coat off so he could see how she was dressed today. So far he'd liked her best in the jeans she'd worn the day she'd lobbed office supplies at him.

"Sort of off-white-cream-ish, don't you think?" he suggested, hoping that whatever perturbed her about white carpeting would not stand in the way of their sitting down to the chardonnay and cheese tray he'd picked up at the wine shop near his gym.

"Actually, I'd call this particular hue Do-You-Have-Any-Idea-What-Grape-Juice-Does-to-a-Deep-Pile white."

"Oh." He smiled. "No, I don't. You'll have to explain it to me. In great detail. May I take your coat?"

After a moment, Nina shrugged out of the thin wrap. "Okay, but only because it's warm in here, and I have a feeling the tour will take a while, because this place is mammoth."

David inclined his head agreeably. She sounded less than approving again, but she was here, and she was staying. He was getting what he wanted. Who was he to argue?

About to say he'd hang the coat up, he decided to toss it over the leather sofa instead. Obviously Nina was having a problem with the formality of his apartment relative to the casualness of her lifestyle. So he'd show her what a casual guy he really was.

Following the direction her coat took, she smoothed a hand over the arm of the sectional couch and whistled in appreciation. "Is this Corinthian leather?"

He nodded in satisfaction. All right, at last she'd found something to admire. The fact that he had no idea what kind of leather adorned his sofa did not stop him from answering, "Yes, it is."

"Uh-huh." She clucked her tongue. "One good jab from a ballpoint pen, and that's a goner."

She was beginning to sound like an inspector for *Better Homes and Gardens* child-proofing edition. David put a hand on the small of her back.

"Come on. Let's get out of here before you notice

the Chihuly glass bowl waiting to be shattered by one good tap of a Nerf ball."

"My kids don't have Nerf balls," she said, allowing him to guide her toward the kitchen. "They have the hard rubber, dangerous kind. I'm only thinking of you."

"Miss Baxter," David murmured as he nudged her ahead of him and sneaked a look at her jean-clad tush, "you've no idea how those words comfort me. Please believe me when I say I'm thinking of you, too."

## Chapter Six

Nina knew she was being disagreeable. She even knew why.

Knowing for sure that David wasn't gay had allowed all sorts of annoying fantasies to disturb her sleep the past two nights.

There was no denying it: She found him attractive, in a what-are-you-out-of-your-mind-he's-your-boss-and-completely-inappropriate-for-you kind of way. Moving in with him would be a disaster—capital *D*, capital *Isaster*.

Which was why she was smart to point out all the flaws in his reasoning.

"Oh wow, you have a stainless-steel fridge." She

ran her hand admiringly along the handle. "Aren't these great? I mean, if you don't have kids. Once you have kids, of course, stainless is the last finish you want on an appliance. They never look clean." She tapped the refrigerator door with her fingernail. "All fingerprints, all the time."

"I'll remember that, Heloise."

"I'm just—"

"Thinking of me." David nodded. "You've got my back."

He took two steps toward her, pressed his palm flat against the freezer door—which would leave a terrible mark—and loomed over her. "I have a nice chardonnay chilling in this impractical refrigerator. Would you like a glass? It might help you relax."

"I don't need to relax."

"Oh, yeah." He nodded broadly. "You do."

"Well!"

Nina tried to glance away. David wasn't encroaching on her space, exactly. He hardly ever did that, she'd noticed. He was far too upright—figuratively and literally. He stood as straight as a tree most of the time. When he leaned toward her, he did it with his eyes.

"I picked up some cheese, too," he said.

Nina's gaze snapped back to him. He didn't look particularly flirtatious. "You bought wine and cheese? For a quick business meeting?"

David angled his head and frowned. "Too stuffy?"

He moved to a cabinet, opened it and looked in. "How about cherry cola and a peanut-butter Ritz?" When she didn't answer, he poked around some more. "Corn curls and apple juice? Molasses snaps? Scooter Pie? Aw, there's only one left." He angled his gaze toward her. "It's vanilla, not my favorite. I suppose I could let you have it."

"Scooter Pies?" she said, incapable of not smiling. "*You* eat all this stuff?"

"Yes, I'm really a casual person, Miss Baxter. Very informal. Just a big kid myself. I get fingerprints all over the refrigerator, too. Cheese-puff crumbs on the bedspread." He wagged his head. "Johanna gets very annoyed with me."

Nina felt the smile slip from her face. "Who's Johanna?"

"My housekeeper. She comes once a week. I was going to hire her another day if you and your kids moved in, which would help her out, but if it's just me there's not enough for her to do." He tossed the information off casually, as if it weren't a tactic to make her agree to the job and the accommodations. "All right, let's see…. I also have chililime tortilla chips." His eyes darted her way. "I won't mention the garlic if you don't mention the garlic."

"I thought you said you rarely eat at home."

His grin was infectious. "You call this eating?" He rooted through the cabinet some more. "Bag of chocolate chips…cinnamon graham crackers…beer nuts… stop me if I'm getting warmer."

Nina swallowed the lump in her throat. *He* wasn't getting warmer, but *she* was. Darn him, why did he have to be…cute? He stretched up to reach the top shelf of the cabinet, and his polo shirt lifted above the waistband of his jeans to reveal a lean, flat middle. When Nina leaned her head a little to the right, she was pretty sure she glimpsed a hint of washboard abs. He was handsome in his suits, yes, but she'd never guessed that he kept himself so fit.

"Do you bring women here?" she blurted with no preamble, save for the one in her own head. "I mean, often? Do you bring them home often…on dates? I'm only asking because I have impressionable pre-teens, and if I were to consider your offer—which I'm really not—but in case I were suddenly to consider it, I would need to know."

He turned toward her. "If you and your children were to move in—which you are not—but *if* you were suddenly to consider it, you have my word that I would not bring women home."

And that should have been that.

But David's response referred to the future, and Nina was asking about the past and the present, too. Which was obviously none of her business and which had nothing to do with her children's welfare. Darn it.

Leaving her post by the refrigerator, she pointed

to a beautiful carved wood door with an etched-glass insert. "What's through here?"

David came up behind her, reached above her head to place a hand on the door and pushed. "Dining area. For casual evenings at home."

The irony of his words struck full-force with Nina's first glimpse of the room. *Formal dining room* would be a criminal understatement to describe the space she walked into.

"Wow."

Huge and decorated to the hilt, the room held a table that seated ten without inserts, a majestic chandelier, and walls covered in a quilted champagne-colored silk.

Nina ran her hands over the back of a chair that had pale striped-silk upholstery and carved blond wood. "Is this where the president sits?"

David joined her next to the chair and sighed. "You're about to tell me what ketchup would do to these chairs, aren't you?"

"Not at all. Because I highly doubt that anything served at this table would require ketchup."

She turned to face him. Deliberately, she had worn her customary Sunday-with-the-kids attire: jeans that were faded because she'd worn them for years not because she was making a fashion statement, a cropped lilac sweater, a pair of clogs. Her hair was scraped into a ponytail, so it looked neat until it reached a thick elastic band and burst into the usual ringlets.

As relatively casual as David appeared today—and he was definitely dressed more casually than she had ever seen him—he still gave the appearance of being neat and conservative. And rich. His leather shoes looked as expensive as his couch.

"I'm not used to all this luxury, that's all," she answered him. "Forgive me if I gawk, but this is like one of those holiday home tours, minus the eggnog."

"I knew I forgot something." He snapped his fingers then laid his hand on the back of the chair, close enough to her hand to make her fidget. "I'll show you the rest of the house."

He led her through the apartment with ease and an enviable nonchalance. Obviously David wasn't overly impressed with his own possessions, but neither did he ignore the impact they had on her, particularly when he and Nina entered the library. Nina heard herself sigh.

The room was a reader's dream. Wall-to-wall carved wood bookshelves, ambient lighting, reading nooks with the kind of chairs you could disappear in. There were books of all kinds. Her children, especially Zach, who loved to read and seemed to have no preference regarding subject matter, would go nuts.

"You even have children's books," Nina said, running her fingers along the spines of hardcover editions of *Harry Potter* and *Lemony Snicket*.

"We have a children's Web site. Gotta keep up." David stood behind her, casually shrugging off the answer.

Nina walked her fingers down the row of books. "You have *A Wrinkle in Time...Roll of Thunder, Hear My Cry...Where the Red Fern Grows....* I bet most of the kids who visit the Web site have never heard of these books."

"Yes they have. I post there."

Surprised and interested to know more, she turned, but David was already walking to the door. He spent time on the Hanson kids' Web site? He posted? Talked to kids? Suggested books? He truly was full of surprises. And his library was designed for use, not merely for looks. What would the other books say about their owner?

Apparently he wasn't going to give her time to find out. David was already heading down the hall by the time she exited the library. She had to trot to catch up. Standing once more in the living room, she realized they'd made a wide U.

"And that completes our tour. Sorry about the eggnog. Check back with us at the holidays." He offered the smile she was coming to think of as gentle and a bit goofy.

In truth, though aspects of his apartment were decidedly elegant and far grander than what she was used to, nothing here was tasteless or overdone, and the rooms that were truly David's—like the library— were perfect.

"So, what's the verdict?" he asked, smile still in place, tone casual.

After a few sarcastic cracks about the formality of the rooms, Nina welcomed the chance to make amends. "It's a wonderful apartment. Really. Sophisticated, but warm. And I'm sure the dining room is exactly what your guests expect—"

"I'm not asking for a critique of the decor." David waved a hand. "Move in and redecorate for all I care. I'm asking whether you're taking the job." He paused, holding eye contact. "I need an assistant soon. You've seen the apartment." He spread his arms. "You've seen me. What's your decision?"

Outstanding bills, the threat of homelessness, fear of failure nipped at Nina's heels, urging her to jump at the job, but she remained as disturbed by the solution as she was by the problem. If she said yes and fell in with his plan, what next? Move in lock, stock and barrel? How would she keep her distance from the boss whose eyes and decency drew her like magnets?

When several bars of upbeat music interrupted the moment, she felt a whoosh of relief. "My cell phone!"

David arched a brow.

"It could be important," she apologized, trying not to exhibit excessive gratitude for the time out as she ran toward her purse. Generally when her cell phone trilled on a weekend, the caller was her grandmother, asking the name of George Clooney's pet pig so she could win a bet with someone at the senior center.

Flipping open the phone, Nina endeavored to answer with more professionalism than her usual, "Hey, Bubby."

For several long moments, all she did was listen. Then she nodded, croaked, "I'll be right there," and snapped the phone shut.

Scooping her purse over her arm and grabbing up her coat, she headed immediately for the door. "I have to go," she muttered, turning at the last minute toward David, who looked as if he'd expected this.

"I really have to go," she said, struggling to stay calm while her chest constricted. "Isaac is in the hospital."

David insisted on driving Nina to the emergency room, and he kept a steadying hand beneath her arm as they walked in, unsure exactly of Isaac's status. The boy had been playing ball at a friend's house when he'd collapsed with an asthma attack. David was not sure who looked more ashen when they were finally by Isaac's bedside—the boy or his mother. Nina enveloped her son in a tight maternal hold, and the preteen didn't seem to mind at all.

"I couldn't get my breath this time," he whispered in his mother's ear while she stroked the back of his head.

Nina's own terror—she'd been silent the entire car ride—was put aside so she could be strong for her son. "I know, baby. I'm here now. You'll be fine. Everything will be fine."

Simple words, but Nina's attendance allowed Isaac to relax. There was magic in her love, in the trust she'd inspired in her children. It soothed. It convinced.

David hung back, but no one questioned his presence, so he stayed to hear the E.R. doctor's opinion that Zach should carry a stronger inhaler from now on. He cautioned against overexertion, an admonition Zach had heard too many times before. David could see Nina's frustration, and he decided to take the steps he'd have taken for his own child. He slipped from the room and made a call.

When Zach and Nina emerged from the E.R., he handed her a piece of paper with a phone number plus the date and time of Zach's appointment with the head of cardiopulmonary at the hospital.

Nina frowned at the paper then turned to her son. "Here's some change for the vending machine, Zachie. You must be starving. Get something decent, like trail mix."

"How about a Baby Ruth? That has peanuts."

"How about trail mix?" she reiterated, and Zach ran off. Nina raised the paper David had given her. "I don't understand. This is a specialist. We weren't referred to a specialist. Where'd you get this?"

"Phil Reed is a friend of mine," David said, trying to keep pride out of his voice, because in truth he felt damned good about being able to help. "We went to school together. Call his office first thing tomorrow, and they'll set up an appointment."

"It's Sunday. Did you call him at home?"

David smiled. "He owes me a favor or two. He didn't mind."

Nina held the paper up as if it were a note from her kids' principal, the kind of thing she didn't want to see. Keeping her voice low, so Zach wouldn't overhear, she said, "We can't see a specialist, because we weren't referred. My insurance won't cover it. Not to mention, I'm not sure how much longer I will even have insurance. There's no way I can afford to take Zach to the head of a pulmonary department. Those guys charge a fortune for saying, *How are you today?*"

Tears David didn't understand sparkled in Nina's blue eyes. He thought she was angry with him until he realized that her anger was directed inward. Shame and frustration tightened her lips and the fist that clutched the now-crumpled note.

"So Zach hasn't seen a specialist in a while?" he ventured, despite her obvious resistance to the conversation. "He doesn't visit one on a regular basis?"

"What planet are you from? The one where there really was health-care reform?"

David scowled. "All right, I get the picture. But fortunately I know Phil…" He stopped himself. Nina's face revealed every emotion: hope, worry, anticipation and ultimately the absolute unwillingness to let him foot the bill. She shook her head.

David felt as frustrated as she looked. "Zach needs this."

"I know!"

"What do you suggest?"

Together they looked toward Zach, who was still trying to decide which button to push on the vending machine.

Nina divided her gaze between her son and David and finally asked, "Does the job come with health benefits?"

"Yes."

"I'll take it."

It was a sunny, windy Saturday morning when Nina and her children moved out of their apartment. Zach had an appointment with Dr. Reed the following Monday morning, and Nina wanted to be settled in their new accomodations by then.

Goodwill had already picked up the larger pieces of furniture Nina didn't need, as David's place was already furnished. Because she drove a compact car, she had rented a small van to haul their TV and the boxes that held all their worldly goods. There wasn't much to shout about.

The kids were indoors, finishing their packing, while Nina lugged boxes to the van. Fearing hernias and unwilling to listen to Bubby complain about having to wear a truss the rest of her life, Nina had banished her grandmother from the proceedings.

Likewise, she'd insisted that Zach fill boxes rather than carry them; she did not want to risk triggering another asthma attack. So, despite the wind and the fact that it was only 11:00 a.m., perspiration made Nina feel soggy and sticky beneath her T-shirt.

Grunting, she hefted the TV onto the van then tried to wriggle it farther into the cargo area. Sweat trickled from beneath her baseball cap.

"I figured."

The displeased tone came from directly behind her. Nina whirled, lost her balance and landed on an elbow on the van floor.

"What are you doing here, and what do you mean, you 'figured'?" Nina demanded as she struggled up. She wiped sweat from her eyes and silently cursed David Hanson for looking like an ad for Lands' End while she resembled a street kid.

Taking her gently but firmly by the shoulders, David pulled her away from the van, climbed aboard and carried the TV all the way to the back. Then, without speaking, he rearranged boxes until they were stacked precisely, so that they fit together like a puzzle, keeping each other in place. When he was satisfied, he jumped down and confronted her on the sidewalk.

"I figured you'd be out here, attempting to move everything by yourself. You are one of the most stubborn women I've ever met." He out-scowled her and demanded, "Where are the high-school boys you said you were going to hire?"

"They wanted eighteen dollars an hour, plus breaks every two hours. You'd think they were unionized. I don't have that much stuff, I can do it myself." She planted both fists on her hips and said, "You told me you'd be working all day." Despite the fact that she and her kids were moving into his condo, Nina had wanted to ease into the new environment without his presence for the first couple of hours.

"You agreed to call if you needed help."

"You agreed to keep quiet and let me do this my way."

"You said your way would be fast and simple."

Nina narrowed her gaze. "Evidently neither one of us can be trusted."

"Evidently." David smiled broadly. "Miss Baxter, I predict that we will make an excellent team. Stay here and guard the TV," he directed. "I'll get the rest of your things."

"No way. This is my show. I'm running it. *You* stay here. I'll get the rest of our stuff."

"You want me to stand here, watching a van while you carry boxes down two flights of stairs?" He crossed his arms high on his chest, rocked back on his heels and slowly shook his head. "Nothing doing. Less than a week ago you suggested I might be gay. My masculinity won't survive another hit."

Observing the belligerent posture, Nina could barely suppress a grin. "You look like Mr. Clean." He refused to budge. "All right." Sighing, she dug into her jeans pocket and pulled out a quarter. "We'll flip to see who guards and who carries."

*Ohmigod, I think I broke something.*

Dropping the box she carried with a loud *thump,* Nina reached around to massage her aching lower back. For the past hour, she'd toted boxes, more than she'd realized they had. Her kids had helped with some of the smaller items, but boxes of books, videos, clothes and toys were heavy, and Nina was seriously reconsidering whether she'd "won" the coin toss.

Wiping her forehead, she glanced at David. Seated on the ground, with one of her kids on either side of him and his legs stretched toward the curb, he laughed heartily at a story Izzy shared. Earlier he'd sent the kids down the block to pick up meatball subs from the Italian deli on the corner. Now the three of them sat with saucy submarine sandwiches on their laps and sodas by their knees, having a picnic. The rats.

She'd ditched her baseball cap when the wind had died down an hour ago, thank goodness, but now she was hot, sweaty and intermittently chilled. All because of a stupid coin toss.

*No, all because you're too dang stubborn to accept help from a man when it's offered.*

Ever since she'd agreed to take David's job, she'd been asserting her independence in other ways, like insisting she could handle the move on her own.

Bubby thought she was nuts, and obviously so did David, but they didn't understand.

Working at Hanson's had given her confidence when her husband had walked out on her. It had given her courage when Zach had been diagnosed with asthma: She could provide for his health care. She could count on herself. Relying on someone else—who might or might not be around for the long haul—was too scary.

Nina swiped moisture from the back of her neck. She was just a sweaty single mother trying to keep her head on straight. Trying to raise two healthy, well-adjusted young people in a world where inconsistency was the rule rather than the exception. She didn't want her children to believe that it was normal for people to walk in and out of each other's lives as easily as they changed shirts. She wanted them to experience stability, not loss. And as far as she could tell, maintaining her independence was the only way to accomplish that.

On the other hand, she'd been pretty independent so far today.

There were only a few boxes left, but she ached from head to toe.

And her stomach growled.

And she wanted a meatball.

Digging into her pocket, she pulled out a quarter and approached the lunch bunch.

"I'd like a rematch," she said to David, flipping the

coin in the air. "I think I've been very unfair, making you sit here, questioning your masculinity and all."

Leisurely he took a bite of his sandwich, chewed, swallowed and said, "No, I feel okay about that now."

She smiled. "Really? Because you look a little…insecure. Let's flip again. Heads I keep moving, tails you take over." She tossed the coin in the air before he could protest. Catching it mid-fly and slapping it on the back of her hand, she said, "Ah, look at that! Tails."

David raised a knee, rested his forearm atop it and eyed her. "And I can trust you on this?"

"Oh, absolutely." She pocketed the quarter.

He nodded toward his paper-wrapped lunch. "There's half of an excellent meatball sandwich here. Can I trust that it will still be there when I return?"

"I hate meatballs."

David stood, brushed off his jeans and gazed down at her. "I heard your stomach growl."

She sighed. "David, if we're going to work together, we're going to have to learn to trust each other, aren't we?"

"You don't need a root-beer float." Nina reached into the corners of the window she had just sprayed with glass cleaner and dug out the dust. "You just had lunch," she reminded David, who had finished packing the van and was now helping her and the kids clean the apartment so she could collect her security deposit.

David removed a long-deceased moth and a very crunchy spider from the inside of the living-room light fixture. Then he borrowed the glass cleaner to spritz the glass dome so it would be sparkling clean when he reattached it to the ceiling.

"Excuse me," he countered as he worked, "but *I* did not have my lunch. *You* had my lunch. And for the record, it's just wrong to lie about disliking meatballs."

"We're almost finished here. If you want, I'll make you meatballs for dinner." She sneezed. "I must be allergic to something in this cleaning fluid."

"Here." David took the paper towels. "You sweep the kitchen. I'll rehang this light and then finish the windows."

"We already swept the kitchen. And mopped. This is all that's left."

"Well, sit on the floor then and supervise."

Because she was exhausted, Nina didn't argue. She plopped onto the carpet, trusted that the kids were cleaning their rooms and watched David climb the step stool and stretch up to hang the light. As he reached, she could see his abdomen beneath his sweater. Nice. Flat and very nice.

He glanced down at her. "So, will you really make me meatballs?"

He sounded surprised, hopeful. As if the notion gave him some deep pleasure. She considered her aching body and, at the moment, equally aching head, and weighed that against his smile. "Yes, Mr. Hanson. I will make you meatballs."

Considering her answer as he screwed in the fixture, he smiled. "To tell the truth, I think I've had my fill of meatballs for the day, and I'm sure the kids have." He hopped down from the step stool. "Let's stop by the market on the way home, anyway, though, for essentials like ice cream. And chocolate sauce. I make a mean soda. It'll knock your socks off, Miss Baxter. We'll call it a housewarming party." He folded the step stool to carry to the van then asked, apparently as an afterthought, "Do you make lasagna?"

Nina had never been as devoted to cooking as Bubby. The domestic goddess gene has skipped her generation.

But she liked the way David said *the kids.*

And he moved boxes.

And he was going to make ice cream sodas.

And every time he was fed, he smiled like a big, happy cat.

"I make such good lasagna," she said, trying—and failing—to ignore the way his brows rose and his smile stretched slowly, pleasurably, across his face. *Aw, hell.* She smiled back. "I make garlic bread, too."

*Chapter Seven*

Within a half hour of moving their belongings into David's condominium, Izzy and Zach were able to make themselves right at home. They loved having their own rooms, exclaimed in joy over the spaciousness of the condo and the electronic amenities. It appeared to Nina that David had picked up a few items, too, since she'd been here last.

The library was now also David's office, while his former office had become a den, complete with a large plasma TV, DVD player, stereo system and PlayStation. A stunning assortment of age-appropriate DVDs and CDs filled a shelving unit. It would have taken most of Nina's salary for the next six months to pay for all those goodies.

There were changes in Nina's suite, too: candles and potpourri and bath salts from an expensive bed-and-bath boutique.

When they'd stopped at the market on the way "home"—a pit stop Nina had unsuccessfully tried to veto—David had made her stay outside with the van while he and the kids had descended on the gourmet market he liked best. They emerged with not merely the makings of a knock-your-socks-off ice-cream soda, but a bulging bag filled with treats from the gourmet deli.

It was 6:00 p.m. by the time all the boxes were stacked neatly in their respective rooms, the van was locked up tight for the night and everyone was ready for dinner. Nina's head was throbbing with more rhythm than a rap album, and she'd have been thrilled to try out the bath salts before pouring her aching body into bed. But there was business to attend to, namely the business of having a chat with two children who were sure they had just walked into paradise.

Before she accompanied Zach and Izzy to the kitchen to prepare their dinner, she sat them down on David's gorgeous leather sofa, where she immediately admonished them never, ever, ever to sit with food, drink or fountain pens. Then she got down to the serious stuff.

Content to have David safely ensconced in his office on a business call, Nina stood before her politely attentive children and began her this-is-how-we-be-have-in-someone-else's-home spiel.

"Most everything in here is designed for adults, not kids," Nina warned, waving a hand to indicate the light carpeting and handblown glass bowls. "If we spill a soda or throw a ball in here—even a Nerf ball—we could wind up paying Mr. Hanson back for the rest of our natural lives. So no eating or playing in these rooms."

"Where do we eat?" Izzy asked.

"The kitchen. *Only* the kitchen."

"What about in the den in front of the TV?" Zach asked. "You're supposed to eat in dens. Teddy's mom says all his dad needs to be happy is a cheese steak, his den and a barking lounger."

"Barcalounger." Nina thought it over a moment. She loved popcorn and a weepy movie. That was how she spent most of her Saturday nights after the kids went to bed. But if she allowed popcorn then she'd have to allow sodas, and she hadn't missed the new chenille-covered love seat in David's former office. "No." She shook her head. "No food in the den. Sorry, buddy."

"We have to remember that I'm here to work. Mr. Hanson will be hosting business dinners. The house has to look good all the time, so we've got to make sure there's a place for everything and everything in its place."

Her children began to look positively horrified, which she decided wasn't an altogether bad thing. She was sure the plasma TV, PlayStation and giant-size bedrooms were planting ideas of permanence in their pre-teenage heads.

Five minutes later, her children's eyes were going glassy and their mouths were turning down at the edges. Nina pressed on with what she hoped were gentle but firm admonishments not to think of this as their home…because it wasn't.

"This is temporary," she stated, lowering her voice a bit. "We're here indefinitely, but only until I can find an appropriate permanent position and our own housing again. So it's important to treat this place the way you would treat, say, Mrs. Watson's house." She named one of Bubby's friends, who had a three-bedroom home in the suburbs and often invited the kids over to play in the yard.

"Mrs. Watson's house smells like mothballs." Izzy wrinkled her nose.

"And she serves broken cookies," Zach added. "Bubby says she buys them for half price at the bakery."

"But we can't tell what kind we're eating!" Izzy shook her head. "We don't like it there."

"All right." Trying to keep her cool, Nina held up a hand to stave off more complaints. "Maybe that wasn't a good example, but whether or not you like it isn't the point. The point is when you're a guest in someone's home, you treat it extra-carefully and with respect."

As if by magic, the mutinous pouts on her children's faces softened. Zach nodded broadly. Izzy looked at him and, taking his cue, nodded broadly also.

Nina used the glimmer of hope and satisfaction she felt to spur her on to a recitation of the house rules.

"If you want to use the telephone here, please ask me first. No friends over on nights when Mr. Hanson is entertaining, so you'll have to check with me first to get the schedule...."

As she continued, Zach and Izzy appeared alert and attentive, shaking or nodding their heads appropriately. They also, however, appeared to find much of what Nina said to be very humorous. Their mouths looked like someone had pulled too hard on drawstrings, a sure sign that they were trying not to laugh. When she saw Zach's gaze travel behind her, she became suspicious and glanced at the mirror above the sofa while she spoke.

David stood behind her, grinning and nodding ridiculously when she told the children what they could do; he frowned deeply and wagged an admonishing finger when she listed a behavior she wanted them to avoid.

"So if it's raining, no shoes on in the house, and *what are you doing?*" Whirling, she caught David mid-wag.

Izzy gasped dramatically and slapped a hand on her mouth. Zach giggled.

David grinned. "That's an awful lot of rules you've got there, Mom."

She blinked. He was criticizing her? He ought to be thanking her! "Pardon me," she said with great dignity and gravity. "I am trying to advise my children on how to behave in someone else's home."

"And I'm trying to make them feel at home. Can we have ice cream sodas now?"

The kids jumped up.

"No!" Nina held out a hand to stay them.

"Why not?"

"You were supposed to say, '*May* we,'" Zach prompted.

"Ohhh." David nodded. "May we have—"

"That is not why! No one is going anywhere until you've been excused."

"May we please be excused now?" Izzy piped up.

Exasperated, Nina flapped a hand at her children. "Yes, fine." She glared at David, who had decided to take Zach's place on the sofa. "What are you doing now?"

"I wasn't excused."

"There are no excuses for you, Mr. Hanson."

"You're right. None whatsoever. I apologize for my, may I say, uncharacteristically juvenile behavior." Then he leaned forward. "I'm having a great time. I realize you're uncomfortable with this situation, so pathetic confession number one—I never had kids of my own, and I was a workaholic when my nephews were young. Being around your kids—who make me laugh, by the way—gives me a chance to live vicariously. Pathetic confession number two." He clasped his hands. Refined, comforting hands. "The thought of filling my very large, very quiet home with the sound of other people works for me right now. Please don't ask your kids to be too quiet here, Nina. This place feels like a morgue sometimes."

Nina felt her resistance to the entire situation drop a notch. Every time she thought she'd shored up her immunity to David, he managed to touch her. Usually by saying something exquisitely simple.

"Is there a three?" she asked.

David cocked his head. "Three?"

"Is there a pathetic confession number three?"

"Ah." He shook his head. "No. Two per day is my limit. I don't like to overindulge." Standing, he smiled with no apparent agenda other than to enjoy the evening. "Except when it comes to ice cream. Time for sodas." He deferred to her with a nod. "All right?"

What could she do but nod in return?

"Good," he said, rubbing his palms together. "Stand back and let a master show you how it's done."

*I think I just have,* Nina thought, knowing already that making the decision to leave here would be more difficult than the decision to move in.

Despite a lingering headache and fatigue that she attributed to the move, Nina spent the following two days organizing the library/office into a functional work space. David suggested she take a couple of days simply to settle in with her kids, but she ignored him. Her children were in electronics heaven, and she needed to focus on work in order to remind herself that their stay here was first, last and in between about business.

It didn't take too long for David to fall into step with her. They worked smoothly together, organizing files and compiling task lists. After the first couple of hours on Sunday, Nina noted a marked change in David's demeanor, however. He started out relaxed and casual, as he had been during the move, but by midday he was the David Hanson she knew from the office—polite, professional and remote.

On Monday she phoned him at the office to tell him about Zach's early-morning appointment with the pulmonary specialist. The visit had offered far more promise than their usual doctor appointments, and both she and Zach had left the office in good spirits. David picked up her call by saying, "Yes, Miss Baxter? What can I do for you?" Nina told herself that the distance, the return to formality—even to a bit of awkwardness between them—was right. It was good.

She worked furiously through Monday afternoon, keeping her mind on business, and by the time she picked her children up from school—a luxury afforded by the job's flexible hours—she was ready to collapse in the wondrously comfortable bed David had given her.

She was on day three of her headache, plus now her body protested every move and her throat was sore. Her children would have been thrilled with drive-through burgers or microwaved frozen dinners featuring a fat and sugar content guaranteed to accelerate the hardening of their arteries. Nina, however, insisted on preparing something fresh and reminiscent of the food pyramid while Zach and Izzy worked on homework at the kitchen counter.

She was sautéing broccoli and red peppers for a pasta sauce and concentrating hard on remaining upright when David arrived home.

He looked tired as he entered the kitchen, leaned against the counter and watched her. He remained like that, not speaking, simply watching her cook, a full minute. Then he straightened, raised a hand carrying a briefcase and pointed at her. "You should not be cooking. You look as if you're about to keel over."

"I'm fine, and good evening to you, too," she snapped, too sick and irritable to admit that he was right. "I'm making pasta. There's plenty if you're hungry."

Nina kept her pounding head lowered and was surprised when the large sauté spoon was plucked from her hand.

"Sit down," David commanded. "You look like

you're about to fall face first into the skillet. You're probably scaring your children."

Nina glanced toward her kids, who should have been studying, but instead were engaged in a discussion about gummy worms. Go figure. Nina smirked at David. "You don't know much about kids. Right now my children's biggest concern is their empty stomachs. Give me back the spoon."

He held it out of her reach. "You look like hell."

Nina's eyes widened, which hurt her head. Apparently their strictly business relationship was on a different footing after five.

Unable to argue the fact that she looked awful, she settled for logic. "You can't stir spaghetti sauce— you're wearing a white shirt." *Nyah, nyah, nyah.*

Reaching into a drawer, David withdrew a large dish towel and tucked it into his collar, letting it drape across his chest. He looked ridiculous. And certain that he'd won the argument. So she let him. Sort of.

At 7:00 p.m., after supervising dinner from a stool at the kitchen counter, Nina crawled into bed with a glass of water and two ibuprofen.

Zach and Izzy were with David, watching *Shrek 2* and laughing uproariously when Shrek passed wind.

Nina had had no idea—none, not a lick, not a clue—that David would be so eager—or that he would enjoy the kids so much. She'd had a very different scenario in mind when she'd finally agreed to move in.

Jerking the covers up on her luscious queen-size bed, she shivered beneath the duvet. She certainly would have stayed up and made sure the kids got into bed okay, but she was so achy she could hardly sit upright and her head was still pounding. David and the kids had urged her to call it a night, promising that bedtimes would be honored and no food would leave the kitchen area. Though David had moaned, "Aw, Mo-om," when she'd insisted on delivering the no-snacks-in-the-TV-room reminder.

Groaning a little from the effort, Nina reached up to turn off the bedside lamp. Apparently she was the only person in the house at present time who did not find this situation comfortable.

No, that wasn't true. It *was* comfortable. It was too comfortable. It was—

Tension filled her chest as she tried to block the word that came to mind.

*Don't think it. Don't think it.*

Perfect.

*Arrrrghhhh!!!* Nina grabbed a goose-down pillow, held it over her head and growled into it. David Hanson was a low-down, dirty double-crosser! The man was supposed to be a stiff-backed executive. He was supposed to socialize with models and socialites and other stiff-backed executives in swanky clubs and five-star restaurants. He was *not* supposed to enjoy whipping up ice-cream sodas or to laugh out loud at flatulent green ogres. If he was going to be so damned agreeable and easygoing, such a…such a…*family man,* then he ought to get his own family and leave single mothers with fantasy issues in peace.

Nina blew a long stream of air into the pillow. He was confusing her. She was getting all mixed up. There had been a moment in his kitchen that first night when he'd very carefully measured chocolate syrup into four glasses then just as carefully added soda. He'd kept lifting the glasses up, eyeballing them to make sure he had the perfect amounts of everything before he'd added his secret ingredient—a little shot of pure vanilla—and the tip of his tongue had rested on his lower lip as he'd concentrated. Nina had watched him, and in one unguarded second she'd thought to herself, *What a wonderful dad.*

She groaned again.

*What a wonderful dad.* That had to be the most dangerous thought a single mother could have about an unmarried man.

In the next second, in that kitchen, she'd wanted to kiss David Hanson. Right on the mouth. And then before she'd been able to preempt it, she'd had a vision of them all on a beach—her, Izzy, Zach and David—with Zach and Izzy racing ahead and her throwing her arms around David's neck while he picked her up and whirled her round and round on the sand. In the vision, everyone was laughing. Everyone was happy. Everyone was going to be together forever.

*Help!* She shook her head. Maybe she was feverish. She felt feverish.

"I've got to stop this train before there's a wreck," she said, her voice muffled by a three-hundred thread-count pillowcase. If she didn't slam the brakes on now, her next fantasy would feature Bubby baking the wedding cake.

She hadn't known she could still harbor such daydreams.

Feeling hotter and more claustrophobic by the second, she tossed the pillow aside and pushed her aching body to a sitting position. She didn't have her own apartment anymore; she couldn't leave now. But she could remind herself exactly why her life plan included her taking care of her family by herself and *excluded* inviting a man into the picture.

Sitting on the bed with the soft light of the bedside lamp creating a private ambience, Nina forced herself to go to the one feeling that could always remind her why she'd decided not to risk loving anyone new.

First she pictured faces, the perpetually smiling faces of her mother and father. Only in their thirties, in love with each other and their bright teenage daughter, they'd had every reason to smile. When Nina was fourteen, they'd gone on a second honeymoon. To welcome them home, Nina and Bubby had prepared a dinner that was the same meal they'd served at their wedding.

Sitting on the bed in David's house, Nina closed her eyes and remembered the anticipation, the excitement as she looked forward to their surprise and to sitting down with her mother to listen to the details of the trip.

"Marry a man whose hand you want to hold all your life," her mother would tell her as she always had when talking about the man she loved.

Nina had waited in the living room with Bubby, watching the clock. And watching. And watching. They hadn't been worried at first when her parents had been late. So many things could happen to delay an arrival from the airport. It had taken an hour and a half for Bubby to grow concerned enough to call the airline.

*Remember. Remember,* Nina commanded herself as she slipped back into the heart of the girl who in an instant had lost the safety and joy she had known. Still, though losing her parents in a plane crash had been devastating, that wasn't what had convinced her to stop inviting people into her life.

From fourteen to twenty-two, she had kept her heart open. Sometimes she'd thought it was her dreams that had saved her: the dreams of creating an intact family again, of recapturing the incomparable warmth of two parents and kids and wanting to hold someone's hand all your life.

She'd been so ready to be married at eighteen. Ready to have two babies at an age when most young women were still in college.

She had not been prepared to raise her children on her own. The end of the dream had felt like the loss of her parents all over again. In some ways it had been worse. For a long while she had found herself more lost, more depressed than before.

It was the depression that had truly frightened her. With two babies and a full-time job, she couldn't afford not to get out of bed in the morning. Thank heavens she'd used her insurance and her lunch hour to get counseling. A sage therapist had taught her that she'd never completely grieved for her parents. That she'd used her dreams to keep them alive and to avoid the deep-down fear that she was somehow destined to be alone.

So Nina had worked on grieving. When she hadn't been at work and when the kids had been in bed, she'd grieved. Slowly, she'd begun to feel better—lighter, more able to stand on her own and to jump into her life feet first.

It had taken only one additional failed romance to convince her absolutely that she would never put her kids through unnecessary pain and loss. Zach and Izzy and she, too, were happy as they were. Why mess with success? Why hand your contentment over to somebody else for safekeeping?

Nina rubbed her face. She was bone-tired. Really beat. But she was cognizant enough to know that the odds against a forty-four-year-old, never-married executive becoming a devoted family man—to a ready-made family, no less—were pretty steep. David was merely trying it on for size, the way he'd try on a new suit by the latest designer.

Well, if he wanted to experiment, fine and dandy. But by damn he could do it with someone else's kids, someone else's life.

Reaching for her pillow, she punched it several times then stuffed it once more behind her head and sighed as she leaned back. Their location may have changed, but she was still in charge. Come tomorrow, she'd show David Hanson who was the boss.

## Chapter Eight

*I'm dying.*

Nina strained her neck to raise her aching head and peer at the clock. It read 7:15 a.m. Tuesday, if she recalled correctly.

"Nnnnnghhhhhmmmmph." Letting her head fall back against the pillow, she scanned her body for any part that *didn't* hurt.

*Right pinkie,* she thought. *Concentrate on your right pinkie.* The old focusing trick usually worked to help her overcome any physical discomfort enough to get moving, but not today. Today the mere thought of being upright made her want to weep.

She had the flu, no doubt about it. Her head was

pounding, she felt cold and hot at the same time, she was queasy; even her eyeballs and her teeth ached.

She seriously considered lying in bed indefinitely, but her children's voices roused her attention. She heard Zach laughing, and Izzy saying, "More! More!"

They sounded too far away to be in one of the bedrooms. When Nina imagined them preparing their own breakfasts in David's pristine kitchen, she heaved herself out of bed and pictured every cell in her body holding a protest sign.

Moving with care, she pulled a robe on over her T-shirt and pajama bottoms then tucked her feet into clogs. She clumped heavily to the bathroom, where she brushed her teeth and scraped her curls into an exploding ponytail. Apologizing to her reflection, she promised herself an open account at Victoria's Secret in her next life.

She hauled herself to the kitchen, expecting to see her children alone, pouring more cereal than any two people could consume in one sitting. Instead, she found both her kids teaching David how to make a tablespoon stick to his nose.

"Rub harder," Zach instructed. "You've gotta make the spoon feel hot."

"Okay, now!" Izzy crowed. "See if it'll stick now!"

Obedient to her children's commands, David let the bowl of a shiny tablespoon rest on his nose, where it held a few moments before it dropped. Laughter filled the kitchen.

"I think that's the first time I ever had a spoon on my nose." David grinned.

"Have you ever put straws up it?" Izzy asked quite seriously.

"Why would I do that?"

"You do it to look like a walrus." She shrugged. "Little kids like it."

"Hmm. I don't think I have any straws."

"Lucky you." When Nina spoke, the words emerged like a strange croak. The threesome in the kitchen turned to look at her.

"Did we wake you up?" David asked, an apologetic expression on his perfectly shaved, perfectly handsome face.

Nina tugged on the belt of her robe, acutely aware that she was the only person present who was not dressed and ready for the day. Not a good way to impress the boss.

*Though a mighty fine reason why you shouldn't live with him in the first place.*

"I'm usually up every morning by six," Nina said. "I don't know why my alarm didn't go off."

"David said we should let you rest, so me and Zach sneaked in and turned it off!" Izzy beamed, proud of herself and her brother.

David held up his hands when Nina glanced at him. "The alarm wasn't my idea. Although I think it was a good one. You looked a little done in yesterday."

*Well, that was good to know.*

"Are you all right this morning?" he asked, his doubtful expression telegraphing clearly the fact that she didn't look any better today.

"I may be coming down with something," Nina admitted reluctantly. "But I'll be fine in a couple of hours. I'll take some zinc." Self-consciously she glanced at her outfit. "I would have dressed, but I wanted to get the kids' breakfast."

On her last word, the toaster popped up.

"Got that covered." David grabbed two plates. "Toaster waffles." He raised a brow. "Is that okay?"

In response, she sneezed. Messily.

"Oooh, gross, Mommy!" Izzy covered her eyes.

Quickly, Nina grabbed a napkin from a Lucite holder on the counter.

"Cool." Zach grinned. "We studied mucus in science class. When you have a cold, the human body can produce a cup of mucus." He looked at David. "How much do you think she sneezed out?"

With a hand at the back of Zach's head, David guided the young scientist to a stool at the breakfast bar. "I think we have more to look forward to."

Zach was in high spirits since his visit with the pulmonary specialist. The doctor took a variety of approaches to asthma, and he was confident that Zach would be able to manage his condition without increased steroids. He'd even told the boy that one of his asthma patients was now a pro baseball player. Zach had excitedly told David the news last night, and David had promised Zach a trip to Wrigley Field, an offer that catapulted him to hero status.

Nina blew her nose and eyed her children's new best friend over the Kleenex.

Meeting her eyes, David asked, "Are you hungry?"

She surveyed the granite counter, set with butter and syrup for the waffles, orange juice and milk. Her sore throat protested at the thought of a single swallow. "Are you eating?" she said, wishing for a throat lozenge.

"I'm an oatmeal man in the morning." He shook his head woefully. "Ever since I turned forty, health has taken precedence over taste. You're lucky." He looked at her with a smile, as if her present appearance were perfectly normal and perfectly attractive. "You don't have to worry about age yet."

"You're *forty years old?*" Izzy exclaimed, blatantly disturbed by the news. "That's almost as old as our principal."

"No it's not!" Zach piped up, rolling his eyes at his sister. "Mr. Kenner's hair is white already. He's probably fifty."

"Well, I hate to break it to you both," David confessed, "but I'm forty-four."

Izzy looked at David as if she were profoundly depressed. "Then you'll probably never get married. Bubby says if a man isn't married by the time he's thirty-five he's either a miser or a schmuck."

"Isabella!" Nina gave her daughter the "angry eyeball," as her children liked to call her best parental glare. The next time she saw her grandmother, Bubby was going to get a dose of the angry eyeball, too.

"Don't worry, David, plenty of old guys get married." Zach spoke with the confidence of a true authority on the subject. "They even have babies. It's old women who don't get married."

"Zach!" For the first time in memory, Nina wanted to stuff a sock in her son's mouth. She sneezed again, blew her nose and apologized to David. "Obviously my children have been watching too much MTV. They're having trouble recognizing that anyone over twenty-five is still breathing, much less capable of having a social life."

Zach looked sheepish. "Sorry, Mom." He lowered his head to his orange juice. "I didn't mean you, exactly."

Izzy spoke while painstakingly pouring syrup into each indentation of her waffle. "You're not old, Mom. You're just stressed because you're single. But you could still get married." When her waffle was filled to capacity, she looked up with a smile meant to be encouraging. "You might even still be able to have babies. But you'll probably need fertilizer treatments, and you could wind up with twins like Rachel Abrams's mom, and then you'll think you ought to have your head examined."

"Oh, my God," Nina said, blushing furiously.

David turned around, rested both palms on the

granite countertop, hung his head and laughed so hard his shoulders shook.

Izzy grumbled, "What's so funny?" Zach shrugged, and they both started eating, avoiding their mother's gaze.

"Go ahead and enjoy yourself, Methuselah." Nina croaked to David above his laughter. "You won't think it's so funny if Viagra is taken off the market."

He sobered immediately. "Have you heard Viagra's being taken off the market? Are there rumors on the Internet?" When Nina laughed, he grinned. "I'll make a deal with you, Nina. I'll keep my ear to the ground for a good deal on fertilizer, and you inform me of any Viagra sales that come to your attention."

Nina nodded. "Deal. I suppose those of us who have a foot in the grave ought to stick together."

His grin eased to a relaxed smile. "My thoughts exactly. So, how about it, Mrs. Dorian Gray? Want to gum some oatmeal with me?"

Nina looked at her children, who listened avidly to the conversation while they ate. "I want to take a shower," she said, "and a couple of aspirin before I eat anything. And I need to drive the kids to school."

"Got that covered, too," David said. "I'll drive them."

"What?" A caring, responsible man who was not her husband, father or brother was offering to take her children to school…after making them breakfast so she could sleep in? The data entered Nina's brain, but wouldn't immediately compute. "No, I couldn't possibly… I mean, thank you, but—"

"Please, Mom?" Zach leaned so far over his plate, his shirt touched his waffle. "David's car is sweet! No one's *ever* come to school in a Mustang!"

"Mr. Hanson's car is not the issue. Get your shirt out of the syrup." She turned to David. "You have to go to work."

"I'll drop them off on my way to the office."

"Their school isn't on your way."

David sighed. "This is going to be one of those annoying conversations that we have. Isn't it?"

She wasn't sure how to respond to that.

"You may as well give in now, Nina. I'm definitely driving them. You're definitely staying home. They'll get to school safe and on time. Scout's honor."

"I don't know—"

"Mo-o-om!" Izzy joined Zach's plea.

David arched a brow and Nina sniffed. "I suppose I could use the extra time to compile a list of caterers. I want to call and get price lists—"

"Give it a rest, Miss Baxter. Literally."

"I'm not that sick. I'd rather get right to work. I—" Closing her eyes, she sneezed into her paper napkin. Loudly. Messily.

"Ooooh, gross!" This time David made the comment, and Zach and Izzy laughed around mouthfuls of waffle.

"Fine, go," Nina said after blowing her nose again. "I'll be able to sneeze in peace."

Zach and Izzy immediately began arguing over who got to sit in the Mustang's front seat.

"Have fun," she said, grabbing several more napkins off the counter and giving her children a little wave. "Come to my room before you go, and I'll give you lunch money. Zach, make sure you take your inhaler."

"Maybe he should leave it for you," David cracked. "You really do sound sick. I'll check back with you."

"No, no," she insisted, shuffling toward her room. "I'm fine. I'm going to take a shower. You three have fun— *Ahhh-chew!*"

Nina got into the tub after she left David and the kids. She decided that a hot soak would ease her sore muscles and wake her up, but an hour later she awoke in a cold tub with muscles that ached more than ever and pounding temples that required additional pain-killers. When she emerged from the bath, even her toes hurt, so she donned her soft chenille robe and swallowed two more ibuprofen.

While she'd been soaking, David had phoned and left a message, asking how she was. Nina had called back, but he'd been in a meeting, so she'd asked his secretary to tell him that she felt much better and thanks for everything. Then she'd crawled into bed for a few minutes…just a few…to finish the nap she'd started in the bath.

That's where David found her several hours later, after clearing his afternoon and leaving her another message to say he intended to pick the kids up from school and take them to the zoo for a couple of hours so she could continue to rest. Just to get a rise out of her, he added that he hoped she really was resting, but that given her obstinate nature, he figured there was a fifty-fifty chance she was out tarring the roof.

At the zoo, outgoing Izzy had waved her hand madly when a performer at the live animal show had requested parent-and-child volunteers. "We can pretend," she'd whispered to David when they'd been chosen. Close together onstage, they had held out their arms so a trained owl could land on them. Izzy had squealed, and David had used his free arm to hold her steady. The owl had cocked its head and blinked, and the audience had cheered. The staff performer had said that David and Izzy made a great team, which had made Izzy smile so widely, David was sure the entire audience had been able to see her molars.

The funny thing was, something inside him felt like it was beaming just as broadly. He'd spent most of his adult life keeping his distance from people, either by design or by circumstance. He'd had some initial concern that Zack and Izzy might become bored with his company. What did he know about entertaining kids, after all? He'd hardly ever been one. But they'd liked having him around, and he liked knowing that.

It had been the most satisfying couple of hours he'd spent in years.

On the way home, he'd found himself mentally planning a trip to the children's museum until he'd pulled on the reins and told himself to slow down. Way down. He needed time to digest the unfamiliar feelings before he waded farther into this particular pool. Yes, he'd invited—all right, pressured—Nina to move herself and her children into his home, but how far they moved into his life was still up to him.

So when he returned to the apartment, he intended to tell Nina they'd had a good time at the zoo. That's it. Just a simple, "Yes, we had a good time," and leave it at that. But the kids ran directly to their mother's room and returned to report that she was sleeping again.

"She sounds like she's got asthma, like me," Zach said. He and Izzy stared at David as if they expected him to take some action.

"Maybe we should call Bubby," Izzy prompted.

"I think we should go in and look at her again," Zach said.

"I think your mother has a cold or maybe the flu and that she needs her rest. You're probably not used to seeing her rest much, are you?"

"I want to go look at her again." Izzy started toward the bedroom.

David tugged the hood of her sweatshirt to keep her in the living room. "I'm not sure that's a good idea."

He guessed the girl was going to awaken her mother in order to reassure herself. In all likelihood this was the first time Nina had gotten time off from her life.

"But Zach says she's breathing funny."

While two pairs of wide, worried eyes applied as much pressure as a boardroom full of investors, David tried to balance reason with caution.

Izzy was used to seeing her brother struggle for air; she knew the result was sometimes serious. It was natural for her to feel more fear than the situation warranted.

David asked himself what he would do right now, what his immediate response would be if Nina Baxter were his personal concern, not only his personal assistant.

*I'd watch over her and make sure she knew she could rest without worrying—about the kids, about health insurance, about anything.*

…And while she lay in bed, trying to sleep off her cold, he would stroke her forehead, her cheeks, the bridge of her nose. He would brush back her hair and when she felt well enough, he'd wash it for her in the kitchen sink….

He swiped a hand down his face. *Get a grip, man.*

"All right, I'll go look at her," he said, feeling and sounding gruff. Zach and Izzy immediately nodded. "I'm not going to wake her up, though," he cautioned. "I'll listen to her breathing, and if she needs a doctor, we'll call one. All right?"

Solemnly, the children nodded again.

"Good. You two get started on your homework. I'll check on your mom, and then we'll figure out something for dinner."

As he headed down the hall, he thought he sounded like a man who had everything under control. That was good PR.

When he reached Nina's bedroom, he pushed on the slightly open door and edged into the room. With the curtains closed, the bedroom was cool and dim. A slice of light from the hallway provided the majority of illumination. Moving gingerly toward the bed, he could see Nina asleep on her back, several scrunched tissues around her head and clutched in her hands.

She was snoring—due, he hoped, to congestion. Her mouth was open; a little rivulet of drool shone in the light. Her masses of curly blond hair were spread across the pillow, reminding him less of a romantic silk waterfall and more of lots and lots of unraveled yarn. Soft yarn.

While he watched her, she appeared to have an attack of sleep apnea. Her head jerked and a loud snort escaped. David jumped back when she started to awaken. Thankfully, she dropped against the pillow again...with several more snorts. She licked her lips, brushed at the drool with the back of her hand then groaned, turned away from him and settled once again into a nice snore.

David felt his frowning brow relax. An odd tightness in his chest eased, and he began to laugh. Silently, but so hard he knew he had to get out of the room quickly.

Creeping out and down the hall the same way he'd crept in, he slipped into his library, closed the door, sat at his desk and let the laughter come until he actually felt tears at the corners of his eyes.

He'd been all over the world, had dated women who shared his background and his lifestyle. Women, who, it had seemed, managed never to have an unattractive moment. Women whose unencumbered lives had allowed him to come and go as he'd pleased.

With all her personal commitments, the baggage Nina would bring to a relationship could fill a moving van. In only a few weeks of knowing her on more than a superficial level, he'd discovered that she was stubborn, always put her family first, had spent more time in senior centers than nightclubs and sneezed louder than any of the men in his college fraternity.

David wiped his eyes and sighed. For a second there in the bedroom, he'd seen his life as it would look with Nina rather than with the type of women he usually dated.

Yes, he'd gotten a good laugh out of that. But what had really struck his funny bone was the realization that in forty-four years, he'd never once thought of wiping someone else's runny nose or of kissing them while they drooled.

Until now.

# Chapter Nine

"I'b weady to wook, I tell you."

"No, you're not."

Nina heard paper shuffling on the other end of the phone she held to her ear with one hand while she jammed Kleenex to her nose with the other.

She had only vague memories of last night. Mostly she remembered being so fatigued that she'd awakened only enough to open her eyes, utter a token protest when David had fed her canned soup and NyQuil, and then close her eyes again and pretend to be asleep already while he'd cupped a palm over her brow to check for fever.

Oh, that palm. Cool and large and immensely

comforting. Drifting in and out of a restless sleep, Nina had sensed someone beside her for what had seemed like a long, long time. It could have been delirium, but her impression was that David had stayed with her for a couple of hours.

Then today she'd dragged her protesting body out of bed at seven to make the kids' lunches and to drive them to school, only to find that David had helped them make their own lunches the night before and had gotten them up early so they could eat breakfast out before, once again, *he* dropped them off at school. They'd all signed a card to her, wishing her a nice, quiet day of rest.

For the first time in years, Nina had felt no need to be in control. She had been the cared for, not the caretaker.

Any single mother with half a brain—make that one tenth of a brain—would have spent the entire day moving from the bed to the jetted tub and back again. She'd have allowed herself a few delicious fantasies about the boss and would have phoned her girlfriends—from the tub—to say, "You are not going to believe the situation I've landed in."

So what had Nina done? She'd read the note, sneezed five times in a row and cried into her tissue because she felt obsolete. Obsolete! It was ridiculous, but she was used to taking care of everything herself, of being the only adult in the family. She was used to feeling, basically, alone. Being taken care of had felt so odd and so good that this morning she was completely off balance and scared. She wanted to find normal again.

So she'd given David time to get to the office and then she'd phoned him to say she wanted to get to work.

David's mellow voice countered that notion. "You'll be of more help if you take the next few days to recuperate. There'll be plenty to do after that."

Nina tried to rise above her congestion. "I peel pine *now*. I cabe hewe to wook and dat's what I'b going to do!"

"To someone, somewhere I'm sure that makes sense." A smile lurked in David's wry voice. After he shuffled more papers, he said, "My housekeeper's name is Johanna. She'll be there at ten. If you need anything, ask her. In the meantime— Wait a sec." He covered the mouthpiece, spoke to someone then returned to Nina. "I've got to take a call from Japan. Relax and concentrate your energy on recuperating, Miss Baxter, not on becoming Secretary of the Year. In good time I expect you to rise like a phoenix and give new meaning to the word *vibrant*."

Nina could say nothing for a moment, then in a small voice she halfheartedly complained, "Dobody talks like dat."

"Rex Harrison did."

"Sixty years ago."

David chuckled. "I'll call you later."

The line went dead, but the phone in Nina's hand felt alive. *Vibrant?* Was that how he saw her?

*Stop.*

She set the phone in its cradle and blew her nose. Standing in the kitchen, she checked her reflection in the glass door of the double oven. She felt weepy and lost and tragic, not vibrant. At least she'd dressed as if she were going to work today—sky-blue blouse, navy skirt and pumps. Her hair was more or less tamed into a bun. In other words, all suited up to sit on the bench.

She wasn't used to staying home with nothing to do and too much to think about. In all her years at Hanson's she'd only used, max, a dozen sick days, and those had been for her kids, not her.

Nina started a coughing jag that had her rummaging through her pockets for the menthol lozenges she'd stashed there. Popping one into her mouth, she pushed it around with her tongue and made a plan.

First, she needed some cold medicine to de-fuzz her brain and decongest her nose. Then she'd call Judy Denton, David's administrative assistant at the office, and ask her what kind of errands, etc., David usually required. And, given the extra work created by layoffs, an offer of help with word processing would surely come as a welcome surprise.

Buoyed by the prospect of an active day to keep her mind busy, she crunched the throat lozenge to get it out of the way, picked up the phone and dialed

Hanson Media again. She'd show David Hanson who needed taking care of around here.

By 10:00 a.m., Nina had returned from the drugstore and taken a decongestant so she wouldn't sound like Elmer Fudd the rest of the day. Judy Denton had proved intractable when it came to sharing her boss's itinerary with anyone, including his new—and still nasal—personal assistant. Her advice to Nina? "It sounds as if you should rest, dear. I'm sure Mr. Hanson will give you directives soon."

Nina wasn't sure about directives, but she had an expletive or two she wanted to try out. She was standing at the door to his home office, chewing on a fingernail and seriously considering the merits of snooping for something to do, when she heard a key in the front door lock.

Jumping at the sound, she trotted to the foyer as a fifty-something woman in a trench coat entered the condominium.

Ice blue eyes raked Nina with out-and-out unfriendliness before a crisp voice with a decidedly British snap said, "I always let myself in. Are you all right with that?" The tone suggested that if Nina happened not to be all right with that, David would soon be looking for a new housekeeper.

"Fine," Nina said. "That's fine." She'd already forgotten about Johanna, the woman who came weekly to clean David's former bachelor-only abode.

Johanna was a tall, handsome woman with skin like ivory linen, gray hair cut close to her head and strong features. Her greeting suggested that she wasn't surprised to see Nina in the apartment. Her expression suggested she wasn't happy about it.

Nina thrust out her hand, realized she was still holding a crumpled, germ-ridden tissue and pulled back. "Hello, I'm Nina," she said, foregoing the handshake, "Dav— Mr. Hanson's personal assistant. I'll be living here with my children."

A thin brow arched to telling heights while Johanna's voice dropped to a telling low. "I heard."

She stomped a few steps past Nina then turned with obvious reluctance. "I suppose now's as good a time as any to get things straight. I clean for Mr. Hanson. Sometimes I cook. *For...Mr....Hanson.* If he's got leftovers it's his business what he does with them. I don't take requests, so don't leave me any notes telling me your children like pasta and cheese."

Nina thought the most politic response would be a simple *okay*, but her throat chose that moment to tickle her violently, so she wound up nodding spasmodically while coughing.

Florence Nightingale she wasn't, but evidently even the unyielding Johanna felt some compassion for the ill. "Nasty cough," she said, shaking her head. "I'll fix that." Before she marched to the kitchen she issued a clear order. "You stay here. I don't want you spreading germs in my kitchen. I'll bring it when it's done."

Nina did not dare ask, of course, what "it" was. She considered herself fortunate that Johanna was willing to let her stay in the house.

"*Oy vey,*" she sighed when the coughing jag was spent. Her boss refused to tell her what to do, and the housekeeper couldn't wait.

Maybe she should have spent the day in bed when she'd had the cha—

The doorbell jolted her away from the wall. She hurried to the door. Surprise flared when Bubby pushed past her into the foyer.

"My granddaughter is dying, and she doesn't even call me." Weighed down by two paper-handled grocery bags, Bubby swept her head broadly from side to side. "That's what I get for minding my own business—silence. Secrets! *Oy,* what can I do?"

"Bubby." Nina knew better than to relieve Bubby of her burdens; she wasn't finished carrying them yet. Shutting the door, she trailed her grandmother into the living room. "I wasn't expecting you."

"Some news flash, Barbara Walters. You didn't give me the address, so why would you expect me?" Bubby stood with her back to Nina while she studied the unfamiliar living room. "Fancy," she proclaimed. Setting the paper bags on the floor with a thump, she turned to eagle-eye Nina. "A couple of days I figured I'd give you to settle in. I don't like to butt in."

"You know I never think you're butting in—"

"Imagine my surprise when I get a call first thing

this morning from David Hanson, who tells me, 'Good morning. Your granddaughter is on her deathbed.'"

"I am not on my deathbed! He didn't say that." Then Nina realized the really important part of Bubby's statement. "He called you?"

"Why not? I've got a phone." Bubby arched a sparse gray brow. "Have *you* got a phone?"

Point made. "I'm sorry. Everything was so hectic here. I thought I'd settle in first and then I'd call—"

Bubby raised her hands. "I don't want anyone to feel bad. You know that crazy Sylvia Cohen? *She* loves to make people feel guilty. Me, I'd rather mind my own business. Who's in the kitchen?"

Nina heard dishware clanking. "That's Johanna," she said sotto voce. "David's housekeeper."

"She's cooking?" The microwave beeped several times. "What is that? What's that smell?" The wrinkle of Bubby's nose suggested she found the aroma only marginally better than something that had been dead for a long time. Nina sniffed the air. It did smell a bit like boiled roadkill.

"Don't say anything," Nina whispered. "She's making something for my cough." Although Nina hoped to heaven that the thing she smelled was not it.

When Bubby heard that someone else was preparing cold remedies for *her* granddaughter, nothing short of a police barricade would have kept her out of the kitchen. Nina knew she'd said the wrong thing when her diminutive grandmother picked up her shopping bags and marched toward battle like General Patton.

Bubby was tough, but Johanna was bigger and knew where the kitchen knives were stored. "Bubby, wait!" She started after her grandmother, but the doorbell rang. "Company!" she singsonged, trying to motion Bubby back. "Company!"

Bubby kept marching. Torn, Nina raced first to the door, flinging it open to a young man who carried a box filled with, from what Nina could tell, plastic containers of food.

"Hi," he said, "I'm from Ciao Chow's. I have a home delivery for Mr. Hanson."

"Oh!" Ciao Chow's was a popular gourmet food mart featuring a deli that offered the best pasta take-out in town.

Bemused, Nina wondered whether to take the box, referee the meeting in the kitchen or run for her purse to get money for a tip. Before she could debate the merits of each option, the hall elevator opened to emit a tall, willow-thin redhead in a dress as brightly pink as a begonia.

Samantha Edwards strode to the door with her customary intrepid stride. She smiled at the delivery boy, glanced in the box he carried and said, "Pasta! Yum!" Grinning at Nina, she held up a paper bag bearing the name of a local health-food store. "David told Jack you were sick. I brought herbs. We'll have you cured in no time!"

## Chapter Ten

Apparently David thought Nina might need company.

So, he'd called Bubby, then he'd asked Jack if Samantha would mind paying Nina a visit, maybe bringing a few of the health supplements she poured down Jack. Then he'd called Ciao Chow's and told them to deliver so Nina wouldn't have to worry about food for the day.

She had to grin when Samantha explained the situation. David had sent her a Jewish grandmother *and* lunch? Boy, did he have a lot to learn. Still, she was…

Touched. Grateful. Very.

Now Bubby and Johanna were both in the kitchen,

striking an uneasy truce, or perhaps playing out their own version of *Iron Chef* as each prepared the one and only true cold remedy.

Samantha had seated herself on the living room couch and was pawing through her bag of supplements and homeopathic remedies.

"I was so surprised when David said he'd hired you and that you were living with him. You've been here—what, a few days now?" Her earrings—a row of flowers and leaves dangling from a long gold vine—swayed as she shook her head. "He's so solitary. You know this is the first time I've been to his place?"

Nina shook her head. She hadn't been acquainted with Samantha long before the layoffs and knew little about the other woman save for the fact that she was dynamic, creative, a strong businesswoman and in love with David's nephew, current CEO Jack Hanson. Samantha and Jack couldn't be more different, but their relationship appeared to work.

"The Hansons never seemed particularly…close," Nina said, treading onto territory she would have avoided had she still been working at the office. "It was nice to see Jack step in and work with David after George died. And they seem to get along."

"Jack respects David," Samantha agreed, examining a bottle of zinc-and-elderberry lozenges. "Although you're right. The Hansons aren't as tight as other families. I know Jack is working harder than he should have to in order to persuade his brothers to come home for the reading of George's will."

Unscrewing the lid on the zinc tabs, Samantha shook two lavender-colored lozenges into Nina's hand. "Let them dissolve in your mouth, one right after the other. Fact is," she said, recapping the bottle, "Jack would love to pass some of the responsibility for Hanson Media over to Andrew—he's the younger Hanson bro. Have you met him?"

Nina frowned, but in thirteen years with the company, she couldn't recall meeting Andrew. George hadn't been the kind of father who brought his sons to work with him. She shook her head.

"Well, Jack can barely get Andrew to return a phone call these days. He's pretty ticked. I think David's going to lay down the law about the reading of the will. Demand that all the boys haul their handsome Hanson tushies home."

Nina smiled. She liked the way Samantha talked. Popping a lozenge in her mouth, she quivered at the first tart taste then spoke around it. "Do all the Hansons have 'handsome tushies'?"

Samantha's smile turned mischievous. "I can certainly vouch for Jack's." She tilted her head. "David's too, come to think of it."

Nina's eyes bugged wide, and Samantha winked. "Fully clothed, fully clothed." She wagged a finger. "Shame on you. Although I must say if I were living with him I'd make sure to take at least a little peek."

Nina almost swallowed the lozenge whole. She started coughing and felt her face flame at the same time. Samantha reached over to wallop her on the back. For a reed-slender woman, she had quite a punch.

"Are you all right?" The outspoken executive appeared a bit worried for the first time today.

Nina pressed one hand to the base of her throat and used the other to wave away Samantha's concern. "Fine," she rasped. She pointed to her neck. "Piece of the lozenge…went down the wrong way."

"Ah." Samantha shrugged. She allowed thirty seconds of silence then said, "I can be a little too plainspoken, or so I've been told. At the risk of not being able to walk out of here because I have both feet in my mouth, let me state for the record that when David told us he'd hired you to be his personal assistant and that you were living with him, Jack and I thought maybe you two had a *thing* going."

Nina opened her mouth immediately to refute that notion, but she started coughing again. Samantha hastened to add, "David set everyone straight. He said the setup between you two is strictly business."

Nina's mouth went so dry, the lozenge felt like it was super-glued to her tongue. "Yeth," she lisped around it, "thtrickly bithneth. Thtrickly." She tried to work a little moisture back into her mouth. "What do you mean 'everyone'?"

Samantha looked uncomfortable. "Oh, no. I meant *a few people*…in the boardroom. Shiguro Taka is coming to town—are you familiar with Taka Enterprises?—and David's going to do a little entertaining, so he mentioned at the meeting this morning that he'd hired you to help out with that." She handed Nina a bottle of chewable Cs. "And about how helpful it'll be to have you and your kids living in the condo, too, because Shiguro's wife and children will be coming with him. That's all."

Samantha futzed with the homeopathic remedy in her hands, twisting the cap to see how many pellets emerged at once. "There were only three…maybe four…I think six of us, not counting me and Jack, who heard him say it. It's no biggie."

"Eight people? He announced to eight people that I'm living with him? Oh, my God! Does the entire office think David and I are having an affair?"

"No, no!" Samantha shook her head vehemently. "Not anymore." She gave Nina's knee a reassuring pat. "I told you. David set the record straight."

She handed Nina the homeopathic remedy. "Follow the directions on this. But wait thirty minutes after the lozenge has dissolved before you take it." Rising, Samantha glanced toward the kitchen. "Something's starting to smell good. I'm sorry I have to go."

Nina rose, too, and the two women walked to the door. "I'd love to get together sometime when you're well and settled in here," Samantha added graciously before she left. "I've been trying my hand at cooking. Nothing fancy." She frowned. "The lasagna I made the other night was a little…crisp. Maybe I'll try a quiche, and we can brainstorm a few creative parties to woo the press. Hanson's could use a little lighthearted PR."

Nina agreed, thanked Samantha for the cold remedies and shut the door. Her head was beginning to feel fuzzy and overly full again, but she wasn't sure that was due to her cold.

Plopping on the couch, Nina realized she still had a zinc tablet in her hand. She set it on the coffee table and curled up on her side.

Holy moly, she was shaking, and something told her she didn't have the chills.

The conversation with Samantha replayed in her head.

What had shocked her was not so much Samantha's comments as her own reaction. What Nina had realized immediately was that she *wanted* to take a peek—just a tiny, quick one—at David's tush.

Curling into a tighter ball, she buried her face in her hands.

Yep, even now she felt an as-of-late unfamiliar warmth spread through her body when she imagined viewing David's nude backside. His nude shoulders, back and legs featured themselves prominently in the fantasy, too.

She rolled to her back and stared at the ceiling. When she pictured David showing up at her apart-

ment and at the hospital and at the senior center…
when she imagined his gaze, so steady, so penetrating…and when she realized that he thought of her
even when she wasn't in sight, she wondered if another man had *ever* made her feel that…held.

She released a shuddering sigh. Long ago she had
decided that being a good mother meant putting her
sexual and romantic needs on hold until her children
were grown and less likely to be affected by her
choices. She'd promised herself she would wear
white cotton underwear and avoid dating until her
children were twenty.

Was it wrong to change her mind in the course of a
morning? To know suddenly that she had missed lovemaking? That she had missed *feeling loved* by a man?

Was it wrong to want sex with David so she could
discover if making love was different in the arms of
someone who knew how to care *for* a woman, not
merely about her?

Because David's bedroom suite was on the opposite end of the condo, a tryst or two would also be fairly
convenient. They could get together when the kids
weren't even home, and no one would be the wiser.

Nina wrapped her arms around herself. *This is what
happened when your mind was idle.* It was all hypo-
thetical, of course. She wasn't even close to making a
decision of such magnitude. But she did wonder….

Now that David had defended her honor, would
he mind very much besmirching it a little?

\* \* \*

Dimly, as if from very far away, Nina heard some-one snore. Because she was perfectly comfortable for the first time in days and because she was having a lovely dream in which she was naked with no cellu-lite on a tropical island, she ignored the sound.

Instead, she felt her lips curve at the edges as an equally nude David Hanson licked her sun-kissed shoulder. It tickled. All over.

"She must be dreaming."

"I'm going to have to make a potato poultice. She'll have a crick in her neck when she wakes up."

"Potato poultice. Does that work?"

"Of course."

Nina's brow puckered. The Yiddish and British-in-flected conversation did not belong in her dream. Brushing it aside, she refocused on David. He was broad-shouldered…beautiful…his skin glowing in the sun…. He was tracing figure eights now over her shoul-der. He smelled like pheromones and coconuts….

"Shake her harder, David. God forbid, she could be in a coma."

"I don't think it's a coma, Bubby."

In the dream, David's voice was rich and low, but he stopped licking and started jostling her shoulder. The dream Nina frowned and shimmied, hoping he'd go back to licking, but he kept on shaking her. Peeved, she scooped up a handful of sand and chucked it at her ill-behaved lover.

A deep, loud *Ooof!* finally woke Nina from her dream. She opened her eyes to see David, fully clothed and bent at the waist. He was not smiling. In fact, his face, mere inches from hers, was screwed into a very tight grimace.

"Nope. Not a coma," he announced, squeezing the words through gritted teeth. Slowly, he backed away from the couch and tried to stand.

"It's going to take more than potato plaster to fix that," commented Johanna, who was standing on the other side of the glass coffee table, next to Bubby, whose blue eyes were the widest Nina had ever seen them.

"I'll get you a nice castor oil pack, Mr. David. Don't you worry."

"Castor oil? That works?" Bubby's eyebrows jerked up. "I work at a senior center. You got anything for prostates?"

Johanna and Bubby adjourned to the kitchen while David attempted to straighten.

Nina sat up and rubbed her eyes. Everything seemed a bit vague and discombobulated at the moment. Tilting her head at David as he tried to take a deep breath, she asked, "What's wrong?"

With his hands on his hips, he looked at her like she was crazy. "What's wrong, Miss Baxter, is that since you were fired from Hanson's, *my* life has been in an uproar." Finally, he took the breath he'd been after. "I think you're fired again."

\* \* \*

A half hour later, Nina poked her head around David's half-open bedroom door. "Knock, knock." He'd retreated to his bedroom—limping—shortly after he'd suggested that she might need to look for work again posthaste. "May I come in?"

David stood at his dresser, putting on his watch. He'd showered and changed into lightweight brown corduroys and a round-necked ivory sweater that emphasized the breadth of his shoulders. When he heard Nina's voice, he turned and narrowed his gaze.

"Are you armed?"

Standing half-behind the door, Nina shrugged. "I wasn't armed last time."

"True. All right, come in. But don't hurt me."

Nina, who had also changed out of the work clothes she'd put on earlier, took a few steps into the room. "This is for you." She held up the castor oil pack Johanna had thrust into her hands.

"I thought you said you weren't armed."

"This is supposed to help you feel less, um, however you feel. Johanna says it's an old family remedy."

Accepting the dubious first aid, he weighed it in his hand. "Old family remedy, huh?" Cocking a brow, he glanced at Nina. "Do you think Johanna's family gets kicked in the groin a lot?"

"Maybe by Johanna."

David grinned. "She can be a little strong-willed. Did she give you a hard time?"

"Not really." Nina slid her hands into the back pockets of the Levi's 501s she'd donned after her shower. "She and Bubby looked like they might rumble at first."

"They seem to be getting along well now."

Nina rolled her eyes. "Too well. After I deliver your castor oil, I'm supposed to head back to the kitchen for my cold cures."

He gestured to her expression. "And you are dreading this why?"

"You're holding a towel soaked with enough oil to fry Big Bird and you can ask me that?" David's easy laugh broke some of Nina's tension. "Bubby's cure is chicken soup," she said, "which would be all right except that she insists we eat the chicken neck. She thinks it prevents pneumonia." David winced, and she nodded. "I have no idea what Johanna uses to cure a cold, and I'm afraid to find out."

"Raw lamb."

"I could be in denial, but right now I'm telling myself I heard you wrong."

"You didn't. She keeps my freezer stocked with raw lamb all winter." He glanced to the door and lowered his voice. "Defrosts it in the microwave then grinds it into little meatballs. Nasty."

"I'm going to gag just thinking about it."

"Don't. If she hears you cough, you're a dead woman walking." Taking her wrist he pulled her farther into his bedroom then softly closed the door. Conspiratorially, he whispered, "You'll be safer in here."

Nina felt like a teenager, alone in a "guy's" bedroom when she shouldn't be. "I can't stay here, forever," she said, wondering if the statement sounded as flirtatious to his ears as it did to hers.

Apparently not because David seemed completely relaxed when he sat on the bed. "No, but you may be able to hide out long enough for Johanna to leave the kitchen. Once she's busy doing something else, I'll show you my disappearing meatball trick. Works like a charm."

He studied the towel Nina had brought him. "It's still hot." Looking up, he mused, "I wonder what effect castor oil is supposed to have on groin injuries?"

It would be humiliating to blush because he said the word *groin*. However, because David's crotch had recently figured so prominently in her fantasies, Nina found total composure difficult to maintain.

"How is it?" She pointed in the appropriate direction.

David looked down, then up again. A mischievous glint lit his eyes. "It's mighty fine."

"I meant your injury!"

He composed his features into an ingenuous mask. "So did I."

*Did not.* Nina knew this was probably the most opportune moment she would have to discover whether David was as attracted to her as she was to him. They were alone in his bedroom…having a conversation about his groin. A woman at ease with her own sexuality, a woman who had the sophistication and chutzpah to honor her own desires, would look him in the eye and say simply, *David, I like you. There's no reason we can't explore a physical relationship if you like me, too.*

That was so proactive, she felt empowered just thinking it. Unfortunately, she was an *un*sophisticated woman with limited chutzpah.

David's eyes had fine crinkles at the corners. As he gazed at her, she had the impression that he was in a very good mood. His king-size bed was roomy, but his height and the breadth of his shoulders suggested that a woman would not get lonely on the big mattress. She had nothing to lose, really, and perhaps a lot to gain by finding out how he felt.

"David," she said, trying to speak above the thunderous roar that rushed to her ears the moment she opened her mouth. She could feel her heart begin to sprint as if she'd run a mile in seven minutes. "David, Samantha mentioned that a few people in the office might have gotten the impression we're having an affair."

She watched him closely. His reaction would tell her a great deal. A man who was interested in a woman would maintain eye contact, smile suggestively and murmur something ambiguous, like, *Does that bother you?*

David bowed his head, pressed a thumb and forefinger to his brow bone and said, "My fault." Lowering his hand, he looked at Nina with patent regret. "My fault entirely."

Not a good sign. Nina felt her heart sink as he stood and walked toward her.

She looked up—way up—into his face as he put his hands on her shoulders. Regret sobered his expression.

"I mentioned that I'd hired you and that you were living with me. I thought it would be better for all of us if I put that fact on the table right away. I've got to host a business dinner sooner than I thought, and I didn't want the party to ignite speculation." His hands tightened on her shoulders. "I intended to defuse interest, not stir it. You have my word that I won't compromise your integrity in any way."

She felt his hands tighten once more and then release her. "On that note," he said, moving to the bedroom door and opening it, "hiding out in here probably wasn't a great idea." His smile returned, along with the wry tone. "If your grandmother or Johanna wanders this way, they'll have us married before the sun sets."

Stepping aside, he waited for her to exit the room ahead of him.

Defeated, she moved forward and caught a whiff of the clean, light cologne he used—or perhaps it was the pheromones she was starting to go nuts for. This wasn't right. Thirty-two, and she couldn't unearth the simple question *Are you attracted to me?* with both hands and a shovel.

Stopping directly beside her boss, she looked up and smiled at him a little weakly. Then she reached over, put a hand on the door and pushed it closed.

## Chapter Eleven

The thing about bold moves, Nina realized, was that once you made one you had to follow it up with something equally bold. Otherwise, you wound up looking like a schlemiel.

So after she closed the bedroom door, she stood schlemiel-like while David gazed down at her in question.

"I'm not upset that people thought we were living in—" She stopped herself right before she said *sin*. How archaic was that?

Apparently she didn't stop herself soon enough. David's deep brown eyes widened. "Living in…?"

Wishing she'd bitten her tongue a sentence ago, she fumbled. "Living in… Dating."

David hooked one brow and deadpanned, "Living in dating."

"No, I mean, dating. Just dating. Never mind. I wasn't upset when Samantha told me what people thought." Because she wasn't used to telling fibs—even harmless fibs in the interest of seduction—Nina's mouth started working on the truth before her mind had a chance to orchestrate it. "Well, I was a little upset. I was pretty upset. It bothered me."

Humor suffused David's expression. Frustrated with herself, she socked him lightly on the shoulder. "What I mean is I wasn't angry with you. Samantha said you set the record straight right away."

"I did."

"Thank you."

"You're welcome."

Nina smiled. And silently said a word she'd once grounded Zach for using. Obviously her flirting skills had not made it into the new millennium; this seduction was too far gone to save.

As her eyes began to ache from sinus pressure, she acknowledged that this was a damned sorry time, anyway, to seduce a man who had dated the most beautiful women in Chicago. Her best efforts today had left her looking like the "before" photo for a NyQuil ad.

The problem with David, she decided, was that he was a chocolate-covered graham cracker. Nina never kept her favorite cookies in the house when she was dieting, because she understood that temptation trumped reason. David was the kind of cookie who should not be allowed in the house.

"Too bad we're single. If I had a boyfriend or you had a girlfriend, our living in the same house wouldn't be such an issue," she said, thinking it would help keep her head on straight, too.

David looked surprised. "If I had a girlfriend or you had a boyfriend, we wouldn't be living together at all, Miss Baxter."

He bent toward her, his lean-jawed face so close she could see flecks of gold in his eyes. "I don't know whom you've been dating," he purred in a liquid voice she'd never imagined her boss using, "but if you were my lover, you would not be sleeping in another man's home."

Nina felt herself sway as if hypnotized. "Oh."

*Kiss me.*

That was her only clear thought. It was just occurring to her that she might have to say it out loud when a bell rang. Multiple times.

As Nina tried to figure out whether the bell was a warning inside her head, David straightened and looked at the closed bedroom door. "Company," he murmured.

In the next moment, Nina heard Bubby and Johanna's voices, followed by a stampede of feet and the sound of her exuberant children. "The kids!" she moaned. She slapped a hand to her forehead. "Oh, no! I wanted to meet their bus."

Saying nothing, David nodded, reached over and opened the bedroom door.

Nina stepped into the hallway, expecting him to follow. When she heard the door click softly shut behind her and realized she was alone, she felt like she'd just ended a date. A bad one.

"You're absolutely certain you want to do this now?"

"Absolutely." Nina blew her nose and nodded vehemently. Her extraordinarily curly ponytail flopped heavily atop her head.

Five hours after she'd left his room this afternoon, David sat with Nina in his library. He peered intently at the calendar spread out on his desk, not because he needed to check dates, but because he didn't want to stare at her.

He'd barely been able to keep from picking her up and throwing first her and then himself onto the bed this afternoon.

Clearing his throat, he removed a pencil from a silver cup on his desk and stuck the tip in the electric sharpener. He had the ridiculous thought that the noise might mask the roar of his thoughts.

Nina Baxter was driving him crazy. He'd had to take several steadying breaths after she'd left his room. Then he'd dressed and joined the others as if nothing were out of the ordinary. He'd said hello to the kids, heard about their experience on a different school bus route, assured Johanna that her cure had worked wonders and had finally excused himself, saying he needed to head back to the office for a couple of hours. In reality he'd spent his time walking along the river, trying to clear his mind.

The instant he'd seen the insinuating tilt of his co-workers' raised eyebrows he had known that he would do nothing, *nothing,* to compromise Nina's reputation or her children's well-being. Didn't mean he'd decided he wasn't interested in something more than a boss-secretary relationship; it merely meant that he would force himself to decide exactly what that "something more" was before he took any action. The conclusion he'd come to while defending her integrity in the boardroom today was that he either had to marry Nina or fire her again so they could explore a relationship.

And then she'd stepped into his bedroom this afternoon. And had flirted. At least he was pretty sure she'd been flirting. He'd never seen it done quite that way before.

Accidentally allowing the electric sharpener to chew his pencil down to a mere shadow of its former self, David frowned, tossed it aside and plunged another helpless stick into the whirring blade.

"All right, let's get down to business," he said, removing the pencil before its demise and tapping the point on Friday of the current week. "You think you can pull together a small cocktail reception by this date?"

Nina leaned forward to view the day in question. She smelled like flowers and menthol, and instantly he had the image of the two of them ten years down the road, leaning over household accounts and discussing college funds.

He sat farther back in his chair. A woman's scent had affected him in the past, but never in that way. Blaming the vision of himself, domesticated in his fifties, on the menthol, he waited for Nina's response.

"Friday. That gives me four days," she said, nodding over the calendar. "Sure. Of course. Absolutely no problem." She swiped the tissue under her nose. "Tell me who's attending, how formal you want it and if you have anything special in mind, and I'll handle everything from there."

She sounded confident, even enthusiastic, but David didn't want to overtax her. His long-suffering secretary, who'd called him a workaholic slave driver for the past twenty years, would hit him with her hole punch if she could read his mind right now.

"Great," he said, in lieu of babying her. "The party is to welcome Shiguro Taka and his wife, and the objective is to convince Taka Enterprises that Hanson Media Group is still a major player. You'll have to do all the hiring necessary. George and Helen used to host the business parties." He frowned. "I suppose you can call Helen and ask for referrals if you want to."

"But you would rather not?" she guessed, studying his face.

David rubbed the shadow of stubble appearing on his chin. "Their parties were always very formal. Big and showy, like George." He smiled wryly at his new assistant. "Frankly, I've eaten enough beluga caviar to last me until the next ice age. I'm wondering how we could achieve a similar effect—enforcing the idea that the company is thriving again—without sacrificing…" David wasn't sure of the word he wanted.

"Warmth?" Nina suggested.

He nodded slowly. "Warmth. Yes. Hospitality."

"Something a little more old-fashioned and homey?" she ventured.

"Do you think old-fashioned, homey and warm can be impressive?"

Nina laughed. He thought the sound, husky and low, was distractingly sexy. "Obviously you've never been to a bar mitzvah."

For the next three days, Nina was too busy with decisions, plans and preparations to spend much time picturing David naked.

Well, she managed a couple of brief fantasies, but she was determined not to stray from her goal: to throw a party that Shiguro Taka would remember and that would make any and all suspicious minds realize that David had hired her because she was competent, creative and smart.

The first thing Nina did was check into caterers, but their ideas for a "warm and homey" soiree all sounded similar: mini hamburgers, hibachi cocktail dogs, custard cups of macaroni and cheese, individual meat loaves. Nina pictured tiny portions of mashed potatoes and gravy served alongside with eensy-weensy utensils. The image made her laugh, but the price of the all-American cocktail party did not. Making a mental note to go into catering if the business world completely dried up for her, Nina hung up with the last caterer and suddenly remembered what she'd said to David: *Obviously you've never been to a bar mitzvah.*

Why not?

She called Bubby. Together they planned the party and worked like fiends every minute that the kids were in school and David was at the office.

When they needed extra help in the kitchen, Nina called Janet Daitch, the grandmother approaching retirement age who had also been fired from Hanson's. And Bubby asked two of her friends from the senior center to bake challahs. All the women were thrilled to be cooking and baking "professionally."

Not only was Nina planning a very enjoyable cocktail party and giving good people a chance to earn a little extra cash, she was also saving David a truckload of money, which inspired her to add a new goal to her agenda: Show him and anyone else who cared to observe that one did not have to break the bank to have a good time. It was better to cut expenses than employees.

Each night when David came home, Nina would tell him only that the party plans were progressing nicely. She didn't want him to know that she and Bubby were preparing the food. She knew he'd balk, though she trusted that his resistance to the idea would stem from concern about her working too hard, not from lack of faith in her ability. That revelation evoked a sweet gratitude that made her all the more determined to plan a party he could be proud of.

For three days and three nights, Nina worked and planned and budgeted. When David arrived home to see her still fussing over her accounts ledger, he retired to his office. But he always emerged in time for popcorn and a movie with the kids.

On Thursday, with the plans and preparations looking good, Nina decided to do something about her own appearance. For years and years, she'd looked like exactly what she was: a single working mother on a budget. One who'd forgotten that even penny-pinching single mothers deserved a decent hairstyle.

Seeing Samantha again had sparked Nina's imagination. David expected her to be the hostess of this gathering; that called for something more than a skirt with a pattern that camouflaged jam stains and a hair claw to scrape her unruly curls into place. Samantha had curly hair, too, but she embraced the wildness. Her wardrobe was eclectic and creative and fun.

So, on Thursday when Nina called Samantha to formally confirm that she and Jack would be at the cocktail party, she stole an informal moment to ask the other woman about hair care.

Samantha did more than advise; she came over Friday on her lunch hour with hair products from Barneys in New York and showed Nina how to work with thick curly hair so that she looked more like Andie MacDowell than Roseanne Roseannadanna.

When Bubby and the other women Nina had hired to work in the kitchen that day noted the change in her appearance, they went to work on her wardrobe, promising to return that evening with items for her to try on.

David returned home after Nina had showered and experimented with the hair products Samantha had left. To her surprise and pleasure she was able to replicate the style Samantha had shown her earlier. Now for the first time in memory, her loose curls were soft and spiraling.

Because she was still waiting to see what the other women had chosen for her to wear, she was dressed in black warm-up pants with a white Maroon 5 T-shirt Zach had given her last Mother's Day.

"Hi," she said as she emerged from her room to find David walking down the hallway toward his office. He paused when he saw her, his expression plainly surprised. "Don't worry," she laughed, "I won't wear this to the cocktail party. I'm going to get dressed a little later."

"You look great."

She plucked at her T-shirt. "If this is 'great,' I definitely need to rethink my style."

David was dressed in his suit from work, his tie loosened, but not removed completely. He *did* look great, although a bit rough around the edges. His eyes were tired, his hair looked as if he'd been pushing his fingers through it, and he could use a shave. He still looked like John Corbett. On a good day. Not the kind of guy you'd kick out of bed for eating crackers.

*Or for any other reason,* Nina thought, immediately slapping a benign smile on her face. This was not the time to lust after the boss.

"We still have an hour and a half before the guests arrive," she ventured, changing the subject in her mind, "and half an hour before the crew shows up. So, I was wondering… It's Friday night, and the kids and I always celebrate Shabbat when we're home. If it's all right with you, I'd like to have a short service with them. Light the candles, say kiddush. Then they're spending the night with friends."

David looked bemused. "I'm not really sure what you're talking about, but sure. Go ahead." He smiled.

Nina smiled, too, and explained. "In observant Jewish families, we celebrate the end of the current week and the start of the coming week even when we're not in a synagogue. Especially when we're not in a synagogue. The Sabbath is a special day set aside for family and for reflection. Ideally," she added, since she'd moved on a Saturday and was working tonight. "Officially it begins at sundown on Friday and ends at sundown on Saturday. There's another service called havdalah that officially ends the Sabbath day."

David listened closely, but his expression was hard to read. Nina laughed. "Speaking of all things official, that officially ends my lecture on basic Judaism. Anyway, we'll be brief, and I'll make sure we don't disturb anything set up for tonight."

"I don't care what you disturb. Do you know your eyes get bluer when you talk about this?"

Nina didn't know about her eyes, but she felt her cheeks turn redder. "It's a passion for me. A way to connect with the past and the future. A way to bless the present."

"Do Zach and Izzy appreciate it the way you do?"

"They're beginning to. Izzy loves to light the candles. Plus there's really good bread and ultra-sweet wine involved."

David grinned. "Count me in. Are you starting right now?"

"Hmm?"

He loosened his tie and whipped it off his neck. "I'd like to join you, if I may. I can shower and change later if you want to get right to it."

Nina's eyes widened. "Oh!" A myriad of responding emotions left her speechless. "We can wait for you."

The anticipation she felt was surely sweeter than it should have been.

*"Barukh ata Adonai Eloheinu…"*

David didn't understand the Hebrew words and couldn't have repeated them if they'd been printed on a paper right in front of him. But understanding them didn't matter, not tonight. He understood that much right away.

*"…melekh ha o-lam…."*

The sounds and sights before him played on his heart…no, on something bigger, something that would never die… It played on his soul like his first glimpse of the ocean, the first sighting of an eagle.

Watching Nina and her daughter, their heads covered in lace, faces bathed in candlelight, eyes closed, lips parted to utter an ancient prayer as they held hands—it was a sight that stirred him more than he'd ever, ever have guessed.

The Friday-night candles were lit and the candle-lighting prayer sung by the women in a family, Nina had said, and David could see the wisdom in that tradition: No man would be able to think of work, of annoying traffic, of the bottom line while watching his wife and his daughter turn into angels right before his eyes.

*If a man had a wife and a daughter.*

David stood on the opposite side of the kitchen counter with Zach, watching and changing a little bit, though he wasn't sure how, with each small ritual of the service.

After the candle lighting, Zach, Izzy and Nina sang a happy song in Hebrew and English about greeting a Sabbath bride. They each listed one thing they had done well in the week past, one thing they were grateful for and one thing they wanted to do better in the week ahead. When Nina looked at David to see if he wanted to contribute anything to that part of the proceedings, he was so filled with emotion, so unsure what he was feeling exactly that he shook his head slightly, something he regretted when her list included gratitude for the work she'd been given and the hospitality she and her children had been shown.

Nina then had Zach bring out a handmade box with Hebrew lettering. She thanked God that her family had "plenty," and that they were able to give daily to others, at which point she, Zach and Izzy all reached into their pockets to place money inside the box. Nina placed dollar bills; her kids dropped in change.

"There are kids in Chicago who have to sleep on the street. That's me and Zach's *Tzedakah* project," Izzy said.

"*Tzedakah* is a form of charity," Nina clarified. "But really it's about remembering that we're all connected, all responsible for each other in some way, so when one person is hurting, we have to notice and care. Izzy and Zach drop in change each day and when they have ten dollars, they give it to a women-and-children's shelter. *Tzedakah* is a daily practice, but it's especially powerful on the Sabbath. It's part of repairing the world."

David dropped in a ten, but watching two preteen kids dig into their pockets and say a prayer, asking God to make the money do good work, left him with a vague unease. Hanson's grand donations and lavish charity events seemed small, almost embarrassing by comparison.

In David's family, no one had ever prayed at home. The family had trekked to church on Christmas and Easter, but once they'd left the building, prayer was forgotten in favor of more business. Always the business. David remembered thinking that for the Hansons, going to church was like visiting an elderly relative: You didn't want to go, the cookies were good, you couldn't wait to leave. He wished now that his parents had talked to him about the meaning behind the moments. He wished they'd talked more, period. And touched.

David emerged from his uncomfortable musing when Zach moved to stand next to his mother and Izzy. Nina put a hand on each of her children's heads, thanked God for "blessing me with these beautiful people," and asked Him to remind Izzy daily that she was strong, loving and kind and to remind Zach that he was compassionate, wise and noble.

David could have sworn that the kids grew taller in that moment beneath the cap of her hand. He had a sudden, disturbing memory of himself seated between his parents in church on an Easter Sunday. His father had opened the paper program and was scribbling office memos over the words to "Amazing Grace." His mother was staring straight ahead, a bland smile on her face, her mind obviously elsewhere. But the parents in the pew ahead had their arms around their kids and when it was time to stand and sing, each parent held a hymnal with one hand and put a free arm around the nearest child. David had inched his own hymnal closer to his mother so she could sing with him, but she hadn't noticed.

It was no wonder he found this moment of candlelight, song and family to be almost painfully full of grace.

He began thinking he might excuse himself, get ready for the party, when Zach announced, "Time for *hamotzi!*"

The boy placed his hands on a plate covered by an attractive embroidered cloth. Izzy and Nina each touched one of Zach's shoulders while Zach said a prayer, again in Hebrew. His mother and sister joined him on "Amen!" and the cloth was removed to reveal a fragrant golden-brown loaf of bread that was braided to resemble a fat blond pigtail.

A bread knife was eschewed in favor of breaking the bread by hand. The inside of the loaf was pale butter-yellow, soft and sweet-smelling, and the rustic appearance of the broken hunk seemed in keeping with the evening's theme of honoring the past while ushering in the future.

The big surprise came when Nina broke off two small bites of bread and placed one each in her children's mouths. Then Zach and Izzy broke off two pieces and took turns putting those in Nina's mouth.

While Nina chewed, Izzy spun around to look at David. "Now you!" she said. She tugged on her mother's shirt. "Someone has to feed David."

Nina raised a brow, silently asking if he was willing. "We feed each other the challah." She raised the larger hunk still in her hand. "It's symbolic."

Something happened in his stomach, some gnawing yearning that was stronger than hunger. He looked at her, springing hair glowing in the candlelight, face and eyes shining from the inside out.

Moving toward the threesome, but unable to take his eyes off Nina, he nodded. *Yes. Feed me.*

Under the watchful eyes of her two children, Nina broke off a piece of the bread and lifted it to David's mouth. From David's perspective, the scene seemed to play out in slow motion.

He opened his mouth and felt the brush of her cool fingers against his lower lip as she fed him the bite of challah. He felt his heart pound, felt the sweet, yeasty taste burst on his tongue. Bread had never been this good.

She began to step away, but David stopped her by reaching for the challah still in her hand. Locking his gaze with hers, he raised the bread to her mouth and felt the same heart-pounding anticipation, the same burst of sweetness as he fed her.

The candle flames danced light around the room and illuminated the pinkness of Nina's cheeks.

"Well, that's how our family celebrates Shabbat," she said breathily, a puff of sweet, self-conscious laughter trailing the words. "Now you know what you've been missing."

"Now I know," he murmured.

But David had an inkling—no, he was certain—that he'd only just begun to discover what he'd been missing.

# Chapter Twelve

"Shiguro Taka just told his wife to get the recipe for the brisket." Samantha waylaid Nina and pulled her into the hallway for a brief conversation. "You're brilliant. Everyone's so into the food they're actually relaxed and chatting like normal people at a party instead of suits with martinis in their hands."

Nina breathed a sigh of relief. Actually it may have been her first full breath since David had put the bread in her mouth.

Samantha looked smashing. Confident and unique as always in a dress made from some filmy material that looked like a watercolor painting. Coming from her, the thumbs-up gave Nina a welcome shot in the

arm. She hadn't had time to trade more than a word
or two with David since the first guests had arrived.
She didn't know how he felt about her decidedly
Yiddish soiree.

Carved brisket, miniature potato kugels, mini bagels and lox, tiny hot pastrami sandwiches on mini
rounds of rye, and chopped liver spiked with port
(which several people had deemed the finest "pâté"
they had ever eaten)—the food was definitely a hit,
devoured with the kind of gusto that would make any
Jewish mama kvell with joy.

Looking over Samantha's shoulder, she watched
the twenty or so guests laugh and mingle with plates
in their hands.

The room glowed, lit by candles and lamps with
amber bulbs. Music was provided by the grandson
of one of Bubby's friends at the senior center, who
sang in low tones and accompanied himself on the
guitar.

"Do you think David is happy with the evening?"
Nina heard the puppy-dog eager-to-please-ness in
her own voice. She may as well have wagged her tail
and peed on the floor. Smoothing the pale blue silk
skirt she'd been lent for the evening, she looked away
as if the answer didn't mean all that much and hoped
Samantha had missed the too-vulnerable tone.

"David's usually a little stiff at these things." The
other woman pursed her lips. "I've asked Jack if the
Hansons have a genetic mutation I ought to know

about, something that makes them sound like European royalty in the 1940s. Have you noticed that?"

Nina nodded. "I told David he sometimes sounds like Rex Harrison."

Samantha laughed. "Jack says his brothers got all the wild and crazy genes. He got an extra dose of responsibility."

"Does that bother him?"

"I think so." Raising a white-chocolate martini to her lips, Samantha let the drink linger on her tongue then giggled. "At least, it bothered him enough to prove to me he can be wild and crazy when it counts."

When Nina's eyes widened at the revelation, Samantha laughed again and patted her shoulder. "Anyway, I've noticed that Jack and David get more formal when there are a lot of people around or when they're nervous."

"You think David's nervous?"

Samantha shook her head. "I think David looks more relaxed tonight than I've seen him at any business function. You've done a great job. Don't worry."

Nina nodded and Samantha trailed off in search of Jack. Nina did worry, though. She knew she'd gone out on a limb tonight. Everything from the food to the decorations to the people who were serving had been organized on a self-imposed budget with Nina's own agenda in mind.

As yet unbeknownst to David, both servers were recently "released" Hanson employees. They had experience in food service, and it had seemed…well, just plain *wrong* to use a catering service when Nina knew that Janet and Gillian were still looking for jobs. They'd been glad to get her call and though they hadn't been happy to be fired, neither did they appear to hold a grudge against anyone at Hanson. Nina was sure they would conduct themselves professionally, but she wished she'd thought to pull David aside and warn him.

Stretching on tiptoe, she looked for him among the milling guests. Before she found him, however, she spotted Gillian.

Circulating with a tray of mini bagels and lox, Gillian had been waylaid by Les Deland, a Hanson exec, who was pointing at her and squinting. Gillian had worked in accounts payable and claimed she'd never mingled much with the Hanson execs or board of directors, but Les looked like he was trying to place her or had already recognized her. More troubling was Gillian's response: Glancing nervously around the room, she appeared to be looking for Nina.

Foreboding crept fingerlike up Nina's spine. What if one or more of the guests really did take exception to her choice in hiring? What if they thought that populating a Hanson PR party with recently laid-off employees was a bad idea? They would blame David.

Heading immediately for the plate-glass windows where Gillian and Les Deland stood, Nina began to entertain a host of worries, all of which ended with

David losing the trust of his colleagues because of her. Why had she tried to impose her values on his party without even checking with him?

When she reached the duo, she heard Les Deland, a portly gentleman with a generally jovial disposition and prematurely receding hairline say to Gillian, "Aw, come on, meet me after the party. We can get sushi. There's a place in my neighborhood that stays open till two."

"Oh, there's my boss!" Gillian said, her voice sounding worried, but her eyes wide with relief as Nina stopped beside them. "I'd better take this tray around."

Les didn't catch the relief part. He patted Gillian's arm. "Don't worry. I've got some pull here." He winked. To Nina, he said, "I hope you won't chastise this lovely young woman for sharing a few words with me. I fell in love with her bagels and lox before I fell for her. Maybe you can convince her to have dinner with me?"

Now that she was close enough to look into his eyes, it seemed to Nina that Les Deland had ingested more bourbon than bagel this evening. Before she could respond to his soggy request, a broad hand slapped Les on the back. "Good to see you enjoying yourself."

David's warm voice betrayed not a hint of disapproval.

"I'm having a terrific time," Les confirmed, raising a glass that contained nothing but ice. "Best party I've been to all year."

"Good. That's what we like to hear. Where's your lovely wife?" David glanced around. "Is she here?"

Les's puffy cheeks reddened. Looking down at his glass, he mumbled something. The only words Nina caught were *visiting* and *sister*.

"Tell her we missed her," David said, still betraying not a hint of censure, though Nina thought that someone who knew him well would surely notice the steel behind the smile. "The Takas were just asking me about tickets to the Oprah Winfrey show," he said, his hand still on Les's shoulder. "Mrs. Taka would like to go. Why don't you look into that?"

While Les nodded, David told Gillian he was sure Mr. and Mrs. Taka would love to try the lox and bagels if they hadn't already, which gave Gillian the chance to slip away.

Nina felt a whoosh of relief now that the incident was over, until David requested, "May I have a word with you, Miss Baxter?" She couldn't help but notice that the conviviality in his expression had grown a bit…set.

*Uh-oh.*

"Certainly, Mr. Hanson," she answered pleasantly, as businesslike as she could be, but that foreboding tingle was back.

"We can speak in my office," he said and led the way.

David walked easily around the pockets of party guests, all dressed in designer clothing and coiffed to studied perfection. He fit right in among them. On the way to his office, he smiled, nodded and traded a word or two here and there, all without actually stopping. The glances from other men were always courteous, sometimes deferential. From the women, he received open admiration and, twice, lingering looks that were frankly flirtatious. David never broke stride. He was obviously a man who had spent his career cultivating respect, and he'd come to take it for granted.

His brother's dishonesty and the ensuing problems at the company must have been an open sore to a man like David. He intended to use this and subsequent parties to heal the wounds. He'd made that clear to Nina. Which once again called into question her decision to hire ousted Hanson employees without even running it by him first. She hoped he would consider the fact that his guests appeared to be enjoying themselves, but her feet began to drag heavily as she trailed behind him. Something in the way he'd looked at Gillian told her that the catering staff would indeed be the topic of their conversation.

By the time she stood in the former library, she'd rehearsed, *We'll leave in the morning,* a dozen times.

"Will you close the door, please?" David spoke

while glancing at some papers on his desk. He didn't even make eye contact with her.

When the latch clicked, David looked up, bland and businesslike. "Have a seat. This won't take long."

"If it won't take long, I think I'll stand."

"Have a seat."

"Don't mind if I do."

She perched on the edge of a designer chair, and waited.

David leaned a hip on his desk, loosely clasped hands resting on one thigh. "I went to the kitchen for an aspirin," he said. "Your grandmother certainly is busy in there."

Nina got the point. She hadn't mentioned yet that she and Bubby had made all the food themselves. She'd decided to wait until after he realized how delicious it was.

"I was glad to see she had help," David continued, his tone deceptively conversational. "Jog my memory. I'm great with faces, but not as good with names. Who is the woman slicing the pastrami?"

"Janet Daitch."

"Right. And I recognize her because she works at Hanson Media Group. Correct?"

"*Worked* at Hanson Media Group."

David's expression did change then, growing somber, tighter. "The laid-off grandmother who was looking forward to retirement." He remembered what she'd told him the day she'd lectured him about firing employees and eating at restaurants with Michelin stars.

"What about the woman Les was bothering?" he asked.

"Gillian." Nina sighed. In for a penny. "Gillian Roesch. Accounts payable."

"Laid off?"

"With the first wave of cutbacks. She has three kids under five. And waitressing experience," Nina said in her own defense.

David's expression remained impassive. "What about the other server? Short dark hair."

"Amanda Barker. She'd only been at Hanson a couple of weeks before the layoffs," Nina said hopefully, as if that would make her decision to hire much more palatable. "And she really prefers waitressing."

He nodded, slowly and without ever taking his eyes off her. Guilt crept along the edges of Nina's mind. She'd wanted to "teach" David and his fellow execs about budgeting and loyalty to employees, but she hadn't shown much loyalty to him. Ever since she'd thrown things at him he had done nothing but attempt to make amends for her job loss. He had tried to improve her circumstances.

She had complicated his.

"If I was half as smart as I think I am, I'd fire you."

Nausea and regret rose in Nina's throat. Under the circumstances she couldn't blame him, but the sense of loss she felt swelled like a wave she needed to jump.

He stood away from the desk, which made him tower over her. "You're wasted here. I don't know what I was thinking. I ought to hire you to assist with in-house public relations. In fact, the more I think about it, the better firing you as my personal assistant sounds."

Perched on the chair while he hovered above her, Nina felt her mind swirl with indecision. Should she begin apologizing now? Walk away with dignity? Beg for her job so her children could eat next week?

She pushed to her feet, willing, at least, to ask that he please allow the other women to finish the night's work.

David's expression was unreadable, his handsome face a construction of chiseled angles and clean curves.

"Do you think I should fire you?" His voice was softer now. Subtle. His warm baritone melded the words together like a song, making her fear subside. Milk-chocolate eyes gazed at her like he was a layer of frosting and she was the cake.

*What was the question?*

"Think about it, Nina. If you weren't my personal assistant, it wouldn't be quite so wrong to do this."

He'd anticipated her resisting. He'd half expected himself to stop before he actually kissed her.

But when David put his hands on Nina's arms and drew her toward him, lowered his head…closer… closer…closer…neither of those two things happened. He didn't stop and she didn't pull away.

There was a world of surprise and awe in that kiss. For David, at least. He couldn't tell what Nina was feeling. At first it was difficult to focus on her response because he was too involved in the taste of her and in resisting the pull to delve his fingers into the masses of thick looping curls. *Go slow, go slow* was the chant that thrummed through his brain, but desire clashed against it like a competing cymbal.

He remembered that he was kissing someone who hadn't asked to be kissed, who hadn't indicated in any way that she wanted to make their relationship physical, so he worked his mouth more slowly over hers, testing and questioning until he knew they were on the same page.

More or less the same page. What David sensed from Nina was that she was willing; he, on the other hand, wanted to end the party now, clear out the house and carry her to his bedroom. And he didn't want to come out for at least twenty-four hours.

Through his suit jacket, he felt her hands curl around his triceps. He wanted to rip off the jacket and growl, "Touch me!" To avoid frightening either her or the guests in the other room, however, he contented himself by releasing her arms to slide his hands up toward her collarbone.

She was wearing a silky pale blue top with a round neck that gave him easy access to the delicate, creamy skin, dusted with freckles so small they looked like glitter. He merely pictured those freckles now as he trailed the pads of his fingers over the silky skin, eyes closed as she shivered and he deepened the kiss. He gave himself another minute before he had to pull away or lock the damned door and take her now on the Berber carpet.

He ran a hand to the back of her neck, slipped his tongue past her open lips and felt himself grow harder than granite as she opened her mouth.

If he'd been twenty years younger he wouldn't have considered stopping. Not when her tongue met his, not when he felt her fingers tighten as if she had to cling to his arms to keep from falling down.

*Yes.* This was what he wanted. This woman. At this time in his life. *Bring your baggage, bring it all, Nina Baxter. And let me touch you, let me inside, because I've never wanted to be anyplace more.*

He slipped a knee between her legs, moved his hands down her back to hold her when she swayed. The fire he was playing with consumed her, too.

*To hell with stopping.* All they had to do was figure out how to get out of here so he could take her to a hotel room. Jack could close the damned party.

David's brain tried to work, but with most of his blood rushing downward, it wasn't easy. He decided to clue Nina in on what he was thinking and gently, with great difficulty, pushed her away.

Lust made his heart pound, which in turn roughened the edges of his voice. "Listen—"

"David, the Takas are leaving, and I— Oh. Sorry! Oh."

Nina jumped when she heard Jack's voice. Swiveling in David's arms, she looked at the door and saw what he did: Jack *and* Samantha stood on the threshold, Jack looking flummoxed, Samantha surprised and trying not to grin. David felt Nina's muscles turn rigid, though they'd been as soft as cooked noodles only a moment before.

David, the soul of patience if he said so himself, wanted to wring his nephew's neck. "Do you knock?"

"I did, actually. Twice." For the first time in ages, sheepish Jack looked more like David's nephew than Hanson's CEO.

The truth was Jack could have knocked a dozen times, and David wouldn't have heard him. Unfortunately he was in no mood to be reasonable. "Well, did you hear me say, 'Come in'?"

"No, that's true. But I, uh…" Jack looked at Samantha. "Why did I open the door?"

Rubbing her fiancé's shoulder, Samantha prompted, "Because we're leaving, and we want to say goodbye like polite guests." She addressed David. "Also Shiguro is looking for you."

"Right." Jack nodded, taking Samantha's hand. "The Takas want to say goodbye and thank you. Les said he saw you heading this way, so I thought I'd…" He frowned at his uncle's still unpleasant expression. Calmly, he turned toward his bride-to-be. "I think we're done here."

Samantha smiled. "Almost. Great party," she said to both David and Nina. "Listen, don't bother to answer now, but will you consider hosting our bridal shower? I want Bubby to cater. I'm mad about the liver or pâté or whatever you want to call it. Think it over." Mischief infused her falsely innocent expression. As the door closed behind her and Jack, she leaned around for one more smile and a huge thumbs-up.

"Subtle, isn't she?" David murmured when the door had clicked. "Hard to believe we're going to be related."

Nina took a step away and shivered. She didn't look at him as she smoothed the top and skirt he'd only just begun to muss.

"Don't even think about walking out of here," he said, drawing a glance of surprise.

"The Takas are looking for you," she reminded him. "You don't want to hide from your guests of honor." Her voice was a bit shaky, not nearly as matter-of-fact as she wanted it to sound. David took great comfort in that.

Reaching for her arm, he drew her close and held her, letting his fingers play in the tumbled cloud of curls the way he'd wanted to all evening. He didn't try to kiss her again; that would have been counterproductive.

"I'm not forgetting the Takas," he assured, weaving a thick curl around his finger while his other hand stroked her back. She shivered again. "But I'm not leaving this room until I can make a G-rated appearance."

Nina pulled back to look at him quizzically. Then her expression cleared, and, to his great delight, a smile played across her rosebud lips when she realized that although he had put the brakes on their kissing session, his body was still very much in drive.

## *Chapter Thirteen*

Nina was rinsing the champagne flutes and matching china plates she'd rented for the evening when David entered the kitchen. It was after 11:00.

The condo was still redolent with aromas from the food they'd served all evening. Tangible reminders of the savory brisket and hot pastrami mingled with the subtle, lingering scents of two-hundred-dollar-an-ounce perfumes.

Mostly what Nina would recall from this evening, however, was the surprise of David's kiss and the way it had excavated an aching awareness of her own loneliness. For years she had buried her personal needs, denied having any that couldn't be postponed indefinitely.

She'd believed she could live for her children, her responsibilities and then remember herself…someday.

It appeared that today was the day.

Every cell of her being had come awake with David's touch. His kisses made her remember why the first flowers of spring were so welcome after a long bare winter. She didn't know if he'd want to pick up where they'd left off when Jack had interrupted, or if he was thinking, *Whew, that was a close call*. But she knew she'd cry in bed tonight if she had to sleep alone.

She would have sex with him if he asked.

The knowledge was exhilarating. Terrifying. Like an extreme sport.

He said nothing as he crossed the kitchen to stand beside her. They were alone now in the condo, guests gone and her children at their friends' house until tomorrow. David stood so close she could smell his skin—warm and musky with the memory of his aftershave. Nina felt her heart wobble as if each beat took all her body's effort. Beneath the running water, her hands trembled around.

David reached for the faucet and turned off the water. Taking the glass from her slippery hands, he set it aside, picked up a dish towel lying over the lip of the sink and wiped her fingers…gently, thoroughly…one by one.

When her hands were dry, he ditched the towel and drew her toward him until their torsos touched… and then their hips…the tops of their thighs…. Fire burned.

David released her hands after he'd guided them around his waist. He'd discarded his coat, and Nina felt the solidness, the strength and power in his body.

He plowed fingers through her hair, tilted her face and kissed her with all the desire and none of the restraint he'd grappled for earlier in the evening.

Nina gave herself up to the kiss. Her hands refused to stay primly around his waist. She wanted to touch his back, his shoulders, his neck where it sloped into collar and chest. She cupped a palm around his jaw and felt it move when his tongue slipped between her lips. Every time she thought of a new place to touch, she followed the desire with action. David did the same.

Two minutes into the kiss, it seemed as if they were merely seconds away from slipping to the kitchen floor to make love. The urgency of his need was evident in the sudden roughness of his hands, the ragged breathing, the hardness that pressed against her pelvis. Nina was more than willing to make love where they stood, without breaking the moment, without thinking or speaking. No space between desire and consummation.

In the end, they moved out of the kitchen and down the hall. David's room was the unspoken destination, though how they got there she couldn't remember later. Clothes were pushed and pulled, hiked up and down, but not removed completely. They fell onto the king-size bed, and the only pause Nina noticed was the one during which he reached into a drawer for a condom, and she tugged off her pantyhose. After that, it was all hungry mouths and even hungrier hands.

He reached for her, made sure she was ready, but words dissolved into groans and groans to gasps. There was no time for teasing, and no patience for it. Like teenagers who hadn't any idea how to wait, or clandestine lovers who couldn't afford to, they tore remaining barriers out of their way. David made quick work of her underwear. Then, breathing like a thoroughbred nearing the end of a race, he opened her body to his and drove inside.

Nina moaned at the pleasure and the pain of re-awakening. David pushed deeper, gave and took, and they rocked together until they could no longer breathe.

David knew true satisfaction for perhaps the first time in his life.

Standing at the window of his downtown office, he looked at the street below, but saw only Nina.

For sixteen hours he'd had her all to himself. They'd slept for part of that time, but she'd been in his dreams, too, and when he'd awakened, he'd opened his eyes to her beautiful face…had felt her touching him.

The first time they'd made love, he'd been almost ashamed of his need, of the urgency that hadn't allowed him even to disrobe fully. But Nina's need had matched his. And he'd made it up to her, later that night and most of the next day.

Gazing out the spotless window, he grinned, finally managing to notice the sky and wondering if Chicago was always this cloudless and sunny in early May.

Making love to Nina had scrubbed away a good quarter century of dusty cynicism.

He'd spent Sunday showing the Takas around Chicago. Even though Nina had begged off to take Izzy and Zach to a music recital, David had thought Chicago never looked better, more interesting, more clean.

That night they'd all been together—David, Nina and the kids—and though he'd spent a good part of the evening wondering whether he and Nina would find a way to make love with two preteens in the house (they hadn't), he'd enjoyed that Sunday night at home more than any in memory.

Now it was eleven-thirty Monday morning, almost lunchtime. David had phoned home twice and had gotten the answering machine. He had no lunch meetings; going home to see Nina, to talk, to make love seemed like a much better plan than eating over his desk.

His secretary buzzed just as he was reaching for the phone.

"Mrs. Hanson is here to see you," she said.

It took a moment for him to realize whom Judy meant. "Helen?"

"She'd like to know if you have a few minutes before your next meeting."

Judy knew he didn't have another meeting until three that afternoon. She was giving him an out he'd love to take, but Helen, his sister-in-law, had never asked to see him at work before. Hoping it wouldn't take long, he responded, "Send her in."

The door opened. Helen entered as she'd entered every room since the first time he'd met her: She swept in; she glided. Blond, tall and as perfectly groomed as a Nieman Marcus mannequin, George's widow was as beautiful today as she'd been when George had first introduced her to David.

There was something different today, though. Something slightly off.

"I'm sorry I came over without calling first." She apologized before saying hello. "George hated it when I did that."

"How are you, Helen?" The perfunctory question emerged as just that: a polite rejoinder. It occurred to David almost immediately as he noted the unusual puffiness around Helen's eyes that if he *really* cared how his sister-in-law was faring, he'd have visited her at least once or twice since George had died. He felt a stab of guilt, though duller probably than it should have been.

She aimed her green eyes slightly to David's left as she replied, "Fine. May I sit down?"

He came around the desk, pulled out a chair Helen

had ordered upholstered in Thai silk the year she'd redecorated the offices.

Sitting behind his desk seemed too businesslike, so David hovered at its edge and waited for Helen to speak. He felt his brows pulling together by the time she formed her words.

"The reading of George's will is coming up," she began, her voice as unusually tentative as her gaze. "We haven't discussed George—you and I—since the funeral. I thought…"

In the uncertain pause, David wondered what, precisely, she wanted to discuss. Given the information that had come to light after George's death, affectionate reminiscence seemed unlikely. Even the eulogy David had delivered at the funeral had focused on George's exuberant personality, his business acumen, his commitment to excellence, but had neatly skirted personal details. George Hanson's death had brought one fact above others into bald relief: David hadn't known his brother.

It had never occurred to him, for instance, that George had kept a double set of books for the business, or that George had been so afraid of failure that he'd been willing to lie to his family and business associates for years.

"I'm not sure what to talk about," David began, deciding there had been enough courtesy. If Helen wanted to take a trip down memory lane, she'd have to find another travel companion; he couldn't do it, not yet. "If nothing else, these past months have proved to me that I didn't know my brother, Helen. I'd like to offer you some comfort…something…. I'm not sure—"

"I didn't know him, either!" Helen blurted, her green eyes large and worn from crying as she looked directly at David for the first time today. "That's why I'm here."

She dug into an ivory leather handbag the identical shade as her dress. David noticed then that the blond hair she'd pulled into a low coil at the nape of her neck was straight and tight, not big and curled, as she'd worn it for years. When she pulled out a large plain envelope, he saw, too, that she'd removed the gemstones that had previously decorated her long fingers.

She held the letter up, looking at David with unblinking pain. "George left me this. I found it a few days ago. He wrote it right before he died, apparently. As if he had a premonition."

She stopped speaking, but David's curiosity was peaked. He reached for the envelope.

As if his fingers were licks of fire, she snatched the letter to her bosom, away from his grasp. "It's written to me. It's…private."

"Then why are you—"

"I don't know!" Helen, truly agitated now, rose and paced the office. "I shouldn't have come. I shouldn't have, but I want to know if George ever said anything to you…about me." She halted and looked at David again. When her lips trembled, she set her jaw with the determination of a fighter climbing into the ring. "Did he tell you why he married me?"

Oh, hell. Apparently there were more surprises from George. David wasn't sure he wanted to hear this. Correction: He was damned sure he didn't. But Helen was genuinely upset and clearly intent on answers, not platitudes.

"George didn't talk to me about personal issues, Helen." He decided to start with broad truths and work his way to specifics. "He always seemed proud of you. Glad you were his wife—"

"Glad to show me off," she interrupted bitterly, her eyes sparking now with more fire than he'd ever credited her. "Did he ever use the word *love?* As in, 'Look at the little lady. Ain't she somethin'? I sure do love her.'" Her lips pursed and she shook her head. "No, I guess not."

Raising the letter, she looked at it as if she couldn't decide whether to rip it to shreds or read it again. "He apologizes in here." She spoke with her eyes on the envelope, and with each word her tone flattened, sounding more resigned. "He's sorry he wasn't able to give me what I needed. Sorry he didn't have the 'emotion' I wanted." Her gaze rose. "He says he suspects I'm smarter than he gave me credit for."

David was stunned. Even in the face of Helen's palpable pain, he found himself amazed chiefly that his brother had, after all, noticed other people's needs. That he'd felt some remorse.

He also realized the letter's less overt implication: George must have sensed that he was ill. Perhaps he'd felt some culpability for the mess he was about to bequeath his family.

Helen took a shuddering breath. When she looked at David, she was still full of emotion, but visibly calmer.

"Damned right I'm smarter than he gave me credit for," she said, admirably more resolute than angry. "Obviously not smart to accept the truth a long time ago—I was George's trophy wife. The second wife usually is, isn't she?" Her lips curled with eloquent irony. "But we trophy wives get older, too, and if we're lucky we grow up. Well, I'm smart enough to realize that my stepsons share their father's flaws. They don't know how to act like family, and they underestimate their stepmother."

She tucked the letter into her purse. "You've always been cordial to me, David. Cordial and, I think, honest. So I'm going to be honest with you. I realize that the Hanson men expect me to take my diamonds and my big house and pretend my involvement in this family is over. But it isn't. Not by a long shot. For better or worse George Hanson made me a stepmother and a shareholding member of Hanson Media Group. I intend to follow through on both responsibilities."

David didn't know exactly what she meant by that and wondered if Hanson Media Group or the Hanson family could survive too many more surprises.

He gestured to the abandoned chair. "Helen, why don't you sit down? It appears we have more to discuss." He reached for his phone. "I'll have some coffee brought in, and we can—"

"Do I sound like I need caffeine?" She managed to laugh. "No, David, that's enough for today." She looked at her watch. "I barged in. We'll talk more another day—when we both have more time, and I'm a little calmer." She offered a self-aware smile through her tears. "May I ask you not to mention this to the boys? Though I'm sure it would brighten their day to know their father cared for me about as little as they do."

The boys. George's sons, who had never been on fabulous terms with their young stepmama.

David frowned, but nodded, because despite her being distraught, today he'd witnessed in Helen a steely strength he'd never before attributed to her. And she was right about one thing: The Hansons didn't know how to be a family. If she thought she could straighten them out, why not give her a crack at it?

"I won't say anything until I hear from you again, Helen," he said. "But I hope that will be soon."

The smile she sent him was grateful. "It will be."

On high, thin heels, she walked out, and David felt suddenly exhausted. Running a hand through his hair, he decided he'd rather not know all that was in that letter. Shoving his restless hands in his pockets, he stalked to the window, but this time he saw nothing at all.

Good God, when he exited this world, would he be like his brother? Would he leave behind the same uncertainty, the doubt and division George had left?

Two of his sons couldn't even be bothered to show up for the reading of the damned will.

"You blew it, George. You had the people present and accounted for, but you didn't know how to turn them into a family."

That seemed to be a problem in the Hanson DNA.

David blinked, tried to focus his eyes, but instead of the Chicago skyline he saw Nina…Zach…Izzy… even Bubby.

*The people. Present and accounted for.*

The need to see Nina *now* welled inside him like lava looking for the top of the volcano.

He didn't want to sneak around, trying to have sex when no one was looking. He didn't want to be the lover who lurked in the shadows of her life.

David wasn't even certain what he was going to say to Nina when he got home. He wasn't sure she'd be there. Neither of those circumstances stopped him from picking up the phone and telling his secretary to reschedule his 3:00 p.m. meeting, then grabbing the jacket off the back of his chair and sprinting through the office until he reached the elevators.

He stepped onto the car with his heart hammering so hard he may as well have been walking up twenty flights of stairs, not taking the elevator down. Watching the numbers above the doors flash in decreasing double digits, he knew only one thing with absolute certainty.

Building a family was harder than building a business. And a whole helluva lot more exciting. Nina, her children and her bubby were the fulfillment he'd been looking for all his life.

## Chapter Fourteen

From the moment she'd awakened Monday morning, Nina had sensed the day was going to be atypical. Usually ready to leap into her week, today she'd gotten in the shower and forgotten to wash her hair. Then she'd scorched the eggs she'd intended to give her kids for breakfast and had substituted a quick bowl of raisin bran with organic soy milk instead. Zach had said the soy milk tasted like "feet," but the new doctor had strictly prohibited dairy products until Zach's asthma was under control.

"I'll buy rice milk today," she'd promised her son, but he'd left for school grumpy and talking about child abuse.

Things hadn't gone much better with Izzy. Over the weekend, Isabella had announced her interest in becoming a vegetarian. Nina had thought her daughter would wade slowly into this new venture—if at all—and hadn't thought twice about making her daughter's beloved tuna sandwich with relish and olives on a kaiser roll for lunch. Izzy said she couldn't possibly eat anything that had had a mother, which eliminated the option of the school cafeteria's hamburger day. To insure that her children ingested something more than chips and soda, Nina had sent them to school then made a new lunch for Izzy, and a dairy-free, sugar-free, wheat-free snack for Zach. She drove to the school to deliver the parcels, and had just returned to the condo. It was 12:15, she hadn't had her own breakfast yet, and her shining face was a makeup-free zone.

She was finally sitting down to a bowl of oatmeal and the *Chicago Sun-Times* when David came through the front door.

A wide smile split her face. Probably had oatmeal between her teeth, but what the hell. She rose from the kitchen counter, crossed to him and moved easily into large, strong arms that promptly wrapped around her.

He rested his face in her hair. "Exactly the greeting I hoped for," he murmured. "Right down to the toes."

"Beg your pardon?"

Without moving to look at the digits in question, he said, "Your feet are bare. I noticed when I walked in. I like your bare feet, very uniform toes."

"Hmm." Nina snuggled more deeply into his embrace. There was definitely something to be said for a man's bulkier muscles; she felt locked in a warm, safe place. If they'd been dating awhile she might have told him all about her crappy morning and looked for a consoling smooch. Under the circumstance, she contented herself with the hug.

"Sit down," he said, giving her an affectionate pat on the rump. "Finish your…" He looked in the bowl and raised a brow. "Breakfast?"

"Late start," she said, wishing he'd go on holding her; in fact, wishing they could sneak off to his bedroom or hers and make love again. Spending all night and most of a day in bed with David had used her body better than it had ever been used before. And it had shut off her mind. Without worries, without burdens, she had been able to experience her body and his, to relax into pleasure in a way she never had before. Nina knew that release had been possible because she trusted David.

The trust, too, was easier, deeper than anything she'd felt in the past. A reluctant sigh accompanied her slipping out of his arms and returning to the kitchen stool.

He smiled. "I like hearing that. Makes a man feel wanted."

"Oh, you are." She picked up her spoon, swirled it through the oatmeal. "But this is a workday, and I assume you've come home to discuss a very important function you want me to arrange. We can go Indian this time if you like. There's a lovely woman from Mumbai in Bubby's building. She's ninety now, but very spry. I'll see if she's available to help cater."

A high-beam smile lit the handsome face that looked as if it had never had a hard knock. "Funny. You're very sassy, Miss Baxter."

She batted her lashes at him. "My boss likes it."

Taking the stool beside hers, he grinned down. "Yes, he does."

They could have grown awkward with each when her kids had come home Saturday night, but the transition back to family life had been far, far easier than Nina would have believed. David had not flirted or tried to see Nina in private; he hadn't expected her to sneak into his bed with her kids in the house. His behavior in front of her children hadn't changed at all. She was grateful.

But he had left her a note tucked into a corner of her bathroom mirror Sunday night. It had read simply, *Miss you, Beautiful.*

This was the first time she'd seen David since she'd found the paper, so she said now, "Thank you for my note."

He cast her an admirably blank look. "I'm sorry, Miss Baxter, we're all about business here. Unless you're referring to a memo, I'm afraid I can't discuss my personal life with an employee."

Nina smiled, just a tad smugly. He was being flip,

but the truth was he couldn't afford to ignore the impact their being lovers might have on his business life any more than she could ignore the effect on her children. Fortunately Nina had already decided on an eminently sensible plan. In fact, it was more than sensible; it was exciting.

She, Bubby and Janet had worked so well together in the kitchen that at one point Nina had mentioned they should all go into the catering business. Janet's eyes had lit with interest until she'd realized Nina had spoken tongue-in-cheek. But during the past twenty-four hours, Nina had decided the idea of starting her own business was nothing to laugh at. Why not party planning? Fun affairs with a sense of humor or a sense of elegance, but always at a respectable price.

*Three Yentas.* That's what they could call their firm. And in addition to party planning, they would provide hot, wonderful meals for busy people to purchase on a daily basis. David would continue to be her client, but he'd contract her as he would any other independent businessperson. He would no longer be her boss. Judging from the response they'd received after his party, they'd be busier than they needed to be in no time.

And, Nina would be able to move out.

Since being widowed, Janet lived alone in a house that she claimed was far too quiet. Nina hadn't asked her yet, but she had a feeling the other woman would agree to a work-rent situation.

Nina had always known she wanted something more than office work. Now she could pursue a career, a business of her own that truly excited her, *and* she could pursue a relationship with David without raising eyebrows. They could go out on dates, for crying out loud!

"What, I wonder, is making you smile?" David's voice rolled softly into her thoughts.

"I was thinking about how much everyone enjoyed Friday night."

He leaned toward her, close to her neck, where she felt his lips graze her ear. "*I* certainly did."

The first whispering touch made her breathless. One minute she was excited to tell him about her plans for the future; the next, she was excited about him.

"I'm sorry," she said, controlling her voice as much as possible, "but, as you pointed out, I'm not at liberty to discuss private affairs in a business setting. You'll have to— Oh!"

David swept an arm under her legs and lifted her into his arms. Nina grinned as he carried her from the kitchen. Her arms curled around his neck. "This is highly unacceptable behavior from a boss."

"You got that right," he growled.

"I don't suppose we're heading to the office for a little dictation?"

"Did I ask you to bring a pen?"

"I didn't finish my oatmeal."

He stopped and frowned down at her. She hid her

smile as he wrestled with good manners and a man's
desire. When he looked at her closely enough to notice the faint curl of her lips, he carried her to the refrigerator, yanked open the door, told her to grab a
can of whipped cream and a jar of peanut butter, then
kicked the door closed.

"Peanut butter?" Nina hooked a brow as she balanced the jar and the can of whipped cream on her
stomach.

Jaw set with determination, David didn't look
down as he strode to his bedroom. "Trust me."

"Oh yes, that is soooo…mmmmm. Why is it so
good like this?" Nina asked from her place in the
middle of David's bed.

"It's the freedom. And the honesty." He reached
into the jar of peanut butter with a forefinger, as
Nina had been doing for the past few minutes, pulled
up a neat blob and ate it slowly. "My guess is you've
been using bread because you thought you had to.
Now, for the first time, you realize there are no
rules."

"God, you're smart." She licked her finger clean.
"No rules for peanut butter." Running her tongue
thoroughly over her lips, she shook her head. "You've
shown me a whole new world, Mr. Hanson."

Grinning and sticky, they leaned forward to kiss.
The sheet and thin blanket on David's bed were pud-
dled around Nina's waist. The peanut butter was a

concession to the fact that he'd interrupted her breakfast, but the whipped cream…

Ahhhh, the things David Hanson could do with a
can of whipped cream…. It was enough to make a
pastry chef blush.

David was also naked beneath the covers, which
dipped low enough for Nina to see the silky hair that
trailed from his flat belly to the V of his legs.

"Is this why you came home from work?" she
asked, shamelessly batting her lashes.

"I came home to talk," David said, replacing the
lid on the peanut-butter jar and leaning over to set it
on the end table. He glanced wryly at the bare
breasts that had occupied him for the past hour. "I
got distracted."

Lightly tackling her, he pressed her down to the
bed. Brushing blond curls from her eyes, he spoke
softly.

"I'm probably going to bungle this, so hear me out
before you say anything, okay?"

Bemused by the frown that drew one thin line between his brows, she nodded.

David reached for one of her hands, raised it to his
lips. "Making love with you has been a revelation.
You're loving, generous, shy one minute and wild the
next." He narrowed his eyes. "Which is a very big
turn-on, by the way." He slid his fingers through hers
till their palms touched. "I love what just happened,
but…" His pause tapped a fissure of worry into

Nina's mind. "I came home to tell you I don't want to sneak around like a couple of kids. I'm too old for that. Conducting a relationship in secret..." He shook his head. "It isn't going to work for me, Nina."

Nina's stomach lurched. Was he about to give her the brush-off? She tried to pull her hand back, but he held fast. "Let me make it clear up front that I do not plan to give up sex with you. But living together, working together, sleeping together—it's thorny."

Suddenly she understood: He really was going to fire her.

Nina wasn't a hundred-percent certain whether she should hit him or kiss him. She didn't like the idea of being fired for sleeping with the boss, but giving up the job—not him—was exactly her plan, too.

"I've been thinking—"

"I've given it some thought—"

They spoke at the same time.

"You first," Nina said.

Releasing her hand, David let his fingers play in the dip between her collarbones. "I have a new job for you. It's big."

He'd found her a different job? "What is it?"

"I want you to plan another party. But this one has nothing to do with Hanson's."

Nina's concern turned to anticipation. "Oh!" She smiled. "Hey, Mr. Hanson, I think we may be on the same wavelength."

He took a breath, held it a moment. "I hope so."

With his index finger, David traced a path between her breasts. "This party will be the biggest I've ever thrown. I know you worry about budgets—"

"On principle—"

"But this time there's no holding back. I mean it. I want this to be a front-page affair."

Nina was starting to get excited, and not only because David's fingers sent shivers racing over her skin. His party could dovetail perfectly with her idea. It could be Three Yentas' first official job.

"How many guests?"

"I'm not sure about the details yet. We'll have to hammer that out as we go along. But I'd like it to take place outdoors...if the guest of honor agrees."

"Who's your guest of honor?"

David rolled over Nina in a most unbusinesslike way. He stared down, looking as serious as she'd ever seen him.

"You."

The moment had not gone at all the way he'd planned.

David had never before asked anyone to marry him. He'd never come close. If he had, perhaps he'd have planned the moment more effectively: champagne, roses, an evening out. His proposal certainly couldn't have gone any worse.

When he'd finally blurted the words, "Let's get

married," Nina had looked like he'd asked her to bungee jump…without the cord.

Now the two of them stood across the room from each other, buttoning their clothes. She'd jumped out of bed first to get dressed, and he'd followed—not a good omen. Seemed that a successful marriage proposal ought to lead to *un*dressing.

Tucking his shirttail into his trousers, he waited for her to snap her jeans before he said, "I take it the answer is no?"

She winced at his tone. "This is happening a little fast, don't you think? I mean we just started…"

"Sleeping together?" he supplied when she stumbled. He heard the sarcasm in his voice, couldn't keep it out.

"Yes." Nina's expression held a mix of pain and frustration. "We haven't even had a first date, David. The word *premature* does come to mind." She shoved a hand into her hair. "I mean, what did you think? That out of the clear blue you'd announce you want to be a father and husband, and I'd jump up and say, 'Yippee, where's the ring?'"

Yes, he'd thought that. That was exactly how he'd pictured it.

He knew it was time to back down, let her have some space. In business, he'd always known when to ease off the pedal and when to go full throttle. He couldn't find that same willingness here. He felt only the drive to turn a no into a yes. At least to a maybe.

It was as if her refusal were turning his blood into something toxic, something caustic that burned with every beat of his heart.

"Let's say we back up." He tried to measure his tone, to sound more equable than he felt. "Let's say we begin again, start going on actual dates. We'll slow everything way down. Can you see yourself getting married this year? Next year?"

It was the wrong question. She didn't like it, and it made him sound pathetic as hell, but he couldn't seem to take it back. Before she started speaking, he knew he wouldn't want to hear the answer.

Like a cornered cat, ready to jump or hiss, Nina said, "I've been married once already. I don't know if I ever want to marry again. If I did, it wouldn't be for a very long time. Maybe after Zach and Izzy are in college." Her eyes entreated him to understand. "My family's welfare has to come first."

She raised her chin in a gesture that bespoke resolution, and though her expression was not without compassion, David knew it was over, just like that. He felt a knife slice his heart as easily as if it were slipping through butter. He'd made a critical mistake; he was not part of her family, yet for an unguarded moment he had allowed himself to believe he could be.

He loved Nina. He was sure of it. He'd seen a new life with her in his arms, and it had felt so good and so right he hadn't wanted to spend another minute alone.

When he'd rushed home, he'd been thinking about his needs, not hers. She didn't need him to make her feel loved or cherished or *full*. She had that already. In one form or another she'd always had it.

He was the one who'd driven through his life with his gauge on empty and hadn't even realized it until now.

Sensations he couldn't identify, wasn't sure he wanted to identify, poured into his chest like blood.

The last time he'd felt this desperate, this hungry, his parents had been packing for yet another business trip that would keep them away for yet another Thanksgiving. David had been six; George had been a young man and had accompanied their folks. While their father and George had taken the luggage to the car, David had flung himself against his mother's legs and begged her to stay with him. He was going to be a Native American in the Thanksgiving play at school.

His mother had been gentle, but firm. She'd reminded him that they all had jobs to do: his was to be an Indian in the play; hers was to travel with Daddy. The housekeeper and the nanny had had to peel David away. The day of the play, he'd thrown up on a pilgrim and had had to lie on a cot backstage until the show was all over.

He hadn't thought of that in years. It was a helluva memory to have now. Classic maudlin, old-wound crap. The kind of thing Oprah would eat up and a hundred-and-fifty-dollar-an-hour shrink would yawn over.

But enough to remind him that he would never, ever be that desperate again. He'd been too hungry with Nina, moved too fast.

And he'd forgotten that you couldn't take what someone else didn't have to give.

## Chapter Fifteen

"I got some news for you." Bubby hovered over Nina, a dish towel in one of the knotty-boned hands she'd plunked on her hips.

"What's the news?" Seated on Bubby's over-stuffed chair, which hadn't been reupholstered since 1979, Nina let her legs dangle over the arm and divided her attention between the bag of white-cheddar popcorn on her lap, the *Fear Factor* Miss USA episode she was watching on her grandmother's thirty-two-inch TV, and Bubby.

On the large screen, a bikini-clad beauty was about to be covered in a garden-fresh medley of maggots, hissing cockroaches and a few nonpoisonous (cross our fingers and hope to die) scorpions. Given her mood, Nina thought it was a sissy challenge.

Bubby picked the remote control off the edge of the seat cushion, near Nina's butt, and muted the terrified screams of Miss District of Columbia.

"The news is this," she said, glaring daggers at her granddaughter. "There ain't enough room in this apartment for the kids, me, you and your pity party. You want to sit around looking bored and depressed, go sit in the apartment lobby. It's all Prozac and checkers down there—you'll fit right in."

"I'm not bored and I'm not depressed," Nina argued, though she'd been both for nearly a week. "I'm just tired from job hunting, and you're making me miss *Fear Factor.*"

She had trouble meeting Bubby's gaze.

*My family's welfare has to come first.* The words she'd thrown at David almost seven days ago returned to clang through her head once every half hour, as reliable as clockwork. She was getting quite a headache.

She'd felt so smug, so righteous when she'd uttered the nobler-than-God statement. No one could argue with such a priority.

She hadn't heard from David since that day, and she realized now she wasn't going to. Probably not ever. And that wasn't what she'd intended. She hadn't meant to end their relationship completely; only to manage it a little because he was getting way ahead of himself and didn't even realize it. She'd been right not to leap into a decision about the rest of their lives.

Maybe that worked on TV reality shows...no, not even there.

She shoveled a handful of popcorn into her mouth. She'd been the voice of reason that day, and she wasn't going to let Bubby or anyone else make her doubt herself.

So why did she feel so lousy?

When she'd crunched the kernels enough to allow herself to speak, she said, "I'm sorry we're taking up so much room here, Bubby. I know this place isn't big enough for three extra people. As soon as Janet Daitch gets back from visiting her family in Des Moines, I'll ask if we can move in with her."

*"Psshhh!"* Bubby waved Nina's comment away. "Since when is room for family a problem? Room, I got plenty of. What I don't got is a granddaughter with an ounce of good sense when it comes to men!"

Nina swung her legs off the arm of the chair so quickly, popcorn spilled onto her lap. "What?"

"You heard." Bubby glanced to the bedroom where Izzy and Zach were spread out, doing their homework. Crossing to the sofa, she sat and pointed to her own temple. "My memory is the only part of me that never ages. Details stand out in my mind, and when I put them together I have a clear picture."

Nina longed for an excuse to get up, to sidestep the sharp blue gaze and whatever point Bubby was about to make, but she knew her grandmother's it's-got-to-be-said look; leaving now would only postpone the inevitable. Working a piece of popcorn from between her front teeth, Nina hunched her shoulders and hoped Bubby would be quick.

"I remember one detail in particular from the summer you turned thirteen," the seventy-seven-year-old began, traveling farther back in time than Nina had anticipated. "There was a boy who moved in next door to your parents' house. Two years older than you and thinking more about his first car than his first girl, I think. But you—" Bubby rolled her head. "Such devotion! You wrote his name on napkins, your father's newspaper, even on a pancake once in boysenberry syrup. Always with little hearts and sometimes a poem. Except on the pancake. You remember?"

Nina was stunned. She hadn't thought about that in years. "I remember I had a crush on a boy named Ben."

Bubby nodded, smoothing her housecoat over her knees. "You were going to ask him to the fall dance when school started. Then your parents flew back east...."

Bubby didn't have to finish that thought. Nina would never forget the phone call to the airline, the official who had come to the door, the feeling of wanting to scream and never stop.

"You cried for two days," Bubby remembered, "then, 'Bubby, don't worry,' you told me, 'I'll take care of you.'" For the first time in a long, long time, Bubby's eyes looked older, worn. "It was supposed to be the other way around," she said. "After that, no more school dance. No more hearts over anyone's name."

Nina stirred uncomfortably, wishing she could keep memories of that time stored in a dark corner of her mind. "I suppose even a thirteen-year-old can have a sense of priorities."

"I suppose." Bubby smoothed her housecoat over her knees. "I got one more story."

Nina was absolutely certain she didn't have the strength to hear it. She pointed to the muted TV. "Miss South Carolina just swallowed a maggot. I'm going to turn the sound up."

Bubby managed to beat her to the remote. "One more, then you can watch Miss Silicone Injections eat *treyf.*" She sat back down. "You were too young to remember your grandfather, my Max, may his memory be a blessing. I was eighteen when I met him, and within a week I knew I wanted to get married. A real love affair, and we wanted kids right away, even though we were so young we could barely afford to pay rent on one room. 'There's always a way,' Max said. And so I got pregnant, and a happier girl you never saw. But the baby, a daughter, came too early, and the doctors couldn't save her. Back then was different. Today—" she shrugged "—who knows?"

This was one story Nina had never heard, and as she watched her grandmother, she saw the moistness in her aged eyes. Here was a story Bubby had found too painful to retell.

"I had prayed and prayed for my daughter to be saved. I named her Liba, 'my heart.' When she died, my heart went with her. No one could talk to me, not even Max. 'We'll try again,' he said, but I didn't want to." She shook her head, closing her eyes briefly. "Such a thing, so unthinkable, had happened once. God forbid it should happen again." She shook her head. "'It would kill me,' I told Max, and I said if he wanted to marry someone else, someone who still wanted children, I would understand."

"He loved you too much to let you go," Nina said, wanting to smooth the pain from Bubby's face.

Bubby opened her eyes. They held all the sadness and all the sweetness of seven decades when she said, "He loved life too much to let me stop living. He would have stuck with me no matter what, but then he said, 'If we give up, Rayzel, we won't know what comes next.' He always looked forward, and I loved him too much to ask him to stop looking."

She reached out, ran a finger softly along Nina's cheek. "What came next was your father. And so much joy." Watching Nina closely, she clucked her tongue softly. "I know what you're thinking, and it's true. I've buried a daughter, and I've buried a son, so where's the happy ending to this story, hmm?" She touched her finger to Nina's nose. "You. And Zach and Izzy. Now you're what comes next, and I'm so grateful I didn't miss you.

"What can we do but love anyway, Nina? We accept how painful life can be and love anyway. It's the most faithful thing a person can do."

"I love my kids," Nina said in a hoarse whisper.

"I know that." Bubby reached for her necklace, gold with a quarter-sized medallion. Working the clasp free, she let the gold puddle in her hand, then held it out to her granddaughter. "My father bought me this on a trip to Israel."

Nina knew what it was without looking: a Torah scroll with the engraved words Be Guarded and Protected.

Gently but with firm intention, Bubby closed Nina's fingers around the gift. "To remind you that you're always safe. And that no risk is too big when it's made for love."

Bubby leaned back, obviously tired. "Draw pretty hearts around some special boy's name again, my Ninele. And draw a few of the hearts a little broken, a little worse for the wear." She nodded her grayed head. "It's okay. They'll be as pretty as the others."

Rising with a soft groan, she headed toward the kitchen. "I'm going to get hot cocoa and raspberry *rugelach* for the kids. So the studying will be sweet."

Nina sat on the chair, the Torah pendant in her closed fist. As she felt the rim of the gold circle press into her palm, she realized Bubby hadn't offered her answers, really. Only courage to live with the questions.

Eleven days after Nina and the kids had moved out, David felt sure he wanted to sell the condo.

Izzy had left a pair of pink sunglasses in the TV room. A corner of Zach's *The Ocean World of Jacques Cousteau* poked out from beneath the desk in the library.

David figured he'd find things for the next few weeks. He considered selling the place lock, stock and barrel. Let someone else find pieces of Nina's family.

Maybe he would start over somewhere outside of Chicago. He began to wonder why he stayed here anyway, why he made himself crazy trying to save Hanson Media Group. None of George's kids were interested in the business. Even Jack would love to get out. So why hold on? For whom?

In the days since Nina's unqualified rejection of his proposal, he'd decided she was right: He'd jumped the gun in telling her he wanted to get married right away and had probably come across like a stalker in the process.

He'd put them all in an impossible situation, the kind from which there was no going back. Now Nina and the kids were gone, and he was left to pick up the pieces of a life he no longer liked.

When the doorbell rang at seven-fifteen on Friday evening, he'd been about to carry his heated Healthy Choice Tenderloin Strips in Gravy to the kitchen counter, where he would doubtlessly stare at it a few minutes then throw it down the garbage disposal. That had been his dinner routine for the past week. He had no appetite to eat alone and no desire to ask anyone to join him.

It was not a hardship, therefore, to leave the TV dinner on the kitchen counter and plod to the door. Maybe Jack had decided to drop in. Uncharacteristically, his nephew had shown up twice in the past week to discuss the reading of his father's will and how to ensure the presence of his two younger brothers.

As David reached for the knob, he decided that if it was Jack, he'd make his nephew go out for pizza and beers. The thought of throwing his frozen dinner out *before* he wasted time staring at it perked him up a bit.

When he opened the door, however, no one was on his threshold or in the hall. Mystified, and disappointed, David was about to succumb to solitude when he noticed a large ivory envelope lying at his feet. The words *Private Invitation* were printed across the front in red felt-tip marker.

Bringing the envelope inside, he stared at it until it felt heavy on his palm. Withdrawing a hand-printed card, he read, *Please join us on the rooftop at 7:30 p.m. Dress casual.* The invitation was unsigned. If this was some impromptu get-to-know-the-neighbors party, he really wanted to pass. Even gelatinous brown gravy would be better than small talk.

When he reread the card, however, David noticed that the lettering was very round and very careful—a child's printing.

His heart pounded, leaving a pain with every beat.

*Could be some other kids,* he told himself, *maybe kids in the building. Could even be a practical joke.* But he glanced at his watch and headed for his bedroom, where he changed his shirt, brushed his hair and teeth, and told himself not to be an idiot. Even if Zach and Izzy were on his roof—and why would they be?—Nina could be miles away.

He took the elevator, then a short flight of stairs,

making himself walk in measured, deliberate paces. When he reached the door that lead to the rooftop, he stopped and read a sign, again hand-lettered, and that's when his body tripped into high gear.

Family Shabbat. Please Enter.

He reached for the door, jerked it open and crossed the threshold onto a rooftop that had been decorated with flowers, a folding table covered by a blue cotton cloth with painted handprints, and a string of twinkle lights that glowed softly against an evening sky streaky with orange and lavender.

Zach ran and Izzy skipped over to him.

"Did you get your invitation?"

"We dropped it off!"

"We had to run to the elevator so you wouldn't see us!"

"We wanted you to be surprised."

Excited, they tumbled over each other's sentences. They didn't hug him, though, and it shocked David to realize how much he wanted them to. He'd become so accustomed in his life to handshakes—starting with his own father—that when Zach and Izzy had first started hugging him hello, he hadn't known quite how to respond. Then he'd realized the only response necessary was to fill his arms with them, and he'd looked forward to coming home in the evenings.

Tonight, they maintained a tentative distance, despite their excitement. There had already been too much time and space between them all; the affection wasn't easy now. He knew he could open his arms first, that they might close the distance if he did. But he was scared to do it; scared they might not respond and even more scared that he would hold on too tight if they did. The realization shamed him.

He glanced up, over their heads. Bubby stood at the cloth-covered table. Only Bubby. A cauldron of disappointment bubbled hotly in his stomach. Nina wasn't here. This wasn't reconciliation. She hadn't decided they should begin again as friends…perhaps go on a couple of dates, see if they could make something fit.

*Idiot,* he castigated himself even as he dredged up a smile for Bubby. He looked again at the kids, realizing that staying here would be painful for him, but that he owed it to them to try. When Izzy tentatively took his hand to lead him to the table, he concentrated on how good the simple gesture felt, rather than on how much he would miss it in the days to come.

Bubby smiled as he approached. Several short candles in mismatched holders huddled together atop the decorative tablecloth. He was going to have a difficult time not picturing Nina, how she had glowed in the candlelight the evening he'd first witnessed this simple, haunting ceremony. He was about to ask Bubby if the rooftop Shabbat had been her idea, when he heard a sound behind him.

Her hair, as blond as yarn an angel had spun and covered by the same lace she'd worn last time, was the first thing David noticed. And then her smile.

Small, aching in its hopefulness, Nina's pink lips curved to match the question in her eyes.

"Thank you for coming," she murmured. *Will you*

*stay?* She didn't voice that part, but he understood and nodded around the catch in his throat.

There was no more talking then. Nina started by striking a match and lighting a candle, like last time. And like last time, David felt the edges of his body blur until he was part of the light and song, part of Bubby and Izzy and Zach. He tried to let his mind and body soften until he became part of Nina, too, but that was more difficult, more effortful. When she waved her hands over the candles, drawing the light to her, and sang the prayers and touched her children's heads to bless them, she was the hub of the family wheel, and David knew she belonged to the others.

He wondered why she'd brought him here. If this was an apology for ending abruptly, a way to say, "We can still be friends," he wasn't sure he could muster gratitude. Hanging onto the edge of their family circle was too painful.

The time to light the remainder of the candles—one for each of them—came, and Nina told her family what tonight's theme was. "Courage. When you light your candle tonight, tell one thing you were afraid to do this past week, and one thing you're going to try in the week ahead."

Bubby went first and said, "I'm going to tell Flo Melcher she needs new dentures. A friend don't let another friend wear teeth from 1962."

Zach talked about standing up for a kid who was being ostracized at school, and Izzy said she wasn't going to let Beth Knox cheat off her spelling test anymore even if Beth did tell Danny Hafner that

Izzy thought he was cute. Nina's eyes widened over that one, and David figured there was going to be a talk between mother and daughter later tonight.

There were two candles left—his and Nina's. By tacit agreement, Bubby and the children headed for the rooftop door.

Surprised, David watched them go then looked back to Nina, whose chest rose and fell on a nervous breath. "My turn," she said, holding the candle in front of herself. "I'm not sure I'll be able to top Bubby the Flo Melcher commitment, but here goes...."

Her gaze held his as she explained, "Last week I was afraid to tell you the truth when you asked me to marry you. I panicked and said the first thing that came to mind—that it was too soon to talk about marriage. But that isn't why I said no."

Even as blood rushed through David's veins, his heart felt as if it skidded to a stop. Did he want to hear this?

"I should have told you that I care about you. That I like being with you. That I like it so much, I could hardly breathe this past week when I thought I might never see you again."

David would have taken her in his arms at that moment, he would have let the single admission be enough, but courage was not a job to be left half-done, and Nina had more to say.

"I dreamed of you, you know. For years I imagined someone strong and steady, someone whose love would make the world feel small and safe." She

David's gaze fell on the single wick that remained unlit. Leaning to his left, he raised the candle, tipping it toward one whose flame already burned bright.

Eyes shining, Nina placed her hand atop his, and they lit the last candle together.

\* \* \* \* \*

# THE BABY DEAL

BY
VICTORIA PADE

**Victoria Pade** is a native of Colorado, where she continues to live and work. Her passion— besides writing —is chocolate, which she indulges infrequently and in every form. She loves romance novels and romantic movies—the more lighthearted the better—but she likes a good, juicy mystery now and then, too.

# *Chapter One*

White sandy beaches. Crystal-clear water washing over coral reefs. Lush, dense foliage below enormous palm trees. Soft, lilting music. The scent of sea and soil and sweet, sweet flowers wafting on a balmy breeze.

Paradise.

Tahiti really was paradise, Delia McCray thought as she looked out over the small table where she sat.

The last night of her vacation.

A trio of Polynesians played guitar, ukulele and drums to one side of the wooden dance floor, where her half brother Kyle and his wife, Janine, and Kyle's and Delia's half sister Marta and Marta's husband, Henry, swayed to the sounds.

Delia smiled at the sight. The five-day trip had been

her treat, a reward for everyone's hard work. It was also her own first vacation in ten years—so it wasn't something she'd done lightly—and it was heartening to see how much everyone was enjoying it.

Despite the fact that the three McCray children weren't full-blooded siblings, they'd been raised by the mother they'd shared and they were close. They'd always looked out for each other, and it was nice that they'd been able to have this time together. Even if Delia was aware of being odd man out at moments like this when the two couples paired up.

Her focus settled on Kyle, who was holding Janine close and saying something to her that made her laugh. Delia had no idea what he'd said, but she smiled, too, warmed even from a distance by what they shared.

Kyle was the baby of the family at twenty-eight and Delia couldn't help feeling proud of him, of the man he was. The man he'd made of himself in a houseful of women.

Kyle was un-tall, as he liked to say, but he was lean and wiry, and while he had Delia's same white-blond hair, his hazel eyes and ruddier skin color were more like Marta's.

Marta, who danced into Delia's view just then and diverted her attention, was the middle child at thirty-two.

As Delia watched, Marta pressed her cheek to the shoulder of her husband, Henry. Henry laid his cheek atop Marta's short-cropped black curls, and his hands dropped lovingly to his wife's curvaceous hips.

It wasn't any surprise that no one ever guessed that

Delia and Marta were sisters. They looked nothing alike. Marta's nose was a bit hooked at the end, while Delia's was turned up. Marta's eyes were a mishmash of brown and green, while Delia's were decidedly blue. Marta's lips were fuller, Delia's skin was much more pale, and they'd never been able to trade bras because Delia couldn't even begin to fill one of Marta's. But despite the external differences, they were soul mates.

"You could be out there dancing, too…"

Delia smiled at the deep voice that came from behind her, feeling the scant brush of breath against the ear her very straight, blunt-cut shoulder-length hair was tucked around.

Andrew.

"I could be out there dancing if I had a partner," she countered, braver and more flirtatious than she would ever have been if she were home in Chicago. Or without the liquid courage provided by the sour-apple martinis she'd been drinking.

Andrew came around to set a tray full of fresh drinks on the table and—again under the influence of the liquor that was making her head light—Delia's gaze went unabashedly to the man she'd only met the day before. He was handsome enough to cause even the splendor of paradise to fade into the background.

Andrew.

She knew him only as that, since they hadn't exchanged last names. He was tall, at least six feet, with broad shoulders, a strong back and pure, solid muscle, the only bulk he carried.

His hair was a sun-streaked light brown and he wore it a bit long on top.

His face was an interesting combination of refined features and a touch of ruggedness that carved the edges of his jaw and his nose into sharp angles. His brow was square. His cheekbones were pronounced. His lips were slightly on the thin side and his eyes were so dark a shade of brown they were the color of Columbian coffee beans.

With looks like his, he seemed to be the kind of man who would squire models on each arm and not fraternize with lesser mortals, yet since they'd met he hadn't appeared to notice any of the women who had ogled him. He'd just fit in as one of the guys—one of the McCrays—and if he were aware of how he put height-challenged Kyle and paunchy Henry to shame, he didn't show any sign of it.

Or maybe he was just so comfortable with his own striking good looks that he forgot about them. Anything was possible, Delia conceded, acknowledging to herself that she didn't actually know anything about Andrew except that he was good company and had been able to tell them where the best spot on the island was to snorkel.

He'd arrived at the resort the day before, had overheard them talking at dinner the previous evening about their plans for their last day in Tahiti and he'd offered his advice. And since he was apparently as familiar with their surroundings as any native, when he'd also offered to show them the spot he'd suggested, they'd taken him up on it and spent the day with him.

As thanks for his guidance, the McCrays had invited him to have dinner with them. And now here they were, at the palapa—the open-air bar and dance area covered by a thatched roof only a few yards from the water— savoring the last few hours of their final evening in Tahiti.

Well, the McCrays' final evening. Andrew wasn't leaving.

He was, however, holding out a hand to Delia just then.

"I'd love to be your dance partner," he said with a smile that flashed perfect white teeth and created a dimple at the left corner of his mouth.

"You don't have to," Delia demurred, some of her bravery flagging suddenly.

"I do, though," he insisted. "These are my dancing shoes."

His own dark eyes dropped to his feet and Delia's followed, albeit somewhat slower as her glance drifted down his taut, polo-shirted torso to his narrow waist, to hips caressed by khaki slacks, to thighs thick enough to hint at their existence within his pant legs.

He was wearing deck shoes, not dancing shoes— without socks—and Delia had to quell a tiny shiver of something that almost felt like arousal at the sight of nothing more than a fraction of an inch of naked foot between the vamp of his shoes and the break of his slacks.

At home, deck shoes and no socks would have been a turnoff. But then at home she also wouldn't have been in nothing more than a tight, spaghetti-strapped camisole that she usually only wore underneath things, a brightly colored sarong tied at her waist over her bikini bottoms and sandals. But she wasn't at home. She was in Tahiti. On vacation.

*And anything goes,* she thought.

Andrew was still holding out his hand to her, waiting for her to take it, to accept his invitation to dance.

"Come on," he said in a deep voice that tempted and cajoled at once.

*Why not?* Delia asked herself, taking the plunge. And his hand. And getting to her feet at the same moment Andrew's extremely handsome face erupted into a grin.

"Good girl! I knew you had it in you," he praised, teasing her.

He led her to the dance floor and swung her into his arms. The movement sent Delia's head spinning, warning her that she really was already under the influence of alcohol.

It didn't matter, though. Not when she felt so good. Not when everything seemed right with the world.

Marta gave her a thumbs-up over Henry's shoulder when she caught Delia's eye, bestowing sisterly approval and encouragement of Delia letting down her hair—an uncommon occurrence.

Delia only smiled in return as Andrew pulled her closer and proved he was as adept at dancing as he'd been at everything else they'd done today.

And it was nice. Nice not to be odd man out anymore. Nice to feel a man's strong arms around her—something that hadn't happened in a long, long while. Nice to be where she was, who she was, with her family and this very pleasant, personable stranger. Nice to be oh-so-relaxed and fancy-free, with nothing to do but have a little fun. Nice, for once, to just go with the flow....

And that was exactly what Delia did for the remainder of the evening. She danced with Andrew and Henry and Kyle. She drank more—and more—sour-apple martinis. She laughed and flirted and had a good time until one by one the other people in the palapa disappeared. Until Kyle and Janine wandered off to their bungalow. Until Marta and Henry wandered off to theirs.

Until Delia was left all alone with Andrew, on the dance floor yet again.

His arms were slung low on her hips. His hands were clasped together at the small of her back. Her arms were hooked over his shoulders. Her brow was against the wall of his chest. His chin was on the crown of her head. And they were barely swaying to the lazy strains of a very slow song.

"Why is it that vacations take so long to get here and then end so soon?" she lamented in a singsongy, dreamy voice.

Above her, Andrew chuckled a throaty chuckle that was all male. "I don't believe in ever letting them take too long to get here," he said. "And who says it has to end? You could change your plans. Stay…"

Delia laughed. She sounded giddy to her own ears but she didn't care. "Stay?"

"You could send Kyle and Janine and Marta and Henry on their way and stay," Andrew said. And unless Delia was mistaken, he was serious.

She lifted her head from his chest to peer up at that face that was too good to believe. "I can't stay," she said, *not* sounding serious even though she was.

"Sure you can. A few phone calls can arrange anything. I know the owner of this resort—I stay here often. I'll get him to let you keep your bungalow. And I'll be here...."

That last part was the real enticement.

Again Delia laughed. "No, no, no," she said unfirmly.

"Yes, yes, yes," he responded, dipping forward enough to press a kiss to the spot just above her ear.

The kiss surprised her. He hadn't done anything like that before. But somehow it didn't shock her. Or put her off. It was just another thing that seemed nice. And tantalizing. Like him.

"No, no, no," she repeated, still not strongly and not even sure herself whether she was saying no to his suggestion that she remain in Tahiti or to that kiss. But either way, it didn't have enough force to mean much.

"A few more days—what harm could it do?"

Delia laughed. "Don't ask me hard questions after I've had so many martinis."

It was Andrew's turn to laugh. He also squeezed her enough to bring her closer still to the solid wall of his body. "I'll miss you if you go."

He made that sound genuine even though Delia doubted it was true.

"I think you'll probably survive the horrors of Tahiti without me," she said facetiously.

"But at what cost?" he asked with a voice full of mock drama, making her laugh again.

The bartender had been working at closing the bar for a while and had apparently finished his tasks, because he stepped from behind it to leave just as the last strains of music came to an end.

"That's all for tonight," the ukulele player announced in French-accented English, and the trio picked up and followed the bartender.

But Andrew didn't pay them any attention. His gaze never wavered from Delia, and he went on swaying as if there were still something to sway to.

"I think we've closed the place," Delia whispered as if it were a confidence, meeting his coffee-colored eyes with her own.

Andrew merely smiled a small, contented smile and then dipped down to kiss her again. This time on the lips. A soft, soft kiss that sent tiny tingles raining through her as if it were midnight on New Year's Eve and someone had just dropped a handful of confetti over her.

He stopped kissing her but the tingles lingered.

"Does this mean our night has to end?" he asked, his voice suddenly so deep it was nearly inaudible.

Delia glanced around at the empty tables, the abandoned bar, the drum set left deserted, and then looked up at Andrew again. Only as she did, she became aware of just how much she *didn't* want this night to be over quite yet.

"We could take a walk on the beach," she suggested.

Another smile spread across his supple mouth, slow and lazy and pleased.

"Better than nothing," he said, swaying a few minutes more before finally bringing their semblance of dancing to a halt.

He caught one of her hands in his to hold as they left the palapa and headed towards the surf.

Delia had no idea what time it was. But as they passed the bungalows—all of them over-water bamboo bungalows with palm-thatch roofs that could only be reached by crossing a wooden bridge to a dock that connected them—she couldn't see a single light on anywhere. No signs of life appeared on the beach itself, either, making it seem as if she and Andrew were the only two people on the entire island.

There was just the sound of the calm sea lapping gently at the shore as Andrew took her near the water's edge and headed away from the bungalows beneath a sky spotted with stars paying homage to an almost full moon.

They didn't talk. They just walked.

Ordinarily a silence like that would have made Delia uncomfortable. But there, then, it didn't. Instead she was absorbed in details like the length of Andrew's legs, the confidence of his stride even on the wet sand, the warm strength of his hand around hers and how much she liked it. All of it. All of him.

The bungalows were only dots far in the distance when they stopped. Shoes were kicked off and they sat on the dry portion of the beach—Andrew behind Delia, his arms wrapping her as if it were something they'd done a million times before.

"Maybe if I just hang on tight and don't let go of you you'll stay," he said, his mouth close to her ear, his voice intimate.

"Can't stay," she repeated, allowing her head to fall back to his shoulder.

To accomplish that, her head was tilted to one side and Andrew pressed a kiss to her neck, sighing a resigned and disappointed-sounding sigh that bathed her skin in a hot gust of breath.

"I guess we'd better make tonight last, then," he said.

Delia wasn't sure what he meant by that. But she knew what was going through her own mind. Although she didn't know why or where it had come from.

What was going through her own mind were thoughts of indeed making tonight last.

In this man's arms...

She couldn't believe what she was thinking. What she was considering.

A vacation fling?

She didn't have flings, vacation or otherwise.

Not that it was unheard of to her. She had a friend who loved telling stories of holiday romances. A friend who didn't consider vacations a success unless she met someone to flirt with, to have fun with, someone to send her home with memories that put secret smiles on her face....

No strings. No attachments. No future. No further expectations. Nothing to answer for.

That was what Delia's friend said was part of the allure. Just a fling at a time when she felt free. Free enough to indulge whatever whim struck her. As if her real self had been left at home while she was in some faraway place where whatever she said or did remained there when she returned to her everyday life….

Never before, when Delia's friend had talked about it, had Delia done more than laugh at the very notion. But now?

Now it seemed to be beckoning to her.

Just a vacation fling …

*Throw caution to the wind,* her friend's voice seemed to say in the breeze.

Andrew was tugging on her earlobe with tender teeth, flicking the edge with the tip of his tongue and setting off more of that confetti tingling through her.

*He's a stranger,* she reminded herself. *And we're out here, on the beach, in the open…*

It wasn't something Delia McCray did. *Ever.*

But tonight she really did have the sense that Delia McCray was back in Chicago, while she—whoever she was at that moment—was here. In paradise. With this broad-shouldered, suntanned, muscled man who was nibbling her jawline even as her nipples grew to taut little knots against his forearm and he pushed back on them to let her know he felt it, too.

He uncrossed his legs from where they'd been at her derriere and stretched one on either side of her, coming up closer behind her. Close enough for her to know his thoughts were on the same course that hers were.

He wanted her. There was unmistakable proof. And

knowing it erupted a whole flood of desires in Delia that she didn't even know she was capable of. Overwhelming desires. Driving needs that demanded their due…

She'd had too much to drink. She knew it. She knew it as well as she knew she wasn't completely in her right mind.

But she wanted this man as much as he so obviously wanted her. She wanted this moment. This vacation fling.

She tilted her head and turned it as far as she could to see Andrew out of the corner of her eye. Realizing all over again how handsome he was gilded in moonglow.

She smiled.

And she flexed her hips firmly back into him.

He smiled, too. An answering kind of smile that said he knew. He understood. A smile so sexy she could hardly stand it.

Then one of his hands came to her breast, engulfing it, grasping it, making her nipple stand at attention in his palm so forcefully she thought that small kernel might actually burst right through the negligible containment of the spandex camisole just to have the unbridled feel of his skin against it.

He craned forward enough to cover her mouth with his. His lips were parted. His tongue wasn't shy in the slightest. And in one motion he turned her toward him.

Her sarong came untied and fell away but she didn't care. She was far more interested in reaching her arms around him, in giving herself over to him completely,

in shedding any inhibitions that might have been
lurking and allowing everything her body was crying
out for to be answered.

There.

Right out in the open.

On that Tahitian beach.

Under the watchful eye of nothing but the moon.

## Chapter Two

*Monday morning. Bright and early. Or funds to your account are stopped. I'm not kidding.*

It was Monday morning. 8:00 a.m. And Andrew Hanson was where he'd been ordered to be. Ordered via e-mail by his older brother Jack. Complete with the threat that if he didn't show up at the Chicago offices of Hanson Media Group, he would be financially cut off from all future support by family funds.

So there he was. Only hours off a plane from Tahiti. Barely showered. Unshaven. Dressed in jeans and a T-shirt. And wishing for eight hours sleep. Wishing even more to be back on the beach he'd been on for the last three months. Or on any other beach for that matter.

It was a common response for him. Especially

whenever anything on the home front got complicated
or unpleasant or became a drag. And things in Chicago
at that moment were complicated, unpleasant *and* a
drag. The death of his father had caused all of that at
once three months ago, and so as soon as the funeral
was over Andrew had done what he had done frequently in the past—he'd hightailed it out of town to
wherever seemed like the best escape, Tahiti, this time.
Tahiti, where he'd fully intended to stay for a long, long
while.

A long, long while that wouldn't have ended, except
that after ignoring numerous e-mails from his older
brother and their uncle David—their late father's much
younger brother—Jack had forced Andrew to come
back to Chicago.

To help with the recent disasters that had befallen
Hanson Media Group, the family business.

A woman Andrew assumed to be a receptionist or
a secretary had shown him to the conference room, informing him that Jack and David would be with him
soon. But he had no idea how soon *soon* was and he
really needed some sleep, so he plopped down on one
of the chairs at the large table and used a second chair
for his feet. Then he let his head fall to the back of the
chair he was sitting in and closed his eyes.

But despite the fact that he was tired and jet-lagged
and could usually doze off anywhere without any
problem, he didn't doze off now.

He just couldn't stop thinking, *What the hell do
Jack and David think* I *can do…?*

Hanson Media Group was in trouble. That much

Andrew knew. Apparently his father, George—who had run the media conglomerate—had not been as savvy a businessman as he'd led everyone to believe. As savvy a businessman as George's and David's own father, who had built Hanson Media Group from the ground up.

But rather than exposing his failings to his family, George had kept two sets of books—one that made him look good and another that told the truth. The truth being that he'd run Hanson Media Group—the source of the wealth that had always supported all the Hanson family—into the ground. To the verge of bankruptcy.

Jack had temporarily stepped in after George's death and discovered the second set of books. Now he and David were in the process of giving it their all to turn things around. But compounding matters, one of Jack's attempts had led to the Internet portion of Hanson Media Group inadvertently being linked to a pornography site that had stirred further trouble for the company with morality groups.

Jack's and David's e-mails had kept Andrew up-to-date on these matters, so Andrew was well aware of the dire situation. He just didn't have any idea why his brother and his uncle thought it was so crucial that he be here in the middle of it, too.

The sound of his brother's voice coming from just outside the conference room alerted Andrew to Jack's imminent arrival. It caused Andrew to open his eyes but not to sit up or even to take his feet off the other chair.

Within moments the door opened and in strode Jack

and David, both in business clothes and looking far more professional than Andrew did.

Andrew saw the other men take note of his casual attire but neither of them said anything.

"Finally," was what Jack did say, clearly in reference to Andrew's belated attendance, his impatience with Andrew ringing in his voice.

"Hi, guys," Andrew greeted in return.

Jack shook his head in disgust and sat across the conference table from him.

David offered a tight smile. "Good to see you, Andrew. We're glad you're here."

"Good to see you, too, big D. I'm just not sure why I *am* here," Andrew responded, cutting to the chase in hopes that this meeting could be quick and he could get back to his apartment for some sleep.

Jack had gone to business school, and to law school as well. Before George's death Jack had been a practicing attorney with ambitions of becoming a judge. Now it struck Andrew that his brother was sitting as stiff-backed as if he were already on the bench.

Jack had brought in several files and now he set them on the table and slid them across to Andrew with a force that sent them sailing to the edge.

Andrew didn't raise so much as a finger to intercept them and if they hadn't stopped on their own they would have ended up on the floor.

"You're here to go to work," Jack announced unceremoniously then.

It wasn't like Jack to make jokes but that struck Andrew as funny. "Work?" he repeated.

"Work," his older brother confirmed.

David, who had always stood up for his nephews, took a more friendly tone as he sat at the head of the table where Andrew could see him without so much as turning his head.

"We need your help, Andrew. The porn scandal caused more problems. That computer hacker who fixed it so that people—even kids—who were surfing our Web pages could inadvertently be switched to a pornographic site nearly did us in. We're still trying to recover, to convince people that it *was* the hacker who did it, that Hanson Media Group has absolutely no affiliation with pornography in any way, shape or form. But we've lost advertisers and that means we've lost revenue we couldn't afford to lose. So we had to lay off a lot of people just to continue making payroll once we realized what financial shape Hanson Media Group is in. We're down manpower—"

"And if you want money from the company you're going to have to earn it," Jack cut in, finishing what David was saying and sounding every bit the big brother who was put out with his younger sibling.

"What can I possibly do?" Andrew asked. "I don't have a clue about what goes on here."

"No, you just cash the checks," Jack said, brusquely.

"We're trying to get hold of Evan, too," David added as if to let Andrew know he wasn't the only errant Hanson being asked to pitch in. "But Evan is being even worse than you were about answering our calls and e-mails," David concluded with a tone that showed his irritation.

Evan was the middle brother—five years Jack's

junior, two years older than Andrew. Evan was more like Andrew in his freewheeling ways and lifestyle than he was the nose-to-the-grindstone, judicious Jack, or their straight-arrow uncle. But Andrew was a little surprised that he'd caved before Evan had.

He didn't say that, though. Instead, still without reaching for the manila folders or claiming them in any way, Andrew cast his brother a dismissive gaze to let Jack know he wasn't taking any guff from him, and then focused on his uncle once more as David said, "We want you to sell advertising. We're hurting badly on that front and—"

"And it mainly involves wining and dining clients and potential clients so we figured that wasn't too far removed from your good-time-Charlie talents," Jack said, completing David's thought for the second time.

"I may know about wining and dining, but advertising? Like I said, not a clue," Andrew insisted, still half wondering if they were joking.

But when his uncle clasped his hands together, laid them on the table and leaned forward, Andrew knew that wasn't the case.

"Look, Andy," David said earnestly. "We need you. There just isn't a choice anymore. We're short-staffed and the only money Hanson Media Group can afford to let out of here has to go to people producing for the company."

"In other words," Jack added, "there are no more free lunches. You can work for Hanson Media Group or you can get a job somewhere else, but one way or another you're going to have to earn a living."

Andrew might not have finished college but he wasn't stupid. He knew he didn't have anything to offer when it came to the job market. But he still wasn't sure his brother and his uncle weren't overestimating his abilities.

"It's not that I'm not sympathetic," he said. "Or that I'm not willing to reduce my living expenses or whatever. But I'm not a high-pressure salesman."

"You'll learn," David assured as if he had every confidence in him. "Jack and I will walk you through things until you get the hang of it all. But you're personable. Likable. You make friends easily. You wow the women without even trying. You can talk to anyone and put them at ease, make them comfortable and open to your ideas, your suggestions. Those things go a long way in sales. That's why we know you can do this."

"I'm glad you think so," Andrew said under his breath.

"You really can do this," Jack said then, curbing some of the attitude he'd been displaying since coming into the conference room. "It'll be right up your alley. You'll just have to put some effort into it."

"*Effort* meaning wear a suit and show up here every day—nine to five? Go to meetings? Do paperwork? Call clients? That sort of thing?"

"Your office is right down the hall," David said as if he were thrilled and relieved that Andrew was on board, when Andrew didn't actually feel as if he'd *agreed* to be on board yet.

"And it won't always be just nine to five," Jack

amended. "For instance, tonight you and I are having dinner with a company called Meals Like Mom's."

David picked up the ball and ran with it from there. "Last month Meals Like Mom's made the list of top-ten up-and-coming businesses in the Chicago area. It's an innovative concept that's taking off. Healthy, nutritious, preservative-free meals can be purchased at reasonable costs either from a few specialty shops or delivered right to people's houses. Busy, working parents can put a dinner on the table for their whole family that looks and tastes like they've spent the day cooking. Or single people or couples can treat themselves to a well-balanced, great-tasting meal without any hassle. Or Meals Like Mom's will send in a hundred or more boxed lunches—we did it on the larger scale at the last board meeting. All with the guarantee that the food will taste like someone has prepared it especially for them, like their Mom would make."

"Okay," Andrew said, only half paying attention.

His uncle continued. "My eyes and ears in the advertising world tell me that Meals Like Mom's has just hired one of the biggest local agencies to do commercials, radio spots and print ads for them. That's all going to have to go somewhere and it might as well be to Hanson Media Group. They could be a huge account for us and they could also bring with them the kind of clean image we need to be connected with right now."

"All the information we have on the Meals Like Mom's organization is in one of those files," Jack said. "You'll need to read it, become familiar with it. The other file will show you the deal we're offering and how it compares—favorably—with other local media outlets. That's something you'll want to use as a selling point. The third file will fill you in on what you're to say should the subject of the porn scandal come up— that could well be a sore spot for a company with *Mom* in the title. The meeting is at six. The restaurant's name and address are on a Post-it in one of the files. I'll meet you there at five forty-five. Suit and tie. Clean shaven. And get your hair trimmed. You look like someone who's been laying on a beach for months."

Without waiting for a reply, Jack stood and walked to the conference room door.

But he paused there to glance back at Andrew. "Welcome to the real world. Time to grow up, little brother."

And out he went, leaving Andrew alone with David.

But if Andrew had any hope of his uncle softening the blow he'd just been dealt, it didn't come.

David stood, too. "Read through the files, commit everything to memory and then go out and get yourself fixed up and dress for tonight. This is important."

Andrew didn't respond. He just stared at his uncle.

David passed by him on his way to the door, patted his shoulder and said, "I know you're up to this, Andy. I have faith in you."

Andrew merely raised his chin in acknowledgement of that, not wanting to say his uncle's faith might be unwarranted.

Then David said, "Let me see if your office is ready for you and I'll show you to it, introduce you around."

And out he went, too, leaving Andrew once again alone in the conference room.

Which was probably a good thing since the expletive he muttered wouldn't have been well-received had anyone been there to hear it.

Sales? he silently shrieked to himself. They wanted him to be a salesman? To sell advertising? He didn't know squat about selling *or* advertising. Or about having an office he had to show up at every day. In a suit and tie.

He voiced another, even more colorful expletive under his breath.

This was the last thing he'd figured he was coming home to. He'd thought Jack and David might have wanted to liquidate portions of the company's holdings, or consolidate things, or that maybe they'd wanted to fill him in on legalities that had arisen out of the porn scandal. He'd figured that there was just something they wanted him to pretend an interest in, to lend his support to. Some kind of family-unity thing or something.

But putting him to work? He hadn't even considered that that was a possibility. Hell, he'd never worked for the company. Or for anyone else. All his life Hanson Media Group had just done its thing and he'd done his, thrilled to have his share of the proceeds deposited in his account every month.

And now those days were over.

He didn't like it.

But whether he liked it or not, whether he liked the idea of being an advertising salesman or not, whether he could do it or not, apparently didn't make a difference. Jack and David were set on this and clearly he didn't have a choice in the matter. Not if he wanted to continue to have an income. And what would he do *without* an income?

He was stuck. And he knew it. With nothing to do but comply.

For now, anyway.

Because maybe those good old days weren't really over. Maybe they were just suspended for the time being. Maybe before too long things would turn around. The scandal would blow over. Business would pick up. Former employees could be rehired. And he could just go back to the life he'd been living.

It helped to think that that might be a possibility— even if there hadn't been anything in any of what his brother or his uncle had said to lead him to believe it. It helped to think that this wasn't permanent. It made it all the more easy to accept that way. In fact, it was the only way he *could* accept it at that moment.

So he sighed, hung on to the notion that this would have a limited run, and finally conceded that he was going to have to sell advertising. At least for a while. And he reached for the files on the table, bringing them to his lap.

Files.

This was *so* not him….

But still he opened the one on top, knowing only when he did which file he was looking at first.

Meals Like Mom's—it was the background information on the company he was supposed to recruit tonight.

Just below the name of the company was the owner's name—Delia McCray.

Andrew took a closer look at that, thinking his eyes and his overwhelmed brain were playing tricks on him.

But no, he'd read it right the first time—the name was Delia.

"Huh," he mused.

Delia wasn't a common name. And now here he was, encountering it twice—three months ago in Tahiti and again today.

Maybe the universe was toying with him, he thought. Because the Delia he'd met in Tahiti had sort of haunted him, and just when he was regretting the fact that he'd heeded Jack's and David's e-mails and left the island, he was reminded of Tahiti and Tahiti Delia all over again.

Tahiti Delia…

Oh, yeah, Tahiti Delia had definitely stuck with him even after she'd left him on the beach at sunrise the morning after they'd spent the night together.

Flaxen hair that was so pale a blond it was like lemons diluted with cream. Flawless porcelain skin that could have been the envy of newborn babies. A small nose that was a little pointed at the end where it gracefully curved up just the slightest. High, high cheekbones that gave her beautiful face a fragile look. Lips that were thin but coy and sexy, too. And oh, man, what eyes she'd had—eyes the color of crystal-clear ocean waves just before they broke against the shore.

Eyes that were a blue like no other. Glistening and shimmering and capable of sweeping a person right off his feet.

Top it all off with long, lanky legs that had seemed to go on forever despite the fact that she hadn't been too tall, a tight rear end and just enough up front, and Tahiti Delia had been something dreams were made of.

And he'd had plenty of dreams of her and their tryst under the stars, there was no mistake about that. Plenty of dreams that had let him relive their encounter, that had left him aching to do it all over again. That had made him sorry that they'd had only that one night…

"Ready to see your new digs?"

Andrew had been so lost in thoughts of Tahiti Delia he hadn't heard his uncle return to the conference room door to poke his head in.

As if he were guilty of something, Andrew yanked his feet off the chair and stood, fumbling with the files he'd forgotten about and nearly dropped, before he snatched them up to take with him.

"Yeah. Sure," he muttered, sounding as distracted as he felt and trying hard to get himself out of that daydream and back to reality.

Trying, too, to find some kind of work mindset and wondering—when a wave of what felt like claustrophobia hit him—whether he was actually going to be able to pull off holding this job.

Especially when it took so little to carry him back to Tahiti.

And to Tahiti Delia.

## Chapter Three

"We'll give him five more minutes and then if he isn't here, we'll go on without him. And again, I can't apologize enough. But as I said, he was just back from vacation today, I dumped a whole lot on him that he hadn't expected, he was jet-lagged, hadn't slept and—"

"Honestly," Delia assured Jack Hanson, "we understand. Your brother is only ten minutes late. It's not a problem."

The tight smile that the acting head of Hanson Media Group gave to Delia, Marta and Gwen—the ad agent handling their account—was enough to let Delia know that regardless of what Jack Hanson said, his brother was in for it when he got him alone after this dinner meeting.

But just then Jack Hanson's expression eased and he said, "Here he is."

They had already been seated at a round table in the restaurant Gwen had suggested and since Delia's back was to the door, she took Jack Hanson's word for it and didn't crane around to see for herself. Neither did Marta—also sitting without easy access. But Gwen obviously saw the approach of the other Hanson brother and seemed to like what she saw, because the smile that had begun as businesslike became something else entirely. At the same time her eyes widened and she sat up taller in her chair, drawing her shoulders back in a way that pushed out her ample chest.

And then Jack Hanson's brother came around the table to the vacant chair that had been left for him. Where Delia and Marta could both see him.

"Oh!" Marta exclaimed as Delia merely peered up in sudden shock.

"Andrew!" Marta added then. "It's Andrew! From Tahiti."

"Delia?" he said, his focus omitting Marta and everyone else at the table as his espresso eyes honed in on Delia. "I saw your name in the file but… You're Delia *McCray?*"

"You all know each other?" Jack asked.

"Sort of," Delia answered, struggling to find her voice and some aplomb to go with it. "We just met— briefly—in Tahiti. When Marta and I and the rest of our family were there. A few months ago."

A million things were popping into Delia's mind suddenly. This was not a situation or a scenario she'd ever imagined. And in the last month and a half she'd imagined many.

To her rapidly increasing dismay, rather than taking his chair, Andrew came back around the table to press a kiss to her cheek. A kiss that was nothing, considering the night they'd spent together. But a kiss that unnerved her even further. A kiss she barely tilted her head to receive.

"It's great to see you!" Andrew said. Then, raising his chin to Marta, he added, "You, too, Marta. I just can't believe it."

"Small world," Gwen contributed as if to remind them of her presence.

"And this is Gwen Davis, the account executive from DeWit and Sheldon—the ad agency handling Meals Like Mom's," Jack said to include the other woman.

"Oh, I'm sorry, Gwen," Delia apologized. "Of course. This is Gwen. Gwen, this is Andrew...Hanson?" Since Delia was only assuming that was Andrew's last name she had to add a questioning inflection at the end of that.

"That's me, Andrew Hanson," Andrew confirmed, holding out a hand to Gwen before he returned to take his seat. And to staring at Delia. "Delia. I still can't believe this."

The waiter arrived with the wine Jack had ordered and after getting his approval for the selection, the waiter began pouring glasses of the ruby-hued brew. Delia's mind was spinning in a private panic and when the waiter reached her it was Marta who snatched Delia's glass out of the way.

"No wine for our mom-to—" Marta cut her own words short, gasping as if that might reclaim them.

And Delia cringed inside, hoping and praying that no one would finish Marta's phrase.

But her hopes and prayers were for naught.

"Mom-to-*be?*" Gwen asked. "Is that what you were going to say, Marta?" But before Marta could respond, Gwen looked to Delia and said, "Are you pregnant?"

It crossed Delia's mind to say no, she wasn't pregnant. To try to connect her sister's comment to the name of her business somehow. But not only couldn't she come up with a way to do that, it also occurred to her that it was futile, that she'd be working with Gwen and possibly with the Hansons, and that there wouldn't be any concealing the pregnancy before long, that it would seem silly that she'd denied it when it was true. So she opted for forging ahead.

"Yes," she answered quietly.

Marta leaned over and whispered, "Go ahead, shoot me now."

But Delia merely forced a semblance of a smile. She couldn't blame her sister for something that had happened naturally. Delia, Marta and Kyle had always been watchdogs for each other, and since Delia had discovered that she was pregnant, Marta had been doing things like that whenever she and Delia were together. Delia knew it was a reflex by now. It was just that ordinarily they were in private when it happened and for this to be the first public announcement couldn't have been worse timing.

"Well, congratulations!" Gwen said as if the news pleased her more than there was any reason for it to.

"So Meals Like Mom's is really going to have a mom," Jack pointed out. "Congratulations."

"Thank you. All around," Delia said, fighting mortification and wishing Andrew would stop boring into her with the gaze she was trying not to return.

"Pregnant?"

Andrew muttered so quietly it was barely audible. Which was good because it left Delia hoping no one else had picked up on the personal note she could have sworn she heard in his voice.

Just when she didn't think this could get any worse, Gwen said, "When are you due?"

Now that she'd come this far in the forging-ahead department, she could hardly stop by refusing to answer a perfectly common question. Even if it did feel as if she were exposing herself even more. But the best she could do was a barely audible, "Six months."

Her sister jumped in. "But that isn't what we came here to talk about tonight, is it?" Marta said, her own voice a touch too bright and an octave higher than it should have been. "We came to discuss advertising and we've put it off long enough."

"My fault," Andrew said.

Delia's glance went involuntarily to him at that, unsure for a split second what he was confessing to.

But then he continued. "I promise to make amends for keeping you all waiting."

"Waiting. Right," Delia said in relief. "Well, let's not wait any longer," she said and ushered them into talking business, counting on Marta to pay close attention because just making it through this dinner was going to be about as much as Delia could pull off. She knew she wasn't going to retain a word that was said about anything from then on.

Not now that the cat was out of the bag.

To a man she'd been absolutely sure she'd never see again.

"Why don't you and I discuss a few more things over a drink at the bar?"

It was Gwen Davis's suggestion to Andrew when the dinner meeting was concluded and everyone had stood to leave. Gwen had been less than subtle all through the meal, making it clear that she wanted to get to know Andrew better. On a personal level.

Delia had repeatedly reminded herself that there was no reason for her to feel anything whatsoever about that. That she had no hold over Andrew. That he'd been nothing but a vacation fling for her. She'd also told herself that it shouldn't matter to her under any circumstances. Not even her current ones.

But Gwen's interest in Andrew still irked Delia to no end.

So it was satisfying when Andrew rejected the advance.

But it was less satisfying and far more stress inducing when he then hung back, took Delia's arm to draw her nearer, and said close to her ear, "Actually, I was hoping to persuade you to have a cup of coffee with me. Alone. I thought we could catch up. Talk…"

Feeling as if she couldn't refuse, Delia said a reluctant, "All right."

Marta had overheard the exchange and with the same apologetic expression that had been on her face every time she'd looked at Delia since the comment that had revealed Delia's pregnancy, she said, "Shall I stay?"

Delia knew her half sister was offering moral support and although Delia really could have used it she couldn't accept it. For whatever reason fate had arranged this that she'd never thought would happen, she was going to have to face it—and Andrew—on her own.

"No, it's okay. Go on home to Henry. I'll see you tomorrow," Delia told her, forcing herself to appear more confident than she felt.

"You're sure?"

"I'm sure. It'll be okay."

Marta looked from Delia to Andrew and back again, then she leaned in to whisper to Delia, "I'm so sorry."

"It's okay," Delia repeated.

Jack Hanson, Gwen and Marta left then and Andrew motioned to the restaurant's bar. "How about in there? It looks quiet."

Delia nodded and, for the third time, said weakly, "Okay."

Andrew ushered her to a small round table in a dimly lit corner of the bar. As he seated her, he said, "I know, no sour-apple martinis. So what will it be? Coffee? Tea? Milk?"

Delia nearly flinched at the mention of the sour-apple martinis that had gotten her into trouble in Tahiti. "Coffee is fine. Decaf."

Andrew called the order to the waitress who had begun to approach them and then sat across from Delia.

Not too far across, though. The table was very small and the chairs were positioned so that when Andrew took the other one his knees were only inches from touching Delia's.

It was something she was more aware of than she wanted to be. Just as she was suddenly more aware of how fantastic he looked in an impeccably tailored charcoal suit, and matching dove-gray shirt and tie.

And all she could think was that she was glad it was too early for her to be showing or to have put on weight anywhere but in her breasts. Breasts that somehow seemed to be jutting forward a bit more now…

"You look great," Andrew said after a moment of studying her, as well. "I still can't believe I'm here with you. I've thought about you more than I want to admit. Tahiti wasn't the same after you left."

His handsome face erupted into a smile that was a little lopsided to let her know he was joking. Or at least that he was joking to the extent that not much could diminish how incredible Tahiti was whether she was there or not. But the mention of the island offered Delia a way to delay the inevitable and she seized it.

"Your brother said you just got back from vacation today. Does that mean you were in Tahiti three months ago and took another trip now?"

The quirk of Andrew's lopsided smile increased. "No, I was in Tahiti all along."

"Really?" Delia said, unable to keep the surprise out

of her voice. "Hanson Media Group must have a liberal vacation benefit."

That made the smile waver and dim somewhat. "To be honest, today is my first day working for the company."

The waitress brought their coffees then, and when she'd left, Andrew said, "But we don't want to talk about that. I've had enough of business for one day. I want to talk about you. And what you've been doing since Tahiti."

There was a quizzical note to his voice, as if he were wondering about a secret romance she might have had.

"I've just been working since Tahiti," she said as if that should have gone without saying.

Andrew nodded but Delia had the impression that he was still on a fact-finding mission, even when he said, "I didn't get to congratulate you before. About the baby."

"Thank you?" she said, forming a question with her inflection because she wasn't sure how she was supposed to respond.

"So, when we were in Tahiti you told me you weren't involved with anyone and hadn't been in a long, long while," he said then. "Were you fudging the truth? Or considering yourself technically free because you were on vacation?"

He was definitely testing her.

"I wasn't fudging anything," Delia said. "I wasn't involved with anyone and hadn't been."

"Then you must have met someone as soon as you got back?"

"Excuse me?"

"The baby—it's due in six months, if my math is right, that makes you three months pregnant."

Delia stared at him, searching those traffic-stopping features for some sign of what was going on with him.

She'd been certain that Marta's comment had spilled the beans. So either Andrew *hadn't* put two and two together, or he was playing some kind of cat-and-mouse game. Was he feeling her out in hopes that he would learn that someone else *was* the father?

As she studied him it struck her that Jack Hanson had referred to Andrew as his *younger* brother. And since Jack Hanson seemed to be about Delia's age, she began to wonder just how old Andrew was. If he was young enough to be that naive.

"Are you all right?" he asked when she'd let silence lapse for too long.

"I'm not sure," she said under her breath, taking another, closer assessment of his appearance.

There were a few lines just beginning at the corners of his eyes, but since he'd told her in Tahiti that he took every opportunity to get to a beach, maybe those lines were more an indication of sun exposure than of age. Especially since he lacked the creases an older man might have around his mouth.

Of course he had the confidence and bearing of a man her own age, but if he was from the media-rich Hanson family and was well-traveled, social status and world experience could account for that.

Actually, the longer she sat there trying to figure out his age, the more she realized that she couldn't and before she was even aware she was going to do it, she heard herself ask, "How old are you?"

"Twenty-eight," he answered without a qualm, but obviously with some confusion of his own at the question that had come instead of an answer to his inquiries about the father of her baby. "How old are you?" he asked then, as if turnabout was fair play.

"Thirty-seven," Delia whispered, stunned yet again tonight as she began to consider the fact that not only had she allowed herself to be seduced by a stranger on a vacation, but by a stranger who was so much her junior.

"Thirty-seven?" Andrew repeated. "You? I've known twenty-year-olds who look older than you do."

"I'm thirty-seven," she said once more. "And you're *twenty-eight*...."

Andrew laughed slightly, still clearly unsure what was going on. "And that means what to you?"

"It means you're nine years younger than I am," she mused.

"So you can do math, too?"

"Better than you," she whispered again.

His well-shaped brows pulled together in a puzzled frown. "You really aren't all right, are you?"

"No," she confessed. "Only not the way you think."

But Delia began to wonder if she had an opportunity here that she'd believed she no longer had when Marta had revealed that she was pregnant. If Andrew was even half thinking that he might *not* be the father of her baby she had the opportunity to keep him in the dark about his paternity.

It wouldn't require much. She could merely say that yes, she had met someone when she'd returned from Tahiti. Andrew would never know the difference. He'd go through his entire life without a thought that her baby was his, too. And she could go on with her own plans, the plans she'd had until tonight when she'd so coincidentally encountered him again—she could have and raise her baby on her own.

*Without a father to complicate it...*

That came from the back of her mind. In the voice of her mother. And it jarred Delia.

*Fathers are just complications,* her mother had decreed numerous times. *We don't need them. We do just fine without them.*

Except that the McCrays hadn't always done so fine without them.

Maybe it wasn't wise to make her decision at that moment, influenced by childhood hurts and before she'd considered all the angles, but on impulse Delia said, "I haven't lost my mind and I also didn't meet anyone—or even date anyone—since coming back from Tahiti."

The frown on Andrew's face deepened. "And you weren't involved with anyone *before* Tahiti...?"

"No."

Delia could see that his mental wheels were beginning to turn faster because he sobered considerably.

"Artificial insemination?" he asked.

She wasn't sure whether or not she was imagining a note of hope in that question, but the mere chance that it was there made her feel bad. It made her almost sorry she'd chosen this course after all.

But now that she'd planted the seed, she knew it was going to sprout one way or another and so she said, "No, not artificial insemination."

Andrew stared at her but there wasn't appreciation or happiness to see her or anything good in his expression now. Now he looked as if someone had caught him off guard with a sharp blow to the solar plexus.

He didn't speak. And Delia could tell that he was unable to bring himself to ask that final, inevitable question.

But she answered it anyway.

"Andrew, the baby is yours."

She saw him swallow hard enough to make his Adam's apple rise above his shirt collar.

"This day can't be real," he muttered to himself.

Delia thought that could only mean that he'd had a particularly bad day that this news had topped off. But bad day or not, it was hardly a heartening reaction.

She sat up straighter, drew her shoulders back and, fully intending to tell him she expected nothing from him, she said, "It's okay—"

"Not by a long shot," he said, cutting her off and standing abruptly.

His dark eyes bored down into hers as he shook his head in denial. "I can't do this right now. I'm sorry. I…I don't even know what I'm supposed to say. Or do. I…I guess I have to think," he rambled.

And then he turned around and walked out.

Out of the bar.

Out of the restaurant.

## *Chapter Four*

Tuesday was a bleak, rainy June day in Chicago. An unusually chilly wind gusted from the west. It was the kind of day that could drag down the energy level of a native Californian all by itself.

But Delia's energy level didn't need help from the weather to be reduced. Although she hadn't suffered any morning sickness, she was more tired than was normal for her. A good night's rest was a must. And she hadn't had it. In fact, she'd had almost no sleep Monday night. Not after Andrew's hasty departure from the restaurant had left her stressed out.

She'd still been awake and checking the clock until almost 4:00 a.m. Then she'd dozed off but for only a couple of hours before she'd awakened with a jolt.

From a dream in which she'd been chasing Andrew down a deserted street, unable to catch him or to make him stop when she called to him.

It had been a ridiculous dream, she told herself as she drove to the Meals Like Mom's kitchens where she spent the lion's share of every Tuesday making sure quality control was being upheld and dealing with any problems at that end of the business.

A completely ridiculous dream. Chasing Andrew? The subconscious was a strange thing to come up with something that absurd. After all, she hadn't even had any intentions of tracking Andrew down, let alone of chasing him or trying to catch him. For any reason.

Yes, at one point when she'd first learned she was pregnant she'd contemplated contacting someone at the resort in Tahiti and seeing if she could at least garner Andrew's last name. But she'd gone through a whole lot of contemplations since learning she was pregnant. Different contemplations for each of several stages she'd experienced.

The first stage, she supposed, had been when she hadn't had her period two weeks after arriving home from Tahiti. She hadn't even entertained the idea that she might be pregnant then, though. Her cycles often varied and it wasn't unheard of for her to miss one, so she'd written it off to travel and stress and time changes, assuming that in a week or two she'd simply get back on course.

Then her second period had failed to appear. And she'd suddenly discovered herself in a state of alarm. Oddly enough, not alarm that she might be pregnant, however. Her initial fear had been that something else entirely was going on. She'd been terrified that she'd contracted some sort of sexually transmitted disease that had come from doing something as irresponsible as having unprotected sex with a stranger.

Punishment. She'd been afraid she was being punished for the one rash act she'd ever allowed herself.

So she'd taken her embarrassment to the doctor, confessed, and asked to be tested for STDs.

It had been the doctor's suggestion to also do a pregnancy test.

Even though it was difficult for Delia to believe it now, the chance that she might have gotten pregnant in Tahiti hadn't occurred to her, and the doctor's insistence that a test be done for that, too, had been the first occasion on which Delia had begun to think about that possibility.

Pregnant?

She hadn't *felt* pregnant. Not that she had any idea what being pregnant felt like. But she'd felt just like herself and it had seemed as if pregnancy would make her feel different somehow.

Of course she had been a little tired, but as a result of that she'd also been sleeping better than ever.

And she'd also been a little more hungry than usual, but she'd been working hard to make up for the time she'd taken off for Tahiti.

Her breasts had been more tender—attributable, she was sure, to the built-up hormones of the missed cycle.

But pregnant? She still hadn't accepted that as a genuine, honest to goodness likelihood.

Except that it had not only been likely. It had been the reality.

No, the doctor had assured her two days after her initial appointment when she'd returned to the clinic, she did not have any STDs. She was as healthy as a horse.

She was just pregnant. According to the blood test, which the doctor had insisted—when Delia had questioned the results—was conclusive.

Delia had taken the rest of that day and the next one off work.

She'd gone home, closed her drapes, changed into her pajama pants, an old sweatshirt and her fluffy tiger slippers, and collapsed onto the couch.

She hadn't turned on her television or stereo. She hadn't eaten. For a day and a half she'd done almost nothing but stare into space.

And think, *I'm pregnant?*

It had seemed inconceivable.

Inconceivable that she'd conceived.

A baby.

In Tahiti.

With some guy she didn't know...

That had been the second stage—total shock. And even worse, shame. And mortification.

She was thirty-seven years old, for crying out loud. And there she was, an unwed mother. No different than a teenager. No different than her own mother...

But somewhere in beating herself up had come stage three—the realization that *she* had come from her own mother's transgressions. That so had Marta and Kyle.

That they were good and valuable human beings who contributed to the world. That they were all grateful to be alive and to have each other. And that Delia's own baby could be just as good and valuable and grateful to be alive…

Father or no father.

And that was when she'd entered stage four—she'd begun to come to grips with the souvenir she'd brought back with her from Tahiti. She'd reminded herself that she was a capable, successful single woman who owned two branches of Meals Like Mom's, who made enough money to support a child on her own. That she *was* thirty-seven and that her childbearing years could be fast approaching extinction. That this might be her only opportunity to have a child at all.

Stage five had begun then. Stage five, where she'd come to feel that this baby was a stroke of fate, one that had given her this child as a gift. A gift she was happy to accept.

At about that point she'd toyed with the idea of calling the resort for Andrew's last name. She'd wondered if she should—or could—locate him somehow. If she should tell him about the baby.

But what if she actually *did* find him and tell him? she'd asked herself.

Andrew had only been an indiscretion she'd had on a trip far away from home. The same thing she'd been for him—one wild night on a tropical beach. After a whole lot of sour-apple martinis. That was the extent of it. What could she realistically expect to come of something like that?

Nothing, she'd ultimately realized. And there wasn't anything she'd *wanted* to come of it. It wasn't as if they'd had a relationship. They hadn't even exchanged last names or places of birth or job descriptions or family histories. They hadn't gotten to know each other in any way. Well, in any way but physically. And just the once. But that was nothing to build on. There was nowhere to go from that. No reason to pretend that something of substance had existed between them or ever might.

And as for the feelings of Andrew and the baby…?

Yes, she'd considered that, too.

But given her own family history, Delia doubted that Andrew would welcome the news that unplanned fatherhood had resulted from their single night together. Instead she'd decided that it was far more probable that her pregnancy would be information Andrew would rather not have.

And the baby? Well, Delia would make sure the baby did just fine. If anyone knew how to deal with a fatherless child and everything that child would think and feel, it was her.

So that had been that.

She'd gone from denial to disbelief to actually wanting this baby and being excited that she was going to have it. On her own. Alone. She'd accepted that. Embraced it. And stayed her own course accordingly.

Only now fate had added another twist. Now she'd met up with Andrew again.

And if that wasn't complication enough, she'd also learned that he was only twenty-eight.

"Nine, count them, *nine* years younger than I am," Delia said out loud. "Maybe being attracted to boy toys is a genetic thing."

In Tahiti it hadn't seemed as if there were any age difference between them. If she had had any inclination whatsoever that there was, she wouldn't have spent ten minutes with Andrew. Marta and Kyle wouldn't have *let* her spend ten minutes with him since they felt the same way she did about older women with younger men. And with good reason.

But there honestly hadn't been any evidence of an age difference between Delia and Andrew. In fact, looking back and analyzing it, she was convinced that Andrew's travels and the knowledge he'd gained from that, coupled with his take-charge attitude, had made him appear decidedly older than Kyle, who was also twenty-eight.

But no matter how Andrew had appeared or seemed, the fact remained that he *was* twenty-eight. *Only* twenty-eight.

"The father of my baby is a baby himself," Delia muttered as she arrived at the Meals Like Mom's kitchens and parked in her spot.

She turned off the engine but she didn't get out of her car. She just sat there, staring at the building's brick wall in front of her, thinking, *Andrew is not only a baby, but a baby who completely freaked out and ran away last night....*

Which didn't make him appear or seem older than he was anymore.

So she had probably been right to conclude that her

pregnancy was something he would rather not have ever known about, she told herself.

But it was too late now. He knew.

He knew and he wasn't still in Tahiti or some other place that allowed distance to aid this whole situation. He knew and he was in Chicago. He *lived* in Chicago. They might even be working together....

No. *That,* at least, she had some say in, she thought to console herself when everything felt as if it were careening out of control. They *didn't* need to work together. She could take her advertising somewhere else.

It wasn't much consolation, though. Not when she was still faced with the other two wrenches that had just been thrown into the works.

Andrew did know about the baby.

And he did live in the same city she did.

But there was nothing she could do about those two things.

There was nothing she could do about anything but her own situation. Nothing she could control except her own actions.

And when it came to that, there was comfort in realizing that nothing else had changed.

It didn't alter her own plans in any way. She would still have her baby and would support and raise it on her own.

And if seeing Andrew again the previous evening had served to remind her how pleasant he could be? How good he was at putting everyone around him at ease? How smart and charming and personable he was?

Well, it was nice to know that her child would have the potential for some positive genes that went beyond Andrew's staggering looks.

And it didn't make the slightest difference to her that one glance at him had made her heart skip a beat.

She was sure that that had purely been a result of the shock of seeing him. Not due to the fact that he was knock-'em-dead gorgeous.

And even sexier than she recalled, too…

"That's it for now. You can all get back to work. Except Andrew. You and I need to talk."

His brother's edict only vaguely registered with Andrew. Of course most of what had been discussed during the meeting that he'd spent the last hour in had gone right over his head, too. He couldn't concentrate. Or do much else. He hadn't slept. He hadn't eaten. He'd barely managed to get to the office in one piece since he'd been distracted by his own thoughts on the drive from his apartment, too. The truth was, in the short course of twenty-four hours so much had happened that he just plain didn't know which end was up.

"Andrew! Where the hell are you today?"

Jack. Right. Jack.

Andrew glanced around the conference room where everything had begun the day before, where this morning's meeting had just been held. Everyone else was gone. The door was closed. Only he and Jack were there. But Andrew had no recollection of the other attendees leaving.

Jack was sitting at the head of the table. Andrew was midway down one side, stiffly attempting to keep from slumping and giving in completely to the weight of all that seemed to have been dumped on his shoulders since yesterday.

"Sorry," he said to his older brother, even though he wasn't quite sure what he was apologizing for. But Jack's tone was impatient so he knew something was wrong.

"Well?"

"Well what?" Andrew asked.

"Well, I just asked you what went on with Delia McCray after I left you alone with her last night. But seeing as how you missed it, I'm back to wondering what the hell is wrong with you. You spent the whole meeting staring into space, unfocused, not responding even when something was addressed to you, acting as if you weren't really here, and now you still can't answer a direct question. What's going on?"

Andrew shook his head and stared at the tabletop, unsure if he should be frank with his brother or not.

"What does that mean—shaking your head?" Jack said, his voice rising a decibel.

Andrew shrugged. "I guess it means I don't know. I don't know what's going on with me. I got in from Tahiti yesterday and apparently when I thought I was opening my suitcase I was really opening Pandora's box instead."

Andrew forced himself to look at his brother in time to see Jack frown fiercely at him and shake his own head. "What does that mean? You opened Pandora's box because you have to work for a living now? Please. The last thing I need is more drama."

"I'm not being dramatic," Andrew said, a tinge of anger peeking its head through his stupor.

"Can we get down to business?" Jack said then.

"Isn't that what I'm here for?"

"We haven't established that you're actually here at all. But if you can pretend to be, for just a minute, maybe you can tell me about the McCrays."

"I met them in Tahiti. There's a brother, too. Kyle."

"And did you all hit it off?"

Andrew shrugged again. "They're nice people. I overheard them talking about snorkeling and offered to show them the best spot for it. Then I spent the next day with them, doing that." He omitted the fact that he'd also spent the evening with them. And the night with Delia. Which had, through the course of the last half day, become something he didn't want to think about.

"Do they like you?" Jack asked, as if the right answer might be tantamount to striking gold.

"I don't know," Andrew responded, his own tone somewhat ominous.

"They were friendly towards you. In a reserved sort of way. And then Delia McCray stayed to have coffee with you."

That was a leading statement. But Andrew didn't let it lead anywhere but to a confirmation. "Right."

"So what happened? Did you close the deal? Persuade her to give Hanson Media Group the top spot on the list of possibilities? What?"

"We didn't talk business."

"How could you not talk business? That's why we were there. Discovering a connection to the client, using it as a springboard, that's a plus when it comes to sales. And you didn't even bring up the subject after I left?"

Jack's anger was growing.

"We had other things to talk about."

"Nothing as important as Delia McCray giving us her advertising," Jack said, raising his voice again.

"Something more important," Andrew said under his breath.

"There isn't *anything* more important right now."

Andrew closed his eyes against the burn of sleeplessness, clasped his hands together, propped his elbows on the conference table and dropped his brow to his thumbs.

"I'm afraid there is," he muttered.

Jack hit the table and even though Andrew couldn't see him, he knew his brother had gotten to his feet. "Dammit, Andrew, what are you talking about? What did you do, fool around with Delia McCray in Tahiti and blow this for us before we even got a chance?"

"Maybe," Andrew said quietly.

"*Maybe?* Maybe what? Maybe you fooled around with Delia McCray in Tahiti or maybe you blew her account for us?"

Jack was shouting now. Andrew knew his brother was under a lot of pressure, but so was he.

He opened his eyes, raised his head from his hands and stared daggers at Jack. "There's no maybe about my *fooling around* with Delia in Tahiti. That baby she's going to have? Mine."

Jack stared back at him and for a moment there was a certain amount of satisfaction for Andrew in seeing that, for a change, he'd dished out the shock rather than been the recipient of it.

But it was only a moment before he realized what he'd just done. He'd just told his brother that he'd fathered Delia McCray's baby. Something he was a very long way from coming to grips with himself yet. Let alone being in any condition to face whatever his brother's response was going to be.

"Tell me that's a joke. A bad joke, but a joke," Jack ordered in a voice that was suddenly so quiet it was much, much more dangerous than any loud rant.

Still, Andrew had reached his own limit and he met Jack's glare eye to eye. "It isn't a joke."

"Sweet holy mother of—" Jack said as he threw his hands in the air and turned away, presenting only his back to Andrew.

But it was enough to let Andrew know that Jack was too mad to even look at him, to trust himself to say or do anything until he gained some control.

Andrew merely waited. What else was he going to do? Pandora's box really was open and there was no closing the lid now.

A full five minutes passed before Jack faced him again. Two fists went to the top of the conference table and Jack leaned on them and let his eyes bore into Andrew.

"Do you have any idea what you've done? Hanson Media Group is still reeling from the porn scandal. The meeting you just zoned out of was about how many more advertisers have pulled their accounts from us. They're leaving us in droves. Our competitors are cashing in on it, luring our clients away. Even clients who have been with us from the get-go are bailing. The wolves are at the door and you just unlocked it."

"Oh, come on. My personal business has nothing to do with Hanson Media Group," Andrew insisted.

"You may think this is just your own personal business, but it isn't," Jack said, his voice rising again. "Word of this leaking out—and things like this always do leak out somehow—could be the last straw. It could be what does us all in. David and I are breaking our necks trying to convince the whole damn world that Hanson Media Group would never be involved in por-nography in any way, shape or form. That we're a fam-ily-owned and -operated company with a commitment to values—family and otherwise. That we're respon-sible and upstanding and as wholesome as apple pie. And now you think it's only your own personal busi-ness that you had a sleazy one-night stand—"

"It wasn't sleazy. Delia isn't that kind of woman."

"Okay, a non-sleazy one-night stand with a poten-tial client. And you think it's your own personal busi-ness that you were too damn stupid and irresponsible to use a condom, and that now that woman—who you are not married to—is *pregnant?* You don't think that reflects back on the family? On the business? That it doesn't give ammunition to every single person who's rooting for us to go under and using morality as leverage against us?"

"Now you have to be joking," Andrew said, holding

on to his own temper, but by only a thread. "This isn't the Victorian era, Jack. People sleep with each other. Yes, sometimes they even have one-night stands. And even though they know better, sometimes they even have unprotected sex. We're human. Even the Hansons."

"We can't afford to be *human* right now!" Jack yelled. "We have to be better than that to prove ourselves all over again."

"Obviously it's too late for me to prove I'm better than anyone," Andrew shouted back, losing his tenuous hold on his own mounting anger. "So what do you want me to do?"

"Fix it! Take responsibility for your actions! Wake up to the fact that you're an adult and start behaving like one! For the first time in your worthless life, surprise me—surprise us all—and be a man!"

"And a *man* would do what?" Andrew asked, his teeth clenched now.

"Marry her!" Jack commanded.

"Marry her?" Andrew repeated in disbelief.

But that was when he saw something in his brother's expression that he'd never seen before. Something intolerable.

He saw disgust.

He heard disgust in Jack's voice when Jack said, "That probably would be too much to expect from you, wouldn't it? Doing the right thing for once?"

Then Jack pushed himself away from the table and stood ramrod-straight, towering above Andrew. "Everything David and I and everyone else around here have done since Dad died, everything I've given up, could all be shot to hell because of you. More people could lose their jobs. This family could lose what's kept it going for three generations. Because of you. I can't even look at you right now," Jack said, spinning on his heels and storming out of the conference room.

*Because of you....*

*Because of you....*

His brother's condemnation seemed to echo off the walls as Andrew once again found himself deserted in that particular office space.

He let his head fall to the back of his chair as wave after wave of emotions washed over him. Fury and anger. Insult. Frustration. Confusion. Bewilderment. Resentment. Fear and worry. And complete and utter dismay.

Marriage? Andrew thought. Jack actually wanted him to *marry* Delia? A woman he didn't even know?

Jack couldn't be serious.

But Andrew knew he had been.

In his brother's eyes it was either marriage or risk the entire fate of Hanson Media Group, of the family finances and of the livelihood of numerous other people employed by the company.

"Because of me."

Andrew took a deep breath and exhaled slowly.

Never in his life had the urge to run been so strong. The urge to simply get on the next plane out of Chicago and head for some tropical isle. The urge to leave behind all the complications, all the emotions, all the burdens, all the recriminations.

Only this time Andrew knew he couldn't do that. And not just because if he did, the money he needed to live wouldn't be forthcoming anymore. Also because it would support what his brother had just said about him—that he was irresponsible. That he was a child.

A stupid, irresponsible child.

Nice. Nice to know that that's what his brother and his uncle and the rest of his family thought of him.

Okay, yes, he'd lived a privileged life, thanks to Hanson money. And yes, that privilege had allowed him few responsibilities. And no, he hadn't done what Jack had done—become super-achiever in spite of all Hanson Media Group had provided. But he *was* a grown man. And just because he didn't have a lot of responsibilities—or hadn't had until yesterday—didn't mean he was *ir*responsible.

But the fact that that's what his brother and his family thought of him…? It was like wearing a hair shirt. It felt bad. Really bad.

But would it honestly take *marrying* Delia McCray to show Jack and anyone else who thought of him like that that they were wrong?

Drastic. That seemed too drastic.

Except, of course, that proving his naysayers wrong wasn't the *only* reason to marry her. She was, after all, pregnant.

Another ripple washed over him. This one something that closely resembled panic. The same kind of claustrophobic panic he'd experienced the previous day when he'd had to accept working here.

But a job was one thing. Marrying someone he

didn't even know was something else entirely. Being a husband—a *father*—was something else entirely…

He swallowed with some difficulty and closed his eyes for the second time, pinching them tight against the sting.

And there in his mind was the picture of Delia.

Odd, but in all of this, he hadn't thought much about her. He'd thought about her being pregnant. About the baby being his. Now he was thinking about what his family thought about him. He was worrying about what kind of an impact his next action could have on people who were just nameless faces outside of his office. But Delia? Sweet, sunny Delia—who had been on his mind a lot since he'd hooked up with her in Tahiti—had not been what he was thinking about since last night.

And odder still, seeing her in his head, thinking about her, suddenly made him feel better. Not a lot, but some.

Yet the idea of *marrying* her continued to just be bizarre.

Marriage?

Him?

To Delia?

No, even just trying the idea on for size didn't help. It still seemed totally surreal.

But was it the only way to redeem himself in the eyes of his family? The only way to *do the right thing*.

*The right thing*—Jack's words.

They seemed old-fashioned. Archaic, even. Or maybe he'd been out playing around for so long that his concept of what was right and what was wrong had progressed too far. Far enough to become skewed. So skewed that the notion of marrying the mother of his child seemed weird to him.

*The mother of his child*—now *that* seemed weird. But that's what Delia was now. And that's what he had to deal with. The consequences of his actions.

Consequences that reached far beyond what they would have been had he *not* been a Hanson. Had he not been in the middle of this Hanson Media Group mess.

But he *was* a Hanson. And he was in the middle of the Hanson Media Group mess. And maybe this was where he finally paid the piper. Where he paid for the luxury and privilege he'd enjoyed so freely.

"So, for the greater good and to prove myself, I have to marry Delia?"

*Have* to…

Another old-fashioned idea. And not a particularly appealing one.

But Delia herself was appealing, he thought. In Tahiti and last night, too.

And as for the baby?

Okay, the thought of becoming a father was daunting. Especially when he considered that he didn't have any idea what kind of father he would make. When he considered that he hadn't had the greatest role model in his own father.

But dealing with *that* wasn't going to happen right away, he reminded himself to keep some sense of control. First things first. And first he'd deal with the hurdles that had been shoved in front of him and get over them, and then he'd have some time to adjust to the other…

So, *was* he actually considering the whole "do the right thing" marriage? he asked himself, slightly surprised that that seemed to be where he was ending up.

Yeah, maybe he was coming to that, he thought. Maybe there really wasn't any other choice. Not if he ever wanted his family to think of him as more than a screwup. Not if he didn't want to spend the rest of his life as the person who just might have struck the final blow to Hanson Media Group's existence. And not if he didn't want to be the kind of guy who got someone pregnant and then turned his back on her.

Which all boiled down to one thing.

Marriage.

To Delia.

"It'll be all right," he said forcefully to reassure himself.

But despite his outward show of bravado, despite his conviction that he wasn't the stupid, irresponsible kid his brother had accused him of being, despite his sudden discovery that he just might want to do the right thing, at that moment, faced with making a living and marriage and fatherhood, he felt pretty unprepared for it all.

Hell, he felt completely unprepared for it all....

## Chapter Five

It was after nine o'clock that night when Delia left her office at Meals Like Mom's headquarters. After spending the day at the kitchens she'd had to return to the main office to do some paperwork. Because everyone but the cleaning crew had been gone by the time she'd arrived—and even the cleaning crew was gone now—she was alone when she left the building.

She wasn't the only person in the parking lot, however. When she got there, there was a second car parked in the spot next to hers—a Jaguar sports coupe—and a man was getting out from behind the steering wheel.

Had she not recognized him instantly she might have been uneasy with the situation. But she did recognize him so she continued the short walk from the building to her car.

"Andrew?"

"Hi," he said, closing his car door without taking his eyes off Delia.

He didn't look good. Well, he was good-looking enough never to look bad—especially in a navy blue suit that rode his broad shoulders and narrow hips to perfection. But it crossed Delia's mind that he must have slept even less than she had because he looked exhausted and drained, and his handsome face was as strained and stressed as any face she'd ever seen.

"Are you okay?" she asked as she came to stand at the front of her own sedan.

"Sure," he said, sounding as if he were putting too much effort into being chipper. "How about you?"

"I'm fine," Delia answered, but with a query in her own tone to let him know she didn't believe he was all right. "What are you doing here?" she asked then, not beating around the bush.

He held up a file folder. "I have the formal proposal based on what we discussed over dinner last night. I thought I'd get it to you as soon as I finished it. And maybe we could talk."

"It's late and I've done about as much work as I'm going to do today. I'll take the proposal and look at it tomorrow." And go home and try to figure out why she was feeling disappointed that that was the only reason he was there.

"It isn't business I want to talk about," he informed her quietly. Then, with a nod at the coffee bar across the street he added, "How 'bout I buy you a cup of decaf? I promise to stick around long enough to drink it tonight."

The half smile he flashed her way was deadly. Even if it did have shades of shame and embarrassment to it. In fact, that made it all the more appealing, somehow.

But Delia reminded herself of all she'd hashed through since the evening before. She reminded herself of their age difference. And of how nothing could ever come of anything between them. Then she said, "I don't think so. I think it's better if we just go our separate ways and pretend we never met."

"I don't think we can do that," he said, his natural charm in the cock of his head.

"Sure we can. Had we not met again purely by coincidence that's what would have happened, so let's just let it happen anyway."

"You never even thought about trying to find me? To tell me about the baby?"

"I considered it. But it didn't seem realistic that I'd be able to find you. And even if I had... Well, I just decided not to."

He nodded slowly, his dark brown gaze on her the entire time.

Delia thought he might be willing to accept what she was proposing, that he would figure that it was enough that he'd come back, made contact, given her the opportunity to take this further if she wanted to. And that since she was making it clear that she didn't want to, he'd feel let off the hook and this would be the end of it.

Which should have made her happy.

But somehow the sense that he was going to do that depressed her a little.

He surprised her though. "I don't want to go our separate ways and pretend we never met," he told her. "I can't do that. I don't think I would have wanted to do that even if there wasn't a baby and we'd met again, but now that there *is* a baby, it really isn't an option."

There was more strength and certainty in his voice than she expected there to be. He wasn't wavering. And not only wasn't he accepting the out she was giving him, he was letting her know he wasn't allowing her to brush him off, either.

"Come on," he said then. "A cup of coffee. Right across the street. So we can talk. That's not a big deal."

"It's late…." Delia said, still hedging, almost afraid to have coffee with him when she could feel herself succumbing to his appeal all over again. Even against her will.

"It isn't late. It's not even nine-thirty," he said insistently. "One cup of coffee. If you're too tired to walk over, I'll drive."

The coffee shop was close enough to make that suggestion funny and Delia couldn't help smiling. She also couldn't help giving in, despite knowing without a doubt that she shouldn't.

"One cup of coffee," she said, warning him with her tone that that was the extent of what she was willing to concede to. "And I don't need to be driven across the street. Even if I am nine years older than you are."

He grinned and leaned toward her as if to share a confidence. "That wasn't an age-related remark."

But there were a lot of other age-related issues that Delia made a mental note to keep in mind as they headed across the street.

When they got to the coffee shop Andrew seated her at a corner table and then went to the counter to get their beverages. As Delia sat there waiting, she felt compelled to watch him. Actually, she couldn't take her eyes off him.

He really was a striking man. Even with signs of fatigue and stress tightening his features. Tall and straight-backed, he emanated power and strength and confidence. More than she would expect of a man not even thirty yet.

The white shirt he wore under his suitcoat was minus the tie she assumed he'd had on all day, and the collar button was unfastened, exposing a thick neck she suddenly remembered—all too well—kissing. Hot and solid, that's the memory she had. With smooth, smooth skin…

"Here we go," he said as he returned to their table carrying two cups of coffee.

Delia yanked herself out of her reverie and silently chastised herself for the direction her thoughts had wandered. Recalling anything about being with Andrew in Tahiti was forbidden—she'd decided that this morning—and she was sticking to it.

"Thank you," she said, glad the place was so dimly lit, because she was concerned that her very fair skin might have some kind of telltale blush to it to go with those thoughts that were off-limits to her.

Andrew sat in the chair across from her and crossed

one calf over the thigh of his other leg, grasping the calf with his right hand.

For no reason Delia understood, her gaze went to that hand, relishing the sight of long, thick fingers, and again flashing back to the taboo of Tahiti—to that hand on her breasts, those fingers…

Again she put effort into altering the course of her thoughts and forced her eyes and her attention back to Andrew's face.

"So," she said to encourage him to say whatever it was he'd wanted to talk about over coffee, hoping to keep herself in line that way since she was failing miserably otherwise.

"So," he repeated, his eyebrows arching in what appeared to be lingering amazement. Tinged with perplexity. "A baby."

"A baby," she parroted him this time.

"Wow."

Delia just nodded.

"Are you…healthy?"

"Very."

"Do you have, I don't know, morning sickness or anything?"

"I've actually felt fine."

Andrew nodded this time, and Delia noticed that he had a death grip on his coffee cup as he raised it to his mouth and took a drink. And if she weren't mistaken, he had some trouble swallowing as she sipped her decaf and watched him over the rim of her own mug.

Then he said, "What about…emotionally? Are you all right with…a baby?"

"I really am," she assured without hesitation. "I admit when I first found out I was kind of knocked for a loop—"

"Right," he said, as if there were finally something they had in common.

"But after a while I realized that I'm okay with it. Better than okay, I'm happy about it."

He nodded once more but Delia could tell it was difficult for him to identify with the concept of being happy about this situation. So she qualified it.

"I'm older, remember? And my 'having baby' days are numbered. So for me, after I adjusted to the idea, I decided maybe it was a good thing. Not something I'd planned, or something I would have gone out and purposely done, but since it happened anyway, I'm okay with it."

Andrew nodded yet again but it was obvious he still didn't share her sentiments. "Well, that seems like a good way to look at it."

He did more tight-fisted coffee drinking. Then he looked her in the eye and said, "I don't doubt the baby is mine. I know we should have used something that night and we didn't and that's my fault. And the timing maps out, and… Well, I'm sure you didn't look up at me unexpectedly last night and instantly figure there's somebody to pin it on."

Delia's expression must have shown her negative reaction to what he was saying because he put both big hands up, palms outward, as if to stop something, and said, "I'm sorry. That sounded bad and I didn't mean for it to. I'm just… I've had a lot of shocks and changes

in the last two days. And no sleep. I'm not firing on all
burners. I'm just trying to say that I know that you
aren't the kind of person who would say the baby was
mine if it wasn't."

"Actually, you don't know what kind of person I
am. But no, that isn't something I would do. I have
no reason to."

"And since I'm not questioning that it's mine, I want
to do what I'm morally obligated to do. I want to marry
you."

Delia laughed. Not because what he'd said had been
humorous, but out of reflex because it was so absolutely ludicrous. "Excuse me?"

"I want to marry you," he said again and Delia had
the mental image of someone holding a gun to his back.

"Because you want to do what you're morally obligated to do," she repeated his words.

"Right."

"Just the kind of proposal every woman longs for,"
she said sarcastically.

"And the answer is…"

"No," she responded as if it were ridiculous to
expect any other answer. "Not on your life. Not in a
million years. Never. No way. Not a chance."

"Did you want to take a minute to think it over?" he
deadpanned with a half smile.

"You really do need sleep. And maybe a psychiatrist
if you're seriously suggesting we get married," Delia
told him. "Why on earth would we do that?"

"It *is* something people do. Particularly people who
are going to have a baby."

"Maybe in some cases, but you and I? We don't even know each other. And I don't need to be made an honest woman of. I'm not going to be shunned or thrown out of the tribe or ostracized or stoned or branded or something. This isn't the Dark Ages. I don't need or want anything from you. Marta is already on-board as my birth coach. Kyle and Janine will come out for the occasion, and between them and Marta and Henry, I'll have plenty of help for as long as I need it after the baby is here. And from then on, I had every intention of doing this myself before last night. Nothing has changed because you and I just happened to meet up again. Certainly you don't have any *moral obligations* or any other kind of *obligations* to me."

"Okay, I've made you mad. I'm sorry. I know I'm not doing this right."

"You don't need to *do* this at all. I'm sure you mean well, but the truth is, having and raising one baby on my own is better than raising two babies at once—the one I deliver in six months and the one who fathered it—"

Delia hadn't meant that to sound quite as harsh as it had, and the fact that her words made Andrew draw back, as if he'd been struck, stalled them.

He inclined his head and breathed a wry sort of sigh. "Two hits on good old Andrew in one day. First from my brother and now from you. Somebody must have declared it open season on me and not sounded the alert."

Delia didn't know what he was talking about but she took a few deep breaths to calm herself before she said,

"I'm sorry. That was uncalled for. All I'm trying to say, is that you can relax. You're not on the hook here. You wouldn't have been if we hadn't accidentally crossed paths again and there's no reason that should change now—"

"What if I want it to change?"

In spite of what he said, Delia didn't have the sense that there was much conviction behind it.

"You're young, Andrew. Younger than I had any idea you were in Tahiti. I can see that you aren't ready for this, while I, on the other hand, am. I'm ready financially, emotionally and in every other way there is. I'm ready to have this baby, to raise it, to love it and cherish it and be thrilled that I've been given it. So there's no reason for you to do what you *aren't* ready for."

Delia stood then, wanting to show him through her actions as well as what she was telling him, that he genuinely was off the hook. "Forget we ever met in Tahiti or again here. Forget my name. Forget I even live in Chicago. Go on with your life and I'll go on with mine, and we'll both be better for it."

She walked to the door of the coffee shop then and had to pause for two couples to enter.

By the time she got outside, Andrew was there behind her.

"What if I don't want to forget you and everything else? What if I think that we're having a baby together and we should do it together? What if I want to be a part of that?"

Delia barely glanced up at him as she headed back

across the street to the Meals Like Mom's parking lot. "What if *I* think this is just some kind of grand gesture that's coming out of a misguided notion that it's what you're supposed to do when the truth is, you don't want to be a father at all?" she countered.

"The *truth* is, you don't know what the truth is because you don't know me any better than I know you. So you can't know whether or not I'm ready for this or might be dying to be a father."

Delia couldn't suppress a small smile at that. "I know enough to know you aren't dying to be a father," she said with full confidence.

They'd reached their cars by then and Andrew insinuated himself between her and the driver's side door, requiring her to look up at his face. "You don't know any more about me than I know about you," he said again. "You can't. And maybe that's really where we need to start."

"We don't *need* to start anything, anywhere," Delia insisted.

"We've already started a whole new human being," he pointed out with a glance downward at her midsection that, for no reason Delia understood, sent a little thrill through her.

Then he continued. "If you won't agree to marry me now, then at least agree to give me a chance. Say you'll spend some time with me, that you'll let us get to know each other, that you'll think about going from here."

*From here to nowhere,* Delia thought.

It seemed obvious to her that what she'd said in the coffee shop had provoked him. That he'd taken it as some kind of challenge. A throwing down of the gauntlet. A gauntlet that he was now determined to pick up. Probably because he *was* so young. But she felt certain that any course set only to meet some imagined challenge to his manhood would be short-lived.

Still, if agreeing to see him was what it would take for him to give up the ghost on this, then it occurred to her that maybe that's what she should do. That maybe if they did get to know each other some, they could even reach a more realistic approach to whatever role Andrew might decide he wanted to have in the baby's life in the future. And that maybe that would be better for all three of them.

"All right," she conceded with a weary sigh.

"All right, on second consideration you *will* marry me? Or all right, you'll spend some time with me, getting to know me?"

"*Some* time," she qualified.

"And you'll do it with an open mind," he said as if he'd been reading hers and knew she was only humoring him because she didn't honestly believe anything substantial would come of it.

"With an open mind," she repeated.

He smiled down at her. "That's all I need," he said with another show of that confidence and charm that had been so appealing in him from the start.

Unable to contain it, Delia returned his smile. "Can I go home now? It's been a long day."

He nodded but his dark eyes held her there in spite

of it as if he were seeing her for the first time. And enjoying the sight.

Then, in a tone of voice that was very like what had gotten her out onto the beach with him that night in Tahiti, he said, "You know, I had no idea you were any older than I am. I even thought I had a year or two on you. So if we're going to forget anything, let's forget the age thing, huh?"

"I doubt I'll be able to do that," Delia confessed.

"Try," he urged in little more than a sexy whisper.

Then he leaned forward only slightly.

It may have been nothing but an alteration of posture. But still it flashed through Delia's head that he was going to kiss her. And she got out of the line of fire in a hurry.

"But we aren't in Tahiti anymore and now everything is different. Now we're in the real world," she warned in a way that could have been only referring to the difference in their ages, or could also have let him know there would be no kissing—or anything else—if that's what had been on his agenda.

But if kissing *had* been on his agenda he gave no indication of it and again said, "Try," as if they were still only addressing the age issue.

Then he slid away from her door so she could unlock it.

He opened it for her when she had, holding it as she got in.

Which she did. Fast.

Because suddenly she couldn't stop recalling kisses

she'd allowed from him before the one she thought she might have just shunned. Kisses she'd participated in.

And how great they'd been…

"I'll be in touch," he promised.

For the second time Delia merely nodded, half wondering if he actually would be in touch.

And half imagining him really touching her.

Really kissing her.

And really doing more to her.

More that she had to struggle to keep from fantasizing about the entire drive home.

## Chapter Six

"I am so, so, so, so sorry!"

Delia hadn't been in her office on Wednesday morning long enough to put her purse in her desk drawer when Marta came in, closed the door and fell back against it to relay her apology. It was the sixth one since Monday night when her slip of the tongue about the wine had revealed Delia's pregnancy to Andrew, his brother and the advertising executive at their dinner meeting.

The first apology had been in a message from Marta on Delia's answering machine by the time she'd arrived home Monday night. But it had been too late for Delia to return the call without waking Henry, so she'd refrained.

Tuesdays were always busy days for both Delia and Marta. Delia spent her time at the kitchens, while Marta was also away from the office at the transportation center to deal with matters there. They almost never had contact with each other on a Tuesday. This week Marta had called five times—with more contrite messages—throughout the day and evening. But Delia's cell phone battery had been dead and when she'd finally collected all the messages and called Marta back, Marta had been away from her own phone so Delia could only leave her a message.

Apparently Marta had made sure to get in early enough this morning to be watching for Delia, though, so they could finally connect.

"I know you said in your message that you aren't furious with me, but are you sure you don't want to just kill me?" Marta continued before Delia had the chance to respond. "I wouldn't blame you if you did. Or if you wanted to disown me or fire me or never see me again as long as you live."

With a laugh, Delia put her purse away, sat in the leather chair behind her desk and finally said, "I'm not furious with you and I don't want to do any of those other things, either. You know better than that."

Marta pushed away from the door and crossed to the visitor's chairs, wilting into one of them. "I couldn't believe it when the words came out of my mouth. Of all the stupid things to do—mention the pregnancy with Andrew there. And *Andrew!* Did you have any idea at all that he *would* be there?"

"How would I have had any idea? I didn't even know

Jack Hanson's brother's name was Andrew, let alone that he was the Andrew from Tahiti," Delia answered.

"Did you just about pass out when you saw him?"

"Just about."

"Me, too. What are the odds?"

"It was pretty amazing," Delia agreed.

"But still, shocked or not shocked, I should never— *ever*—have opened my big mouth about the baby in front of him."

"Actually, he didn't put two and two together. I ended up telling him myself. So you didn't really do any damage. I could have said just about anything and he would never have questioned it."

Marta's face showed her disbelief. "It didn't occur to him that the baby was his?"

Delia shook her head. "No. I thought he had figured it out, too, but he hadn't. He didn't have even an inkling that it's his."

"Seriously?"

"Seriously."

Marta rolled her eyes. "Men. They can be so dumb sometimes."

"Especially the really young ones," Delia said somewhat under her breath because she wasn't eager to get into that part of the story despite the fact that she knew there was no avoiding it.

Marta looked appropriately confused. "The really young ones?"

"How old did you think Andrew was when we were in Tahiti?" Delia asked.

"About your age, I guess. I didn't really think about

it. You two looked so good together and he fit in so well—"

"I thought he was about my age, too," Delia said. "But when he seemed kind of naive about the baby stuff Monday night I asked how old he is."

"And?" Marta urged when Delia dragged her feet about revealing what she knew would be as big a sticking point with Marta as it was with her.

"He's twenty-eight," Delia said with a grimace.

"*Twenty-eight?* Kyle's age? No."

"Yes. Twenty-eight. *Nine* years younger than I am."

Marta sobered considerably and Delia read into it.

"I know. Boy toy. Deep down I must be as bad as Peaches."

"You aren't like our mother," Marta said forcefully. "Andrew didn't seem at all a boy toy, and that was always part of the appeal for her, if you'll recall. They were always incredibly immature and very obviously a gazillion years younger. That isn't true of Andrew."

"I don't know…" Delia hedged.

"Andrew isn't obviously young and immature. I thought he was older than Kyle and you know what an old soul Kyle is," Marta insisted.

"When I told Andrew on Monday night that the baby is his he ran like a rabbit—right out of the restaurant. Just like when Peaches told Kyle's father about Kyle when he was three—remember?"

"I remember. He was in such a rush to get out of there that he knocked over my bicycle."

"Well, if there had been a bicycle in his way Monday night, Andrew would have knocked it over, too. I thought that was the last I'd ever see or hear from him again. Just like Kyle's father."

"But you've already seen or heard from Andrew again?" Marta guessed.

"He was in the parking lot when I left here last night. He wanted to talk, but he looked like he was facing a firing squad."

"Still, he came back and wanted to talk," Marta said, surprising Delia by defending Andrew. "What did he have to say for himself?"

Delia told her, omitting nothing. Including Andrew's marriage proposal.

Marta's eyes widened when she heard that. "What did you say?"

"What did I say?" Delia repeated as if she couldn't believe the question that had been asked reasonably. "I said no, of course."

Marta didn't respond to that except to raise her eyebrows.

"What? You think I should have said yes?" Delia demanded as if that were the most absurd idea yet.

Marta shrugged. "I just don't know that I find the idea of you marrying the father of your baby as outrageous as you seem to."

"It's too early in the morning for jokes, Marta."

"I'm not joking."

"You have to be. This is a twenty-eight-year-old guy I don't even know."

"Right. Who also happens to be your baby's *father.*"

Delia deflated slightly in her chair, resting her head on the back of it to stare at her half sister.

"I'm just thinking," Marta continued, "about how much you and Kyle and I craved having a dad around when we were growing up. And what if your baby is a boy? Since we're reminiscing, remember the first jock-strap fiasco when Peaches took Kyle to buy one?"

"She made him try it on over his jeans in the aisle of the store," Delia recalled.

"Right. And after that poor Kyle did everything he could to find a male influence. He was on the list of every mentoring program he ever heard about. He was always beating the bushes for someone to toss a foot-ball with him or take him to a baseball game."

Delia was beginning to feel less certain of the position she'd taken with Andrew.

But even if it showed it didn't keep Marta from going on anyway.

"And what about you?" Marta persisted. "That's how we ended up in Chicago in the first place. It's why you live in the house you live in. Maybe you should think about whether or not you really do want to turn up your nose so easily at the opportunity to give your baby what none of us had—a live-in dad married to its mom."

Delia hadn't thought about it like that. She'd just rejected Andrew's proposal out of hand because it had seemed so utterly insane to her. Putting it in the terms Marta had just put it in, though, gave her pause.

Still, there were other things—important things—that were unchanged.

"But he's only twenty-eight, Marta," Delia said.

"And proposal or no proposal, I don't think he has the kind of staying power or tenacity that Kyle has. He's… I don't know, I just had a really strong feeling that he was proposing because he thought he had to, that he was going through the motions, not that he was doing anything he honestly wanted to do."

"So you said no without considering it."

"Yes."

"And did he breathe a sigh of relief and say he was glad you hadn't taken him up on the offer?"

"No."

"What did he do?"

"He said we should get to know each other," Delia admitted, thinking for the first time that Andrew's persistence said something positive about him in spite of his age—and she was giving him credit only now that her sister had pointed out that he *hadn't* breathed a sigh of relief because she'd turned him down.

"Getting to know each other seems reasonable," Marta remarked. "And like a mature way to proceed."

"I don't know how mature it was. It was just… It was just like an excuse not to end everything right there and then. Which was what I was trying to do."

"But you didn't succeed," Marta guessed.

"He wouldn't have it. I ended up agreeing to see him again, to spend some time with him and get to know him, but I still had—and have—my doubts about whether or not I'll hear from him again."

"And if you do?"

"I guess I'll have to stick to my word and see him. Get to know him."

"Give him a chance," Marta said as if finishing what Delia had been saying.

"Give him a chance at what?"

"Maybe making things work out between you? For the baby's sake?"

Delia shook her head, having difficulty believing what she was hearing from her sister. "There isn't anything between us *to* work out. And *for the baby's sake?* Are you actually suggesting that I try to have a relationship with and maybe *marry* someone just for the sake of the baby?"

Marta shrugged. "I'm just thinking, Dealie," she said, using the nickname Marta and Kyle had had for her since they were all kids, "that you liked Andrew well enough to sleep with him in Tahiti. There must have been *something* there or you wouldn't have done that, because that is *sooo* not you. And even if you don't end up marrying the guy, maybe you should at least try to be on friendly enough terms with him that he can be *some* kind of a dad to the baby—if nothing else, an 'occasional phone call' kind of a dad, or an 'exchange cards now and then' kind of dad. But just a dad the baby can know is out there in the world for him or her, if he or she needs him."

Delia gave her half sister a sympathetic smile. "Is there a little of your own childhood wish fulfillment in this, too, maybe?" she asked gently.

"Okay, yeah," Marta admitted. "I wasted a lot of time calling my father, trying to get him to visit, trying to get him to say I could turn to him if I needed to. But that's the point, hon. Kyle did the mentoring thing, I begged for acknowledgment and a safety net, and you came all the way to Chicago—what it boils down to is that every one of us went to extremes to put a father or a father figure into our lives somehow. Just in case your baby wants to know his or her father, wants him in his or her life, maybe you should give Andrew a shot. And who knows? He could surprise you."

Delia was glad to get home Wednesday evening at the end of another long day. Another long day of work and worry, and of the added strain of half hoping that every phone call her secretary informed her of, every opening of her office door, might bring Andrew into the picture again. That he might actually make good on his claim that they should get to know each other.

Not that it was for her sake, she made sure to tell herself a hundred times throughout the day. But after having talked to her sister, it did seem as if maybe, for her baby's sake—as Marta had said—she should keep the lines of communication open with Andrew.

And if she'd felt disappointed each time the call was *not* from Andrew? That was for her baby's sake, too, she told herself. Only for her baby's sake. Not because deep down she might have been hoping to hear Andrew's voice on the other end of the line.

And if she'd felt the same kind of disappointment each time there had been a knock on her office door and it had opened to reveal her secretary or Marta or someone else she worked with…? That had definitely been for the sake of her baby and not because she was hoping to glance up and see the carved features of

Andrew's remarkable face or that honed body that managed to inspire far too many memories for her.

It was only the baby she had in mind. The baby and the baby's future. A future that Delia was beginning to think would be fatherless after all, when her doorbell rang.

She was upstairs in the circa-1945 house she'd inherited from her grandmother five years before. She'd just changed out of her dress clothes into a pair of jeans and a gray hoodie T-shirt. Zipping the hoodie up, she descended the steps that ended in a small entryway only a few feet from the heavy walnut door.

When she looked through the peephole, she discovered that face she'd been hoping to see all day long. Distorted by the wide-angle lens and barely lit by only the illumination of her porch light, but that unmistakable face nonetheless.

Andrew.

And there she was in her laying-around-watching-television clothes, with her hair caught up in a rubber band at her crown just to get it out of her face.

Still, if she ran back upstairs to put on something better and redo her hair without answering the door, Andrew would think she wasn't home and leave. So, wishing she looked a whole lot more fabulous than she did, she opened the heavy wooden panel to him.

He smiled and raised both arms from his sides, showing her multiple bags with various fast-food logos emblazoned on them.

"Burgers, fries, tacos, burritos, chicken sandwiches,

salads, chili, hot dogs and fried chicken—can we have dinner?"

Delia had to laugh. "For about two weeks. If you want to die young," she answered, bypassing any greeting, too.

"Or we could order pizza," he added.

"Feeling gluttonous?"

"No, I just want to find something that will get me in the door."

"Then you should have brought donuts and cookies," Delia confided guiltily.

He grinned and looked over his shoulder at his car parked at the curb. "I can go back if that's what it will take."

In spite of having allowed herself to be convinced that continuing contact with Andrew might be what she should foster for the baby's sake, and despite all her disappointments during the day when it hadn't been him on the phone or at her office door, Delia still didn't think she should feel quite as elated as she did to have him standing on her front porch. Because seeing him again pleased her so much she actually felt giddy, and that didn't seem like what she should be allowing to happen.

So she tried to temper it by taking a deep breath, reminding herself that he'd run scared on Monday night and that on Tuesday night he had appeared looking as if he'd been through the wars in coming to the decision to see her again. And although none of that haggard appearance was there tonight, she didn't think she should lose sight of the difficulty he'd clearly had in making himself set this course.

"Okay, I'll give you a minute to think it over," he said when she let too much time lapse while her mind raced.

Still, Delia didn't rush to invite him in. Instead she took a closer look at him, searching for lingering signs of reluctance. But the haggard appearance was definitely gone tonight. He was wearing slacks, a T-shirt and a short, lightweight leather jacket that added to the effect and seemed just right against the still blustery June weather.

"Come on, what do you say?" he cajoled when she really had left him standing there longer than she should have. "Can I tempt you with junk food or do I need to go in search of donuts and cookies to sweeten the deal? Because I'll do it, if that's what it takes. Even though you *did* agree to spend some time with me and this is some time…."

The way he looked hadn't aided the cause of toning down her giddiness, or her pleasure in seeing him again but she finally stepped aside anyway and said, "I do need to eat," as if that were the only reason she would let him in.

He stepped across the threshold, out of the way of the door so she could close it. Once she had, Delia turned back to him, finding him standing in the center of her entryway.

Against the aged and scarred dark wood paneling that was on nearly every downstairs wall outside the kitchen, it struck her that Andrew was like a diamond in the rough in her modest, dated house.

He glanced around—into the living room to the

right, up the stairs, down the hallway that led to the kitchen in the rear—and said, "This is not what I expected of someone who owns two branches of a very successful business."

"No?"

"Not that it isn't an interesting old place with possibilities for improvement," he amended. "But—"

"I know, it needs a whole lot of remodeling and refurbishment. But I inherited it as is, and I've needed to devote all my time and energy since then to getting Meals Like Mom's going in Chicago in order to stay here. So I haven't been able to do anything. The remodel is in the works, though. I've hired a contractor and a decorator, and we're getting started by the end of the month so everything will be redone by the time the baby is born."

Andrew again held the bags aloft. "Why don't we eat while this stuff is hot and then you can give me the tour and tell me what you're planning?"

That seemed innocuous enough. "Okay. There isn't a dining room—that's one of the additions I'll make. So that leaves us either eating at the kitchen table or the coffee table in the living room. Your choice."

From the distance of the entryway, Andrew eyed the oval-shaped coffee table in front of her white sofa. "Doesn't look like that's big enough for all this stuff. We'd better do the kitchen."

"Good choice," Delia said, adding, "It's back here," and leading the way to the family-sized space that sported a beautiful round pedestal table surrounded by cane-backed chairs.

The table and chairs were the only nice things among the cupboards that were painted to match the walls and appliances so out-of-date Delia was surprised they still worked.

"It's Incredible Hulk green," Andrew commented as he followed her into the space lit poorly by a single fixture in the center of a high ceiling.

"I know, it's awful. The kitchen will have to be gutted. Everything's going—cupboards, appliances, the chipped and speckled linoleum, and the color, for sure."

"The table and chairs are nice," Andrew said as Delia took him there and he set the sacks of food down.

"The furniture is all mine."

"Then you *do* have taste. That's a relief," he joked.

"You doubted me?"

"Not until I saw this place," he said with a laugh.

He took off his leather jacket then and for no reason Delia understood, she couldn't tear her eyes away while he did. Why such a thing should intrigue her seemed completely irrational, but there she was, drinking in the sight of those broad shoulders spreading like an eagle's wings. That strong, powerful chest thrusting out to stretch the confines of his T-shirt. And something inside her went weak.

So weak she actually felt the need to pull out a chair and sit down.

Although when she did, that put an entirely different portion of his anatomy into her line of view. And looking at his zipper brought a whole other element to mind.

"Sit," she said a bit urgently as he hung his coat over the back of the chair across from her.

He finally did as she'd commanded and Delia forced her gaze to his face. His oh-so-handsome face…

"Tell me again what all we have here," she said, turning her focus to the safety of the food to prevent herself from any further ogling.

"A little of everything," he answered, naming each item as he peered into one bag after another.

"So what'll it be?" he asked when he'd listed everything once more.

"I'm a sucker for the Mexican food. I'll go with a burrito. And maybe a little salad. But I don't know what you're going to do with the rest of this stuff."

"My roommate will eat anything."

"You have a roommate?" Delia asked as Andrew took one of the burgers for himself and set the French fries between them so she could have a few of those, too.

"Mike Monroe," Andrew answered. "We've been friends since we were kids. It was sort of an upstairs-downstairs kind of a thing, I guess you'd say. His mother was the nanny for a family that lived near where I grew up. Part of her work arrangement was that she keep Mike with her while she was with the family's kids and that Mike be sent to the same schools. His mom thought she was getting a better education for him and letting him hobnob with kids who could end up being business contacts or names to know when he got out into the world. The trouble was, everyone knew he was the nanny's kid and they just gave him a hard time."

"Everyone except you?" Delia asked as they both ate.

Andrew shrugged. "Trust fund aside, I had more in common with Mike than with anyone else and couldn't have cared less who his mother was. Actually, I thought he was just lucky not to have a stepmother, the way I did."

That last comment was fraught with disdain but before exploring it, Delia said, "And the two of you— you and Mike—still live together?"

"Mike disappointed his mother by not becoming some big-deal businessman or something. He's a writer. A good one, but still he's doing the starving artist thing. So we share my place. Hanson Media Group pays the rent and all the utilities and insurances and whatnot—which means Mike doesn't need to contribute anything to that—and his being there gives me someone to take care of whatever comes up when I'm traveling. It works out for us both."

Delia imagined a fraternity house, but she didn't say anything about that. Instead she addressed something else she was wondering about.

"So was Hanson Media Group paying for everything even before Monday?" she asked.

"Yes," Andrew responded, as if he didn't quite get the question.

"It's just that you said Monday was your first day on the job," she explained.

"Right," he confirmed after washing down a bite of

burger with one of the sodas he'd brought. "But before Monday Hanson Media Group—or at least the Hanson fortunes—paid for everything without my working for the company."

"Did you work somewhere else?"

"Nope. Not a day in my life," he said, clearly having no clue how that unsettled her.

Then she recalled something else he'd said. "Last night you mentioned a lot of shocks and changes—I'm assuming the baby is one of the shocks…"

"That's an understatement."

"But it seemed as if there were other shocks and changes, too," Delia said in a quest to learn what was going on with him. "Was one of the others that you needed to go to work?"

"That was definitely another shock and change. I was told on Monday that if I want to keep the money coming in, keep the apartment and the rest of the perks I've enjoyed, I now have to work for the family business—hence my new job as advertising salesman. That was a *substantial* shock and change."

"How do you feel about that?"

He grinned at her. "Doesn't seem like as much fun as snorkeling in Tahiti."

In other words, he wasn't enthusiastic about the idea. Any more enthusiastic than he was about the idea of the baby.

"You *have* had some shocks and changes," Delia remarked.

He merely smiled at that, giving no clue as to what

else he might be thinking or feeling in regards to the severely altered course he'd encountered.

He *had* given some indication of his feelings about his stepmother, though, and so it was that that Delia returned to.

"You said something about thinking Mike was lucky that he had a real mother rather than a stepmother. Were your parents divorced?"

"My father was widowed. My mother died when I was fifteen and the next thing we knew—"

"We?"

"My brothers and I. Besides Jack, there's my brother Evan, the middle son," Andrew explained. "The next thing we knew, my father had gone out and married Helen. Without any fanfare, he just sprung her on us one day, announced that they'd gotten married. He was fifty-eight, she was thirty-one. His trophy wife."

"And she was an evil stepmother?" Delia guessed.

"No, she wasn't evil. She certainly tried with us. But…I don't know, we just never liked her. We resented her. She was… Well, she was his trophy. He dressed her, jeweled her, gave her elaborate gifts to make sure everyone knew how successful he was, but when it came to Helen, Jack, Evan and me? We just never connected."

"Not even now? As adults?"

"'Fraid not. I can't speak for anyone but myself, but I hated that my mother had just died and here was this other woman as some kind of replacement part plugged into the slot. Even if that worked for my father, it didn't work for me. So right out of the gate I didn't like the *idea* of Helen. From there, no matter what she did, I just didn't have it in me to play son to her. I pretty much dismissed her as a nonentity. She was nothing more to me than someone who coexisted in my house. And as soon as I could get out of that house—or what I felt was left of our home after my mother's death— I got out and away from Helen. I went to college."

He said that as if there were something amusing about it.

"So you *did* go to college?" Delia said to urge him to explain himself.

"Two years' worth. Not enough to get a degree even if I *had* passed everything. But the truth is, I spent more time partying than studying, so I barely got by before I dropped out. I was hardly what you'd call a serious student. But at least by then I was old enough to be on my own, to get the apartment. Which kept me far away from Helen, and that was what I wanted."

"Do you speak to her or see her now at all?"

"Unfortunately. I'm civil to her, but that's about it. I definitely don't have any soft family feelings for her. But then I don't think we Hansons are really what anyone would consider a particularly close family— not the way yours is. It isn't as if you'd ever find the four of us vacationing together in Tahiti," he said with a wry chuckle.

"Not even you and your brothers?"

"We go our separate ways. In fact, old Jack is beating his head against a brick wall right now trying to get Evan to come back and help out with Hanson Media Group, too, and apparently isn't having much luck.

And he and my uncle—David—are both up in arms about it."

"So not even your father's death has brought you all closer?" Delia asked.

"It's brought me back to Chicago and in close proximity, and it will probably eventually bring Evan back, too, but beyond the fact that we'll all be here again? I don't know that we'll end up the way you seem to be with Kyle and Marta."

"That's sad," Delia said.

Andrew merely shrugged as if it didn't affect him that way.

Delia had all she wanted to eat and apparently he had, too, because he pushed away the wrapper he'd been using as a plate and said, "So why don't you show me around this dungeon and tell me what you have planned for it?"

Delia assumed the question was a hint that he wanted to change the subject.

Since she thought that it might be better if they did before she learned more about him that made him seem young and at a very unstable time of his life, she said, "Okay."

She gathered all their used wrappers, containers and plastic utensils into the empty sacks and took them to the trash under the kitchen sink. Along the way, she said, "That was the first thing I thought about the house, too—that all the dreary paneling down here makes it seem dungeonish. But wait till you see the orange bathroom upstairs and the candy-cane pink bedroom. They'll make you wish there was paneling hiding it."

"Was the person who lived here before color-blind?" he asked with a laugh.

"I don't think so, but to tell you the truth, I don't know," Delia said. "I don't know anything about her."

Turning back to the table, Delia realized that there was still a lot of food left in the remaining bags there.

"We'd better put the rest of this stuff in the fridge until you go home or your friend will end up with food poisoning," she suggested.

"I'll do it," Andrew volunteered, taking it all to the short, chubby refrigerator.

He dwarfed the antiquated appliance and Delia was again struck by both the glory of the big, strapping man and how ill-suited he was to these surroundings.

And to her, too, she thought, telling herself that that was something she needed to keep in mind.

But all she was really thinking about at that moment was that the evening wasn't ending yet.

And that she was unreasonably happy about that fact.

## Chapter Seven

Once the leftovers were stored, Delia led Andrew out of the kitchen and began the tour, first of the downstairs and then of the second level where there were four bedrooms and a single—orange—bathroom.

"It's easier downstairs to add on along with using the mudroom in back to expand the kitchen and add the dining room, family room and half bath. But up here it would be more complicated, so I'll combine the two smallest bedrooms into a master suite with its own bath and much better closet space than I have now."

Andrew poked his nose into the bathroom and then into the bright pink room. "Color-blind. I'm convinced," he joked.

"I'm using the pink room as my own now," Delia

continued. "The other two smallest rooms are what will be combined for the new master suite and bath. When that's finished, I'll move in there and the pink room's closet will be broken down to make it a decent-sized guest room that will also be connected to the main bath. The nursery will go in the original master bedroom, which is a fairly decent size already and only needs paint and carpeting to be ready to go. That makes it the easiest to redo, so I can be sure it's finished in case the addition and remodel takes longer than planned," she explained, feeling strange talking about the baby with him. So strange she wasn't even sure she should have.

"Quite a project," Andrew commented.

The fact that he hadn't responded in any way to her mention of the baby or the nursery made her wonder if he might rather she not mention the little souvenir she was carrying at all.

"It's a huge project," Delia agreed, trying to ignore his omission. "But at least the basic electrical wiring and the pipes are okay. If that had had to be redone, too, it would have been even worse."

Andrew moved to the guest room to glance into it, too, but he never went anywhere near the room that would be the nursery.

Delia had the feeling that he not only didn't want to see it, he wasn't even ready to acknowledge the need for it. And she thought that was something to take as seriously as she took their age difference.

"It should be nice when it's finished," he said then. "It's a great old house. Solid. Interesting."

"I think so, too," Delia said, fighting the sinking sensation in the pit of her stomach. Even as she told herself that Andrew's lack of interest in her nursery plans shouldn't matter.

She headed downstairs again with Andrew following behind.

"I can make coffee," she offered then, sounding more chipper than she felt.

"Not for me, thanks."

"Tea?"

"No, I'm fine," he said as they reached the entryway once more.

*This is where he runs again,* she thought. *Where the pregnancy and the baby have become real enough to scare him away.*

*Well, fine,* she told herself in her internal dialogue. *Go! And don't come back. Don't drag this game out any longer than necessary. Get out and leave me alone and let me do this the way I planned to do it before Monday night. It's better like that anyhow....*

She was so certain that running out was exactly what Andrew was going to do, that she actually headed for the front door to open it for him.

And then he surprised her once more.

Rather than running out on Delia the way she'd convinced herself Andrew would after she'd shown him her house and he'd shied away from every reference she'd made to the baby and the nursery, Andrew nodded toward the living room from the entryway and said, "How about if we sit in there?"

"Oh. Okay," Delia agreed, barely concealing her shock.

Then, correcting the few steps she'd taken toward her front door to let him out, she made a quick—and she hoped subtle—detour to go into the living room ahead of him.

She turned on the lamps on each of the end tables that bracketed the sofa as Andrew sat in the center of it and patted the spot beside him in invitation to her.

Delia didn't want to appear rude by going to the overstuffed chair positioned to one side of the couch, so she accepted the invitation. But not without getting as far away from him as she could, sitting with her back pressed tightly to the arm of the sofa and angling to face him with one leg upraised in front of her as a barricade. Just in case.

"Did you say you *inherited* this house?" he asked then, turning slightly in her direction so he could look at her and settling one long arm on the top of the sofa-back.

That brought his hand only a breath away from the knee over which she was peering at him. Close enough for her to see every well-tended nail, every knuckle, every inch of that hand that she suddenly recalled touching that same knee. Squeezing it before taking a slow slide up her thigh and around to the inside of it...

"Delia?"

She was still staring at his hand rather than answering him and he'd caught her at it. She altered her focus quickly and went just as quickly back through her memory, searching for what he'd asked her.

She was grateful when it came to her.

"I did say I inherited the house, yes," she confirmed, hoping he hadn't asked her anything else after that that she'd missed.

Apparently he hadn't because he went on naturally from there. "How did you inherit a house from someone you don't know or know anything about?"

"How do you—"

"You said it a little while ago, when I asked if the person who lived here before was color-blind. You told me you didn't know because you didn't know the person who lived here before."

Delia had forgotten.

"That's right," she mused, flattered that he'd been paying more attention than she had and appreciating the fact that he was trying to get to know her.

"So how did that come about?" he prompted when her thoughts distracted her from answering immediately once again.

"I inherited the house from my father's mother," she informed him.

"Your grandmother? And you didn't know her?"

"We never met. I didn't know she even existed. Until she didn't anymore and the attorney who was handling her estate tracked me down in California to tell me she'd left me the house."

"Was your father on the outs with his family?"

Delia wished a simple family feud was what she could tell him about, because even now it embarrassed her to reveal her background to anyone.

But in the interest of her own child, she swallowed

her embarrassment and plunged in. "I never met my father, either."

Andrew's eyebrows arched. "You never *met* your father?"

"I wasn't raised…conventionally. None of us were— not me or Marta or Kyle. Our mother—who we were never to call Mom—"

"What were you supposed to call her?"

"Her name—Peaches."

"Peaches? You're kidding?"

"No, that was her name, Peaches McCray. She was not what you'd call a traditional kind of mother. She was different. A lot different. A lot more…freewheeling, I suppose you could say."

"How could she be anything else when she'd been named Peaches?"

"Oh, she named herself Peaches. She was born Beatrice McCray on a farm in Kansas. But the day she turned eighteen she went to court and changed her name legally to Peaches—because that was her favorite food. Then she got on a bus and left town."

Delia could see that Andrew didn't know whether to laugh or sympathize because his expression was a combination of both humor and astonishment. And she'd only begun.

"Okay. Peaches," he said. "Go on. I'm still waiting for the part about how you never met your father and inherited this house from his mother."

"Right. Well, Peaches wanted to be a movie star. Not an actress, there was no studying of a craft or anything. She wanted to be a star—with a capital S and an exclamation point. So she took the bus to Holly-wood, where she was sure she would be discovered and never was. But she also never stopped thinking that it would happen and given that, it was important that she maintain the illusion of eternal youth."

"Are we talking past tense or present? Is she still living and wanting to be a movie star?"

"No, she died nine years ago in a jet-skiing accident. But what was true of her when I was a kid was true of her until the day she died."

"Did she look anything like you?" Andrew asked as if that would have been a good thing.

"Marta and Kyle think I'm the spitting image of her. For better or worse."

"For better," Andrew judged. "So appearing younger than she was must not have been too far out of her reach."

"No, it wasn't. But her own looks were not the only thing she used to keep up the illusion that she was per-petually twenty-five—"

"She also didn't let her kids call her Mom," Andrew said, proving he was listening now, too.

"Right again. Having kids—*three* kids—aged her, so we were introduced as the younger siblings she was raising after a tragic tornado had killed our parents."

"And her parents..."

"Were alive and well until not long ago. Living quietly on the farm in Kansas, not ever understanding what made their daughter tick."

Andrew's eyebrows arched even more. "Okay," he

said with an amazed sort of tilt to his head. "But we're still not up to the unmet-dad part."

"I'm getting there," Delia assured. "It *is* kind of a long story, though. Maybe you don't want—"

"No, I want to hear the whole thing."

"If you're sure."

"I am."

"All right then. Not only did Peaches use her looks and her story about Marta, Kyle and me as her siblings rather than her kids to keep up her eternal youth profile, she also absolutely refused to consort with men over a certain age. Your age, actually."

"Twenty-eight?"

"Twenty-eight was the crest of the hill, anything past that was over it for Peaches, and she preferred her male friends much younger. She was convinced that being with very young men made her seem like she was that young, too. And, to be honest, that was just where her taste in men ran. My own father was twenty-three when I was born. Peaches was thirty. Marta's father was barely twenty. Kyle's father was twenty-one."

Delia tried not to show her own discomfort with that fact. Or how ashamed she'd felt of her mother's affairs growing up. "Three kids by three different fathers and all without the benefit of a marriage or even a long-term relationship in the bunch. The fathers—like the other men who came before, between and after—were all just her boy toys...."

Delia stumbled over the term Peaches had reveled in. The term that had been used for Andrew this week, as well.

"I'm surprised Peaches had kids at all," he said.

"We were her accidents. That was actually how she referred to us. Affectionately, but as her three little accidents," Delia said, knowing it would never, ever be something she said to her own child. Not even affectionately. It had always stung anyway. And made her feel unwanted.

"Oh," Andrew responded as if he didn't know what else to say.

"I told you, Peaches was not a cookie-baking, storybook-reading, mother-earth kind of mom," Delia reminded.

"Did she not want to marry any of your fathers?"

"Absolutely not. Starlets—which was what she always considered herself, even as she got older and older—were not married. And none of our fathers wanted to marry her, either. They were young, most of them trying to be movie stars or actors, too. They were guys she met doing work as an extra on a movie or at one of her other odd jobs."

"How *did* she support three kids? I assume there wasn't a lot of child support paid by boy toys."

Delia didn't like that term any better when Andrew used it and felt a little ashamed of herself for referring to him as that when he said it with such disdain. "No, there was no child support. And we didn't live well, that's for sure. Peaches got all the work she could in the movies—being an extra in mob scenes was her biggest claim to fame. Otherwise she did whatever she could that was near to movie studios, hoping—"

"To be discovered."

"Exactly. She worked in a dry cleaners, waited tables, drove one of those buses that take tourists by the homes of famous people. She never kept one job for long because the minute she thought it interfered with something she believed would launch her into stardom—for instance, if her boss wouldn't let her off for a cattle call—she'd quit. Right there and then. Mainly we did a lot of living in studio apartments or trailer homes, and sneaking out in the middle of the night because we were months behind in the rent and didn't have the money to pay."

"How did you feel about living like that? About having a mother like that?" he asked, clearly trying not to sound judgmental. But Delia could tell he was passing judgment in spite of it. She understood that it was difficult not to.

"There were mixed feelings," she answered candidly. "I hated the uncertainty of it all. I hated having to move around and I definitely didn't like doing it like cat burglars. I really hated it the couple of times when we got caught and there were ugly scenes and the police were called on us...." Delia knew she wasn't helping the impression Andrew had so she cut that part short. "And of course there were always things that I wanted that we just couldn't afford. But I wasn't a miserable, unhappy kid, either. Some of Peaches's flamboyancy was fun. Nothing ever got her down—"

"Not even having the police called on her?"

"The few times that happened she'd managed to cajole the landlord out of pressing charges by the time the police actually got there, so everything worked out all right. And Kyle and Marta and I were closer than we might have been under other circumstances. I'm actually thankful for that because we have a great relationship. We've always looked out for each other, taken care of each other, known we could trust each other and depend on each other no matter what. I guess in a lot of ways, we found stability through that."

"So, are there parts of the way you were parented that you'll repeat?"

Delia laughed. "Don't sound so worried. I'm about as different from Peaches as it's possible to be, and beyond loving this baby unconditionally and being accepting of just about anything it is or does—which was true of Peaches—I have every intention of being as traditional a mom as I possibly can be."

Andrew seemed relieved to hear it. Relieved enough to return to what they'd been talking about before he inquired about her feelings about her mother. "So in all the time you were growing up there was never even a stepfather? Or one of the real dads who played a role in your lives?"

"Nope. Kyle's father didn't even know he existed until Kyle was three, and after Peaches told him about Kyle we never saw him again. Kyle doesn't have any clear memories of him but he did go to great lengths growing up to try to find a replacement." Delia grimaced slightly. "Marta's father showed up occasionally, but that was almost worse."

"Why?"

"He and Peaches sort of had an on-again, off-again thing. He was trying to act, too, so they'd meet up at different auditions. Plus whenever he moved, he'd let her know where he was, and she did the same whenever we moved. But he was… I don't know, he was *so* young when Marta was born and he wasn't the brightest bulb in the box, and he certainly wasn't a kid person. The rare times when he did appear he was awkward with Marta, standoffish. He just didn't seem to know how to relate to her and he definitely didn't give the impression that he wanted to. The trouble was, Marta wanted so desperately for him to love her, to be a dad to her, that as soon as she learned to dial a phone she started calling him, begging him to come see her or let her go to his place or take her somewhere. Begging him for some semblance of a father-daughter relationship that just never happened."

"Not ever? Even now?"

Delia shook her head. "Marta knows where he is and calls him once or twice a year to say hello and see how he's doing, but there's just no effort from the other end. He has nothing to say beyond that he's fine or getting work as a stand-in here and there. He doesn't show an interest in her or give her any indication that he feels a connection to her at all. When she and Henry got married she asked her father to walk her down the aisle—she even said she'd send him the plane ticket to come to Chicago so it wouldn't cost him anything. He said he was in a bind with his landlord and would rather she send him cash than a plane ticket."

"And did she?"

Delia nodded sadly. "I'm pretty sure she did. Kyle ended up walking her down the aisle, and her father didn't even call that day or send a card to congratulate her. She's just had to accept that he isn't ever going to be a father to her. Reluctantly, but there hasn't been any other choice."

"Which brings us to your father."

"Which brings us to my father," Delia conceded with a sigh.

"Who you never met."

"Well, I'm told that he showed up once when I was three days old, but I don't count that as my having met him."

"That was it?"

"That was it. He was from Chicago and I have no idea if he came back here after that or what. All I know is that he told his mother about me, about Peaches, that he died of hepatitis two years before his mother had a heart attack, and that since I was the only living relative left, his mother decided after his death to have a will made that gave me the house—the only thing she owned. She knew my name. My mother's name. And that we were last known to live in California. So when she died, her attorney got on the Internet and found me to notify me of the inheritance."

"That must have come as a surprise."

"It did. The attorney I spoke to had been hired by my grandmother after she found his name in the phone book so it wasn't as if he knew her or could tell me anything about her. She had just told him that her son—my father—had died and she didn't want the house to go to the state, so it should go to me."

"That doesn't inspire any warm fuzzies," Andrew said sympathetically.

"No, but at least she was letting me know that she knew about me and thought of me as some sort of family."

"And that was enough for you to leave California and your business there and move here?"

Delia smiled. "It wasn't that cut-and-dry. Marta and I came here to see the house, thinking that I would just list it with a realtor and sell it. But once we got here..." Delia took a deep breath and when she exhaled, it came out with a shrug and the need to fight a welling up of emotion that made her voice softer. "I don't know. Until that point I'd thought that I had dealt pretty well with the lack of a male parent in my life. Yes, there had been times when I'd wished for a dad. When I'd missed having one. But on the whole, I thought I'd adjusted better than Kyle and Marta had. That I had accepted things the way they were."

"And then you got here," Andrew said to invite her to confide in him what he seemed to realize wasn't easy for her to admit.

"Then I got here," she said. "And I guess the house felt like the closest thing I was going to have to a connection with my father or his mother, and I sort of wanted to absorb what I could of that."

Andrew took that hand she'd been so engrossed in earlier and used it to squeeze not her knee this time, but her arm where it was hugging her leg. A comforting squeeze that somehow managed to send little shivers of something sensual through her even as he succeeded at consoling her.

"The place gave you roots," he said.

Delia smiled and blinked back some moisture that had suddenly dampened her eyes. "Even if the roots were only peripherally mine," she joked. "I suppose a psychiatrist would have a field day with it. But for whatever reason, something about being here just felt like home to me. A tie to family, even if it wasn't much of a tie. Even if there wasn't a family anymore by the time I got here. Still, it was the best I could do, so I stayed and started the Chicago branch of Meals Like Mom's."

Andrew gave her a moment to gain some control of her emotions and then, just when she was wishing he'd say something else, he said, "And how did Marta come to stay with you?"

The fact that her sister had made her own home here had been a source of comfort and support for Delia, it was something she was grateful for, and so it made her smile again. "Henry was the realtor I was going to list the house with. Marta and Henry hit it off, so she stayed here, too."

"And that left Kyle to run the California end of the business?"

"It did. Which was good for him. It gave him more autonomy than he'd had before and he's really flourished with it. He's expanded operations and taken production farther than I probably would have if the status quo hadn't been disrupted."

"And you ended up with two branches of Meals Like Mom's."

Delia laughed. "Yes, but I've already gone on and on with the saga of my own background. I can't talk about the business stuff tonight, too."

"Okay, we'll save that for another time," Andrew said as if he were making a promise. "I do have one more question about the non-business end, though."

He took his hand away from her arm and Delia felt a wave of disappointment.

Still, she hid it and said, "Okay, one more question but then that's it for me tonight."

"Did you decide not to even try finding me to tell me about your pregnancy because of Peaches's track record with the fathers of her kids?"

"That was part of it," Delia answered honestly. "I've witnessed firsthand three examples of male response to unplanned pregnancy, and none of them led me to believe it would make a whole lot of difference if I did track you down and tell you."

"So you thought 'why bother'?"

"I'm afraid there was an element of that in the decision."

"But all three of you have gone to some great lengths to get even a semblance of a father in your lives. Seems like that might have factored into your decision, too."

"Except that the only one of the three of us to actually have the real thing around was Marta and that has been more negative than positive."

Andrew made a face. "That doesn't bode well for me."

Delia shrugged, not wanting to say that the ball was

in his court when it came to that, but thinking it just the same.

He read the shrug correctly. "Okay, so it's up to me to make it a positive or a negative. But now that I do know, and want to be involved," he added pointedly, "you don't have any objection, right?"

She still wasn't convinced that he really did want to be involved, wondering if he might simply be going through the motions. The way Marta's father had. But Delia didn't say that.

"Reservations, maybe. But no objections, no," she said with a tentativeness to her tone. "Although you should also know that if it turns into a negative—"

"It won't," he said with something that sounded as much like bravado as conviction.

Then he gave her a killer half smile so full of mischief it was infectious and said, "Or you could make sure it's a positive that I'm around by marrying me."

Delia laughed and teased him. "Who says that would make sure it was a positive?"

"It would be more a positive than if we aren't married, wouldn't it?" he challenged.

"Not necessarily."

"So what is that? Another no, you won't marry me?"

"Another no, I won't marry you," she said un-equivocally

"I guess I'll just have to keep trying, then," he countered, sounding undaunted.

Or maybe he was just able to sound that way because he was relieved that once again she'd rejected his proposal. Which Delia thought was more likely when she recalled his earlier reaction to her mention of the nursery and his total lack of interest in it.

He checked his wristwatch then and stood. "I took up your whole night. I'd better let you get to bed."

Delia didn't do anything to stop him. But she did discover another rise of disappointment in her. This time that she was losing his company the way she'd lost his touch before.

But again she concealed those feelings and stood, too.

"Don't forget the leftovers for your roommate," she reminded.

"I'll get them. My coat is in the kitchen, too," he said, heading in that direction.

Delia let him go, turning off the living room lamps while he was gone.

He had on the leather jacket again when he returned with the fast-food sacks in hand, and Delia led the way to the front door.

"Thanks for dinner," she said then.

"For what it was worth," he answered as she opened the door and he stepped near to the threshold.

He didn't go out, though. Instead he stopped there and turned to face her. "I had a good time," he said.

"I didn't bore you too much with the story of my life?"

"Not a boring life, not a boring story," he said as if he meant it.

There was honesty in his dark eyes, too, as they met hers and held them. Honesty and warmth and a huge helping of that appeal that had sucked her in so effect-ively in Tahiti. An appeal that kept her looking up at him and made something inside her soften.

*He's only twenty-eight,* she silently shouted to herself.

But at that moment it didn't actually register. At least not as anything important enough for her to break off that eye contact and send him home.

It didn't even register enough for her to rear back the way she knew she should have when he began to lean forward. Or when he got close enough for her to be sure he was going to kiss her. And kept on coming.

Then he did kiss her and even as she was wonder-ing why she was letting him, she was kissing him back. She was savoring the feel of supple, talented lips parted over hers. Tantalizing hers with memories of that night in paradise while still providing an entirely new expe-rience, since this was the only time he'd kissed her when her mind wasn't fogged with martinis.

And heaven help her, she liked it. She liked kissing him. She liked him kissing her. She liked it all more than she wished she did.

Enough so that she was sorry when it ended at just the right length for a first kiss that wasn't truly a first kiss at all.

When it had ended Andrew smiled down at her, his expression slightly dazed. "I remembered enjoying that. I just didn't remember how much," he said almost more to himself than to her.

Then he muttered a good-night and finally went out onto her porch.

Delia made herself close the door right then, when she was inclined to keep it open and watch him go all the way to his car.

But it was a minor gesture that didn't revoke the fact that she'd just let him kiss her. That she'd just kissed him.

And for some reason, even though she told herself forcefully that she shouldn't have done either of those things, self-loathing wasn't what she felt.

She felt all warm and soft and tingly.

She felt like she wanted him back there right then.

To do it all again...

# *Chapter Eight*

"'Morning," Andrew said to announce his presence as he left his bedroom bright and early on Thursday and came across his roommate with a pretty brunette standing at the front door of the apartment he and Mike Monroe shared.

"Hey," Mike greeted in return, sounding as if he hadn't been awake long.

There was more evidence of that in the fact that Mike was wearing nothing but pajama bottoms. The woman around whose hips Mike's arms were draped, however, had on a running suit.

"Melanie, this is Andrew," Mike said then, performing a casual introduction. "Andrew, this is Melanie."

No last names. Andrew knew what that meant—Mike didn't know the woman by anything but Melanie.

"Good to meet you," Andrew said, moving on to the kitchen to leave them alone for what appeared to be a kiss he'd interrupted.

"You, too," Melanie called after him.

It was a variation of a scene that had played out innumerable times in the apartment, both for Andrew and for Mike. Bringing someone home to spend the night was hardly an unusual event. But for some reason, as Andrew went into the kitchen, this time it struck him as a stupid thing for them both to have done so capriciously.

Maybe because of where his last one-night stand had landed him.

He heard the apartment door open and close, and Mike wandered into the kitchen, too.

"New girl?" Andrew asked with an edge of censure to his voice that had never been there when he'd made the same inquiry in the past.

"I've been jogging again," Mike answered, giving no indication that he'd caught the tone. "I keep meeting Melanie on the path. We've talked a little. Joked around. Last night I finally invited her to come by for a post-run cooldown."

The pleased-with-himself smile Mike cast Andrew just prior to opening the big stainless steel refrigerator set off another wave of that same feeling Andrew had had only moments earlier.

Apparently it was reflected more in his expression than it had been in his voice, because when Mike turned around with the orange juice container and faced Andrew across the marble island counter, Mike finally took notice. "What? Do you know her or something?"

"No, I've never met Melanie before," Andrew said.

"So how come you look like that?"

"How do I look?" Andrew asked.

"Like you don't approve or something," Mike said, pouring two glasses of juice and sliding one to Andrew.

"A lot's happened with me since I got back from Tahiti," Andrew muttered darkly. "I guess I'm seeing things differently."

"A lot's happened, huh? Is that why I haven't seen you for more than five minutes? I wondered. Usually we've had our catch-up night out by now." Then, as if it had just registered with him, Mike added, "And what're you doing out of bed so early? Wearing a *suit*. Don't tell me there's been another death in the family."

"No, nobody else died," Andrew said. "But there's been plenty going on since my dad died."

Mike used his juice glass to point to the opulent living room just beyond the kitchen. "Let's take it in there, huh? I didn't get any sleep and I'm beat."

Andrew watched his friend walk to the other room and plop down on one of the leather and chrome chairs without a care in the world. And he envied him.

Maybe he envied him the night he'd just spent with Melanie, too. A night like so many Andrew had had himself—a night of fun and flirting and the excitement of being with someone he'd never been with before….

Andrew took his own glass and joined Mike, sitting

slightly slumped in the center of the cosmopolitan sofa that matched the chair.

Totally at ease, Mike put his bare feet on the glass coffee table and crossed them at the ankle. "So what's the story? Even if nobody else died, you look about as happy as if you *were* going to a funeral."

"Things are a mess," Andrew said, glancing from the big-screen TV in front of him to the wall of floor-to-ceiling windows that looked out over a park and made the apartment prime property.

It was strange, but seeing Mike with that woman had added an element to Andrew's feelings that he hadn't anticipated. No, he wasn't thrilled with the idea of a nine-to-five job selling advertising for Hanson Media Group, but seeing Delia again, spending a little time with her, had begun to make that portion of what he'd come home to slightly okay—only slightly—but slightly more palatable.

Now, though, seeing Mike, knowing Mike would go on the way they both always had, while Andrew might end up actually married with a kid, made that seem daunting again.

Could he really turn his back on this lifestyle? Tie himself to one woman? Raise a kid? Never have another night like the one Mike had just had?

"Geez, man, what's going on? This looks bad," Mike said with alarm when Andrew still hadn't explained anything.

Andrew glanced back at his friend and for the first time since he'd been home and everything had been dumped on him, he spelled it all out to someone.

By the time he'd finished, Mike didn't seem at all relaxed anymore. He'd taken his feet off the coffee table, placed them flat on the floor and was sitting hunched over, as if the full weight of Andrew's problems was bearing down on him, too.

"So now you're working *and* you're supposed to *marry* this woman? Just like that? Overnight?" Mike asked.

"That's what I've been told," Andrew confirmed.

"And your brother and your uncle are all over you to make you do both whether you like it or not?"

"No job equals no money, no apartment, no nothing. And if I don't get Delia to marry me… Hell, I don't even know what I'll be up against if I don't get *that* to happen. I thought Jack was going to pop a vein when he heard she was pregnant. He seems to think the whole future of Hanson Media Group is riding on my getting married and *doing the right thing. For once*—as he put it."

"But is that what you *want* to do?" Mike ventured.

"Get married? No, it isn't what I want to do," Andrew said, feeling a twinge of guilt over the fact that that was true, and that he was presenting the exact opposite impression to Delia. Delia, who he honestly did like. Whose company he enjoyed. Who he was still so attracted to that he'd imagined taking her into that upstairs bedroom of hers when she'd given him the tour of her house last night and seeing what it might be like to make love to her on a bed rather than on a beach….

But marriage? That was a whole different ballpark.

"Can't you reason with Jack?" Mike asked. "He can't think it's a good idea for you to be forced to marry somebody you don't even know."

"There's no reasoning with him. Or even with David at this point. They're doing everything they can to save the company and that's all they can think about. They need manpower, so I have to work. And they need the morality problems to go away, which they believe won't happen if I *don't* marry the woman I got pregnant."

"Man…" Mike breathed, shaking his head. "I'll bet you would never have had *that* one-nighter if you'd had any idea this could be the end result. I know I wouldn't have."

For no reason Andrew understood, he felt defensive of Delia.

"It isn't as if Delia isn't great," he said suddenly. "She is. She's gorgeous and fun to be with and smart. She owns her own business, she's ambitious, successful. She's… Well, she's someone you *could* settle down with—"

"Just not now, with a shotgun at your back."

"And it isn't even Delia holding the shotgun, it's my brother," Andrew agreed wryly.

"But it's still a shotgun," Mike said. "What about her? Does she want the whole marriage thing even if she isn't the one insisting on it?"

"No, not at all," Andrew said, only telling his friend about the age difference then, and Delia's reluctance to have anything to do with him, let alone marry him. "To tell you the truth, it freaked her out when I told her how old I am, and I think it would have been fine with her if she never saw me again. She had plans for having the baby and raising it alone and was okay sticking to those plans. But I've been pushing and she's let me come around, she's been nice about everything. There's no pressure from her, but she hasn't slammed the door in my face, either. Like I said, she's great," he concluded.

"So you *do* like her," Mike said.

"Sure. I *like* her—"

"But *like* isn't the same as being so crazy in love with her that you're jumping at the chance to shuck everything else and stick with her forever."

"I don't know," Andrew said because he didn't want to admit his friend might be right. And because he felt even more guilt over that fact.

"So what're you going to do?" Mike asked.

Andrew shrugged. "I'm doing everything I can to convince Delia to marry me and I'm going to go on doing that."

"Seriously?"

"Seriously."

"Because your brother says you have to?"

"And because I can't be the last straw that broke Hanson Media Group's back. And because…" Andrew shook his head and shrugged his shoulders, hating the sense of being helpless against the tides of fate that came over him. "And because out there in the world there's going to be a kid I made. A kid I'm responsible for. A kid I can't just act like I didn't have anything to do with," he said, voicing something that he'd realized after hearing Delia tell him about her own father and those of Marta and Kyle. After picturing himself turning his back on his own flesh and blood the way they all had and coming to the conclusion that that wasn't the person he wanted to be.

"Are you telling me to rent a tux?" Mike said, half joking, half honestly asking.

"No," Andrew said. "At least not yet. And if it comes to that, you can just wear one of mine."

*If it comes to that…*

The words echoed in Andrew's mind as he sat there morosely staring at the dark television again.

*Would* it really come to that? he wondered.

And if it did, could he handle it?

Could he handle putting his bachelor days—and ways—behind him?

Kissing Delia the night before *had* been good, he reminded himself. Better, even, than he remembered kissing her in Tahiti had been.

But kissing was one thing. Putting his bachelor days— and ways—behind him was something else entirely.

And he wasn't confident that he could….

"I don't know. It's all a mess," he said in conclusion then, standing to put a complete end to the conversation. "And now I'd better get to *work*."

"Oh! You scared me!" Delia said in fright when she opened her front door to leave for work and discovered Andrew standing on her porch.

"Adrenaline—better than caffeine for starting your day," he countered. "I was just going to ring the bell."

"What are you doing here?" Delia asked, still in the throes of that adrenaline he'd sent rushing through her. Adrenaline mixed with a dash of pleasure at seeing him again, no matter what the reason and in spite of the fact that she'd been with him until late the night before.

"I want today and tonight," Andrew announced in answer to her question about what he was doing there.

"Excuse me?"

"I want today and tonight," he repeated. "I was headed into the office and I just decided that I want us both to ditch work and spend today and tonight in a speed courtship—"

*"Courtship?"* She parroted the word that seemed outdated. "As in horses and buggies? You've come a-courtin'?" she teased him, unable to keep from smiling at how silly that sounded.

"No horses or buggies, but that's about it, yeah," he confirmed. "I've come a-courtin'. First date, second date, third date, maybe even the fourth—all rolled into one. Today and tonight."

"You've lost it," Delia decreed.

"I have not," he said, pretending affront. "The way I look at it, we don't have much time. Three months have already gone by. After three more days you still won't marry me," he said as if that were unfathomable, "so I want to speed things up."

"With a speed courtship?"

"Now you're getting it," he said as if she were finally seeing the light.

"And you think that will accomplish what?"

"At best? You'll fall victim to my spell and say you'll marry me."

"Really, you've lost it," Delia said again.

"You promised to spend time with me," he reminded.

"I spent all last evening with you. But today is a workday. For us both. Or aren't you aware that it's bad form not to show up for your fourth day on the job?"

"Today you're more important than the job," he said. "Come on. Run away with me just for today."

"And tonight."

"And tonight—dating needs a night on the town."

"And at worst?" she asked. But when the question put a confused frown on his brow she clarified. "You have some misguided notion that at best I will fall victim to your spell so I'll marry you. And at worst?"

He leaned forward and confided, "We'll get to know each other some more—which you said you would do—and we'll both get a day off work." He straightened up again. "So what do you say?"

The entire exchange had taken place with Delia's old wooden screen door between them and she went on staring at him through it. But even filtered, his appeal didn't diminish. Because there he stood, tall and broad-shouldered, his sun-streaked hair in perfectly artful disarray, his sharp jaw freshly shaven and the rest of his remarkably handsome face looking rested and ready for mischief. Plus he was dressed in a pair of charcoal-colored slacks, a summerweight heather-gray cashmere sweater and a black peacoat that really did make him look too good to resist.

And the longer she studied him, the lower her resistance got.

"I don't know," she hedged when she knew full well that she shouldn't write off work for the entire day and spend it with the man she was beginning to worry was getting under her skin even if she were trying to prevent it.

"Come on," he repeated. "You're the boss, you can do whatever you want. Just call Marta and tell her to take over for the day. I'll make it worth your while," he added temptingly.

So-oo temptingly…

Temptingly enough to make her think out loud. "I suppose I don't have anything on deck that Marta can't do or that can't wait."

"Then you don't have any excuse."

But what she did have, she was afraid, was the same weak spot that she'd had for him in Tahiti. A weak spot she told herself she should be toughening up, not succumbing to.

On the other hand, she never took a day off work. Most weeks, she worked Saturdays, too. And sometimes Sundays. Taking an impromptu day to do nothing but play was just too unlike her not to have it's own allure. Especially when it meant playing with Andrew, who had made her last day in Tahiti more fun than any of the ones that had come before it. Taking a day off to spend with him made it seem like a minivacation.

"I shouldn't," she said, but without much strength.

"Doing what you shouldn't is what makes it all the better," Andrew assured with that touch of devil-may-care that put a special flair in his own brand of charisma.

"I'm dressed for work," she said as if the skirt and sensible shoes she was wearing were steep impediments.

"So change," he said, solving the problem that simply.

But if she did that Delia knew she'd be changing a whole lot more than her clothes. She'd be changing from die-hard workaholic Delia to...

Well, to someone with a little adventure in her soul.

Or at least to someone who just might, for once, do something out of the ordinary. And that felt exhilarating.

It made her feel a little like she'd felt that night in Tahiti.

That night that had gotten her into trouble.

But she was already pregnant, there wasn't a whole lot more trouble she could get into. And she deserved a day off now and then. A day of rest and relaxation. Wasn't Marta telling her that all the time?

*Or am I just rationalizing so it doesn't seem like I'm doing this to be with Andrew?* she asked herself.

But she didn't want to look too closely at that possibility and ruin the excitement she was feeling over playing hooky for a day, so before she could think more about it, she said, "Okay. Today and tonight. But this isn't a courtship kind of thing," she qualified to make herself feel better. "It's a 'getting to know each other' thing."

Andrew grinned. "Whatever you say. Just pack up

some fancy clothes for tonight—the restaurant I'm
taking you to isn't far from my place so we can go there
and dress for that. Now can I come inside while you
call Marta and change for today or do I have to go rent
a horse and buggy?"

"This is *not* a courtship thing," she reiterated more
forcefully, pushing her screen door open to let him in.

But his "Uh-huh," let her know he was only humoring her.

## Chapter Nine

Andrew took Delia to breakfast at a small waffle shop not far from her house and then they went to the art museum.

Lunch was panini sandwiches at an Italian deli, followed by shopping in some small boutiques before going to the dress rehearsal of a play in which two of Andrew's friends had parts.

After the play they went with the cast for coffee and gelato at a nearby bistro, where Delia learned that Andrew's friends were more interesting than the characters they were performing.

Then Andrew brought Delia back to his apartment to change from casual clothes to less casual. There she got to briefly meet his roommate, who was on his way out as they were arriving, and to see the spectacular view from the ultra-chic digs that Hanson Media Group had provided and paid a designer to decorate.

All in all it was a whirlwind day that didn't end when dusk fell. Instead Delia was led to the opulent guest room to shed her slacks and shirt, and slip into the red lace dress she'd brought with her.

The dress was completely form-fitting over a flesh-colored liner that made it look as if more of her was showing through it than actually was. It also had a stand collar, long sleeves and a hem that barely made it to midthigh. She'd only worn it once before and knew she wouldn't be able to wear it much longer, but for now she could still get it zipped up the side without any difficulty.

Nude-toned hose and a pair of three-inch strappy sandals finished the outfit before she brushed out her hair and twisted it into a French knot at the back of her head. Then she reapplied blush, mascara and lipstick, and added a caramel-hued eyeshadow as a finishing touch for the evening that she warned herself she shouldn't be looking so forward to.

But warning or no warning, after a day of Andrew's unfailingly upbeat, charming company, she just couldn't help it.

He was waiting for her in the living room when she left the guest bedroom. He'd gone from his daytime clothes to a deep brown suit that matched the color of his eyes. A suit so fluid it had to have been handsewn to his own personal measurements. The pale tan shirt and tie beneath it matched in elegant perfection, making him a sensational sight to behold standing in the midst of his impeccable apartment that bore absolutely no resemblance to the fraternity house she'd imagined when he'd told her he had a roommate.

And it struck Delia that culture, breeding and sophistication provided more of an air of maturity than her mother's younger men had ever possessed. She thought that that explained why not only had she not realized in Tahiti that Andrew was so much younger, but also why it had been easy for her to forget their age difference throughout the day, too.

Still, it wasn't something she *wanted* to forget, she warned herself even as his dark eyes seemed to devour her.

"You look fantastic," he said with enough appreciation in his tone and in his expression to make her believe it.

Delia humbly inclined her head. "Thank you. You're not too shabby yourself," she countered.

"Good enough to marry?" he joked.

"Good enough to have dinner with," she amended.

"Damn. I knew I should have gone with the blue suit," he muttered, picking up her coat from where it was draped over a chair and stepping to Delia to hold it for her.

She turned her back to him to slip her arms into the sleeves and caught the reflection of Andrew's face in a framed mirror on the wall in front of her as his eyes dropped to her derriere. Apparently he liked what he saw there, too, because a tiny smile lifted one corner of his mouth before he actually settled the coat on her shoulders.

But even if she hadn't spied him ogling her backside he would have given himself away when he said, "I didn't think it was possible for you to wear anything that beat the sarong, but this dress does."

With her coat in place Delia turned to face him again, pleased with the flattery but beginning to feel a little self-conscious. "Are you going to feed me tonight or not?" she demanded, to change the subject.

"Whatever you want," he answered, swinging an arm in the direction of the door to let her know to go ahead of him.

The restaurant he took her to was in a private club that had a reputation for a membership of only the most elite of Chicago's movers and shakers. Andrew was greeted by name and as the maitre d' did that, two men stepped out of nowhere to simultaneously remove both Delia's coat and Andrew's. Then they were escorted into a dimly lit, wood-paneled enclave where enough space was left between the linen-clothed tables to make sure conversations weren't overheard.

After they'd ordered virgin cocktails and hors d'oeuvres, they were left with menus that looked like leather-bound books.

Andrew didn't open his, he merely set it aside. "They do a beef Wellington that's great. But just about everything here is great."

Delia didn't bother with her menu either, placing it out of the way, too. "Sounds good," she said, more interested in the man she was with than in the food, and wishing that wasn't the case.

But since it was, she focused her attention on him

and said, "How did your brother take the news that you weren't working today?"

"I don't know. I just left him a message," Andrew answered with a smile that said he might enjoy it if he'd irked his brother. "I can always tell him it was business, that I was just doing my job and wooing a potential client."

"Is that what you're doing?" Delia asked, a bit disappointed that that might be the case.

"Have we talked business today?" he countered.

They hadn't. They'd talked about art and movies and books they'd both enjoyed, they talked about other plays they'd seen, and food they liked, but they'd never touched on business. Which, now that Delia realized that, made her feel better again.

"Maybe we *should* talk business," she said, thinking that it might be safer to head in that direction than to continue in the personal vein that had made her like him all the more today.

"Okay, tell me about how Meals Like Mom's came to be."

"I know you haven't been at this long but my work history isn't relevant to selling me advertising."

"I'm not here to sell you advertising," he said as if he were telling her a secret. "Even if that's what I tell my brother, we aren't going to get into that tonight. My brother wants your business. I want more than that."

The room was just the right temperature but his words sent a tiny shiver of goose bumps up her arms anyway. Delia cautioned herself against being too susceptible to this man and his charm and instead answered his question just to get conversation going on a more surface route.

"Meals Like Mom's was sort of an evolution," she said. "It all started when I was fourteen and wanted an expensive lipstick."

"Lipstick? Your business was built on a lipstick?"

"I was a freshman in high school and I got asked to the spring dance by a junior—Damon Simosa—and I didn't think I could possibly be seen with an older man without this lipstick."

"But Peaches didn't have expensive lipstick budgeted in," Andrew guessed as their drinks and appetizers arrived.

"She said she had plenty of lipsticks I could wear. But I had my heart set on this one particular one. I just didn't have the money for it. So I lied about my age and got a job fixing trays with a catering company."

Andrew sampled his virgin daiquiri.

"You really could have had a drink, I don't mind," Delia repeated what she'd told him when he'd ordered the same liquorless drink she had.

"It seems only fair that I abstain if you have to," he said, urging her to taste one of the mushroom caps stuffed with lobster.

After she'd marveled over how good it was, he said, "So at fourteen you went to work for a catering company fixing trays."

"Right. But this is pretty boring stuff, you may not want to hear it."

"You haven't bored me yet," he assured. "And we're talking about your business to appease my brother, remember? If you don't tell me you'll be making a liar out of me. So give me the whole saga of your meteoric rise from tray fixer to company owner."

"It wasn't meteoric," Delia amended with a laugh. "I stayed with the company, basically learning every aspect of the business, saving my money—"

"With the exception of buying expensive lipstick."

"With the exception of buying expensive lipstick, and when the owner decided to sell out, I used what I'd saved, supplemented it with a small business loan, and bought the company—which was Cartwright Caterers then."

The waiter returned and Andrew placed their dinner order. Once he had, he went right back to their conversation. "But unless somebody has led me astray, Meals Like Mom's isn't technically a caterer."

"The longer I did the catering, the more I turned toward organic foods, healthier ingredients, things that were fancy enough for parties or weddings, but that were also not full of preservatives or chemicals. I made sure to put that into my advertising—"

"See? Now we've talked advertising and I'm legitimate," he pointed out, making her smile. "Go on."

"Well, when people hiring me would see that the food was wholesome, too, they started making comments about how they wished they could have every-night dinners catered that way for their families. I thought there might actually be a market for meals that were as good and healthy and hearty as moms made—"

"Not your mom, though."

"No, but meals like I'd often fantasized that my mom might make. So I branched off from the catering business into packaging meals for one to however many. I already had the kitchens, the equipment that we used for the catering end of things, and the accounts with organic food wholesalers, which meant I could keep costs reasonable—that's a big thing when you're up against drive-through windows at fast-food restaurants that are easy to hit on the way home. So mainly it was a matter of packaging, *advertising*—"

"Twice. We're doing good."

"And distribution and delivery. But the idea ended up taking off to such a degree that we closed the catering business and got rid of its more complicated headaches, to concentrate on Meals Like Mom's. And here we are."

Their salads were served then and when their waiter left them alone again, Andrew said, "So you've always been ambitious."

Delia laughed. "Maybe living the way we did in pursuit of Peaches's dream of being a starlet taught me hard work was a better route."

"I admire that," he said.

"But you wouldn't have traded traveling and having a good time," she guessed.

His smile was unashamed. "I have had a good time."

"But now it's nose to the grindstone. Or at least it was for the three days before today," she teased him.

"You could make me a star and send me back to work tomorrow with the advertising accounts of Meals Like Mom's," he challenged.

"Not tomorrow, but it's still under consideration," she said as their entrées were served.

"Glad to hear it. I'll report that. But no more business talk," Andrew decreed, going on to make her laugh with the sordid history of the club that he claimed had been a speakeasy and notorious casino in the 1920s.

Dinner was followed by nightcaps and dessert at a hotel lounge, where a blues singer with a stupendous voice was a nice finish to a day and evening more full than Delia's social life generally was in a year. Only then did Andrew finally agree to take her home.

"Thanks for this," he said as he walked her to her door.

"For what? You were the one to whisk me away, arrange for everything, entertain me and take care of all the details *and* all the checks. It's me who should be thanking you."

"I'm just glad if you had a good time," he said, taking her keys from her hand and unlocking her door before giving them back to her.

He didn't make any move to go beyond the porch, though, standing with his back bracing the screen door open as Delia took only one step inside.

She flipped on the entryway light and then turned to face him again. When she had, it struck her as strange that something about him had changed in just that moment that she'd lost sight of him. His expression was more thoughtful, more open somehow.

"You're an interesting woman, do you know that?" he asked her as his eyes delved into hers and seemed to infuse her with a warmth that protected her from the cool late-night air.

"Oh, I don't think so," she demurred.

He smiled a small smile that seemed to say he knew she would say that. "Hey, how can anyone who had a mother named Peaches be anything but interesting?"

"Peaches was interesting but that doesn't make me interesting by default."

"You're independent, you're a visionary, you're brave and strong and determined. You're different from most women I've met up with. I like that."

"I suppose working women are sort of a novelty in your circles."

"Not only women who work, but women who have any substance. I'm probably not worthy of that."

She could tell he wasn't merely saying that. That he was feeling it, too. But not in any self-pitying way. It was more that he was simply recognizing what he *did* feel.

"I'd give it everything I've got to *be* worthy, though," he added then. "If you married me."

"It doesn't have anything to do with worthiness," she said quietly, again wishing away her own feelings since having the courage to show her a hint of his vulnerable side only made him all the more appealing. "You have a lot to offer. You're personable and sweet and thoughtful and you have a real knack for making everyone around you feel comfortable and appreciated and good about themselves. You're fun and full of energy and I know you're trying hard here, but—"

"I don't want to be one of the dads like yours and

Marta's and Kyle's, Delia," he said so earnestly Delia could tell what she'd told him about her family had impacted him in a way she'd never meant it to. That it had impacted him enough for him to apparently make it his goal *not* to abandon the baby.

But good intention didn't bring with them the same thing that age and experience and hard-earned maturity did. His good intentions allowed Delia to hope for the best when it came to him actually being some sort of father to the baby, but his good intentions weren't enough to convince her to jump into a relationship—let alone a marriage—with both feet. Even though she was surprised to discover a small part of her that almost wanted to.

He smiled down at her after a moment of the silence her thoughts had caused and lightened his tone to joke slightly, as if he knew what she'd been going to say before he'd interrupted her. "I know, I'm Superman *but* there's the age thing, and the 'we're still strangers' thing, and probably more things than you're even telling me. But you could marry me anyway and just in case there's even an ounce of you that's tempted to, I want you to know that I wouldn't make you sorry if you did."

Delia smiled, too. "But I'm not going to marry you," she whispered to ease the blow this time, not admitting that there actually *was* an ounce of her—maybe even more than an ounce—that was tempted.

It concerned her to realize it, and she decided that on that note she should definitely put an end to this day and evening that had actually done what he'd wanted it to do—it had put a crack in her barriers and resolve, and cast some of that special spell that was Andrew's.

"I'd better go in," she said then.

"You *are* in," he pointed out with a nod of his chiseled chin in her direction. "What you really mean is that I'd better go home."

"You'd be uncomfortable sleeping in your car," she joked rather than giving him outright encouragement to leave.

He took a deep breath and sighed elaborately. "Okay, okay, you still won't marry me and I have to go home. I get it."

But he didn't leave. He continued to stand there, staring at her, studying her, looking as if he didn't want to stop.

Then he bent at the waist just enough to meet her lips with his in a kiss that Delia had the impression he'd only intended to be a simple kiss, like the one from the night before.

Only right away it wasn't simple at all.

She didn't know why, whether it was the day they'd just spent together, or the talking they'd done that had brought them closer, or if it was some sort of chemical reaction, but that kiss that she'd been sure had begun as a customary goodbye was suddenly much more.

Delia wasn't even conscious of him moving and yet in an instant Andrew had pulled her nearer. He'd wrapped his arms around her. He was cupping her head as it inched back with the deepening of that kiss.

His lips parted over hers and hers parted in answer, making way for his tongue when it came to trace the edges of her teeth, to greet her tongue tip to tip, to circle and spar and introduce an entirely new element as their bodies pressed front-to-front and his arms tightened around her.

But it wasn't merely Andrew who had altered that initial kiss. Delia discovered herself doing her part, too. Meeting and matching his tongue with her own, playing any game he initiated and initiating a few herself.

She also found her arms somehow around him. Her hands pressed to the breadth of his back. Her nipples hardened to twin peaks at his chest, demanding to be acknowledged, too.

She even began to wonder what would happen if she pulled him inside her house....

Picturing it, she could see herself tugging him across the threshold into the entryway. She could see herself kicking the front door closed behind them. Continuing to kiss him the way she was, only with even more fervor, more passion, more of the urgency that was mounting in her with every passing moment.

But the longer she considered it, the more caution prevailed.

She'd already ventured further than she should have with him today. Tonight. She'd already missed work— something that was unheard of for her. She'd already ignored her responsibilities. She'd already given Andrew hours and hours she shouldn't have given him. She'd already done so many things that were unlike her—not even counting Tahiti. And she knew she just couldn't go on doing that. Doing what went against the grain for her.

So she reminded herself of every reason she absolutely should not be kissing him in the doorway, let alone bringing him inside to do more. She mentally yanked herself out of that spell Andrew had put her under and forced herself to regain some control. She ordered herself to end that kiss rather than urging it on.

It was no easy task. But after another few minutes of that toe-curling kiss, she finally put her hands between them and pushed until Andrew got the message and stopped kissing her.

"I know," he mock-complained in a voice affected by what they'd both just been absorbed by. "Go home."

Delia smiled. "Yes, go home," she confirmed.

"All right, all right. But not happily," he lamented, kissing her forehead before letting her loose.

He butted the screen door away and side-stepped out of its lee, pointing a long finger at her. "But you haven't seen the last of me," he warned before he turned on his heels and really did leave.

And tonight Delia couldn't make herself close the door without first watching him walk all the way to his car and get behind the wheel again.

Because tonight she couldn't refuse herself every last minute of him.

It was something that gave her fair warning that she was treading on thin ice when it came to this man.

But with her lips still singed from the heat of his kiss, the fair warning was difficult to take to heart.

And even more difficult to take to bed with her.

While memories of the kiss?

Those traveled very well....

## Chapter Ten

Andrew had been awake many, many mornings at 5:00 a.m. The difference between those other mornings and this one, though, was that he was usually just rolling in from a long night of partying. *This* morning his alarm went off and he needed to roll out of bed. And he decided on the spot that he far preferred 5:00 a.m. as the end of the night rather than the beginning of the day.

But in spite of the fact that he'd only had about three hours sleep, he turned off the alarm, sat up and swung his feet to the floor.

For a moment he propped his elbows on his knees and rested his face in his hands. But only for a moment before he felt himself drifting off again. Then he shook his head like a dog shaking off water and flipped the switch that turned on the overhead light.

Of course it blinded him and he squinted against the pain, blinking repeatedly until he could tolerate the glare. Once he could, he reached for his cell phone on the bedside table, knowing he needed to get into gear.

He had a plan and if he was going to pull it off, he had to get started. Really, really early.

He knew his stepmother wouldn't be awake yet, but that didn't stop him from punching in her number. He required something from her and knowing her, she'd be so glad he was asking for a favor she'd overlook the pre-dawn wake-up.

"Helen? This is Andrew," he said when she answered on the third ring, sounding sleepy and alarmed at once.

"Andrew? What's wrong?"

Of course she would think he was calling with bad news of some kind. It wasn't like him to call her at all, let alone at this hour.

"Nothing's wrong," he assured quickly to allay her fears. "I apologize for waking you but I need something, I need it in a hurry—an incredible hurry—and you know the people and have the connections to help me make it happen."

"I'm sorry, Andrew, I'm groggy. You're sure nothing has happened?"

She seemed to have stalled on that.

"No, honestly, nothing has happened," he assured, feeling slightly guilty when it occurred to him that this call might be bringing up some sort of flashback for her. He wasn't exactly sure of the details of how Helen had been told of his father's death, but his father had had a heart attack at night, at his office, and Helen had been the first one notified.

"I would have waited for a more decent hour if I could have," he said. "I know this must seem insane to you—calling you at five in the morning—but it's important to me and to Hanson Media Group, and in order to do what I want to do, every minute of today will count."

"It's okay," Helen said, beginning to sound more alert. "I'm always here for you. For you and Jack and Evan. Whenever, wherever, whatever."

She was trying. Just as she always had. Trying to help. To be agreeable. To be a parent. A friend. He had to give her points for that. Even if it didn't change his feelings about her.

And in this instance her desire to play a role in his life that neither he nor his brothers had ever accepted her in was going to work to his advantage, so he appreciated it.

"Are you thinking clearly yet?" he asked.

"Better. My eyes are open, anyway," she said with a light laugh. "I'm glad to hear from you at any time. I learned through the grapevine that you'd come back to Chicago. And about the baby…" She faltered over that, as if she might have had second thoughts about saying it once she had. "Can I… Should I congratulate you? Or is it a sore subject? I know Jack has pushed you to marry the woman and you weren't altogether happy about that, but maybe that's changed? Maybe it will all work out?"

She was rambling without so much as taking a breath, and Andrew forced patience he didn't genuinely feel. But then, he'd never felt comfortable with his stepmother, and the harder she tried to connect with him, the more uncomfortable he was.

However, he reminded himself that she could do what no one else he knew could, and so he said, "Helping me meet Jack's requirements is sort of what I wanted to talk to you about. It's what I'm attempting to do. And that's where you come in. Today, at least. And why I'm rousting you out of bed."

Andrew heard what seemed to indicate that she was sitting up and possibly turning on her own lamp.

Then she said, "Okay, what can I do for you?"

Eager. She was so damn eager to please when it came to him or either of his brothers. It was kind of a shame that she hadn't learned yet that things between them all weren't likely to change. That neither he nor his brothers would ever embrace her as a part of their family.

But again, he needed her.

So he jammed his fingers through his hair, sat up straighter and kept his tone level as he laid out his plan.

When he'd finished and Helen had promised to put him in touch with everyone she could to make sure he accomplished what he'd set out to do today, he said, "I'll let you go so you can make those calls for me. I have to get hold of Jack, too."

"If I were you I'd wait until he's been up a while and

had his coffee," Helen cautioned. "I stopped by the office yesterday and he wasn't too happy that you hadn't come in. David was complaining that Evan still hasn't responded to any of their messages, and Jack was saying that if Evan was anything like you, it didn't matter because all they got out of you was three days work and then you'd disappeared."

"In the first place, you know as well as I do that they don't just need Evan in Chicago for manpower, we can't have the reading of Dad's will until he gets here with the rest of us. And in the second place, I didn't *disappear*," Andrew said, taking issue. "I called in. And being with Delia is what he *told* me to do—both for her business and to *do the right thing*."

"Oh, I didn't mean to make you angry," Helen said in a hurry. "I'm just saying not to call him right now."

"Yeah, okay, I suppose I can wait until office hours," Andrew conceded, knowing that his brother wasn't going to be any too happy to find out that he wouldn't be in today, either....

"Kyle? It's me. Did you give up hope that I'd ever call you back today?" Delia greeted her younger brother on her cell phone.

"Just about," he responded. "I'm in my car, on my way home from work."

"Me, too."

"You, too? It must be, what? Eight o'clock there?"

"My dashboard says eight-o-seven," she informed him.

"What are you doing working so late? Especially on

a Friday night? And in your condition?" Kyle repri-
manded.

"My *condition?*" she repeated with a laugh. "I
played hooky yesterday so I had the stuff I didn't do
then and today's work to do today, too—that's why I
had to stay so late."

"Um-hmm," Kyle said knowingly. "I heard you
actually missed yesterday."

"Marta said she'd talked to you."

"About a lot of things. I understand our boy Andrew
appeared from out of nowhere."

"He appeared from Tahiti, where we left him three
months ago," Delia said.

"Long vacation."

"Apparently until this week he was living the lush
life of a trust-fund baby and a three-month vacation
wasn't unusual," Delia informed her brother, going on
to explain Andrew's job and family situation to Kyle as
she drove.

"He honestly never worked before this week?" Kyle
marveled.

Kyle had begun delivering newspapers from his
bicycle when he was barely ten years old and hadn't had
a gap in his employment history since. It was no wonder
it was difficult for him to believe Andrew had *never* had
a job.

"Honestly," Delia confirmed.

"But he's selling advertising for his family's company now?" Kyle asked as if that redeemed the other
man. To some extent, at any rate.

"Well, that's what he was doing the first three days

this week. Yesterday he was with me and I don't know about today. He could be back in Tahiti by now," Delia said wryly.

"Except that I thought he was hanging around, trying to persuade you to marry him."

"Ah, you and Marta really did talk about a lot of things."

Kyle didn't bother denying it. The siblings had never been secretive with each other. Instead he said, "She told me he's my age and that pushed your negative buttons."

"Because *I'm* not your age," Delia pointed out unnecessarily.

"And because you aren't Peaches," Kyle guessed.

"This would definitely be right up her alley."

"Andrew's a good guy, though. We all liked him in Tahiti."

"I'm not disputing that he's a good guy," Delia agreed, trying not to think too much about just how much of a good guy Andrew seemed to be. Or how much of a good time she had when she was with him. Or how good he made her feel. Or how good he kissed...

"Seems like his being a good guy should carry more weight than his age," Kyle said.

"You're on *his* side?"

"I'm not on anybody's side. I'm just saying that he isn't a creep, it's his baby you're having, and he wants in on the whole thing. Maybe you should cut him some slack."

"He's twenty-eight. He's only held a job for a few days in his entire life. He has a roommate because he travels so much he needs someone else to watch his place. What about that shouts 'ability to make a long term commitment to you'?"

"K.C. did it for me."

K.C. was Kyle's and his wife Janine's five-and-a-half-year-old son. The baby Janine had been pregnant with before she and Kyle had gotten married. The *reason* Janine and Kyle had gotten married.

"You know I didn't think I was ready to get married when Janine turned up pregnant," Kyle continued. "But it was just what I needed to make me grow up."

"Who are you kidding?" Delia said with another laugh. "You wanted to go to the first day of kindergarten in a suit and tie. You were born with an old soul. You were always grown up."

"Andrew didn't strike me as a big baby," Kyle observed.

"Maybe not a *big* one…"

"Come on, he's not a kid."

"But just how much of an adult is he?"

"Adult enough to want to be a husband and a father to his child. That makes him more adult than any of our fathers or any of Peaches's other boy toys."

"In theory Andrew wants to be a husband and a father, but I'm not so sure he's thought about the reality of it. Or the fact that it doesn't end. Or at least isn't supposed to."

"But you aren't even letting it begin."

Delia groaned. "Come on, be on my side."

"How about if I'm on the baby's side?"

Delia had feared that was the route her brother's opinion would take. "I know what you're thinking."

"I'm thinking that I wanted a father," he said decisively and without shame.

"I know, Kyle," Delia muttered compassionately.

"I'm thinking that in one way or another, we all did—even if you hid it better than Marta or I, and even if it didn't come out in you until later in the game," Kyle said, obviously running along the same lines Marta had voiced when she and Delia had discussed this earlier in the week. "And I'm thinking that the father—the real, genuine, father of your baby wants you and wants to *be* a father to your baby, and that you shouldn't blow that off so cavalierly."

Had she blown it off cavalierly? Delia asked herself, feeling guilty suddenly to think that might be the case. To think that her baby might grow up and think and feel the way her brother did and decide she *had* blown off the baby's chance to have a father without giving it serious consideration.

"Come on," she repeated, beseeching her brother's understanding. "Don't be so hard on a pregnant woman."

"Maybe somebody has to be," her brother said gently. "It sounds to me like Andrew is trying, Dealie. Yes, I agree that unplanned pregnancies—especially with somebody you just met for one day on a vacation—aren't the best foundations for marriages. But an honest desire to try to make things work out goes a long way in having it happen. Look at Janine and me. We're happy. We may not have come to our marriage without complications, but we did come to it willing to give it our all, and that's been just as good—if not better— than getting married in some unrealistic haze of hormones."

Wasn't that similar to what Andrew had said the night before? That he'd give it everything he had if she would marry him?

"I don't know, Kyle...." Delia hedged.

"Maybe not, but maybe you should do some more thinking about it. Considering it. And Andrew. Rather than just writing him off," Kyle concluded, again making it clear he and Marta were of a similar mind on the issue.

"You're really being mean to me tonight," Delia complained.

"Not *really*. I just don't want you to make a mistake that you and the baby might regret forever. The baby— and you—deserve at least the possibility of having a second parent in the picture."

"Hmm... I just turned onto my street and it looks like the man in question's car is parked at my curb. He's not in his car but there are lights on inside the house," Delia said, seizing the discovery as a method of not answering her brother's pressure on her to change her decision.

"Does he have a key?" Kyle asked.

"No, he doesn't. Apparently he knows a little something about breaking and entering."

"See? He does have a skill," her brother joked.

"Gr-reat," Delia said facetiously.

"Since you're home and have company, I'll let you

go. But think about what I said."

As if she was going to be able *not* to.

"I'll talk to you soon," she countered before they said goodbye and she turned off her phone.

But as she pulled into her driveway wondering what Andrew had up his sleeve tonight, she realized that her brother's words might have had a stronger impact at that moment, because she was already coming to feel more and more torn.

Torn between what her head was telling her to do—or *not* to do—and the direction she was worried her heart might be beginning to lean.

"But for some reason he *did* break into my house," she told herself out loud just to help keep even a semblance of balance before her heart—and her brother's and sister's opinions—swayed her too much.

## *Chapter Eleven*

As Delia climbed the steps to her porch after having talked to her brother on the drive home from work her emotions seesawed.

On the one hand she wasn't exactly thrilled that Andrew had taken the liberty of getting into her house when she wasn't there. Why would he do such a thing? she wondered, unable not to feel a bit intruded upon as she mentally catalogued if she'd left her bra hanging to dry in the bathroom, if that laundry basket of underwear waiting on the dryer to be folded could be easily seen from the kitchen, if there were dishes in the sink or mail scattered on the countertops or if her unsightly old bedroom slippers were in the living room by some chance.

But on the other hand, she also couldn't help imagining an entirely different scenario from the one in which Andrew discovered she owned a few pairs of granny-pants underwear and wore slippers that should have been thrown away years ago. She couldn't help imagining that he'd found his way into her house when she wasn't there to set up some romantic welcome-home for her tonight. A candlelit dinner, maybe?

Or maybe he was upstairs in her bedroom. His marble statue's body stretched out on her bed, wearing only that pair of blue jeans he'd had on the night he'd arrived in Tahiti that made his rear end look amazing; his broad, honed torso bare, braced on one arm, the biceps bulging mounds of muscle. She pictured that devil's own smile on a mouth that was just waiting to begin again what she'd had such trouble ending the night before....

"Okay, but he *broke* in," she told herself out loud as a reminder she hoped would cool down the internal heat that that vivid image had turned on.

When she reached her front door she tried the handle before putting her key in the lock to see if it was open. It was, allowing her merely to turn it and push the door wide.

"Andrew?" she called before stepping inside, suddenly considering the possibility that her burglar might just drive the same kind of car—as unlikely as it was that a burglar would drive a Jaguar.

But it was Andrew's deep, distinctive voice that answered. From upstairs.

"Follow your leaders."

Her leaders?

Waging a second battle against the fantasy of him laid out on her bed, Delia stepped over the threshold and discovered tiny stuffed animals set one per step all the way up her stairs.

"My leaders," she repeated, assuming the toys were what he was referring to.

She closed the door behind her and set her purse and briefcase on the entryway table. Then, she did as she'd been told, bypassing a bright yellow monkey, a pink bunny, a black-and-white loppy-eared dog, an elephant, a giraffe, a turtle, a dolphin, a camel, a lion and a floppy moose to reach the second floor landing.

Her eyes went immediately to her own room. The door was open—the way she always left it—but there was no light flooding out. Instead a frog, a teddy bear, a fluffy kitten and a buffalo continued across the hardwood floor to the room she had designated as the future nursery.

Light *was* shining from that open door and with her curiosity at peak capacity, she made her way to it.

But it wasn't a semi-nude Andrew she discovered when she did. He was fully clothed—in those jeans she'd been fantasizing about and a plain white T-shirt with the long sleeves pushed to his elbows. And he was standing at the opposite end of a room that was no longer four scarred, lavender walls with uncurtained windows. A room that had been transformed as if by magic into the nursery of her dreams.

"What's this?" she whispered, almost unable to believe what she was seeing.

"What's it look like?" he asked with a quizzical arch of his eyebrows.

Delia didn't rush to answer. Instead she stepped farther into the room and did a very slow pivot to take it all in.

The awful lavender walls were now a soft, creamy color, divided at chair-rail height with a border of baby forest creatures frolicking merrily through trees and bushes and scampering across bubbling brooks. The floor was no longer covered with indoor-outdoor carpeting but now sported a thick shag that matched the color of the walls.

And no longer was the room empty of furniture, either. Now, angled in one corner just to Andrew's left there was the very crib she'd seen in her decorator's catalog—a white crib with each end a high, graceful slatted arc that looked like white rainbows. Now there was a changing table, bureau and armoire that matched the crib. There were softly drawn-back curtains on both sets of windows. There was a toy box and a play table and toys on shelves that lined one wall. There was a rocking chair cushioned in a downy pad near the crib, and a table lamp to one side of it. There were even picture frames awaiting baby pictures.

All together it was serene and beautiful and cute, too. It was whimsical and fun and still well-organized and user-friendly. And she loved it.

Her gaze came full circle to that spot where Andrew stood waiting for her to answer his question.

She wasn't sure if he was worried he might see disapproval of his efforts in her eyes and so couldn't meet them, or if he was simply afraid she'd missed the mobile of the same woodland creatures that frolicked on the wall border, but he glanced away and reached a long index finger to flick the bunny's tail and set the entire mobile into motion.

"You've been busy," Delia understated, finding her voice small and cracked with the same emotion that was flooding her eyes with tears.

"Boy, have I," he said with effect. "Beginning with calling Marta before she was out of bed this morning to tell her what I wanted to do so she would help me get in. She let me borrow her key."

Then he must have realized how emotional this had made her because he said, "This isn't supposed to make you cry."

She *was* crying by then, though, as the tears became too much to contain and rolled down her cheeks. "They're happy tears, if that helps."

"Well, a little, I guess," he answered, closing the distance between them in two strides of those longs legs and taking her into his arms to comfort her.

Powerful arms that pulled her in close to his body where she could rest her cheek against his chest.

She didn't dare stay that way for long. Not when, almost instantly, other emotions found life, too. The kind that had spurred the night they'd spent together in Tahiti, the kind that had erupted during the heated kiss of the previous evening, too.

Struggling to keep control of *something,* Delia blinked back the moisture in her eyes and raised her head from Andrew's well-defined pectorals. "I'm getting your shirt wet," she said, dabbing her damp cheeks with her fingertips.

VICTORIA PADE 165

"It's okay," he assured, but he made way for the arms and hands that came between them and she increased the slight distance by standing straighter and taking another look around at the room.

Even on second sight it took her breath away.

"How did you do this?" she asked.

"You told me you'd hired a contractor and a decorator to do your remodel, and I saw the decorator's card near your kitchen phone when we were in there the other night. I recognized it because my stepmother has used that same designer. And I knew which room you were planning to use as the nursery—"

"I didn't think you were that interested."

He merely frowned at that notion and continued with his explanation. "So when I got this idea, I enlisted my stepmother. I figured the decorator would do anything for her—Helen is a valued customer—and I was right. One call from dear old stepmom and your designer dropped everything today to work solely with me."

"Impressive. But my decorator couldn't have done all this."

"No, but she did know what you were leaning toward in here when it came to the colors and furniture. And she could put me in touch with your contractor. I did some wheeling and dealing—"

"With the contractor?" Delia interrupted Andrew a second time in astonishment. "The contractor is who's holding us up until the end of the month. You didn't get him in here *today*, did you?"

"I did. Him and his whole crew."

"How?"

"I told you, wheeling and dealing. I found some common ground and used it. He's a motorcycle buff. I happened to own a vintage Harley-Davidson that I used as a bribe."

"You got him to do this by promising to let him ride your motorcycle? That's all it took?" Delia asked.

"Not quite. He's now the proud new owner."

Delia hadn't thought that Andrew could surprise her more than he already had, but that accomplished it. "You sold him a vintage Harley-Davidson motorcycle in order to get him over here today?"

"Sold would not be the right word. Let's call it an incentive gift."

Delia's eyes widened this time. "You *gave* it to him? What must that have been worth?"

"This," Andrew said with a nod to the room in general and without missing a beat, stunning her.

Then he said, "I'm not fooling around, Delia. I told you, I'm willing to do anything and everything it takes."

For the first time, Delia believed him.

And something about that made her tear up again.

But she didn't want to cry anymore so she went back to what they'd been talking about before the motorcycle issue.

"Still, you did this in one day?"

"I had a whole parade of workers waiting around the corner while I watched your place from up the street first thing this morning. The minute you left for work, we moved in. Painting came first so gigantic fans could dry the walls, and then we went from there."

Delia glanced at the evidence of his work, thinking about the effort that had to have gone into accomplishing this. "I think you're kind of amazing."

"What? Only *kind of?*" he joked.

But before Delia could respond the doorbell rang.

"Pizza," Andrew informed her. "I've had next to nothing to eat since I got up at five this morning and I was beginning to think you'd never come home tonight, so I ordered delivery. I'll go get it, you kick off your shoes and sit down, we'll eat up here and break the room in."

Apparently he'd taken command today and was still in that mode. But Delia didn't mind. Actually, it was nice….

While Andrew was downstairs, Delia forced herself to leave the nursery just long enough to use the bathroom and make sure her hair was still caught neatly in its ponytail, her mascara hadn't run and that the simple black slacks and red sleeveless shell sweater she'd worn for casual Friday weren't too wrinkled. Then she did remove her black flats to toss them into her own bedroom before returning to the nursery in her bare feet.

She took away the two tiny chairs that were pushed into the kid-sized play-table so they could use it for their dinner and sat cross-legged on the floor to continue to study Andrew's handiwork until he rejoined her.

"You look like a little kid sitting there," he said
with a laugh at her when he did.

"You're the kid," she countered. But she was only
teasing him because as she watched his approach with
their dinner in hand, it occurred to her that she was
seeing him in a new light. One that didn't count the
years difference in their ages. One that made her think
that maybe there was more to him than she'd given him
credit for.

He deposited their meal on the play-table and sat on
the floor, too.

"You must be exhausted," she said.

"I think I'll survive," he assured.

Endless energy—an advantage of his youth, Delia
thought as she doled out the salads, opened the pizza
box and handed him a soda can.

"So," he said once they were both situated with full
plates of food. "Is everything okay or do you want to
make changes? Because it's all right if you—"

"It's perfect. I don't want to change a thing," Delia
said without the need to even consider the possibility.
"I still just can't believe you did it."

"Hey, I had to do something to show up the es-
teemed Damon Simosa."

His reference to the high school boy she'd told him
about the night before made Delia laugh in spite of the
bite of pizza she'd just taken.

"After all," he continued in the same vein, "I don't
see you doing menial labor to buy lipstick to wear for
me, so I'm just trying to figure out how I can rate. Or
is it only older men who do it for you?"

"Apparently it isn't *only* older men," she said pointedly, tossing another glance at the nursery. "But there have been only older men until you, now that I think about it."

"Really?"

Delia nodded. "'Fraid so."

"On purpose?" Andrew asked after a drink of soda to wash down salad.

"Yes."

"How much older are we talking about?"

"There's been a pretty wide range," she hedged.

"Among the hundreds you've been involved with?" he teased.

"I'm guessing *hundreds* is closer to your number than to mine."

Andrew toasted her with his soda can as if to concede.

"Honestly? You've been with hundreds of women?"

"Either the light in here is bad or you just lost all the color in your face," he said with a grin that was too endearing not to get to her. "No, I haven't been with *hundreds* of women."

"How many *have* you been with?" Delia persisted.

"Probably more than my share. But it isn't as if I keep score."

"How many have you been seriously involved with? Because those are the ones who count. Not people you've seen casually now and then."

Andrew took another slice of pizza, since he'd polished off the first.

"Ones I've been seriously involved with..." he repeated. "In that case, I'm a virgin."

"You haven't been seriously involved with *anyone?* Ever?"

"If I'm assuming that by seriously involved you mean have I been with anyone for a long period of time, considered marriage and proposed, then no. You're the first to hit two out of those three."

"Oh, dear," Delia breathed, a little alarmed to learn that just when she thought she was seeing more depth in him she might be mistaken.

Andrew must have noticed her concern because he gave her a reassuring smile.

"It isn't as if I've been down on marriage or anticommitment or anything. I just haven't stayed in one place for any extended period of time, and once you've been gone for months and you call the person you were dating before you left, well, you usually find that they've moved on."

"But being gone for months was a matter of traveling for pleasure. You *could* have stayed in one place long enough to have a relationship if you had wanted to," Delia reasoned.

"I guess I never met anyone who inspired that in me. There were a few women I asked to come along on trips with me, if that helps. Women I liked well enough to want things to continue with them. If they'd come, who knows? Those relationships might have developed into something serious. But no one ever took me up on the offer."

"Not many people have the kind of freedom you've had," Delia pointed out. "And when whoever you asked to go along couldn't leave for months, apparently you packed up and went anyway. Rather than staying around to let the relationships develop."

Andrew watched her face, a bare hint of a smile playing about his lips as if she amused him. Then, after a moment, he said, "And what are you thinking? That I'd do that with you? That I'd get a notion to take off, ask you to, too, and if you wouldn't, I'd go anyway?"

"It seems possible," Delia admitted, worrying about that exact thing.

"Okay, I'm guilty of never having been more than infatuated with anyone, so yes, I packed up and went anyway," he conceded. Not on the defensive, though. More as if he were clarifying things for her. "But what I've done in the past doesn't mean it's what I'll do in the future. It only means it's what's already happened and what's already happened with everyone else has never been too serious. But now what's happening between us *is* serious and that changes everything that will happen from here on."

Did he honestly consider what was happening between them serious? And if so, why? Was it only because of the pregnancy or were there feelings that were going beyond infatuation that were making it serious in spite of the baby?

Delia couldn't bring herself to ask. Or maybe she just couldn't bring herself to hear the answer. But he did get a gold star for the fact that he was approaching their relationship as something of more importance than any he'd had before.

"So what about you?" he said then, tossing the ball back into her court. "Not hundreds of guys, but no husband or real commitment that I've heard about for you, either. And you've had more time at it," he added jokingly, successfully lightening the tone.

"No, no husband. Or serious commitments," she answered, realizing that she didn't have a whole lot of room to judge Andrew's failure to commit when she'd never done it herself. And feeling slightly better about his history when she considered that.

"But there have been three guys who were long-term," she added, seizing her only claims to even flirting with permanence. "And one of those might have gone the long haul if we hadn't been at different stages of our lives at the time."

Delia had finished eating so she repositioned herself to lean her back against the solid base of the crib for support.

Andrew had another slice of pizza. "And all three guys were older than you?"

"They were. The first guy was five years older and the third guy was eight years older."

"And you didn't marry them because…"

"It didn't get that far with either of them. They were both just guys I saw for extended periods of time— fifteen months and eighteen months respectively—until things just fell apart the way they do, and we knew the relationships *weren't* going anywhere so we called it quits."

"Then there's the second guy," Andrew reminded. "You skipped him, so he must have been the close-to-serious one and the oldest."

Delia laughed at the accuracy of his guess. "You're good," she said as if granting him an award.

"How old and how close to serious?"

"Daniel was seventeen years older than I was."

Andrew's brows headed for his hairline. "*Seventeen* years older?"

Delia nodded. "And don't give me any armchair father-figure analysis," she warned.

"*Seventeen* years?" Andrew repeated as if that were begging for comment.

"I was twenty-six, he was forty-three. He was well-educated, suave, sophisticated, established in his career, stable. He knew what he wanted and how to go about getting it—"

"And what he wanted was you?"

"He'd reached his career and financial goals. He was ready to settle down, get married, have a family, really devote himself to the next phase of his life."

"With you."

"With me," Delia said, feeling the twinge of sadness she always felt when she thought of or talked about Daniel.

"But I assume you didn't feel the same about him," Andrew said.

"I really liked him. I enjoyed his company. We had a lot in common and if the timing had been better I think we would have had a future together. But like I said, we were at different stages of our lives—because of the *age thing*." She emphasized the phrase both she and Andrew had used frequently since discovering their own discrepancies in that department.

"Actually," she went on, "it was an age-*related* thing. While Daniel's career was on cruise control, I was just getting Meals Like Mom's going and I was determined to make it work—that meant late hours, weekends, whatever it took. Daniel was a strict nine-to-fiver by then and he wanted someone to be at home when he was, someone whose job came second. But mine came first at that point and so we ended up saying goodbye."

Andrew had finished eating and he crawled on all fours like a big jungle cat until he reached her side. Once he was there, he did an athletic sort of spin that landed him sitting next to her with his back against the crib, too. He took her hand in his, weaving their fingers together before resting them on his thigh.

Studying them, he said, "That isn't the same as you and I, you know."

"No, I don't know that," Delia answered, glancing at his striking profile. "Meals Like Mom's operates with or without me at this point. I keep late hours because I want to, not because I have to anymore. When the baby comes I plan to keep work to a minimum, to delegate, to set up my office so the baby can come to work with me. I plan to do everything I need to to be a full-time mom. It's what I want to do now. It's where I am in my life. But you... You'd still be on a beach in Tahiti if it had been your choice. And even though it hasn't been your choice and you're here now, it isn't a sure bet that you'll stick to this course. Especially when it wasn't a course you were ready to be on—and that goes for the job and for the baby. Definitely different stages of life," she concluded.

Andrew shook his head, calmly denying that. "I think that the only thing that really matters is that we're here now—regardless of what got us here. You didn't plan this and neither did I. You've had a little longer to accept it and adjust to it than I have, but I think I've come up to speed pretty quick. I won't tell you that I'm still not having moments when I feel sort of overwhelmed. But I'm dealing with it. And the point is, we're sitting together in our baby's room—*our* baby's room. Same time. Same place. Same stage of life—we're going to be parents. You've embraced that. I'm in the process of embracing it. But that slight discrepancy doesn't put us far apart. And that's what's important."

He went from looking at their hands to looking her in the eyes again. To smiling a smile that was even more endearing, more irresistible than the earlier one.

"And when it comes to our pasts," he added, "think of it this way—I don't have any baggage or war wounds to rear up and cause trouble for us. I don't have any preconceived suspicions or mistrusts or expectations that you're going to do me wrong the way someone else did. And it doesn't seem like you do, either. That puts us on a pretty level playing field in that department, too. So age thing or no age thing, again—it seems to me that we're at about the same stage of life."

He could be very persuasive. And it didn't hurt that all during that heartfelt speech he'd been stroking her hand with sensual brushes of his thumb. Putting her qualms to sleep even as he awakened little shards of glitter in her veins.

He raised her hand to his mouth then, kissing it gently, sweetly, before he looked into her eyes once more with such earnestness that it gave her confidence in everything he'd just said. It caused her to think that maybe she could trust it. Trust him. Such earnestness that, for the first time, she actually had a glimmer of hope that things between them really might work out.

But before she could tell him any of that, he kissed her and turned those little shards of glitter to bright, sparkling diamonds. Sparkling diamonds of desire that seemed to have been waiting just below the surface since he'd kissed her the night before.

And all Delia could do was kiss him in return. All she wanted to do was kiss him in return. Give herself over to it, to him, suddenly.

She raised her free hand to the side of his face, slightly rough with the day's growth of beard, drinking in the feel of whiskers and warm, taut skin over the sharp angles of that face she could see in her mind even though her eyes were closed.

His lips were parted over hers and she willingly parted hers, too. Willingly greeted his tongue when it came to toy with hers in that oh-so-sexy way he had, tip to tip, chasing circles, sparring just a little.

Andrew let go of the hand he held, wrapping one arm around her to bring her nearer, and slipping his other hand behind her head. With more aplomb than she would have expected him to have at such a thing, he removed the clip that held her hair in a ponytail and combed his fingers through her pale blond locks.

It made her secretly smile inside to think that he'd wanted her hair loose and had taken the initiative to free it. She only wished she had the courage to take that same initiative when it came to his T-shirt. The T-shirt that stood between her other hand at his back and the feel of his bare skin beneath it.

She was brave enough to caress that broad back, though. To massage it and explore every rise and fall of muscles she remembered ogling as they'd snorkeled in Tahiti—honed and tanned and gleaming with wetness...

Had she been the first to open her mouth even wider than his? To deepen that kiss? To take it up another notch?

Maybe. Not that it had been premeditated. It was just that picturing him in Tahiti, having him there with her now, holding her, kissing her, was turning her on with such speed her thoughts couldn't keep up.

Andrew could though.

With their mouths still locked and tongues still tantalizing each other, he lowered them both to lie on their sides on the thick mat of new carpeting. His body ran the length of hers but with enough of a separation to make her wish there wasn't one.

She felt her nipples knot and push against the confines of her lacy bra as if reaching out to close some of that distance between them. Her back arched all on its own in silent plea, bringing those tight crests into scant contact with his pectorals. Scant enough that it didn't seem as if it would arouse him even more. But a quiet groan rumbled in his throat and he seemed unable to resist drawing a hand down her side, to the hem of her sweater where he slipped underneath it.

Oh, better still!

Warm and big and strong—that was how his hand felt on her bare rib cage before he let it rise higher. High enough to encompass her straining breast.

It was Delia who moaned then. She couldn't help it. She'd been aware of the fact that pregnancy had rendered her breasts more sensitive, but she'd had no idea just how sensitive. She actually writhed beneath his touch, pushing herself more deeply into his palm, begging him with her body to get that bra out of the way, to give her the full, unfettered sensation.

Which was what he did. Sliding fingertips first inside that cup, replacing it with that hand she was in awe of as it kneaded and massaged and explored the nipple that stood proudly out to meet him.

Andrew rolled her to her back and came to lie half on top of her then. Mouths were wide and seeking and growing more insistent by the minute. Both of Delia's arms were around Andrew and her fingers were digging into his back, urging him on.

And on he went, insinuating his leg between hers, pressing the proof of what she was stirring in him against her thigh, raising his leg high enough to awaken that portion of her body as well.

He ended their kiss then, at the same time his hand left her breast long enough to raise her sweater so that he could take that yearning orb into the hot cavern of his mouth. To suck and knead and flick the kerneled crest, to only lightly nip at it with careful teeth, to tug and tease until Delia was nearly wild with the need for even more.

More of him that merely plunging her own hands underneath his shirt to his naked flesh didn't satisfy. More of him that merely flexing into the juncture of his legs didn't complete. More of him in every way...

But just when she wanted more, she got less.

Slowly, as if it was the fight of his life, Andrew stopped. One final, deep pull of her breast into his mouth and he released it, kissing her stomach as he replaced her bra. One final pulse of his knee into her most private spot, of his most private spot against her, and he took his leg away. Two very, very cautious fingers at the hem of her sweater tugged it down over her exposed torso again.

"I want to do this," he said then, his voice deep and gravely, confirming his claim. "But I won't. Not again. Not until you marry me."

"Oh sure, take me to the brink and then give me an ultimatum," Delia joked, staring up into that exquisitely handsome face, into those dark, penetrating coffee-bean eyes.

He smiled crookedly. "Whatever it takes."

He sat up and tugged her to sit up, too. Then he got to his feet and helped her to hers.

"Marry me, Delia," he ordered forcefully.

A flood of things went through her mind. Her conversation with her brother and the points he'd made. The nursery they were standing in and all Andrew had done to finish it. The lengths Andrew had gone to in so many ways to persuade her to make a go of things between them. All he'd said himself and the points he'd made—better points even than Kyle's.

And it suddenly occurred to Delia that maybe she should give Andrew the benefit of the doubt. That maybe she should swallow her pride about the differences in their ages. That maybe, like that night in Tahiti that had been like no other night of her life, she should throw caution to the wind. That she should give in to what he wanted. To what Marta and Kyle thought she should do in providing her child with the father none of the McCrays had been allowed. That she should stop suppressing her own feelings for this man who never left her thoughts, who she wanted with every ounce of her being no matter how she denied it. That maybe, she should take the leap of faith....

"What if I say okay?" she tested.

"Okay, you'll marry me?"

Delia nodded. Tentatively, but she nodded.

Andrew's responding smile was a bit lopsided. "You'll make me a happy man," he said softly.

"Will I really?"

"You really will."

Still Delia hesitated, hoping, praying, that she was doing the right thing. For herself. For Andrew. For the baby.

But then she said, "Okay. I'll marry you. If you're sure…"

## Chapter Twelve

The collar was too tight. It was choking him.

Andrew ran his index finger around the inside of it and stretched his neck.

No, there was plenty of room. Maybe it was the tie.

He loosened it but that didn't help either.

"Dammit!" he muttered under his breath, not wanting his voice to travel outside of Delia's downstairs bathroom where he'd just dressed and was on the verge of going out to greet his family and the judge his brother had arranged for to perform the ceremony.

The wedding ceremony.

It was Saturday evening, a week and a day after Delia had agreed to marry him. A whirlwind week in which he'd had to make up the time he'd missed the week before that at work *and* help arrange for tonight's wedding. A week in which he'd hardly had time to think.

But now here he was, on the verge of actually getting married.

And he felt as if he were being choked by the collar of the white silk shirt and tie he had on under his best Italian suit. Even though neither the collar nor the tie were anywhere near to choking him.

Was it the idea that he was getting married that was really doing it?

Married. He'd be married. Married, with a job and a kid on the way.

And he just kept thinking that this was going to be his life from now on—up every day at the same time to go to the same place to do the same things before he came home each night to a wife and a kid and that whole bucket of responsibilities. No more hopping a plane for places unknown when the mood struck. No more free and easy living when he *was* in town. No more lying on a beach for endless days until he was good and ready to go home, regardless of how long that took. No more random pursuit of any and every woman who caught his eye just to see if he could make the conquest.

No more life.

At least no more of life as he'd known it. And enjoyed it. And wanted it to continue.

"Not what you're supposed to be thinking half an hour before your wedding," he lectured himself with a glance up from the vanity to the mirror above the sink as he put the folded white silk square into his breast pocket.

But he didn't seem able to stop the thoughts.

Thoughts about how his entire life had changed and was changing in ways he hadn't been prepared for it to change. Ways he wasn't sure he was prepared for it to change now. Thoughts about the fact that he hadn't had a choice in any of this. About the fact that a part of him felt as if he might never have another free choice at all. Ever. Not another choice that wouldn't have to be made with a wife in mind. And what she wanted and approved of and consented to and wouldn't be hurt by. Not another choice that wouldn't have to be made with a kid in mind…

Choking. There was the choking sensation again.

Obviously not the shirt or the tie. Obviously the situation.

But there was no way out. Not this time. This time he had to stick around. He had to marry Delia. He had to work for a living. He had to be a father….

The walls of the bathroom seemed to close in on him. The room suddenly seemed too small a place for him to be shut up in.

Too small a room.

Too tight a collar and tie.

"Get a grip," he told his reflection. "You can do this. Last-minute jitters—that's all you have. Everybody gets them."

Of course not everyone took a job they didn't want and got married because their family forced them to.

Never in his entire twenty-eight years of living—

including since his brother and uncle had dumped the job and the ultimatum and the pressure to marry Delia on him—had he wanted so badly to run….

A knock on the bathroom door startled him to such an extent that his body jolted as if he'd had an electrical shock.

"It's me," his roommate announced from outside. "You all right in there?" Mike asked.

Andrew didn't feel all right. But he said, "Yeah. Sure."

Mike apparently knew him well enough not to believe that because after a moment's pause, his roommate's voice came again in a confidential whisper, "Hey, man, it'll be okay."

Andrew laughed a mirthless laugh and opened the door a crack. "Easy for you to say."

"I know. But it's the truth," Mike assured. "Delia's great and you like her. Everything else will fall into place."

"Is there a manual for best men that tells you what to say?"

"Nah, I mean it," Mike claimed. "I was just upstairs and I got to see her. If you don't want her, I'll take her."

That made Andrew chuckle more genuinely. "She looks nice?"

"Too good for you," Mike goaded.

"There's never been any question about that," Andrew answered wryly.

"Seriously—are you gonna make it? You look kind of green around the gills."

"I'm fine," Andrew lied.

"Then I'm supposed to tell you it's time to get started."

Suddenly there was such a knot in Andrew's throat that he couldn't speak. He merely nodded and closed the door, trapping himself inside again and suddenly finding that preferable to the idea of leaving the bathroom to face what he was about to face.

"What are you going to do?" he whispered to his reflection as if he were challenging someone else. "Are you going to leave Delia standing at the altar while you hide in the bathroom?"

He didn't know why, but hearing her name when Mike had said it and again now that he said it himself, thinking about her, actually helped.

Delia.

He never had these feelings when he was with her. He felt great when he was with her. He felt as if he could be with her forever. That was not only okay, but also a good thing.

*Delia—just keep thinking about her....*

He did have fun with her, he reminded himself. He could be himself around her. He could talk to her, trust her, tease her, joke with her. He could relax with her. Totally and completely.

Oh, yeah, it helped to think of Delia.

She was beautiful, too, his friend was right about that. He could stare at her for hours and not get tired of the way she looked. One flash of those big baby blue eyes and he felt as if the sun had come out from behind clouds. And she had a tight little body that didn't quit.

Plus, she was nice. Sweet. Pleasant. Smart. And he was hot for her. Hell, he'd just about gone out of his mind keeping his hands off her this past week.

But marriage? Shouldn't marriage be based on more than what amounted to a strong attraction? Shouldn't it be based on feelings people had for each other?

Okay, he was headed for dangerous territory again, he warned himself.

*Just think about Delia. Only Delia...*

Besides, he reasoned, it wasn't as if he didn't have any feelings for her. He did. He even thought he cared for her. In a way that he'd never cared for any other woman.

"So maybe Mike is right about that, too. Maybe it will all be okay," he said.

Hell, it was going to have to be because he couldn't get out of this now.

Just think about Delia, he repeated. Just think about Delia....

And that's what he did.

Steadfastly.

To get himself out the bathroom door.

Where all the eyes on all the guests seated in her living room waiting for the ceremony to begin suddenly turned towards him.

And if there had ever been a time he'd actually considered booking it the hell out of someplace, it was at that moment.

But he didn't do it.

He tried to smile.

He moved into place beside Mike.

And he waited for his bride.

"Congratulations, Andrew. It was a lovely wedding."

Andrew had avoided his stepmother all evening but she was standing with his brother Jack and his Uncle David when David motioned for him to join them, so he couldn't put off talking to her any longer.

He also couldn't help stiffening up when she squeezed his arm and raised up to kiss his cheek.

"Wouldn't it be more apropos to say 'Thanks for taking one for the team'?" he responded snidely.

"Oh, I hope not. I know everything that's come about for you in the last two weeks has been thrust upon you to a great degree, but I really like Delia and I think she'll be good for you. I would hate to believe that's honestly how you feel about her or about marrying her," Helen said.

Andrew's late father's widow wasn't the stereotypical-looking trophy wife. She was attractive but not in any overblown way, and she was nothing if not impeccably tasteful. But Andrew's remark had caused her flawlessly made-up face to sober into a forlorn-looking frown that, when Andrew had been a teenager, would have pleased him.

Now he just felt guilty for the petty comment. Not because it had been an ungracious way to accept congratulations from Helen, but because Andrew regretted making such a tasteless comment when it came to Delia. She didn't deserve that.

"You did the best thing," David praised, taking up where Helen had left off. "All the way around. For yourself, too. At least I think that's what you'll come to see in time even if it isn't clear to you now."

"Finding good women has only improved David's and my life," Jack concurred with a glance in the direction of the buffet table where Jack's own bride, Samantha, and David's former personal assistant and new wife Nina were chatting amiably.

"Might have been nice to be able to take *my* good woman on a honeymoon," Andrew countered pointedly, since his brother and uncle had both vetoed that notion.

"We know your pattern too well," Jack said. "If we let you out of here for a honeymoon it'd be the last we saw of you for who knows how long. Besides, you just came back from a three-month vacation and now you have a job to do."

"You did terrific at work this week, though," David added, clearly to soften the blow of Jack not mincing words. "That new chewing gum account is a big one. It's going to help."

"Don't tell me you even managed to get a new advertiser this week while planning the wedding?" Helen inquired.

Andrew thought he knew where that was headed. Helen had been expressing an unusual interest in the business lately and it seemed to him that she might well want more involvement. She never had liked being excluded. From anything.

But when it came to the company, that was the way

it was and Andrew wished she would get used to it. She was his late father's trophy wife and nothing more. And she'd never *be* any more. Not in the eyes of Andrew or his brothers and not when it came to Hanson Media Group, either.

He wasn't in the mood for it tonight, however, and assuming his brother, uncle and stepmother had summonded him to give him the family pat on the back for doing what they'd wanted him to do, he figured he could make his exit from their little gathering.

With that in mind, rather than addressing Helen's comment about the new account, he said, "I should get back to Delia."

"Wait," Jack said to delay him. "We've finally heard from Evan."

That did spur Andrew's interest.

"Finally," David repeated with a full measure of his own irritation over the middle Hanson brother's tardiness in responding to every attempt to contact him.

"I got an e-mail from him just before leaving home tonight," Jack continued. "He'll be in Chicago Thursday. I called the estate lawyer the minute I got the e-mail and arranged for the reading of the will."

"Again—let me just say *finally*," David said.

"When will it be?" Andrew asked.

"Friday morning. The attorney is coming to the office to make it convenient for us. We can all meet in the conference room," Jack said.

"And we really need to get your father's will read," David pointed out. "We've gone too long with things up in the air waiting for you and Evan. That's another reason we couldn't have you taking off on a honey-moon—we knew Evan had to get back to us any time now, and then we could get this all taken care of."

"Hanson Media Group first and foremost," Andrew muttered like a fight song.

"Things do need to be settled," Helen said in a con-ciliatory tone of voice.

Which, for no rational reason, just rubbed Andrew wrong even when he knew she was only trying to make nice the way she always did, and that they were all right and the will did need to be read so the company and everyone connected to it could proceed from there.

But still, he reacted to the irritation he was feeling rather than to the logic of it all. "Well, you know I'll be there. You've all made sure of that. So if that's it, I really should get back to Delia."

"That's it," Jack confirmed.

This time it was David's hand that reached out to take Andrew's arm and halt his retreat. "Make the best of this, Andy," he said. "You won't be sorry."

Delia had come into Andrew's sight just then and seeing her helped to smooth the inexplicable rough edges that had developed during his talk with his family.

So instead of saying anything to his uncle's words of wisdom, he merely nodded as if he were taking the advice to heart before excusing himself and heading for his wife of two hours.

It was after twelve that night when Delia closed the door on the last wedding guest. Andrew was standing right behind her and once the lock was securely in place he proved just how close behind her he was by reaching over her head to brace his weight on his hands as if to prevent the door from opening again to let anyone else in.

Delia could have slipped out from under the archway his body provided but she just wearily dropped her forehead to the carved oak instead.

Andrew kissed the back of her neck, left fair game because her hair was caught up and away from it in a classic French knot.

Then he said, "When my uncle offered to have the wedding at his apartment I turned him down because I thought it would be nice to be married here, in the house that means family to you. It didn't occur to me that that meant we wouldn't be able to slip away when we wanted to."

Delia laughed. "Not only the bride and groom, but the hosts, too. Still, it *was* nice to have it here."

She used what little space was between them to turn around so that her back was to the door and she could look up at him. "Hi," she said as if this were the first time she'd had the opportunity to greet him.

He dipped down to place a miniscule kiss on her lips before answering. "Hi."

Another kiss sent a wisp of warmth through Delia before Andrew raised up and peered into her eyes. "I didn't even get a chance to tell you how beautiful you look."

Delia smiled. She'd fallen in love with her dress the moment she'd seen it at the bridal shop—it was an ankle-length white satin A-line with a lace overlay that reached higher than the sweatheart-shaped bodice that ended just above her breasts, giving a peek-a-boo effect before the lace made a scalloped, off-the-shoulder neckline itself. But she was pleased to know that Andrew liked it, too.

"Your expression brightened up so much when you first saw me I sort of got the idea," she demurred anyway.

"One look at you—the antidote for wedding jitters."

He kissed her once more.

"Did you have wedding jitters?" she asked when that kiss that lasted only slightly longer ended.

"Didn't you?"

She smiled again. "Some," she confessed, unwilling to tell him that she'd been awake the entire night before, hoping she wasn't making a mistake and that this would work for him, for her, and for their baby. But the most she would add as an explanation for her own admission of nerves was, "This has all happened pretty fast."

"And yet some things haven't happened fast enough," he countered with a voice full of innuendo. "At least not fast enough the *second* time…"

That was true enough. After turning her on that night in the nursery and every night they'd been together all week, Andrew had still left her unsatisfied. And with all those pent-up desires just below the surface, Delia took her hands from where they'd been behind her since she'd turned to face him and used them to loosen his tie.

"You were the one who gave the ultimatum, not me," she reminded. "*Not until you marry me*—I believe those were your exact words. And all this last week, you said you wanted to wait. So we waited."

This time it was Andrew who smiled. A wickedly sexy smile that let her know the wait was over. "I was just too afraid that if you got what you were after from me I'd never get you in front of the judge tonight."

Delia took a deep breath and sighed it out resignedly. "True, you might not have," she deadpanned, unfastening his collar button. "I did only agree to this for one reason."

"I knew it!"

"I'm sorry you had to find out this way."

"With you undressing me?"

She *had* unbuttoned his shirt to the middle of his chest.

"Shall I do them up again?" she asked.

"I wasn't complaining," he whispered in her ear, turning up the heat in her another notch with his breath against her skin.

She undid two more of his buttons.

"You looked pretty fantastic yourself tonight," she told him as she did.

Andrew bent low enough to kiss first one of her bare shoulders and then the other.

"So you approved?" he inquired.

"Mmm. Very much," she breathed, leading with her chin to place a kiss underneath his. "Even Kyle and Janine commented on the difference between how you looked tonight and in your beachwear in Tahiti."

Delia's brother, sister-in-law and nephew had flown in for the wedding so that Kyle could give Delia away.

"Little did they know that under these pants I'm wearing bright orange tiger-striped Speedos."

Delia laughed yet again. "Liar. You didn't even wear Speedos in Tahiti."

"Maybe you should check to be sure," he suggested lasciviously as he traced the edge of her scalloped neckline with his nose and sent tiny shivers all through her.

"You want me to take off your pants in the entry-way?" she demanded as if the idea scandalized her.

Andrew mimicked her earlier sigh. "I suppose there are more appropriate places."

"Like the beach."

He took a turn at laughing, too.

Then he kissed her again, this time with his mouth open wide, his tongue running rampantly in to meet hers, and with no doubt left that he'd spent this last week struggling with celibacy as much as she had.

When he ended the kiss, though, he did a push-up off the door and took one of her hands to tug her away from it, too. "No beaches near enough tonight," he decreed, using his free hand to flip off the lights from the main panel near the door. "I guess we'll have to use the bedroom."

"Novel idea," Delia said as he led her up the stairs.

She couldn't resist peeking at his terrific derriere along the way. He really had looked remarkable tonight and watching him even from a distance when he wasn't by her side had only made Delia wish they *could* have started their wedding night earlier. Because of all the things she worried about, a lack of attraction to him was not one of them.

Her bedroom was lit by candles on either side of the bed when they arrived there—something Delia had no doubt her sister had done before leaving shortly before.

"Marta," she said in answer to the quizzical glance Andrew shot to her when he saw them.

But that was the last bit of attention he paid to the lighting, taking Delia to the foot of the queen-sized bed that had also been turned down for them, facing her at the same time he pulled her nearer and kissed her again.

A bedroom kiss. Different than those in the entryway. Different than any they'd indulged in during the week leading up to this moment. His mouth came to hers with an instant passion, open and seeking, hungry and bold.

Not that Delia had any reservations herself. She'd imagined having him here in her room all week. She'd fantasized. She'd relived that night they'd shared on the Tahitian beach. But that kiss was still mind-bending.

Her head fell far back to accommodate it. His tongue did wickedly delicious things to her tongue, to the roof of her mouth, to every inch he could reach, convincing her that there was some merit to a man who had had as much experience as he'd had.

When he released her hand to wrap his arms around her, she found his shirtfront and tugged the tails from his trousers so she could finish the job she'd started.

Then, feeling a surprising lack of inhibition, she slipped her hands inside, to his flat stomach. She let her palms ride the rippling muscles of his washboard abs, upward to curve over his honed pectorals, rising to his expansive shoulders where she slid all the way over them and then down his biceps to shed him of shirt, tie and jacket at once, not caring that the finely made clothing landed on the floor behind him.

Then she kicked off her shoes and let herself have a moment of nothing but that kiss, the feel of his naked back beneath her hands, and his fingers working free the twelve tiny pearl buttons that traveled the length of her spine.

She thought it would take him longer than it did to get all the buttons open. Or maybe she was just so lost in his mouth over hers, in the tightening of her nipples in response to it, that she lost track. But suddenly she felt her dress loosen and Andrew slipping it off.

The bodice had a built-in bra and without the gown, Delia was left in only lace bikini pants and thigh-high nylons. And she wasn't about to be the only one of them that exposed. Especially not when she wanted Andrew equally rid of barriers. So as his hands massaged her back in a preview of what was to come, she went right for his waistband.

It made her smile to discover just how much he wanted her. In fact he was straining behind his zipper to such an extent that she had only to unfasten the hook at the top of it and that long, hard evidence did the rest of the work. From there it required only a nudge to send his pants to join the rest of his clothes.

Delia broke off their kiss to grin at him. "Am I mistaken or are there no Speedos?" she asked without glancing downward. Even though she wanted to.

Andrew grinned back at her. "Okay, so they're just boxers," he confessed. He began to trail kisses along the side of her neck. To her shoulder. Finding her breast even before the hand she'd anticipated, and sending a shockwave of pleasure through her as he divested himself of his own shoes and spun her around to ease her to the mattress.

Then he was gone.

Well, not actually gone, just not touching her or kissing her or doing any of those wonders with his mouth at her breast.

Instead he was standing above her, looking down at her as if he were absorbing every inch of her with his dark eyes.

Delia might have felt more self-conscious, but she was too enthralled by the sight he presented— magnificence personified in a body better than she'd even remembered, muscular, dynamic, perfectly proportioned.

His handsome face erupted into an appreciative smile and with his eyes holding hers, he rolled down her hose and followed them with her panties as Delia reached up to pull the pins from her hair and shake it free.

And then he was on the bed with her, partially beside her, partially on top of her, and it was as if everything broke free at once.

His hands and mouth were everywhere and so were hers. And between the fact that Delia had had no idea how alcohol-numbed she'd been that night in Tahiti, and the fact that hormones had apparently raised all her nerve endings closer to the surface of her skin, an entirely new array of sensations awaited her.

Every stroke of his fingers was intensified. Every kneading, sucking, flicking of her nipples was almost enough to send her right over the edge all by themselves. Every kiss, every trail of the tip of his tongue was a miracle unto itself.

It wasn't only what he was doing to her that took her step by step higher up the stairway of desire. The warmth and tautness of his skin was like French silk over steel, elevating her need to feel all the more of him. The bulge of each muscle was something to be explored, learned, reveled in. The tightness of each tendon, the power in each sinew, took her another step higher, inching toward what they were both striving for.

And the feel of that shaft when she reached for him, when she sheathed him in her hand, the sound of the deep, guttural groan that rumbled in his throat, the writhing he did in response, were all more heady than any martini she'd ever consumed.

Then, just when she needed it most, he was above her again, this time on the mattress, between her thighs, pulling her legs to wrap around his waist as he found his way inside her. Carefully. Gently insistent. Until he was embedded within her.

Slowly at first, they moved together. Rhythmically. As if they really were back on the beach, mimicking and maintaining the motion of the waves. Until bodies and needs demanded more, and Andrew began a quicker pace, a race up what remained of those stairs.

Delia kept up, her fingers digging into shoulder blades that seemed more than able to take it, meeting him and matching him, striving for that peak that came closer and closer and closer...

And then like heavy drapes thrown wide over a window at the top of the stairs, bright, brilliant sunshine flooded her and Delia reached the ultimate crest. She couldn't move with Andrew any longer, she could only cling to him as her body, her entire being succumbed to pure, exquisite ecstasy that held her in its velvet grip for one timeless moment of splendor.

Gliding down from that pinnacle when it had spent itself she discovered Andrew in the ending throes of his own climax. She felt him shudder slightly before he stiffened above her, within her. Like a glorious work of art, there he was, tensed and frozen for a moment of his own bliss.

When it had passed he also began the descent. It was as if the starch were being drained out of his muscles by slow increments. His hands were on either side of her head, his arms stretched straight, and as he relaxed he lowered himself to her, covering her with the welcome weight of his body melding itself to hers.

Then he pulsed inside her and reared up only enough so that he could kiss her forehead.

"Are you... Is everything okay? I swore I was going to be more in control just in case, but—"

"Everything is great," Delia assured him, laughing lightly at his concern.

He seemed relieved—and satisfied—because his supple mouth stretched into a cocky, lopsided grin before he dipped down to kiss her mouth.

Then he slipped out of her and rolled to his back, bringing her to lie at his side, wrapping her tightly in both arms to bring her close.

"So this marriage thing? Using a bed rather than a beach? Not so bad?" he asked.

"Not so bad," Delia confirmed as many, many things caught up with her and exhaustion began to take its turn. "What do you think?" she managed to ask.

"Better than not so bad," he said as if he meant it, sounding as worn out as she felt.

Too worn out to say more because Delia heard him exhale as fatigue overtook him, too.

She didn't have anything left herself to fight it, so after glancing one more time at the wedding ring on her finger, at her hand resting on her new husband's chest, she closed her eyes.

Drifting off to sleep with a warm, wonderful sense of security that she hoped would last forever.

## Chapter Thirteen

"I'm on my way, Jack."

Andrew was rushing around the kitchen, trying to find his car keys when his cell phone rang. He and Delia had just said a lingering goodbye before she left for work and when the cell phone's display told him in advance that his caller was his brother, that was how he answered it, figuring Jack was annoyed that he was late.

"Tell me what day this is, Andrew," Jack ordered, his own temper clearly on the verge of erupting.

"Uh, I believe it's Thursday," Andrew said facetiously, peeved that his brother was being such a stickler. Again.

"Now tell me why it was important for you to get in here on time."

"Well, let's see," Andrew mused as he gave up on

finding his keys in the kitchen and moved into the living room to continue the search, drawing a blank as to what his brother was alluding to. "The reading of Dad's will is tomorrow, so that can't be why it was important for me to be there at the crack of dawn today. Was I supposed to bring breakfast or something?"

He heard his brother draw in an enraged breath and breathe it out through nostrils he imagined flaring.

"Right—tomorrow is the will reading," Jack said through what sounded like gritted teeth. "But today—*Thursday*—was the meeting with the Geltrace Chewing Gum people. The meeting that was to close the deal for us to do their advertising. The deal *you* were supposed to be here to close."

Andrew paused in scanning the living room to take his phone away from his face, throw his head back and mutter an expletive to the ceiling.

Then he brought his head down, put the phone back to his ear and started flinging sofa cushions out of the way in hopes that his keys had fallen from his pocket and lodged there.

"I forgot," he confessed. Because at that point, what else was he going to do but admit it.

"You forgot," Jack repeated.

"I've had other things on my mind, other things needing my attention." He didn't want to give details because the distractions all involved Delia and the fact that they hadn't been able to keep their hands off each other since the wedding on Saturday night. They'd both been leaving work early every day this week, spending most of their time in bed, and still hadn't been able to forfeit morning lovemaking in order to get to work on time each morning. Including this one.

But his brother didn't seem to care what his reason for missing the meeting had been, because from the minute he'd said that he'd had other things on his mind, Jack had been reading him the riot act.

And even though Andrew was only half paying attention, it was enough to make him angry. He was getting more and more sick of his brother as his boss.

Cutting Jack off, he said, "What happened with the gum guys? Did they walk or did you close the deal?"

"I shouldn't have had to close the deal. It was *your* deal. And David and I both had to dance around the client's doubts about just how trustworthy we are. Do you have any idea what it does to client relations when they show up, get led to a conference room and then have to sit on their thumbs waiting for the one person who's handling their account? Do you have any idea how David and I looked assuring them that you'd be here any minute and then finding out that the assistant we'd sent to try to reach you couldn't even get you on the phone? And why the hell *couldn't* we get you on the phone?"

"I didn't hear it. It was downstairs and I was upstairs," Andrew said, coming as near to the real reason he was late as he was going to.

"The client nearly walked out. David and I had to offer even more incentives to keep the account and all the while you were where? Sleeping in?"

Was his brother honestly that obtuse? Or was it just that Andrew's marriage to Delia was so completely a business arrangement to Jack that Jack couldn't fathom what *else* Andrew might have been doing upstairs and didn't see that he should be cut some slack to do it when he'd been denied a honeymoon in any other form?

Andrew's aggravation increased.

"We didn't lose the account so what's the point of this?" he demanded defiantly.

"We didn't lose the account but we could have!" Jack railed. "And we can't afford to lose anything. We can't afford to have word get out that George Hanson's playboy son lures clients in but may or may not show up to see the deal through."

Andrew had had it and he snapped.

"I'm not George Hanson's *playboy* son anymore, remember?" he said, his voice loud. "As much as I'd like to be, you made sure *that* changed. So what else do you want from me?"

"More than I'm getting!"

"More? You want *more* from me? I sacrificed my whole personal life for the good of this company. I freaking got *married* so there wouldn't be any *more* ugly scandals to smudge the almighty Hanson name, the almighty Hanson Media Group. And if you think that postponing your big dreams of being a judge compare to that, you can think again. I'm sick and tired of taking what you've been dishing out even when I do everything you ask. So get off my back, Jack! Because if you don't, keep in mind that if I'm going to have to work for a living anyway. I can do that anywhere and for anyone—it doesn't have to be for Hanson Media Group and it doesn't have to be for you.

I can be someone else's *manpower.* And believe me, I'd rather be selling surfboards in Hawaii than selling advertising in Chicago."

With that Andrew turned off his phone, closed his eyes and tried to unclench his jaw.

Selling surfboards in Hawaii and never having to listen to his brother rag on him again—there was an appeal to that.

But after a few deep breaths Andrew calmed down, reminding himself that not showing up for that meeting this morning was a really bad thing to have done. Especially after having given his word to his client that he would *personally* see to it that they were taken care of to their satisfaction.

"Damn!" he said.

Shaking his head at his own screwup, he opened his eyes and spotted his car keys on the floor in front of the sofa.

Picking them up, he stormed out of the house, slamming the door behind him in anger as much at himself as at his brother.

And without any idea that he hadn't been alone in the house after all.

When the doorbell rang at ten o'clock that night Andrew spun from his path pacing the living room and ran for the entryway.

"Delia?" he said in a panic even before he had the door open.

But it wasn't Delia on the porch outside. It was Marta and Henry.

"Oh, tell me this isn't as bad as it looks," Andrew said, more to himself than to his new sister-in-law. "Is Delia all right?"

"She's fine," Marta said in a strangely clipped tone.

"Where is she?" Andrew demanded, ignoring it. "Has she been in an accident or something? She never came home. I've been calling the office, her cell phone—you guys—and when I couldn't get anybody, I even tried the police and the hospitals. I've been out of my mind worrying about her."

"She hasn't been in an accident," Marta said.

It occurred to Andrew only then that he should step out of the doorway and invite his in-laws in, so that was what he did, pushing the screen door open.

But neither Marta nor Henry took a step toward coming inside. Instead, Marta said, "I don't think so."

Andrew didn't have any idea what was going on but he was having some trouble feeling reassured. "Where's Delia?" he repeated.

"She's gone," Marta said flatly.

Andrew glanced at Henry where the other man stood partly behind his wife. Since Marta was being less than cooperative, Andrew was hoping to gain a little help from her husband. But Henry merely gave him the hard stare, offering no information himself.

So returning his gaze to Marta, Andrew said, "What do you mean Delia's gone?"

"She's gone," Marta said again. "And we've come to tell you that you're to get all your things out of here immediately."

"Is this a joke?" Andrew asked, wondering what else it could be.

"It's not a joke," Henry said. "Delia wants you out."

Andrew actually laughed a little. They had to be kidding. The last time he'd seen Delia was this morning when he'd lifted her onto the kitchen table where they'd shared not only a goodbye kiss but enough sexy groping and rubbing up against each other to delay both their departures for work another fifteen minutes before Delia had insisted they postpone what they'd begun until tonight.

But here it was tonight, and rather than having Delia back here, on the kitchen table, he was standing in the doorway facing her sister and brother-in-law, both of them looking stern and angry and disgusted. And for the life of him, Andrew didn't have any idea why that could be unless this was some kind of practical joke.

"Okay, I'll bite—why would Delia want me out of the house?" he asked.

"It's over, Andrew," Marta informed him in all seriousness. "The cat's out of the bag. She knows. We all know now."

"Know what?"

"That you're a liar. That you've been lying to her this whole time. That you didn't want to marry her or be a dad to the baby. That you only did it because your family made you."

"Delia heard you on the phone to your brother this morning," Henry supplied.

Andrew had had a day from hell even before coming home to spend the evening frantic and worried about his wife and he wasn't at first sure what Henry was talking about.

"On the phone to my brother this morning?" he re-iterated, trying to think how that was possible. "Delia left before I did. Before I talked to Jack."

"No, she didn't," Marta said. "She went back up-stairs to get her umbrella and you were talking—screaming at your brother—on her way back down the stairs. She heard the whole thing."

The whole thing? Andrew had been fighting with Jack all day. He had to mentally work his way back-ward to recall what he'd said on the phone that morning that Delia might have overheard.

But when he did that and remembered the gist of it, he knew he was in trouble. And he instantly felt even more rotten than he had moments earlier.

"Oh, man," he moaned, shaking his head.

"Kyle and I were the ones who talked her into giving you a chance," Marta said, unable to control her own rage any longer. "She'd have never let you get to her otherwise. She knew better. But Kyle and I both gave you the benefit of the doubt. Probably because we've had our own issues about fathers. Neither of us will ever forgive ourselves for this. For what you've done, you—"

"Just tell me where she is," Andrew said soberly, morosely.

"She's gone!" Marta shouted. "She's not even in Chicago so you can't get to her. And she's not coming back until you're out of here."

For the second time Andrew focused on Henry, hoping for any amount of help or understanding. "I need to talk to her. This is bad, I know. But—"

"I'm not telling you where she is, either," Henry said flatly, making it clear that there was no support from that quarter.

Marta seemed to have regained enough control to return to the cold, flat tone of voice again as she said, "Delia told me to tell you that she'll be contacting her lawyer on Monday. She'll ask if the marriage can be annulled but if it can't be, she'll file for divorce. She wants it quick and clean, she doesn't want anything from you, she doesn't expect anything from you. She'll go back to her original plan to have and raise the baby on her own, and you can tell your family that she won't even name you as the father so there won't be any kind of *scandal* to do damage to you or your business. No one will ever know the two of you even met, let alone that there's a baby." Marta seemed so furious she almost shuddered before she added, "And just for your information and the information of the rest of the big-deal Hansons? She would never have done anything that would have made any of you look bad or anything that would have hurt your precious dynasty. That isn't her style."

Andrew closed his eyes and shook his head, wondering when the hell things were going to get better instead of worse for once.

"This is all wrong...."

"I doubt if you even know the difference between right and wrong," Marta exploded again. "We're all hoping that you *do* go sell surfboards in Hawaii and keep your perpetual Peter Pan routine as far away from Delia as you can get! You might as well, you're free again, free as a bird—just the way you wanted to be all along."

Once again Henry contained his wife, this time with an arm around her shoulders before he said to Andrew, "Just get your stuff out of here and make yourself scarce. The least you owe Delia is to do whatever she wants from here on." Then he squeezed his wife and to her said, "We're done. Let's go home."

But Marta didn't leave without letting her eyes bore into Andrew a moment longer, her expression rife with disappointment and disillusionment that were harder for Andrew to take than anything she'd said in anger.

Then she allowed Henry to turn her around so he could take her to their car where it was parked at the curb, leaving Andrew with nothing but his marching orders.

He watched them go, still feeling a sense of disbelief that this was happening. But once Henry had closed the passenger door after Marta he shot another glance at Andrew and said, "Don't make this any uglier than you already have. Just get out."

Andrew didn't respond to that, he simply stepped aside so he could close his own door on the scene outside.

But he couldn't seem to move away from that spot once he had. He could only fall back against the heavy panel and slide to the floor, knees bent, elbows on each one, staring straight ahead at nothing in particular, and thinking, *Delia's gone. She knows and she's gone....*

It really had been one hell of a day. Worse even than that first day back from Tahiti when Jack and David had leveled their initial job ultimatum, and then he'd found out that same evening that Delia was pregnant.

Hanging up on Jack this morning had only made his brother more mad. They'd argued again at the office, to the point where David had had to step in. Then David had taken Jack's side and let Andrew know how he'd felt about Andrew missing the meeting with the chewing gum people. That had led to more shouting. More threats. More guff Andrew had ultimately had to take.

Then he'd come home to what he'd thought was going to be a night that would wipe away all the misery of the day only to find no Delia. To find himself increasingly terrified that something had happened to her.

And now this.

And even though the guilt—the almost intolerable remorse—he felt, he reached a point where he thought, *enough is enough.* How bad could selling surfboards in Hawaii be compared to all this? he asked himself. Sunny skies. Sandy beaches. No pressures. No responsibilities. So what if he didn't have a fraction of the money he'd always been used to? He also wouldn't have the rest of this garbage to deal with. He really would be free. Free as a bird—as Marta had said.

"Out of advertising. Out of the family mess. Out of the marriage," he told himself. "Say the hell with it all."

For a moment he thought he might do just that. He might go upstairs, pack his bags, and take off. Let Jack and David—and Evan, when he got there—deal with Hanson Media Group and all the problems, let them have whatever his father left, wash his hands of the whole damn thing.

And as for the baby? Delia could have that. She could have it and raise it exactly the way she was going to before they met up again by sheer coincidence. Exactly the way she'd decided she would when she'd opted not to even try to find out who or where he was to let him so much as know she was pregnant.

Life would go on without him. Everything and everyone would go on without him.

And he'd be free...

So why didn't it *feel* like he'd be free?

That seemed strange. Was it because he knew the family and the family company was in trouble and needed his help?

Was it because he knew now that there *was* a baby—*his* baby?

Did just knowing mean he'd never be free?

He thought about that and came to the reluctant conclusion that yes, it did. But there was more to it than simple knowledge not allowing him to be free of everything if he left it all behind, he realized as he analyzed it.

For the first time in his life, he felt the weight of his responsibilities. Now that he'd been in the trenches at Hanson Media Group, now that he'd begun to contribute to the family business—this morning's meeting notwithstanding—he could see how he could be of value. He wanted to be of value. And discovering that in himself made him realize that he couldn't simply turn his back and take off. It made him realize that the responsibilities and what he owed his family were real to him.

And so was his responsibility to Delia and the baby. *His* baby. *His* wife…

But it wasn't only the weight of the responsibilities that he felt, either. There was more than that when it came to both the job, and to Delia and the baby.

He'd liked the sense of accomplishment when he'd gotten that chewing gum account. He'd liked the challenge, the chase, and he'd liked succeeding when it had all paid off. He'd been as mad at himself all day as everyone else had been at him for missing that meeting this morning to close the deal, because he'd liked contributing something. Doing a job. Doing it well…

Well, doing it, anyway. Missing that meeting hadn't been doing the job well. But still, he'd done the job and he'd liked it. Liked that he'd been able to help the company by bringing much-needed business in, rather than only taking, taking, taking.

So yes, he'd had a truly lousy day at work and with his family, but no, he didn't want to turn his back on the job or Jack or David and take off.

But even more, he knew deep down, he didn't want to take off on Delia. That a big part of the job and the satisfaction he'd found in it was that it had made him feel worthy of her. It had made him feel equal to some of the things about her that he admired.

Because really, it was all about Delia.

He hadn't known that until tonight. Until he'd thought something might have happened to her. Until now, knowing that she'd left him, that she wanted him out of her life. But it was the truth.

Delia.

Pregnant or not pregnant, it was Delia who he thought about every minute of every day. Delia who he hadn't been able to wait to tell about the ad account. Delia who he couldn't wait to share even his smallest victories with. Delia who he wanted to be with to share everything.

He didn't know when it had happened or how. He only knew that it was the truth. That in the short time he'd known her, she'd become the most important thing to him.

Important enough to make him want to succeed at work. Important enough to make him want to meet all his responsibilities. Important enough to want to rush home to her every night, to be with her, more than he wanted to be on any beach in the world. Important enough to want to have this baby with her, to see what the two of them had created together, to be her partner in raising it and watching it grow and flourish into someone—with any luck—who would be as incredible as Delia was. Important enough to make him aggravated with his brother when Jack had acted as if his and Delia's marriage was nothing but a business arrangement when his marriage to Delia—no matter how he'd entered into it—was very, very real to him.

But Delia probably didn't know that. Not after hearing what he'd said to Jack on the phone this morning.

He wished he could turn back time and make it so that he hadn't said any of those things he never wanted her to know.

Things that had hurt her. Things that must have made her think of him in a way he didn't ever want her to think of him. Things that had caused her to leave him. To want him out of her house. Out of her life...

His elbows stayed on his knees but he raised his hands and dropped his head into them as if he had a horrible headache. When in fact, he had a horrible heart-ache.

"What the hell have you done?" he whispered to himself.

But he knew what he'd done. The real question was, could he fix it?

And how could he even begin to fix it when he didn't know where Delia was?

He'd never felt so low in his life. So hopeless. So rotten.

He had to see her.

He had to talk to her.

He had to get her back. To get everything back to where it had been before that damn phone call this morning....

Then something flashed through his head and he recalled Marta saying that Delia wasn't even in Chicago. But he knew Delia well enough to know that she wouldn't cut herself off from both of the people who had been her support system all her life. If she wasn't with her sister, she'd go to her brother. In California.

Andrew didn't have anything more than a hunch about that, but he trusted it. He had to. He had to have something to hang on to or he thought he might go out of his mind. Delia was in Los Angeles with Kyle, he just knew it.

And he could get there tonight if he took the next plane out.

But if he did that, his own family wouldn't be able to have the reading of his father's will tomorrow morning. The reading of the will that had been postponed for months now. That *needed* to be done. That left everything hanging in the balance until it *was* done.

Mending fences with Delia was Andrew's first concern, his first priority. A future with Delia made everything else worthwhile.

But there wouldn't be any "everything else" if he didn't at least stick around through tomorrow morning for the will reading, so he knew he had to do that.

The minute it was over, though, he would be on the first plane to California. To Delia, he promised himself. No matter what.

With the decision made, Andrew raised his head from his hands and tipped it back to the door, staring up at the steps in front of him, picturing Delia at the top of them, overhearing what he'd said to Jack this morning and actually feeling a wave of what she must have felt.

"Tomorrow," he said as if she were standing there now. "Just hold on until tomorrow when I can get to you."

But it wasn't only Delia who needed to hold on.

It was Andrew, too.

He needed to hold on and get through the hours until he *could* get to Delia.

He needed to hold on and just hope that he was going to be able to repair the damage he'd done....

*Chapter Fourteen*

In spite of the bombshell that had been dropped by his father's will, as the estate attorney left the conference room after the reading on Friday morning, Andrew checked his watch for the time. He had a plane to catch.

Luckily he wasn't scheduled to leave for the airport for another twenty minutes because the moment the lawyer was gone, his brother Evan revealed his displeasure in a snort of disgust.

"I'm so glad I came back here to be a part of this family again and do what I could for the business when I didn't get so much as a mention in the old man's will."

The omission of the middle son *had* been glaring.

"Why'd I bother?" he added.

"Please don't feel that way," Helen said, jumping in to console him. "We want you to be a part of the family, of the business."

"And you're in the position to say it, aren't you, Helen?" Jack said, obviously still reeling—as was everyone else—by the revelation that their father's trophy-wife had just inherited the controlling interest in Hanson Media Group. That as owner of fifty-one percent, they were all suddenly working for her.

"None of this has to be a negative," Helen insisted. "I've been honest and open with you, Jack and David about how much I want to be involved in the resuscitation of Hanson Media Group and now I really can be."

"The offices are already decorated, Helen," Andrew contributed wryly. Knowing his marriage was hanging in the balance had sent him into this meeting with little patience. What little there was had been stretched even thinner to learn that his barely tolerated stepmother would now be running things. Just when he'd thought it was difficult enough to be working under the jurisdiction of his uncle and brother, the situation became more difficult to tolerate.

The attractive Helen sat up straighter in her chair and leveled them all with an unwavering stare. "As a matter of fact, it was your father's wish that I stay out of the workforce as long as he was the breadwinner in the family. But I happen to have an MBA—"

"We don't really buy it," Andrew said.

"I also have ideas that none of you have given me

the chance to share," Helen insisted. "I can be more of an asset than you all realize."

"And now you have the power to *make* us all realize it, don't you?" Jack said.

Andrew couldn't blame his brother for being even more angry than he was about this turn of events. After all, everything Jack had left behind in his own life in order to take over the helm of Hanson Media Group since their father's death now seemed like a waste since he was working for Helen just like the rest of them.

"Please, can we call a truce?" Helen beseeched them. "Can we put the past behind us and simply work together as a family?"

"A family minus one," Evan said, his anger seeming to gain steam the more it sank in that he'd been overlooked by his father.

"We are *not* a family minus anyone," Helen said forcefully to the middle son. "And keep in mind that George may not have included you directly, Evan, but any kids you have will be in line for their share of the twenty percent interest in Hanson Media Group that's to be held in escrow for all Hanson grandchildren. And there was also nothing in the will that prevents you from working here, from holding just as high a position as any of the rest of us. That's something you and I can work out together."

"Can we?" Evan said facetiously, clearly leery of his stepmother's overture when the truth was that he and Helen had even less of a relationship with each other than Jack or Andrew had with her.

But Helen seemed determined to develop one now

because she met his sarcasm head on and said, "Yes, we can."

Andrew was surprised to see his brother's eyebrow arch as if Evan might actually be willing to hear her out at some point.

Then to the room in general Helen said, "I think we should look at this as a new beginning, not as something divisive. As a basic structure from which we can now all join together to rebuild Hanson Media Group for the benefit of every one of us and for the benefit of all the Hansons to come after us."

"She has a point," David finally chimed in after a prolonged lack of contribution. "Evan, I—"

"Yeah, yeah, yeah," Evan cut him off, pushing himself away from the conference table and abruptly getting to his feet. "I get it. Helen is in charge. She'll try to find something for the black sheep to do so we can all pretend that isn't what I am. I need some air," he concluded, storming out of the room.

"As I was saying," David continued, "I agree with Helen that we should look at the will as just a foundation to work from. Now we know where we stand, what we have to work with and we can proceed accordingly. Now we really can move forward. With Helen at the helm, but with none of us inconsequential."

"More than just not inconsequential," Helen was quick to amend. "Vital—every one of us in this room, and Evan, too, is vital to getting Hanson Media Group back on its feet. The bottom line is that we all just have to work together."

Andrew checked his watch again and with no more

time to spare, he stood. "That does seem to be the bottom line," he said, thinking that nothing—not even the prospect of working with his stepmother—was as important as getting to Delia. "And now I'm sorry to duck out, but I have some personal matters that have to be taken care of. I'll see you all on Monday."

Andrew expected Jack to jump on that, to question him, to demand that he work the day, to play the role of super-boss that he'd been playing since Andrew came on board.

But instead Jack pushed his chair away from the conference table and stood, as well. "To tell you the truth, little brother," he said with a sigh, "I think a three-day weekend is what I need, too." Then to their stepmother, he added, "I guess we'll see you here first thing next week, Helen."

Helen's expression was slightly forlorn and Andrew almost felt sorry for her.

But he had enough problems of his own to deal with. She'd just have to make her own way when it came to running Hanson Media Group.

It was eight o'clock Friday night when the doorbell rang at Kyle's and Janine's house in Los Angeles. Delia was finishing dinner cleanup with her nephew while Kyle and Janine went for donuts.

"I'll get it!" K.C. announced the minute the bell sounded, leaping off the chair he'd been standing on at the kitchen sink beside Delia in order to hand her plates to rinse and put in the dishwasher.

"Hold on," Delia called after him, grabbing a towel

to dry her hands before racing after her five-and-a-half-year-old nephew.

She reached the front door just as K.C. opened it.

Then she stopped cold.

Standing on the other side of the open portal was the last person on earth Delia wanted to see.

"It's that guy from your wedding, Aunt Dealie," K.C. told her without first greeting their visitor.

"Andrew," Delia said flatly, feeling a sudden resurgence of all the pain, all the disillusionment, all the embarrassment, all the disappointment, all the betrayal she'd felt since overhearing his phone conversation the morning before.

"Go away," she added when the feelings she'd been contending with and trying to keep at bay all washed through her.

"We need to talk," Andrew said, not bothering with a greeting either.

"No, we don't. I've heard what you *really* have to say. I don't need to hear anything else from you."

She also didn't need to see him looking the way he did. She didn't need to see those refined features, which any soap opera actor would have envied, tense and strained. She didn't need to see those dark, dark eyes that looked troubled now as they stared at her from above the faint bluish-gray hammocks left by no sleep. She didn't need to see the day's growth of beard that shadowed his sharp jawline and proved he hadn't been thinking about his appearance enough to shave. She didn't need to see the two vertical lines that formed from his brows pulled together, or the downward curve of his lips or the rumpled blue suit and less than crisp shirt he wore that were evidence that he'd been too distracted to pay attention to his clothes.

She just plain didn't need to see him. Or to feel—even amidst the awful things he'd just caused her to suffer again—the warmer, softer feelings that had grown for him since they'd reconnected, since they'd gotten married.

No, she definitely didn't need to feel *those* things....

After a moment of staring at her as hard as she was staring at him, Andrew altered his line of vision to take in K.C. instead.

"Hi there, buddy. I came to talk to your aunt. Think you can give us a minute alone?"

"This is his house. He doesn't have to go away, you do," Delia said before K.C. could answer, not wanting to lose her nephew as a chaperone. Or as a barrier between herself and Andrew.

"It's okay," K.C. said. "I can't have a donut unless I put away my puzzles, remember?"

And with that reminder, the little boy dashed around Delia and went down the hallway of the ranch-style house to his room, leaving her without a buffer.

But that didn't mean she was any more eager to be with Andrew.

"Please go," she said firmly, taking the edge of the open door in hand, making it obvious she intended to close it.

But Andrew crossed the threshold before she could, making it necessary for her to step out of his way.

"I'm not going anywhere," he said. "Not before we talk."

"I don't have anything to say to you."

"But I have plenty to say to you," he countered, taking the door from her grip to close it behind him.

Delia backed farther away from him. As far away as she could get before she came up against the archway that separated the entry from the Spanish-style sunken living room of her brother's home. But it felt good to have the bolster of the wall bracing her spine so she stayed put.

Andrew didn't come any closer, apparently getting the message that he needed to keep his distance. He merely stood in the center of the entry, tall and broad-shouldered, handsome and haggard at once.

"I know that you heard what I said to Jack yesterday morning on the phone," Andrew said then, cutting to the chase. "And I know it must have sounded bad—"

*"It must have sounded bad?"* she repeated. "It *sounded* like what it was—the truth. And yes, bad. Really, really bad."

"It wasn't the truth—"

"It wasn't?" she said, cutting him off again. "It wasn't the truth that you gave up your *playboy* status and life-style against your will? It wasn't the truth that you had this marriage shoved down your throat? That you were *forced* to marry me? That you sacrificed your personal life for your family's company to avoid more scandal? It wasn't—isn't—the truth that you would rather be on a beach in Hawaii than chained to me in Chicago?"

"No, it wasn't and isn't the truth."

"I don't know what's worse—that you're here because your family made you do this, too, or that you're still willing to stand there, look me in the eye, and go on lying to me."

"My family doesn't even know I'm here."

"Because you didn't want to tell them that you blew your cover and I left you because of it? You're hoping to mend fences before they find out?" Delia said snidely.

"My family doesn't know I'm here because it wasn't any of their damn business," Andrew answered.

"Oh, I don't know, since this marriage was a business arrangement it seems to me that that's exactly what it is. In fact, that's about *all* it is—part of the family plan for the family business."

Andrew closed his eyes and shook his head.

When he stopped and opened his eyes again, he said, "What I said to Jack came out of being mad at him and at myself. It was dumb. It was stupid. It was—"

"All the truth."

"Okay, yes, it was all the truth. But only at first."

That sounded too heartfelt not to be honest and Delia couldn't bring herself to refute it this time so she didn't. She merely stared at him, waiting for him to go on, torn between being glad he was dropping the façade and being struck yet another blow to hear that what he'd said the morning before really had all been the truth at *any* time.

When he did continue he told her about the pressures his brother and uncle had put on him to do the right thing by her, to marry her. He admitted that that might not have been the route he would have taken initially without their insistence.

"But the only thing that actually got me down the aisle was thinking about you," he said then. "Not that I realized what that meant last Saturday, but I came home after work yesterday and spent too many hours scared to death that something had happened to you to explain why you were never getting home, and then Marta and Henry showed up and told me why, and after another flirt with thoughts of flight, it all came together for me."

*More thoughts of flight...*

That stuck in Delia's mind as he went on to tell her about going from those thoughts to the rest of what had gone through his head both about his work and about her.

"That's when it occurred to me, Delia, that thinking about you to get myself down the aisle was only the beginning. That I've spent this past week wanting to get home to you. Wanting to see you, to spend every minute I could with you. Wanting to share my fledgling successes with you. Wanting to do everything, share everything, with you. And not because my family *made* me. Only because of the way I feel when I'm with you. The way you make me feel. I realized that pregnant or not pregnant, family pressures or no family pressures, you're the best thing that's ever happened to me. You're who I want. Being married to you is what I want."

Delia's eyes filled with tears she wouldn't allow to fall. But they weren't happy tears. Because as she looked at him, as she listened to him say words she could only wish to believe, she knew two things.

First, she knew that he'd made a strong case for her to marry him based on sentiments much like what he'd just relayed. But he'd already admitted that that had been something he likely wouldn't have done at all if not for his family forcing him to. Which meant that regardless of how convincing it had been, it had been an act. Just as this could well be.

And second, she knew that he was young and hadn't been ready to settle down. That she'd been right about him early on when she'd seen that vast difference in where they both were in their lives. When she'd told him that while she was at a place in time where having this baby, becoming a parent, were things she could embrace, he wasn't at that same place in time.

So she merely shook her head no.

It clearly wasn't something Andrew wanted to accept because his voice gained strength and frustration echoed when he said, "I'm telling you that the responsibilities are real to me now, Delia. The responsibilities to my family and the business, to you, to the baby. That they're as real to me as if they actually were things I was carrying around on my shoulders. And I'm not only willing to meet them, it feels *good* to meet them. To take them on. To know I can handle them, that I can be more, do more, contribute and take care of what I should be taking care of—"

"That has the ring of burden to it," she pointed out the way it seemed to her. And she didn't want to be a burden any more than she wanted to be the wife he was unduly influenced to have.

"Okay, sure, it was all daunting at the start. But now that's not how it is. Now it's nice to be…" He let out a half laugh. "This sounds hokey, but it's nice to be a full-grown man instead of some kid who flies off to the beach of the moment whenever the going gets tough. It's as if I've had my eyes opened to the person I can be and I like that person a whole lot better than the person I was before."

"I'm happy for you," Delia said, meaning it.

"Then you'll come home to Chicago with me and we can go on the way we were before that damn phone call?"

She was genuinely happy that he'd achieved what he had. But that didn't change the situation for her. And for her, the situation was that this was a much younger man who was just now growing up because he had to, not because he was necessarily ready to or had chosen to. A much younger man who was reveling in his newfound ability to carry some weight.

But it was new to him. Too new to consider him stable or reliable in that role. And she couldn't bank her own future and the future of her baby on something like that. On someone who could very well, at any moment, decide that having responsibilities wasn't his cup of tea after all and abdicate them—as Marta's father had done despite even his feeble attempts to be some part of his daughter's life.

And Delia definitely couldn't trust her own future or her baby's future to Andrew when she couldn't get that phone call out of her mind—the words and the tone that had made it obvious how close to the surface was still that inclination to blow off everything and go back to the lifestyle he'd loved and only left because other people had forced him to.

So again Delia shook her head. Only this time she said, "No."

"No?" he parroted as if the answer confused him.

"I'm glad you've come to some sort of place where you can accept the changes in your life and try to make the best of them, but that still doesn't make a good basis for our being married. It isn't why I'd want you to be married to me or why—"

It was Andrew who cut off her words this time. "There's more," he said with a drop of his eyes to her middle.

"The baby isn't basis enough, either," Delia said quietly.

"I'm telling you that I want you, Delia! That *I want you*," he repeated more strongly.

But yet again she only shook her head.

"I'm in love with you!" he shouted then.

But to Delia it seemed like a last-ditch effort and it only brought more tears to her eyes. "Was that the big gun you were going to use if nothing else worked?"

He looked as if she'd hit him in a weak spot. And now it was Andrew who shook his head, whose eyes actually seemed more moist than they had a moment before. "It was the big gun I didn't want to trot out and have used to shoot me down if you didn't feel the same way. Which apparently you don't."

Then he turned and walked out.

And when the tears in Delia's eyes began to stream down her face she wasn't sure if they were from the hurt he'd caused her, or the hurt she'd caused him.

## Chapter Fifteen

"Breakfast in bed?" Delia said on Saturday morning when her brother knocked on the guest room door and then came in with a plate and a glass of milk.

"Your share of the donuts from last night—one chocolate glaze and one cake with white frosting and chocolate sprinkles. And milk to dunk them in," Kyle answered, setting everything on her nightstand as Delia sat up against the headboard.

"What time is it?" she asked as she broke off a piece of the chocolate donut and tried to pretend she had an appetite for it when her stomach was still in too many knots to be hungry.

"It's a little after ten," Kyle informed her.

"I slept till after ten in the morning?" Delia asked

in astonishment. "I haven't done that since I was a teenager."

"You were up until four," he reminded, propping a hip on the edge of the mattress and settling in.

"So were you. And Janine."

Kyle and his wife had kept a miserable Delia company as she cried until her eyes ached and rehashed her entire relationship with Andrew down to the last detail. Several times.

"Janine is still sleeping," Kyle said. "K.C. got me up. But he's off on a playdate now and even though I probably should have let you go on snoozing, too, I wanted a few minutes alone with you. I have some things to say."

Her brother looked serious and reluctant to have this conversation, and that made Delia particularly curious. Ordinarily Kyle had no qualms about telling her anything.

"Okay," Delia agreed. "Shoot."

"Andrew has called here four times already this morning."

Just the mention of Andrew's name made Delia drag her legs up so that her knees were almost to her chin. Then she wrapped her arms around the tent formed by the sheet and blanket, hugging her shins with both arms as if she needed protection.

"I hope you told him to go back to Chicago," she said.

"He called, asked to speak to you, I said you were sleeping and he hung up. Each time."

"So you *didn't* tell him to go back to Chicago."

"No, I didn't," Kyle said firmly. Then he glanced at the door he'd closed behind him when he'd come in, and said, "I've had Marta on the phone half a dozen times since Thursday so I know she blames herself and me for encouraging you to give Andrew a chance. She thinks he should be shot or beaten with a blunt object or something equally as dramatic. And I listened to Janine do the girlfriend thing all last night, rallying 'round, supporting everything you said—"

"Without you saying much at all," Delia said, only realizing in retrospect that her brother had been unusually quiet.

"Without me saying much at all," Kyle confirmed. "It seemed like last night you needed that whole girl thing kind of support so I stayed out of it. But I'm not so sure support for the way you're thinking about all this is what you need for the long run. Or that Marta and I were wrong in the first place."

That surprised Delia.

It must have shown in her expression because before she said anything, Kyle continued. "Let's just say that I have a different perspective on this whole thing and I think you should hear it, too."

"The male perspective?"

"I don't think it's male or female. I just seem to be seeing some things that no one else is."

"Okay. Like what?"

"Well, like I keep wondering what you expected from this guy?"

Delia's eyebrows arched. "What I expected from Andrew? Nothing."

"I don't mean that the same way you do. I don't mean in the way of money or child support or something. I mean, what did you expect from him when it came to this whole situation and marriage and relationship? Did you think he wouldn't have any insecurities about it? Any doubts? Any misgivings? Any regrets? Because it seems like that's the direction you've been going and I think it's a mistake."

Delia's surprise was mounting. "So you think I was wrong to react the way I did when I heard him say what he said on the phone Thursday morning?"

"I don't think there is any right or wrong. Yeah, I think what he said was hard to hear. Yeah, it stinks to find out that his family pushed him into marrying you to avoid a scandal. But the way I see it, you and Andrew both have two things going on and they're close to being the same two things. Even though you keep saying you're at different places in life because of the age gap."

"We are at different places in life because of the age gap," Delia insisted.

"You're both in a marriage—a first marriage—that came out of unusual circumstances. Age has nothing to do with that. And I'm here to shed some light on the similarities rather than supporting the disparities."

"Okay," Delia said again, unable to conceal the fact that she wasn't particularly happy with where her brother was headed with this.

"Look," Kyle reasoned. "You and Andrew like each other, you're attracted to each other, you enjoy being together, there are feelings, undefined or not, but feelings for each other—that's the good side. The romantic side that everyone has been counting on to prevail, and it's true of you both."

Delia confirmed that with silence and a slight, negligent shrug of only one shoulder.

But Kyle was undaunted and went on. "But this whole thing hasn't run a common course. You hooked up in a one-night stand that produced a baby. You accidentally met again, did a whirlwind courtship and got married. That's bound to come with fears and worries and concerns and regrets and the occasional freak-out when that stuff comes to the surface—that's the bad side. The second thing that's going on. For *both* of you. You, Dealie, have had a lot of your own fears and worries and concerns. But you seem to think that yours are warranted and his aren't."

"You think I'm being unfair?"

"A little bit. This whole thing hasn't had the smoothest, most leisurely start—that's a given," Kyle continued. "But consider this—Andrew only threatened to take off. And he made the threat to his brother, not to you. You're the one who actually did it. You're the one who's ready to throw in the towel on everything because you overheard Andrew say some things that shouldn't have come as too much of a shock. Well, except for the family pressure part of it."

"Not an insubstantial part of it," Delia reminded. "The man married me because his family made him."

"Come on. They may have pushed him or twisted his arm, but do you really believe that if he hated you, hated the whole idea, he would have gone through with it? Because I don't. He could have done a lot of other, honorable things to make it work out for everyone. He could have made arrangements with you for child support and visitation and been father to the baby no matter what. He could have gotten you to agree to some kind of gag order to keep it quiet, if that's what it took to appease his family. Or he could have just said to hell with it all and literally gone to sell surfboards in Hawaii. But he didn't do any of that. And I think he didn't do any of that because of the side of him that's attracted to you and enjoys you and has feelings for you—and I'm betting he really does have feelings for you, that he loves you or he wouldn't have said that."

"He might have," Delia said, holding out because the more her brother talked, the more guilty she felt for her own part in this fiasco.

"He didn't," Kyle said definitively. "And I'll tell you something else. I don't believe that without some pretty potent things going on in you, you would have spent that night with him in Tahiti or let him sweep you off your feet in the short time since your paths have crossed again. And then there's been this last week when you've been on cloud nine every time I've talked to you, and Marta said you were late to work every morning, and left early every evening—has that all been a sign that you don't really like the guy?"

Just the thought of the way she'd spent the past week made Delia feel flushed and she couldn't bring herself to answer her brother's question.

"Actions speak louder than words," Kyle said then. "And consider this—along with the fact that it was you who bolted, you gave Andrew his own easy out. You left Chicago, you said you'd get an annulment or a divorce, that you wouldn't cause any more problems for Hanson Media Group. You left him scot-free. If that was what the guy wanted on any level, why did he chase you all the way here? Why did he take what you dished out last night and come back for more today? He had freedom in the palm of his hand and he didn't want it. So what it looks like to me is that it's really you running scared and regretting this more than it's Andrew."

Kyle reached a hand to the top of her head and ruffled her already sleep-tousled hair in true brotherly fashion. "It's all right if that's the case," he assured then. "I'm with you if knowing the truth behind this is too much to take and you've decided you want out. It just seems to me that there's more between you and Andrew than you're paying attention to. More that must be pretty intense to cause you to do things that you've never done before. And if there's really something there, maybe you shouldn't turn your back on it because you've had a freak-out of your own. Seems to me—"

Delia rolled her eyes at him. "A lot of things *seem to you* today."

Kyle grinned and went on anyway. "Seems to me that if you've gone the 'give the guy a chance' route, you should really give the guy a chance, and not just bail on him before he can bail on you the way Peaches's younger men all bailed on her and on us."

Delia flinched. "You think that's what I'm doing? A preemptive strike?"

Kyle shrugged this time. With both shoulders. "I'm not saying that Andrew hasn't given you cause. I'm just saying that unlike Peaches and her boy toys, you and Andrew might genuinely have something that could work." Kyle leaned forward to nudge her legs with his shoulder. "And forget the whole age difference. Like I said, you're both basically at the same place anyway."

"Tahiti, Chicago, now California," she grumbled. "Every time we're in the same place I get into trouble."

"Yeah, well, just don't blame the whole thing on the guy. You're in this, too," her brother cajoled teasingly, lightening the tone.

"I knew this was a 'boys sticking together' thing," she joked back as if he'd revealed himself.

Kyle sat up straight again. "Marta and Henry and Janine and I are with you no matter what—we just want you to be happy. But think it over. Seriously. And from more than your own perspective."

Delia's brother got up and left the room then.

When he was gone and she was alone behind the closed door again, Delia dropped her forehead to her knees.

Had she bolted from Andrew before he could bolt from her? Was she the one doing the running? she asked herself.

It certainly wasn't a thrill to find out that Andrew had married her—or even presented the idea of marriage to her—because his family had made him. But had she used that as her bail-out clause? Her excuse to put an end to the bad side of things that Kyle had talked about—to put an end to all her own fears and worries about their age difference, about marrying someone she hardly knew, about whether or not she and Andrew really could have a future together?

When she considered it, she thought she actually might have done just that.

Because she had to admit to herself what she hadn't told anyone else in the last two days—that there was a secret part of her that had felt relieved that the worst had happened right away, before she'd gotten in any deeper.

But she knew she was already in pretty deep because with the exception of that secret part of her that felt relieved—and it was a very small part of her—she'd been miserable since making her decision to end things with Andrew. To call the marriage quits. And she knew that that wouldn't be true if Kyle wasn't also right about the fact that she had more feelings for Andrew than she wanted to admit.

The kind of feelings Andrew had revealed to her, and she had thrown back in his face.

"What a mess," she muttered to herself.

But when she took her brother's advice and seriously and objectively thought about the way things had been between herself and Andrew—in Tahiti and since the minute they'd laid eyes on each other again—she couldn't deny that there honestly was something that drew them together. Something that was bigger than both of them. Something that ignored conventions. Something even more than the fact that they were having this baby.

She and Andrew connected. They clicked. No matterr what the difference was in their ages. No matter how uncommon were the circumstances that had brought them together. No matter how many worries and fears and concerns they each might be harboring. When they were in the other's company, when their eyes met, when their hands touched or their bodies even came close, everything else faded into insignificance.

And really, wasn't that what was important? That and the fact that somewhere along the way, genuine feelings had developed and grown?

"Feelings you threw in his face, you idiot," she repeated to herself, aloud this time, but suffering even greater guilt and remorse for it.

Because yes, she realized that whatever it was that connected her and Andrew was what mattered most. They were what meant the marriage should be given a chance to survive. They were what meant that the baby should be born into it, raised in it.

And that was really what she wanted. Andrew. A future with Andrew. Regardless of how scary that might be when the insecurities and worries and concerns cropped up.

It was Andrew she wanted. Andrew she needed. Andrew she craved and desired and honestly thought was worth weathering everything else to have....

And then something just awful occurred to her.

What if Kyle was wrong about the reason behind

Andrew's repeated phone calls? What if he was calling to say he was accepting her offer to give him his freedom? What if he was calling to say that he actually was flying off to Hawaii or somewhere even farther away?

Delia bolted upright. "Oh, you really could have blown it," she moaned.

But maybe even if Andrew was calling to tell her the worst, she could still get to him, tell him she was sorry, that she loved him, too. Maybe she could stop him before it was too late….

## *Chapter Sixteen*

As Delia stood outside of Andrew's hotel room an hour later she was so tense she could feel her heart pounding. Kyle had called hotels and motels near his house until he'd learned where Andrew was staying and had relayed the information to her. But now that she was there, Delia was terrified that when Andrew opened the door, she'd discover that he was packing his bags to leave.

Her confidence wasn't boosted by the fact that he hadn't called again after the four times her brother had told her about when he'd come into the guest room to wake her up. That didn't seem like a good sign and only encouraged her thinking that Andrew was taking her up on her offer to cut him loose from the marriage.

But she'd never know for sure until she talked to

him, she told herself, and so she finally forced a timid knock on the hotel room door.

Then she waited. And waited.

The door never opened.

She knocked harder, hoping that Andrew just hadn't heard the first one. But when there was again no answer her fear that he'd already left her behind grew and in response she dropped her forehead to a spot just below the gold 1346 that labeled the room.

"Delia?"

Startled, she jumped back from the door at the sound of her name from down the hallway.

A quick glance in that direction proved that she wasn't imagining it—Andrew was coming toward her. Looking freshly shaved and great in a pair of jeans and a bright yellow polo shirt that accentuated his broad shoulders.

"You're still here," she said the first thing that popped into her head.

"Where else would I be?" he asked as he drew near and pulled out his room key.

Adrenaline only made her stress worse and Delia wished she hadn't said that. She didn't want to begin this by letting him know she thought he might have taken off for a faraway beach after all. It seemed like the wrong tone to set.

So thinking as fast as she could, she said, "I wasn't sure if you had to get back to Chicago right away or not."

Andrew opened the door and then waited for her to go in ahead of him.

He seemed calm. Calmer than he'd been the evening before. Delia was afraid that didn't bode well for her cause. Maybe now that he'd accepted that his freedom would be restored, he was no longer as intense as he'd been when he'd shown up at Kyle's house trying to salvage their marriage.

Even though that possibility made her feel all the more awkward, she didn't know what to do except precede him into the hotel room anyway.

"You're not wondering why I'm here?" she asked as he followed her in and closed the door behind them.

"I'm just glad you are," he answered quietly.

"So you can say thanks for letting you out of this?"

She couldn't believe she'd actually said what had flashed through her mind again. And she hated that not only had it come out so spontaneously, but that she sounded so small, so full of dread.

Andrew didn't respond immediately. He tossed his room key onto his unmade bed before he glanced back at her with a serious expression lining his features.

"No," he said as if he didn't have any idea where a question like that would have come from. "I made up my mind last night after licking my wounds that I wasn't leaving here without you. I just went downstairs to make sure I could have the room as long as I need it, and I came back to get the keys to the rental car so I could show up on your doorstep again."

"Not to tell me you were accepting the annulment-divorce?"

He shook his head. "I'm not letting you call it quits just because I said something stupid in the heat of a fight with my brother. That's not grounds for an annulment or a divorce." Then, on a lighter note, he added,

"I was going to try bringing flowers today, though, to see if that might help."

Apparently with age didn't necessarily come wisdom, Delia thought, feeling foolish for having been so ready to end everything over an eavesdropped phone call when Andrew was taking a more rational view of the situation.

"Would the flowers help?" he asked then. "Because I can still go downstairs and get them."

"No, I don't need flowers," she answered before quietly confiding what she hated going through her mind. "I just want not to feel like the ugly cousin your mother made you take to the prom. But I don't know if I can."

"Because of the forced marriage thing," he finished for her.

"You made me believe that getting married was what you wanted," she accused.

"Would you have married me if I had told you what was really going on behind the scenes?"

"No."

"Nobody would," he said as if he didn't think anyone should.

"And you wouldn't have married me *without* what was going on behind the scenes," she said, but it stabbed her even as she did.

"Maybe you could think of it like this," Andrew suggested. "We're at the first summer camp dance of the season. The boys are lined up against one wall across the rec room from the girls on the other wall, and no one will make the first move. But everyone knows that you and I kissed down by the campfire at the end of the last year, so my friends give me a shove away from the wall to put the wheels in motion. Now, I could balk and elbow my way back against the wall. Or I could cross the room—"

Which he did right then as if he were demonstrating, stopping only a scant foot in front of Delia where she'd ended up after going only far enough into the room to allow him to close the door.

Then he continued with his fictitious scenario. "I'm nervous about it—scared out of my head, to be honest—but I cross the room. And once I'm standing right in front of you and I take a good, long look at you again, I do ask you to dance. Because in spite of the push I needed to get me off that wall, there you are. You're as beautiful as I remember you. As beautiful as you were in all my memories of the summer before, all my fantasies. You're as smart and fun to be with. You're an amazing, incredible person, and I want you every bit as much as I wanted you the year before at the campfire."

Delia had been reluctant to look him in the eye and, as a result, had been staring at his chest. But now she tilted her chin, looking up into his dark, piercing gaze as he said, "That's how this was. I picked you myself, if you'll recall. In Tahiti. Without any help from anyone. It wasn't as if my family put a personal ad in a newspaper and then told me I had to marry the one woman who answered it. And I think I would have come to the idea of marriage myself after the baby news had sunk in and I'd had some time with you again to hash through that, to get to know you. But to do it instantly? That took a nudge," he confessed. "Only a nudge, though, Delia. The baby business threw me for a loop—I'm not denying that—but it only took a little while of being with you, getting to know you, getting to know what a great person you are, to realize I wanted you myself. Like I said last night, that's what got me to the altar last week. Not my family."

"And if I tell you—or even sign some kind of legally binding contract—that I'll never reveal your paternity or cause a single shadow to be cast over you or any of the Hansons or Hanson Media Group to cause a scandal? Then what would you say?" she tested, because as much as she wanted to believe him, she was still afraid he might be doing this for reasons other than his own.

"I'm not going to let you hide that this is my baby. And this stopped being about my family or about Hanson Media Group a while ago. I really knew it had stopped being about anyone or anything but you and me on Thursday night when I was going out of my mind thinking something might have happened to you. I wasn't just saying it when I told you that I love you. I *do* love you. And I'll fight tooth and nail to keep you and this baby, even if it means a media scandal of its own. I'm not letting you or this baby go. Not now, not ever. And if you think about it, consider how we spent last week. Did any of that seem like it was family mandated?"

That made Delia smile involuntarily. They'd made love more times, in more places, with more urgency than any honeymooning couple she could imagine. The man hadn't been able to keep his hands off her any longer than she'd been able to keep hers off him. Because there genuinely was something overpowering between them. Something far stronger than any family mandates.

She couldn't deny it and if there were any doubts left in her after all he'd said, she had only to remind herself that she'd given him a way out—no strings or scandals attached—and he still hadn't taken it.

"Are you saying I'm stuck with you?" Delia managed to joke, feeling suddenly much better than she had since Thursday morning.

"Permanently," he confirmed. "Although I would like to hear you say that if this was last week at this time, you'd marry me all over again. In spite of my big mouth."

"It seems just the right size to me," she said with an innuendo-laden tone.

He reached for her then, pulling her into his arms and wrapping them tightly around her. "And here we are, within inches of a hotel bed...."

"Plus it's our one-week anniversary...." she contributed.

That was all the encouragement he needed to kiss her. A deep, reconnecting kiss that let Delia know he meant all he'd said, that he genuinely did want her. As much as she wanted him.

And even though it hadn't been long since they'd last made love, it was as if eons had passed because suddenly clothes were flying off—her sundress and sandal and panties, his shoes and socks and jeans and shirt—and they were on their way to the hotel bed with mouths still clinging together hungrily, with hands already exploring, seeking, finding and arousing by the time Andrew gently laid her on the mattress and joined her.

But despite his tenderness in getting her there, what erupted between them from that moment on was explosive. Needs, demands, desires ran hot. By then each knew what the other liked, what spots were sensitive, just the right amount of force, of finesse to use to build anticipation, eagerness, pleasure.

And neither of them held back. Instead, as if all inhibitions had been set free, they came together in a way even more powerful than they ever had before, culminating in a simultaneous, blindingly potent peak that left Delia feeling as if they had physically sealed once and for all the bond they'd formed under less than ideal circumstances. A bond they gave new life— just as they'd created new life that night on the beach.

Afterward, exhausted, spent, satisfied, Andrew held her close, stroking her arm from elbow to hand and back again where her wedding ring once again shimmered from her finger resting on his chest.

"I love you," Delia whispered then. "And I'm sorry for what I said to you last night when you said that to me."

Andrew squeezed her even tighter. "That *was* pretty tough to hear," he said. "But probably not as tough as what you heard from me."

"I'll forgive and forget if you will," she proposed.

"Done." He kissed the top of her head. "And you know why?"

"Why?"

"Because I really do love you."

"I really do love you, too," Delia repeated, kissing the masculine mound of one of his taut pectorals.

"And the age thing—I'd like it if you'd let go of that," he told her.

"Your reaction to what's happened since Thursday morning was more mature than mine was," she admitted. "I kind of decided when that occurred to me that maybe it was time to forget the age thing, too."

"Finally!" he shouted at the ceiling.

Then he let out a sigh that she recognized. It was what he did when he was relaxing for sleep.

But she was ready for a little of that herself and so she gave up the fight against the fatigue that had settled over her, too, and closed her eyes.

Their legs were entwined, their bodies rested together in the perfect meeting of curves and valleys, his chest was the best pillow she'd ever had, and as Delia reveled in that sublime comfort and let it all cushion and embrace her, she also took secret pleasure in knowing that Andrew would still be there when she opened her eyes again.

And that was when it struck her that paradise wasn't only an island in the South Pacific.

That right there in Andrew's arms she had her own private slice of it.

Her own private slice of paradise into which she would bring their baby.

A baby she had no doubt Andrew would be there to greet with her when she delivered it into the world.

Just as she had no doubt he would be there for her from that moment on.

\* \* \* \* \*

*Don't miss three linked stories available next month in By Request. Look for* Beyond Business *in February 2011.*

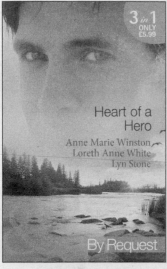